CW01278787

ATOMIC UNDERWORLD

ATOMIC UNDERWORLD

Jack Conner

All characters in this book are fictitious. Any resemblance to actual persons, living or dead, is purely coincidental.

ISBN-13: 978-1537607467

For Hua.

Chapter 1

The three moons shone high over the Atomic Sea the night Frankie found him.

Tavlin was playing cards at Savver's, a tavern situated on a rooftop garden perched atop a tall, gargoyle-encrusted building of weathered stone. Lightning flickered up from the harbor in a thousand electric tongues, and somewhere a gas pocket exploded out over the waters, but Tavlin was too far away to hear the thunder or the boom, and he was winning besides.

"Match and raise," he said, flicking in several chips.

"You're cheating," said Verigga, a hulking woman with a scar across one eye and half her face.

The others at the table quieted. They were a rough lot, hard and tattooed and grim. Smoke wreathed up from their cigarettes and cigars, but that was the only movement at the table.

"I'm in a good mood, so I'll pretend I didn't hear that," Tavlin said.

"You're a cheat," Verigga said. Her scarred eye was white, and milky clouds drifted across the pupil. "I been studyin' you. I admit I don't know how you're doin' it, but I know you are."

Tavlin relaxed. *She can't prove anything.* "Apologize."

"Do what?"

"Else I'll have to consider your accusation as calling me out."

"I'm not apologizing."

With exaggerated calmness, he stuffed and lit his pipe. The tobacco was an alchemical concoction, and the smoke that curled up from the bowl bore a greenish tint.

"I choose knives," he said, then waited. *Please work.*

Verigga paused, as if his choice had actually made her rethink her accusation, then made a decision. She climbed to her feet, knocking her chair to the floor (which was more dramatic than Tavlin thought strictly necessary), and stabbed a finger at him. "That man's a cheat or I'm a beauty queen, there ain't no two ways about it."

Tavlin felt himself grow cold. His reputation wasn't good enough to survive such allegations. He'd already been banned from multiple gambling houses, which is why he shivered on a rooftop garden two hours past midnight with this lot.

Slowly, making a show of it, he mounted to his own feet, placed his pipe on the table, and glared at Verigga. There was still a chance to scare her off.

"Are you calling me out?" he said.

"I damn well am."

"Knives, then." His reputation in knives was something he had paid very well for.

Too well, as it turned out.

She spat. "Do I look like I fear knives, Tavlin Two-Bit—or anything else?"

"Maybe a shower."

Apparently that was the wrong thing to say. She reached to her waist and ripped out the largest knife he'd ever seen. It should have been wielded by some knight of ages past against some lumbering reptile or monstrous bug.

"Shall we take this somewhere else?" she said. "I hate to get blood on the money."

Tavlin glanced to the others. They traded looks, but none volunteered to help. Likely they wondered if Verigga might be right.

A dark figure appeared behind the woman. A short sharp length of metal glimmered at her throat. A voice croaked, "Leave now or go home shorter."

Verigga seemed about to move against her assailant, but the knife twitched, and blood leaked down her neck.

With a snarl, she shoved her own weapon back into its sheath. The blade at her throat retracted. She spun about, but the other knife was still out, and it danced back and forth as if taunting her. Its wielder stood in shadow.

"This isn't over," she said to Tavlin, then gathered up her money and stormed off.

Tavlin wiped sweat from his forehead. "To whom do I owe the thanks?—not that I needed the help, mind."

Out of the shadow stepped a squat figure, more toad than man, with dark green skin, bulbous neck and torso, and jutting, wide-lipped batrachian mouth. He was obviously infected. Mutated. Many of the infected lived here in Hissig, constant reminders of the nearness of the Atomic Sea. What was more, Tavlin recognized him.

"Frankie."

Frankie's webbed hands moved, and the knife disappeared. His eyes stared at Tavlin, unblinking. "We need to talk."

Tavlin cashed in his chips—this was not a formal casino, but there was an independent bookie—and followed Frankie into a shadowed corner of the tavern garden. Midnight blooms nodded all around, lacing the night with a lavender fragrance, and from somewhere drifted the sounds of jazzy music, crackly and fitful, as if emitted from an old gramophone, not one of the newer record players. It echoed strangely through the misty spaces between this building and the next. The drinking and gambling continued, but here Tavlin and Frankie had a sphere of privacy.

"What's this about?" Tavlin asked. If he hurried, he could get back to the game without missing more than a hand.

"There's trouble."

"There always is."

"This ain't like most trouble."

Tavlin felt a sinking sensation. "I'm afraid to ask, but you still work for Boss Vassas, don't you?" When Frankie said nothing, just stood there stone-faced, blinking his frog eyes slowly, Tavlin grimaced. "This trouble . . . it wouldn't have anything to do with him, would it?"

"Who else?"

"Shit. Listen, Frankie, I want no part of this. I don't even know what this is and I want no part of it." He started to leave.

"I'm afraid I ain't askin'."

Two large figures materialized from the darkness. They were infected, too, huge and piscine. Their fish scales glistened wetly in the moonlight.

"Sonofabitch." Tavlin glared. "Alright, what's this about?"

"Now you're talkin'. And it's better to show you. Come'n."

Frankie set off for the stairs. Reluctantly, Tavlin followed, knowing it would be better to miss the game than to offend Boss Vassas. The two goons trailed him. The group reached the stairs, took them to the next level down, then a fire escape. This led to a gravel-lined surface, and from here they took a bridge of bolted metal pipes over to another rooftop. Wind howled about them, bringing with it drops of moisture and flapping Tavlin's coat out behind him. It was a cold, wet night, but he navigated the aerial highway with practiced ease. To the west, lightning flickered up from the seething, toxic water of the Atomic Sea, and Tavlin tried not to think about the monstrous things that lived in it. One of them—or something derived from them, anyway—slithered up a wall across the way: a fur-covered octopus, or drypuss, searching for a rat to eat, or maybe a family pet or infant if it could get in through a window.

"You shouldn't have helped me," Tavlin said. "What if word spreads that I can't take care of myself? Which I could have, by the way."

"Yeah," Frankie said. "She looked like a pushover."

"Even so."

Frankie shrugged. "You seemed like you could use the help, and I need you alive. Ain't my job to look after your career, or whatever the hell it is. Just what are you doing up here, anyway? You had a life down below."

Tavlin scowled at Frankie's wattled neck. "I have a life here."

"Yeah. Some life. Livin' outta rats' dens, cheatin' lowlifes at crummy bars. Why d'ya cheat, anyway? You're pretty good on your own."

"I don't cheat."

"Listen, I saw you. That cyclops may not've seen the cards up your sleeve, but I did."

Tavlin said nothing. On one hand, he was relieved that Frankie had helped him. If he'd won the duel against Verigga and had killed her, he would have had to drink himself to sleep for many nights afterwards. It would have been different if she'd been wrong, but to stick someone for catching you actually cheating seemed like bad form. And of course, he might not have won.

"Whatever," Frankie went on. "You're goin' below now."

Tavlin repressed a shudder. "Must we?"

"Yes."

"And you won't tell me why?"

"You'll find out soon enough."

"As long as it's not about some debt I owe . . . It's not, is it?"

Frankie's grunt was his only answer.

They passed down through the city, the crowded, ancient metropolis of Hissig, capital of Ghenisa. Fog curled through the streets, and moisture beaded the smoked glass above. Thick domes fashioned of stone and massively encrusted buildings loomed in the darkness, moisture dripping from the horns and teeth of gargoyles and serpentine dragons, and from the breasts of six-armed goddesses and other creatures of myth. Great stone buildings and monuments hunched like sentinels, interspersed with occasional skyscrapers. The older buildings showed countless pocks and scars from war, most notably the Revolution fifty years ago and the dark times of the War of the Severance hundreds of years before that, but there was still some signs of the debaucheries and madness of the Withdraw nearly a thousand years ago.

Tavlin passed a window through which a radio hissed and crackled: " . . . which the Archchancellor of Octung denies. He continues to claim the expansion and development of the Octunggen military is for defensive purposes only. Meanwhile he and his party members have been giving stirring speeches to packed crowds in Lusterqal and elsewhere, and there is much activity around the temples to the Collossum. Reporters are being shut out and even evicted from the country . . ."

"Damned Octung," Frankie snorted as they scrambled down another fire escape. "They'll make their war, you can be sure of that."

Tavlin knew Frankie was probably right. And Octung was only half a continent away from Ghenisa. When the war started, Ghenisa would be hard pressed. Already refugees seeking asylum or a boat out were beginning to arrive in Hissig.

"We'll hold," Tavlin said with more confidence than he felt.

They reached street level and passed through the swirling, acrid fog until they arrived at a manhole cover. Tavlin watched skeptically as the two goons jimmied it up. The manhole cover groaned as metal grated on asphalt, and the big men rolled it away. Revealed in its place was a dark, gaping pit. A fetid reek curled out. As Tavlin stared at the darkness, a wave of dread seemed to settle in his gut.

"I don't like this."

"You don't have to," Frankie said. "Just get your head out of your ass and come on."

Frankie slipped into the hole, having to squeeze his slimy bulk through, and descended via the rungs bolted into the sewer wall. The goons prodded Tavlin toward the hole, and for a moment he thought of running—it was starting to feel like a good idea—but he knew if he ran he would have to keep on running. With a sigh, he followed Frankie down. Instantly the stink of the sewer wrapped him in its embrace, and he felt his gorge rise. He tried to resurrect his old immunity to the reek, but it didn't come.

He lit on a concrete surface, and darkness surrounded him—almost. The large men had replaced the manhole cover, but a thin slice of light came from overhead, and it glimmered off the slowly-moving river that ran by the walkway. Tavlin tried not to look at it for long, and its stench made him want to retch. His eyes burned.

"I better get paid for this," he said.

"That's up to you and the boss."

That gave Tavlin some hope. He wasn't being taken to his death, then. At least not directly. And profit was always something to look forward to.

The rough men lit flashlights, and the group set off. They passed down this hall, then another. The walls were composed of rough-hewn stone blocks, scored by time and marked by graffiti, some of which looked quite old, written in languages Tavlin didn't even recognize. He knew the sewer system was a composite thing, built over centuries by the different nations that had occupied Hissig. Much of it had been carved out of the earth thousands of years ago, back when the Empire of L'oh had ruled the continent. He thought the section he was walking through now was probably built by them. But some of it was built in even *older* times, by civilizations thriving before humans had walked the planet.

Something splashed in the fetid river, and one of the goons shone a flashlight on it. Nothing. Then: a white shape breached the surface, slipped back under. It had gills and whiskers. "Wish I'd brought my net," said the man.

Tavlin tried to resist curling his lip. The sewers merged with underground tunnels that ran to the Atomic Sea, and the waters had become mixed with the sea's strange energies. Now an entire ecosystem lived down here, but it was an ecosystem that Tavlin would prefer not to dwell on.

They walked for a ways, sometimes ducking down narrow, slimy tunnels, sometimes crossing bridges over the river—bridges that seemed formed by the secretions of some awful insect—sometimes descending stairs beside ancient locks, coming into a lower part of the sewer, and finally the tunnel they walked through spilled out into a great chamber, one of the huge cisterns where someone could shout at one end and not hear his echo for minutes afterward, if at all. Here the ceiling arched to a dome overhead, so high up Tavlin couldn't see it, and the river became a lake. In the center of the lake lights blazed and shapes shifted and swayed to unknown rhythms. Tavlin saw boats lashed together, ancient piers and docks, buildings rising from the chaos. Sounds drifted across the waters. Tavlin heard music.

"Welcome back to Muscud," Frankie said.

Boats were tied up at a pier on this side, and for a price the boatman took them aboard one, started up the motor, which smoked and shuddered and sounded as if it had seen better days, and made for the town on the lake.

Shapes swept down from above, and Tavlin winced as a drop of mucus fell on him. He shook it off. The shapes wheeled about the boat, then moved on, but not before he caught a glimpse of winged slug-like creatures with tendril-fringed, sucking mouths. Flails. They infested the sewers, stinking and dripping, living mostly off the slime that coated the walls. There were predatory varieties, however, and he kept an eye out.

The city—so its residents called it, anyway—of Muscud drew nearer, and Tavlin looked on its familiar outlines with apprehension. Infected people tottered down the lanes of the makeshift community, slouched along the docks, called to each other from the balconies of listing buildings. Everything was worn, paint peeling (where there was paint), wood blistering, rat-things shimmying in the gutters, some structures built of stone, others from stolen debris sagging and about to collapse.

At least it smelled better here. Alchemical lamps hung from the buildings, blazing redly out over the canals, and they drove back the stink, making the air not only breathable but actually pleasant, and slightly musky.

Jazzy music from the bars and whorehouses rang out, blending with the cacophony of thousands of mutants talking and laughing and fighting and crying and carrying on their daily lives.

"Good to be home, eh?" said Frankie.

"This isn't my home," Tavlin said.

The boatman tied them up to a dock, accepted Frankie's tip, and waited for them to clamber off. Tavlin was just glad to be away from the stench and out of easy reach of the things in the water.

They stepped into the streets and entered the town, passing the lashed-together boats, piers and platforms that composed the city's foundation, and the great shabby buildings that rose from it. Canals ran all through the city, and boats came and went. Tavlin saw one mutant emerge from the water, dripping and holding a white fish in his mouth. Children ran down the streets, laughing or fleeing, clutching stolen purses and burned rats. Whores leaned against cracked pillars, and piano music drifted from between batwing doors. Tavlin saw shops and businesses, just like a real city almost—well, a human one, he amended. There were no autos or horse-drawn carriages down here, but there were bicycles and motorcycles, and they careened around the corners, scattering pedestrians before them like sodden leaves.

One mutant with the chameleon-skin of an octopus stood on a podium before a small crowd, shouting over the babble, ". . . and see the error of your ways. Convert and accept the divinity of Magoth, and you will be saved when he descends from the Holy House …"

Tavlin chuckled. "Magoth has a promoter now?"

Frankie didn't give the expected answer. "That guy's not just some madman. He's a preacher, one of several at the church."

"A *church* . . . to Magoth? It's just some boogeyman of the sewers!"

"I wouldn't say that too loudly. I know when you lived here there was only a few that worshipped it, it was just another cult, but it's caught on lately. It's a regular religion now."

Tavlin nodded noncommittally, but he didn't say what he was thinking. He didn't know what Frankie had bought into.

They arrived at one of the largest and proudest of the buildings in Muscud, a large stone structure held aloft by pillars anchored into the artificial lake bed. Stone steps led up past decorative if chipped columns to an impressive doorway spanned by colored beads. A man with a tongue like an anemone and striations like a sea bass parted the beads when he saw Frankie, and held it open as Tavlin and the goons filed past. They entered the Hall of the Wide-Mouth, most notorious den in Muscud. Shady-looking mutants played pool, gambled at large tables, drank at the bar under a cloud of smoke, engaged in private dealings in the booths. Whores of all descriptions prowled among them, stroking arms, whispering in ears, and occasionally leading a man or woman up to the second floor where the real fun took place. It all stank of smoke, cigarette and otherwise, seaweed and grease. The latter came from the kitchens, and fried things that were likely caught down here and quite unprocessed were shoved before hungry mouths.

The smells relaxed Tavlin for some reason. This had been his home, or at least the place where he had spent the most time, for nearly a decade, though that time had long since passed.

"It hasn't changed much," he said.

Frankie raised a hairless eyebrow. "Oh, there's change, all right. You'll see. C'mon. We have to meet the Boss."

They moved into the backrooms, and the sounds of revelry from the front diminished into a vague roar. Here secretaries typed notes and hard-looking men cleaned guns. Several looked up as Tavlin walked past, and he noted familiar faces. "Hey, it's Tavlin!" one said. "What gives?" "You back or what?"

"Or what," Tavlin replied, though he couldn't resist a small smile. He was rarely greeted with warmth in the world above.

They moved toward a certain back room. Its stone walls were thicker than the others, yet even so Tavlin heard grunts and smacking sounds when he drew close. Two toughs stood beside the door. One was tall, slick and pale. He had no nose, at least not a human one, but a rounded lump with holes in it like a fish might have, and his eyes were solid black, shark-like. He was Galesh, the Boss's right-hand man. The other man, Edgar, was shorter and more human-looking, though he possessed the gills of a fish, which pulsed weirdly on his thick neck.

"Boss's busy," Galesh said, when Tavlin and Frankie approached.

A smacking sound came from the other side of the metal door, and a curse.

"He'll see us," Frankie said.

Galesh studied him a moment, then rapped on the door, and someone on the other side slid away the small panel. A short exchange followed, locks popped and the door banged open, revealing a small, dingy stone room lit by a hanging alchemical lamp; its red fluid flowed slowly, making the light shift in languid motions. A man strapped to a wooden chair hunched in the middle of the room. Bruises covered his face and body, and blood soaked his hair and pretty much every other part of him. One of his arms had the texture of a sea horse. He looked even redder with the light on him, but Tavlin figured he was red enough.

Boss Vassas stood over the man, shirtsleeves rolled up, blood dripping from his fists, chest heaving. The Boss was of medium height, but his chest was deep and his arms thick. His mutations were subtler than some; he bore a slightly piscine cast, his mouth a little too wide, his lips thick, his skin grayish, but nothing overt. He could almost pass for an uninfected. He had a rugged face, with bushy black eyebrows and short wavy black hair, now with as much salt in it as pepper, normally combed back from his broad forehead but at the moment disheveled and sweat-soaked. An old scar curled up from his right eye, disappearing into the hairline over his ear.

"Where the hell is it?" he demanded of the man in the chair. "Why'd you take it—*why*? And why'd you *kill* her, you fuck!" He balled a fist and struck the man in the face. The man listed backward and would have fallen but for the nails sticking the chair to the floor. Even so, the wood creaked, and Tavlin supposed the Boss would soon need a new chair. "Damn you!"

The man spat blood. "I'm t-telling you, w-we didn't take it. It wasn't us. And I d-didn't kill anybody!"

Boss Vassas started to punch him again, then sighed and lowered his fist. "You sure can take a lot of punishment for a liar."

Frankie cleared his throat, and the Boss swung his gaze in the direction of the newcomers. He took in Tavlin and nodded in acknowledgement. Tavlin nodded back, feeling his throat constrict. There was a desperate, harried look about the Boss that he had never seen before. Vassas's eyes were bloodshot, his complexion even more ashen than usual.

"You made it," Vassas said. "Good."

Tavlin indicated the man in the chair. “Mind if I ask what he did?”

“I-I didn’t do nothing!”

Vassas backhanded him across the face. “Let’s talk outside,” the Boss told Tavlin.

He led the way out of the small room and Galesh closed the door behind them. When they were out of earshot of the beaten man, Vassas said, “Truth is, I don’t know who did it. I thought it must be that creep’s gang, they’re the only ones stupid enough to come into my territory lately—but maybe not.”

“That was one of Grund’s boys, wasn’t it?” said Frankie, then with an aside to Tavlin: “Suvesh Grund runs his own crew outta the Blighted Quarter. He’s trying to expand.”

“Idiot,” Vassas said with sudden violence. “It can only lead to war, and that’s the last thing any of us need.”

Tavlin tried not to think of the ragged man in the chair. He had seen Boss Vassas beat people before, but for some reason it shocked him all over again, and he reminded himself why he had left this life.

“I don’t get it,” he said. “What exactly did you think that man did?”

Boss Vassas didn’t answer at once. He motioned to Edgar, who produced and lit a cigar for him. Smoke wreathed Vassas’s head, and his bloodshot eyes peered through the smoke at Tavlin. “That’s why I called you here. I hope you haven’t eaten.”

* * *

Tavlin hadn’t eaten, and he was glad of it. It was only after the implications sank in, though, that he felt truly queasy.

Boss Vassas ushered him up to his suite on the third and highest floor. Half the floor was devoted to rooms for his boys, the other half was his private penthouse. Few went into the penthouse save Vassas and his women. He had two women that lived with him, though they weren't permanent and frequently rotated with the women on the second story—at least historically that had been the case. Around the time Tavlin had left, a girl he knew named Nancy had taken up residence with the Boss, and Vassas had fallen so hard for her he'd invited her to stay for good, and so she had, demanding only that she be the only woman there. He'd agreed, and from what Tavlin witnessed they'd been very happy together. In the time since he'd left, rumor ran that little had changed save that Nancy had only grown more lovely and strong-willed and had begun exercising some authority with the crew, which Vassas actually encouraged.

Tavlin had rarely been to the penthouse before, and he saw that, as he'd remembered, the suite was large and opulent. Ancient tapestries hung on the walls beside priceless paintings, and thick animal hide carpets draped the floors. Idols and statues of various empires stood all about, surely stolen or looted. Many of the statues were nudes. Vassas had fine taste in art and furniture, and though he acted rough in front of his men Tavlin knew him to be a sensitive and intelligent man in private.

Bodies lay all over—though at first Tavlin didn't realize what they were. There were five of them—one woman, Frankie said, and four of Vassas's soldiers. "They musta heard her scream and come runnin' in, then they got what she got," Frankie said.

What they got exactly was obviously the source of Vassas's unease (or part of it), and it was clear why it unnerved him. The bodies no longer looked human. The flesh had been turned translucent, slightly whitish, and been made rubbery, like the flesh of a jellyfish. Tavlin could see the internal organs through the flesh, and they had been turned translucent as well. The bodies had been ripped apart, as if by a blast or an animal attack, and pieces of them were strewn all around the room. They stank somewhat of ammonia but did not emit the normal odor of a human corpse, which Tavlin to his chagrin was all too familiar with. One didn't live amongst the mob for a decade and not see a few bodies. Whitish flesh hung from the walls, the furniture, sagging and stinking. An overhead fan spun, making the ribbons of flesh flap and stream.

Seeing the corpses hit Tavlin hard, perhaps because he hadn't seen dead people in a while, but also, he was certain, because of what it meant.

Something *unnatural* had happened here.

"What could have done this?" he said, hearing the numbness in his voice, one hand over his mouth and nose to block out the stench of ammonia. He staggered through the room, cataloguing what he saw, trying not to step in anything wet.

"If I knew, my blood pressure would be a lot lower," Vassas said. He stared about the room and shook his head. His blood-shot gaze landed on the body of the woman, and a long sigh escaped his lips.

"That was Nancy?" Tavlin said, and Vassas nodded raggedly. Tavlin thought he might have been crying earlier. His eyes were *very* red. "I'm sorry," Tavlin said. "Nancy was a good woman." She had been a friend of Sophia's, too, he remembered, but he didn't say so. "When did this happen?"

"Coupla-three hours ago. I figured it was Grund at first and sent some boys to get him or one of his men for questioning. But it just didn't feel right—how could that bastard have done … *this*? So I sent for you, too."

"I don't know what I can do." Tavlin made his way through the room. Frankie hung back by the doorway. None of the other men had accompanied them. "Who else knows about this?"

"Just you, me, Frankie and Galesh," Vassas said. "And that's the way it stays. The other boys know somethin's up, but they don't know what. Shit, I don't know how we're gonna get rid of the bodies. Can't let the boys see 'em like this."

Tavlin wanted to ask why, but that would be disingenuous. He knew Vassas feared any questioning of his power. An unfathomable attack in his very lair resulting in the deaths of five people under his protection would rattle his organization to the foundation. If it had just been straight murder with normal corpses, that would have been bad enough, but this . . .

Tavlin found his way to the largest statue of all. It stood before Vassas's huge wooden bed, a cluster of small black obelisks, with the central obelisk rising higher than the others, though how high it was impossible to tell, for the statue had been broken off, and black stone shards littered the floor around it.

Tavlin eyed the broken top. "Why would they take the top?"

"There was this gem, a bloody red gem big as your fist," Vassas said.

"I hated that thing," Frankie said from the doorway. His eyes were on the bodies, and he looked nervous. "Always gave me the creeps." To Tavlin, he added, "It looked like it *burned.* There was some fire, deep inside."

"It was beautiful," Vassas said. "Got it from a merchant from Taluush. Said he found it in some ancient ruins."

"How ancient?" asked Tavlin.

"Pre-human, he said. Some inhuman thing built that statue. I always liked to think the gem gave me power. Maybe that's why someone took it. I want it back. But that's secondary." His eyes misted as they returned to Nancy. "I want *revenge.*"

The Boss's voice shook, and Tavlin felt something twist in his heart. Nancy had been a hell of a gal, even a friend. By the expression on Vassas's face, she had been something more to him than that, more even than a lover.

"I'm no assassin," Tavlin said. "I'm a card-player. And, lately, not a very good one."

"I don't want *you* to get revenge for me," Vassas said. "If I know who did this, I can get that myself. But I need to know who. Here's why I had Frankie get you, Tavlin: I need someone, someone I know, someone I can trust. You ran my gambling hall for ten years. You're a good man, and we been through a lot of shit together. You helped make me the most powerful boss in Muscud. I don't know why you left, but I let you go and never thought about doin' anything else. Now I need you back. Somethin' dangerous is out there, and I don't know what it's up to, but it ain't good. It killed five people by unnatural means to *obtain* something unnatural." His voice hardened. "What do you think it's gonna do with that gem?"

"I can't imagine."

"Me, either. But these sewers are home to all sorts of things that have fallen through the cracks o' regular society. Secrets lost long ago up top are still shakin' things up down here, and some are still waitin' to be found. And some shouldn't *ever* be found."

"You think this is one of those."

Vassas nodded. "If I send one of my men to poke into this thing, word will get out. People will find out what happened here. Whatever did this will find out I'm on its trail." Vassas ran a hand across his face. "I don't want that."

"I wouldn't either."

"But you … they won't suspect you. You've been gone long enough to be seen as independent. So that's it, Tavlin. I need you to figure this mess out and end it before it gets any worse. I'll pay you for the trouble, but I know you. You liked Nancy almost as much as I did. You'd probably do it just for her. But pay you I will. What do you say?"

Chapter 2

A motorcycle nearly ran Tavlin over, but he was so wrapped up in his thoughts he forgot to give its driver the finger as he crossed the street, coughing on the diesel fumes.

He pressed his way through the thickly-packed gathering on the cracked sidewalk, making his way down streets that had once been familiar but were now subtly alien, though he couldn't define exactly why. Strange buildings of crumbling brick, stone and mud huddled over him, and weird light bathed their windows. He passed a concert hall and heard the singing of a fish woman. It was unsettling but oddly beautiful. A man with a tentacle where his right arm should be played a guitar as he lounged against a peeling wall. Stroking the strings with his suckered limb, he accepted donations out of a patched hat at his feet. A pretty little girl with yellow curls and the stunning colorations of a rainbow fish passed out fliers; Tavlin accepted one and saw that it was for the Church of Magoth. He crumpled it up and threw it away at the next fly-covered trashcan … which needed emptying.

A man that looked like a great anthropomorphic clam, his white skin glistening, sold fish that must be diseased on a street corner, and Tavlin blanched at the sight. Diseased fish from the Atomic Sea was what contaminated most people in the first place—that and unprotected sex with an infected person, or birth from same. Seafood had to be carefully processed to be safe, but some were too poor or too hungry to care, and so they ate black market seafood regardless of the risk. The result was mutation or death, sometimes both. Once they were mutated, they didn't seem to care anymore, and they would eat diseased food willingly, perhaps even preferring it to clean food, but the sight turned Tavlin's stomach. Of course, the infected down here were different in some ways; many were descendents of the original mutants from the Dark Times, and as such they held themselves with more pride than first-generation mutants and would exalt in thumbing their noses (if they had them) at an uninfected.

Here and there throughout the city he saw them—normal people, uninfected, true humans like himself. They were people who for one reason or another had left mainstream society and joined the mutants. Most were on the run from the law, debt collectors, the sanitarium, or some combination of the three. Tavlin couldn't remember what exactly had driven him down here all those years ago. He'd been a junkie and a thief and he thought he remembered having some vague notion of getting clean and starting over again. He hadn't believed in the cities in the sewers—like most people he thought them an urban myth, though one that had lasted for hundreds of years—but his underworld connections had led him to Muscud, and there he had stayed. He'd gotten clean like he'd promised himself, had even found a respectable job, by his standards, and he had found a lot more besides. Until . . . Jameson.

He sighed, kept going.

At one point he nearly collided with an unusual form clad in a trench coat, but he quickly saw that the coat was merely to hide the being's true shape. It was one of the Ualissi, the gelatinous pre-human race that occupied its own ghetto of Muscud. Its mucus had penetrated the trench coat, making it sticky, and Tavlin wiped his hands on his pants as he gave the creature space to pass on by. Above and below the trench coat the being pulsed with bioluminescence, and Tavlin had to admit it was beautiful in its own way, if eerie. And sticky. Mostly the Ualissi kept to their own quarter, and he was surprised to see this one out and about, but then they did have errands that took them beyond their area of town, and who knows, maybe they had become more outgoing since he'd been away. Then again …

The ruby.

As casually as he could, Tavlin scanned the thing's pockets for any suspicious bulges. They were all wet and pasted against its swollen form. If there had been any pre-human gems hidden upon the creature's being, Tavlin would see them. He could find nothing, though. The creature was innocent—of this, at least.

Tavlin pressed on. Soon he found himself before a tall building crammed between two others. It had a gabled roof and a wide front porch. Music drifted out from it, something swinging and light, and there were lights and the sounds of laughter. A wooden sign proclaimed THE TWIRLING SKIRT.

He mounted the front porch, passed a couple necking on the swing bench, its chains creaking, and crossed into the parlor where people danced on hardwood floors and others reclined on sofas or chaise lounges, while a jazzy band played on a dais, their saxophones flashing like molten gold, violins sawing like grasshoppers. The women dressed scantily, some barely dressed at all.

A pretty young woman with iridescent scales on half of her face approached Tavlin and stroked his arm. "And how are you doing this fine evening, handsome?"

"Fine, Maya, how are you?"

Her eyes widened. "Tavlin Two-Bit! Can it be? It's been ages!" She gave him a big hug and drew him aside, making him sit on an unoccupied sofa. She reclined next to him. He could feel her thigh pressing into his own, and smell her heady, cloying perfume, like some overripe orchid. "What brings you back Muscud-way?"

"Boss Vassas, he . . ." Vassas had sworn him to silence on the subject of the strange deaths. One reason Vassas had wanted an outsider on the case was because he would be less likely to spread the news. "Well, he has work for me."

"Got tired of the life above, huh? Well, I don't miss it either. I mean, I miss the shops, and the fine clothes, and how clean and nice everything is—but who needs it? To be looked down on, treated like a plague victim . . ."

"I know." Mutants were contagious and thus ostracized in the world above, at least in Ghenisa. There was more to it than that, of course. The long-ago wars over the Resettling had left their mark, and there was the fact that Hissig, a proud fishing port with a well-regarded processing industry, saw those infected by the sea as a blemish.

"I was hoping Madam Saraja could give me a room for the night," Tavlin said. "The Wide-Mouth is full, and I'm supposed to lay low—no pun intended."

She appeared surprised, then a pained look entered her eyes. "You didn't hear? Madam Saraja died a year ago."

"That's terrible. How?"

"A shooting. Two bravos from different gangs. She tried to stop it but got gunned down. She lasted two weeks at the hospital, but you know the doctors down here, and the supplies they have."

"Damn."

"Boss Vassas is good at keeping order, but sometimes one of the smaller gangs gets restless, and that just encourages the others. Then the Boss has to clamp down hard—which is a good thing, I think."

"I guess Madam Saraja would agree."

"Elana's our new madam." She indicated a plump woman talking with one of the girls near the dance floor. "Maybe she'll give you a room."

"Thanks."

She kissed his cheek, and he was careful not to wipe it in front of her; the contagion was passed through bodily fluids. "Give me a call if you're in the mood for a tumble. For you, half price."

Before she could leave, he grabbed her arm, and she looked back at him in surprise. He gathered his courage and said, "Sophia. Where is Sophia?"

She shook her head. "This isn't your night for good news, dear."

Something balled in the pit of his stomach. His voice suddenly hoarse, he said, "She's not . . . she didn't . . ."

"No. But she left Muscud when Saraja died."

The fist balling in his stomach unclenched—somewhat. He still felt the ache were it had been. "Where did she go?"

"I don't remember. Still in the under-towns, I think. Maybe Netherlusk. Or Cor. I'll ask around."

She squeezed his hand and rejoined the crowd, seeking out her next client. For a while Tavlin stayed on the couch, taking it all in. The music seemed far away now, as if a veil of cotton separated him from it. When a girl with a silver platter bearing complimentary drinks passed by, he snatched one and downed a long swallow without glancing twice at its contents. The whiskey burned his throat, and his eyes watered. Healing waves of warmth traveled through him, and he finished off the glass in another swallow.

Thus fortified, he made his way to the new madam, Elana, a big woman in a loose red dress practically spilling out her voluminous breasts, which were only barely contained, half tease, half threat. Her eyes were bulging and somewhat fish-like, and her skin bore the faint suggestion of scales. Currently she was whispering with a john, possibly negotiating the price for one of her girls. It gave Tavlin time to study her, and he realized that he recognized her. Elana had been one of the aging prostitutes under Madam Saraja, one of those who had fought for power within the ranks of the Skirt.

When finished with the john, she turned her bulging eyes to Tavlin. "How may I help you? Wait, I know you, don't I? Yes, you used to come around calling on Sophia."

"That's right."

"You ran the gambling hall over at the Wide-Mouth, didn't you? Yes, I remember because you're uninfected, and I always thought it strange that in a city of mutants, only a human could appear so flashy. But you were especially so."

He smiled. "I think that was a compliment."

"Just an observation. You did have style, I'll give you that." She gave him the once-over. "What happened?"

He wished he had another drink. "Listen, I need a room for the night, maybe several. Just a room, no girls. I'm trying to avoid the inns. I don't want to be noticed."

"Like I said, a human in a city of mutants is going to get noticed. But I suppose you're not the only one, and I do have a few empty rooms currently making no money. I'll give you one for five crowns a night."

He arched his eyebrows. "Bit steep, isn't it?"

She put her hands on her wide hips. The hands were slightly webbed. "It's you that wants special accommodations, dear, not me. Are you willing to pay for it? That price, by the way, pays for breakfast in the mornings. You can eat with the girls. But don't get any ideas. No toss under this roof without compensation."

"Fine." He started to hand over the coins, but she shook her head.

"Do I look like a cashier? I'll send someone to collect the money." She turned to a girl who was straightening her bodice. "Henrietta, will you take this gentleman to Room Twenty-nine?"

"Sure thing, Madam." She finished straightening up, appraised Tavlin, and said, "Right this way, honey."

She showed him out of the parlor and up a narrow, creaking flight of stairs, and he admired the sway of her hips as she took the stairs ahead of him. The glossy green fabric over her buttocks was stretched very tight, and he could see every flex and roll of her round cheeks—as, no doubt, was intended.

"This way, hon," she said when she reached the second story, and led down a certain hall. Frayed rugs of surprising fineness lined the way, and a split chandelier that looked as if it had been looted from a garbage dump, and probably had, lit the musty space. She ended at the last door and nudged it open with her knee, letting him see a flash of leg through the slit in her ruby skirt. The door was off-kilter and its paint peeling badly. What with the heat and humidity of the city, plus the strange fumes rising from the sewer, the buildings were constantly eaten away by the elements.

"This is it," she purred as he stepped close. She ran her hands up his right arm, and he felt a prickle of gooseflesh. "The room looks awfully lonely. Maybe you could use some company. Don't worry, I have protection. Don't want you to sprout gills, do we?"

Tavlin hesitated. He still had his winnings from earlier that evening . . .

"No," he said. "Maybe later." The memory of those mutilated, transformed bodies lingered in his mind.

She rolled a naked shoulder. "I'll be here. Or maybe I won't."

She sauntered away, swinging her hips as she went, and he watched her go. She glanced back at him, winked, then disappeared down the stairs. He sighed, entered the room and closed the door behind him. The unit was small and faded, the window directly opposite the door streaked with grime and cracked in the middle as if someone had thrown a stone at it. Oh, well, he was lucky to get a window at all.

The bed lay along the right wall, and its length was pretty much the depth of the room. Opposite was a sink in disrepair overhung with the remains of a mirror. Tavlin moved to the sink, turned the faucet—the plumbing banged and squealed, but it worked, if fitfully—and nearly gagged at what came out. Quickly he shut off the water, or whatever it was, and watched as the blackish goop bubbled and swirled about the drain, regretfully leaving its stink behind. When it was as gone as it was likely to get, he braced himself against the sink, took a deep breath, and stared into the mirror.

What he saw was a man slightly above average height, lean in build, with a likewise lean face, long nose and high forehead. Thick eyebrows perched atop eyes that seemed wary and alert, hiding in deep sockets. The lips, full and wide, noted for their smiles, frowned at him. He had cultivated a seedy appearance over the last few years, and his face reflected it – stubbled and unwashed, a scar on the cheek, another over his right eyebrow, hair unwashed and over-long, his flesh scoured by the sun. Once he had worn bright, flashy clothes, but now the clothes he wore were drab and ragged.

He didn't want to look at himself for long—it was too painful—so he reclined in the window seat and went about the motions of stuffing his pipe. He lit the bowl, drew the alchemically-treated tobacco smoke into his mouth, swirled it about his teeth and gums, prodded the smoke with his tongue, enjoying the faint lift it brought to his mind as it was absorbed into his bloodstream, and blew it out the window in a fragrant green cloud, which rose up and out. The great cistern chamber was large enough to produce breezes, and a faint acrid gust tore the smoke apart. In its place was revealed the panorama of Muscud.

Lights blazed from shabby houses and shops, and mysterious alleys emitted weird noises and shadows. It was quite late—early morning, really—but time didn't mean as much down here, in this place forsaken by the sun. To the left stretched shops and homes, ragged apartment complexes, while directly before him sprawled the business district, merging with the industrial sector, such as it was, on the right, a rash of smoking factories and listing aluminum warehouses, some surprisingly large, and throughout it all, right, left and center, sprouting like mushrooms, the various churches and temples. Just ahead loomed the Temple of the Three Sisters with its white towers and silver dome, and Tavlin found it odd that an underground community, whose members rarely saw the sky, would worship the moons. However, it was a very popular religion up top and many of the dwellers of the sewers had been raised in its faith, so it was not too shocking that they continued in it even after becoming infected and moving below. Other churches dominated, however. Several were devoted to the worship of slug god Caryth, or Vorgost, the mythical giant white squid of the deep sewers, or Meblang, the Queen Flail. But there were darker places of worship, more sinister ones: the churches to the variously named gods sometimes known as the Ung'zain, or sometimes the R'loth, those awful beings that mutants had worshipped after the Withdraw, during the Dark Times. It had disturbed Tavlin years ago when he'd learned some mutants still worshipped them, and it still did. He didn't like it, but he understood it.

What he didn't understand were the new churches he saw, the ones he couldn't name. He supposed one must be the Church of Magoth. What others might there be? Had the mutants taken to worshipping all the bogeymen of the sewers? He knew the under-cities were only tiny points of light in a vast, alien darkness, a system of tunnels ancient and strange and massive, and there were all sorts of things reportedly living out there in the darkness, but to worship them seemed . . . what? Wrong? Insane? He was not particularly religious himself, but he understood the need for it. Life was chaos, and religion gave it order, meaning.

Speaking of which ...

The attack tonight—what was the meaning behind *it*? He turned his mind to the problem, tried to understand what might have done that to the bodies. Some strange technology? Some weapon? Had some *thing* done it? And why had the perpetrator/perpetrators taken the jewel?

He decided he would talk to Vassas's men, surreptitiously, see if they'd noticed anything out of the ordinary. Then he would research the jewel itself and the race it came from. There was a decent library on Lovell Street, or had been. If it was still there, it might hold some helpful information. Perhaps if he knew more about the jewel, and the strange alchemy that apparently went into its making—*Like it was alive,* Frankie had said—he could figure out what the thieves wanted with it, and where/who they might be. If the Lovell library didn't help, he would ascend to Hissig proper and its great library on Haslehg Blvd.

He finished his pipe and paused before refilling it. It was late. He should sleep. He wanted to send down for an overnight kit, a toothbrush, razor and so on, but he was too tired. He did manage to leave the room briefly, find one of the public toilets—the one for the johns—and use it. At the urinal a man was bragging about his just-finished tryst with the Eel Twins. Tavlin tuned him out. Wearily he washed and made his way back to his room.

Just as he turned the knob, Tavlin heard a long, terrified scream.

* * *

He stood stock-still.

The scream came again.

Blood pounding, Tavlin ran toward it, up a flight of stairs, then another. Prostitutes surged around him, crying out to each other in confusion.

"What was that?"

"It sounded like the Madam!"

"Could it be?"

"Maybe we should get some help."

"Get to her room!"

Breathless, fighting his way through the tide, Tavlin emerged onto the fourth and highest floor and flowed along with the women toward Madam Elana's rooms at the end of the hall. She didn't possess half the floor like Boss Vassas did, but she did have a large suite (Tavlin had seen it before, when it was Saraja's) and a large, elaborately-worked door.

The girls banged on it. When no one answered, two of the larger women kicked it down. Tavlin volunteered to help, but they pushed him aside.

As the door splintered, the girls rushed inside. Tavlin reached for the knife he always kept in his jacket pocket, although usually it was just for show. With it in hand, he entered the Madam's suite. Elana had kept much of Saraja's belongings, the lacy curtains and delicate lanterns, but she had added a profusion of figurines of toads and toadstools, and she had many surprisingly lovely paintings of swamps.

Her body lay in the middle of the room. Like the ones at Boss Vassas's place, it had been transformed into an inhuman mass of whitish, translucent material, blown apart as if by great force so that, in addition to the main mass oozing on the floor, pieces of the jellyfish-like flesh hung on couch and lantern, dripped off wall and overhead chandelier. It all stank of sulfur and ammonia. Tavlin placed his free hand over his mouth and nose and tried to breathe shallow. Several of the girls made gagging noises, and two rushed from the room. Others knelt over the Madam's body, or stood carefully away from it, exclaiming in horror.

"Is that the *Madam*?"

"What could have done this?"

A gentle breeze stirred Tavlin's hair. He looked to the window, which was large and elaborately framed.

And open.

Without thinking, he moved to it and peered outside. Rooftops and rooftops. Nothing else save for a swirl of down-sweeping flails, slippery and glistening in the light of a street-lamp. Whoever had done this must still be nearby.

He placed his hands on the windowsill, swung a leg over it, feeling the chipped edge dig into his thigh through his corduroy pants, and carefully lowered himself onto the thin ledge that was the window's bottom edge and that ran in both directions, becoming the bottom edge of the next window and wrapping around the house. At its corners, mismatched gargoyles glared out over the little city.

"What are you *doing*?"

The words, so close to Tavlin's ear, made him jump so that he nearly fell off the ledge. He turned to see Maya looking grief-stricken and shocked.

"Going after him," Tavlin said.

"You're crazy."

He wanted to say it's what he'd been hired to do, and the murderer had possibly just saved him a good deal of time and effort—not perhaps the most charitable thought, he admitted to himself—but instead he concentrated on stepping sideways along the narrow ledge. A flail swished past him, its mucus spattering his cheek and its wings making thick wet *wack-wack* noises. When Tavlin reached the corner, he was able to brace himself against the gargoyle there, turn about and use the crenellations and ornamentation in the walls as handholds and toeholds. He used to be a thief, and though those skills had long ago rusted they were still present, if atrophied. With a grunt, he hauled himself up, hand over hand, foot over foot, until he could heave himself over the edge. He flopped onto the roof, braced against the gutter that channeled the ever-present drip from above, and lay gasping. He had only climbed a few feet and already he was out of breath. *You're getting old, Tav.*

He forced himself to his feet, climbed the peaked roof of the Twirling Skirt and swept his gaze over the surrounding rooftops. All the buildings in this section of town were pressed up against each other—the columns that supported the platforms on which they stood being thick and ancient—and it would be easy for a thief to navigate roof-to-roof. Tavlin had done so back in the old days, and that had been in the city above where it wasn't as easy. Many of the residents of Muscud kept rooftop gardens, and weird fungus, pale ferns and lichenous growths sprouted from the darkness, lit only by the few lights still blazing in the buildings and by the occasional street lamp below, each one beset with moths and other, slimier things. The lights shifted and swayed as the clouds of moths and other creatures became denser, then more fluid.

Among all this Tavlin did not at first see the slim dark shape speeding away from the whorehouse, but he had good eyes, used to seeing in the darkness, and at last he saw it. He swore. The shape was already far away.

He crossed to the next rooftop, moving in the direction of the killer, but lost his footing and stumbled. *Shit!* He caught himself at the last moment. Gasping, he stared down at the pavement he would have landed on. *Too close.* Gathering his resolve, he pressed on.

A gun cracked.

He was just passing a crumbling brick chimney, and chips of brick exploded under the bullet's impact. The shrapnel sliced his cheek. He ducked behind the smokestack.

When a second gunshot did not immediately follow, he grabbed a loose brick and stuck it out. Nothing. He rushed out, ran to the next chimney and threw himself behind the low wall that bordered the rooftop garden. He could smell the ozone stench of the albino ferns and the pine of the mulch.

No gunshots. He swore. He was breathing heavily and sweating. Part of him would have been relieved if he'd had to go back.

Instead, he hauled himself to his feet and continued pursuing the assassin. He couldn't see the figure but went on in the direction he'd seen it go. He found it odd that the killer would be armed with both a pistol and whatever had slain Madam Elana. *Maybe the unconventional weapon has little ammunition—that or it's expensive.*

The enemy moved into the open. Darting from one chimney to another, the assassin picked his way over rooftops, scrambled up a peak, then half slid, half scurried down the other side, almost vaulting over this rooftop to another.

Tavlin ran after him.

The killer swiveled. A flash of fire signaled another gunshot, an instant before the crack reached Tavlin's ears. Even as the assassin spun, Tavlin flung himself to the roof. The bullet whizzed overhead.

Then Tavlin was up and moving again, the killer disappearing and then reappearing between chimneys and peaks and walls. Tavlin followed. The assassin made his way into the industrial sector. Here the roofs were further apart, and the man scaled down the walls and alit on the streets. Tavlin clambered down a fire escape and followed. He could smell the stink of the sewers now; they were on the edge of the city, close to the shore, where the influence of the scented alchemical lamps was weakest.

The assassin emerged from the cover of the buildings and ran along the docks, down Eyersly Blvd., which bordered the shore and encircled much of the city. Warehouses and factories still lined one side. As soon as Tavlin went after him, the killer turned and fired again. Tavlin reeled back. When he judged the killer too far away to fire accurately, he reemerged.

A tentacle rose from the black water and curled toward his leg. The huge suckered limb attempted to lasso his ankle. He leapt it, barely. *What the hell?*

Another tentacle rose, then another. Huge fleshy bodies strained against encrusted bars that just breached the lake's surface. Someone was transporting illegally-caught giant squid from the Atomic Sea, probably for use as either circus fodder or expensive menu items.

Tavlin swore and ran on. At last he saw the killer stop at a gate in a fence surrounding a particular factory, show some I.D., then be admitted through. The man spoke with a figure at the gate, pointing back.

The figure withdrew a pistol and started for Tavlin.

Shit, thought Tavlin, and stopped. Panting, sweating, joints aching, he watched the dark shape approach. As the light of a passing street-lamp revealed it, Tavlin saw glistening black flesh, huge black eyes and a thrusting snout. It was one of the Suulm, a salamander-like race that lived in underground caverns, typically dwelling near black lakes. They were creatures that loved the water and disdained man and man's technology, thus it surprised Tavlin to see one near the foul sewer water, carrying a pistol and clearly cooperating with men.

Tavlin ducked behind a corner just as the Suulmite lifted its gun and fired at him. The bullet struck chips from the wall.

Tavlin waited for the creature to approach, then popped out and threw his knife at its head. It had to adjust the angle of its gun to deflect the oncoming blade. The gun fired anyway, but the bullet passed harmlessly over Tavlin's head and struck a warehouse wall.

Tavlin rushed the wet, dripping Suulmite, and slammed hard into it. He grabbed its wrists in his hands, forced them up and kneed it in the crotch. The Suulm apparently were not so sensitive in this area, and the creature opened its large snout and snapped vicious teeth at Tavlin's throat. He wrenched himself away, taking the gun with him.

He aimed at the Suulmite's chest. Before he could fire, a strong black hand swatted the gun away and sent it hurling end over end down the docks. It landed atop one of the squid cages and nearly fell through. The Suulmite's other hand made a fist and crashed into Tavlin's jaw. He staggered backward, keeping his feet with an inelegant flap of his arms to balance himself as starbursts flickered in his vision.

Enough. Tavlin edged around the Suulmite, making for the gun.

The Suulmite wasn't about to let him get to it first. The creature leapt to all fours and waddle-ran toward it, tail wagging for balance behind it. The Suulmite moved on all fours faster than Tavlin could run, but Tavlin had a head start. Still, they reached the gun almost at the same time. Tavlin just barely scooped it up and fired—not at the Suulmite, who was low and moving, but at the thick padlock just before him.

Freed, something massive and misshapen erupted from the cage in an orgy of tentacles, huge eyes and snapping beaks. Tavlin ran, screaming, but his screams were not as loud as the surprised Suulmite, who was immediately caught up in a dripping limb. Tavlin did not look back to see the Suulmite's fate, but the salamander creature's screams lasted longer than Tavlin would have supposed, then ended abruptly.

Dear gods, I just killed a man. Or whatever a Suulmite is.

Feeling sick, Tavlin reached a space where the docks stretched out over the lake, and many boats of various sizes bobbed on the calm waters, heaving up and down very slowly to the small swells that rippled across the lake, mostly caused by the movements of the town itself. He sucked in deep breaths and grabbed his knees for support. Sweat stung his eyes. His legs shook. If his hands had been steady enough, he would have stuffed and lit his pipe. Behind him, he could hear the thrashing of the squid-thing, the breaking of wood, the groan of metal and the shouts of townspeople rushing toward it in order to contain the thing, but the noises were far away now. He was safe for the moment.

What had the Suulmite been guarding? What was in that factory, and who owned it, and why did they need whatever the killer had been bringing to them?—if he *had* been bringing anything. Tavlin thought he'd seen a pouch on the man's belt, but he couldn't be certain. Still, he had to assume the man had been about the same business he'd been about earlier that night when he'd killed the five people at the Hall of the Wide-Mouth. If, of course, it had been the same man. Perhaps Tavlin should double back, try to sneak into the factory . . .

He shook it off. They would be on high alert now.

"Shit," he said, partly just to hear his own voice. It didn't sound as steady as he'd like.

As he was standing there collecting his thoughts, a white mist rolled in off the water. At first he barely noticed it, but when it moved closer his eyes were drawn to it. It flowed across the lake, a contained cloud of whiteness, coming straight toward him. At first it was just a dark, amorphous shape at the edge of the city lights, then the roils of darkness became roils of whiteness, and the cloud streamed toward Tavlin as if driven by phantom winds. It was coming *straight for him*, and only him, there could be no mistake.

The hairs lifted on the back of his neck. His knees turned to jelly. A pit formed in his stomach, and he felt cold. If he'd been able to reason logically he would have run, but an odd paralysis had come over him.

The cloud rushed toward him.

I'm safe here on the docks, he thought. Whatever it was, it must be limited to moving on the water. Surely.

It reached the docks and sped across them, a churning cloud whose summits rose higher than Tavlin was tall. It bore down on him.

Before he could shake off his terror to run, the cloud slowed, and the tendrils of vapor sloughed away from its central mass, revealing a beautiful young woman. She was all of white, not like porcelain, and not quite ghost-like, but somewhere in the middle. He could see the suggestion of shadows through her, but she was not *quite* translucent. She glowed, very faintly, a pulsing whiteness, and when the light pulsed bright her limbs glowed like glass. Flowing blonde or blonde-seeming hair fell to her delicate shoulders, and it was almost like vapor as it swirled there.

She came straight toward Tavlin. She stopped when she was near, and he gasped as he stared up at her, buoyed as she was on her cloud. He could not see her feet. Vapor swirled all around her.

She was beautiful. She possessed an otherworldly splendor, an inhuman exquisiteness, that he had never before been able to imagine. Her nose was small and straight, her lips full and round, but not overly so, her brow fine and high, her cheekbones chiseled as if from ivory. But her eyes . . .

Luminous, startling, possessed of an indefinable color, they pierced him. He felt their presence as if her gaze was a physical weight, settling on his shoulders, driving the breath from his lungs.

He stumbled back. He felt as if he were about to pass out.

She flowed toward him. One of her slender arms rose up to his face, and he realized for the first time that she was utterly naked. Clothed only by the clouds, and this only barely, she stood before him nude, phantasmagorical, otherworldly. If she had been human, he would have placed her in her late teens, but there was no telling. She was slender and supple, delicate and graceful.

Her bone-white hand reached toward his face, and as if in a dream he let it approach. She smiled softly at him, and he was struck again by her luminous eyes. They transfixed him. Speared him.

Her fingers brushed his cheek, and they were soft and warm but light, oh so light, almost as if they didn't exist at all.

"Tavlin . . ." Her voice was like a sigh.

"Lady . . ." He wanted to kiss those perfect lips.

Her hand seized his throat and squeezed. Pain like fire filled him. Her beautiful, angelic face twisted into an expression of wrath, and her eyes burned. *"Why did you take it?"*

"Wh-wh—" He gasped around her hand but couldn't speak.

"Why did you take it?"

She shook him like a rag doll.

He tore himself away, and for a long time he knew nothing save the vague patter of his feet. Dimly he realized he was running, but to where, or from what, he did not know. Often he looked over his shoulder, as if making sure something wasn't following him, but he wasn't sure why.

In the morning he awoke in an alley. His head throbbed and he was covered in grime. He remembered everything. He couldn't stop the shaking in his hands and legs.

Chapter 3

He returned to the Twirling Skirt. Entering through a rear entrance, he cleaned himself off in his room, used the lavatory and descended to have breakfast with the ladies of the establishment. He was still trembling. Never could he remember being so out of sorts—but he was also hungry. Ravenous. His stomach growled loud enough to hear from several feet away. The women of the Skirt smiled at him, but the smiles were sad.

The food smelled heavenly, eggs and biscuits, tainted seafood of various sorts, mutated mollusk, diseased zappers, fried flail, plus orange juice, toast and jam of questionable freshness. Tavlin filled his plate (eschewing anything that came from the water or had contact with same), sat down at one of the crowded wooden tables whose scars were hidden under frayed but pretty checkered tablecloths, and commenced eating. His trembling began to subside, but slowly.

Young women (and a few men) filled the room, trickling in a few at a time. The women assigned cooking duty would cook all morning, so there was no hurry. Many of the prostitutes rubbed red-rimmed eyes, and all looked sad and scared. Groups huddled and spoke of Madam Elana and of what had happened last night. Several made tear-filled speeches. Tavlin began to feel bad about listening in—he was an outsider here, after all—and rose to leave.

As he reached the doorway, someone squeezed his arm. He turned to see Henrietta. She was clad in a flimsy shift, though the illusion of sensuality was somewhat ruined by the curlers in her hair and the thick, fluffy orange leg warmers that crawled halfway up her thigh. She too looked as if she had been crying, and she flung herself against him and sobbed into his chest.

He patted her back. "There, there."

"You were so *brave*." She lifted her face to look into his eyes.

"I—what—"

"Going after her killer last night—oh, that was so amazing! Did you get him? Did you *kill* him?"

Other girls glanced up, and many clamored to know what the result of last night's activities had been. They seemed a bit too bloodthirsty for Tavlin's liking.

He gently disengaged himself from Henrietta. "I didn't get him."

There came a disappointed *ahhh.*

"But I think I know where he went."

Their eyes lit up.

"What are you going to do now?" asked one, and others echoed the sentiment. Tavlin knew that Muscud did have its own mayor, and the mayor employed a single police officer, but both were eminently corruptible and unreliable. If you wanted something done in Muscud, you pretty much had to do it yourself—or, apparently, get Tavlin to do it for you. Despite that, he felt his chest swell as the women's eyes seized on him like graphite shards to a magnet.

"I'm . . . going after him," he said. The words were easy to say, at any rate.

Henrietta smiled, somewhat insanely. "Good."

"Tell me, did Elana . . . was anything missing last night?"

The women looked at each other. Then one of the older ones, with threads of white in her red hair, said, "Yes. Her favorite necklace. Why?"

"Was it . . . was there anything odd about the necklace?"

More strange looks. The redhead said, "Yes. The stones set within it were taken from old ruins, or so Elana always said, and I believe it. Ruins from one of the pre-human races—the Iuss'ha, I think. The stones . . . sort of glimmered. Like a fire was somewhere way down inside them, and they weren't clear exactly. You couldn't see into their depths. They were sort of . . . smoky. But they were the most beautiful stones I ever saw, like honey-burgundy, a color I've never seen before. Never seen their like, either."

Tavlin nodded. It's what he had expected. "I mean to make sure you see them again."

These were more bold words, of course, and as he stepped out onto the street several minutes later he began to regret them.

*   *   *

The air smelled of musk, rust, stone, an underlying, hardly-noticeable foulness, the scents of various restaurants and streetside vendors—fried rat, squid, egg wraps, grilled slugmine, bagels—and a thousand strange secretions.

It was too early to visit the Wide-Mouth. Deciding he could do with some coffee, Tavlin made for a place he used to frequent and dry-swallowed his daily pollution pill on the way. All non-infected coast dwellers carried a supply on them just in case; skipping even a single day was risking infection. The pills were lifesavers and, coupled with the air processors up top, they allowed humans to live along the coasts of the Atomic Sea. They still weren't enough to protect someone from contaminated food, water, or swapping bodily fluids from someone already infected, however.

As he made his way through the streets and over the canals, he remembered strolling these same avenues before. Many of those instances had been with Sophia. They had been through here countless times together. They had likely explored every square inch of Muscud, from the Razor Quarter to the Shingles, from Dockside East to Dockside West, from the depths of the Innysmere to the heights of the Spire, even a brief foray into the Ualissi Quarter. He remembered casting pennies with Sophia off the Waythern Bridge; there were said to be spirits in the Way Canal that granted wishes. Sophia had believed it. Together they would often picnic in the Syssl, a rooftop garden with an unparalleled view of the city, or grab a hot dog along Liechsmarg Canal; she knew the vendor there and was always assured of the hot dog's safeness. Of course, that was only for Tavlin's benefit, as she had been infected long ago, before they met.

Her mutations were subtle, one webbed hand, some scaly skin, gills. He remembered he used to trace the left side of her torso, from her ribs up over her breast, to her collarbone. The whole expanse was covered in glittering silver scales, and when she moved it flashed brilliantly. It was oddly beautiful, and the smooth, cool, raspy feel of it had sent tingles down his whole hand. Sometimes she would shudder at the caress, at the twist of a blue nipple, and when she did her gills would flutter briefly, and her gorgeous hazel eyes would widen, and her toes flex.

Those days were over now. After Jameson . . .

Tavlin switched the thought off. Better to think of other things, things that he could make some difference in. There was no changing the past.

He found his coffee bar, Gezzyr's, perched on an old stone bridge above a canal, and he reclined on the terrace smoking his alchemically-laced tobacco, drinking coffee, and trying to come up with a plan. Below him boats came and went, the early morning traffic of Muscud. The fog that had crept throughout the city during the night at the lessening of activity now broke up and faded away as boats whipped it aside, but that fog made him remember …

The girl in the cloud.

Did that really happen?

She had been like a ghost, he thought. But ghosts didn't exist. Did they?

Horns blew through the still-hazy air, and mutants called to each other, or honked the horns of their motorcycles. Somewhere music played so loudly that it echoed off the stone ceiling that was Muscud's sky high, high above, stirring the flails that nested there in their dripping stalactite mounds.

Tavlin smoked on. Thinking.

When he was done, he moved swiftly toward the industrial sector. Though his skin crawled as he neared the factory he'd seen the assassin vanish into, he forced himself closer. It seemed just as busy today as yesterday, only he saw no Suulmites at the moment, only mutants. Then again, the Suulm were nocturnal creatures, in as much as they recognized the time of day. Tavlin found the address without getting too near, then ducked down an alley, climbed a building and squatted on its roof for some time, studying the comings and goings of the factory. It was a hive of activity, with much traffic in and out, some of it from beneath the docks.

The industrial sector was raised above the level of much of the town, and boats made pick-ups and drop-offs under the docks from trapdoors in the factories above. Tavlin could not see what it was the boats picked up or dropped off, of course, which was likely intentional. No smoke issued from the factory's smokestacks. He wondered what they might be making.

After a few hours of spying, he climbed down. He drew on his pipe as he made his way back through town, thinking as he went. At last he found his way to the library, a listing building of wood, brick and stone several hundred years old, scarred by smoke and covered in grime. Several flails sucked on the walls in the alley he passed, making squelching noises, and he saw orphan mutants preparing traps for them.

The library was ancient, and as Tavlin entered the small, two-story building he had to wrinkle his nose at the smell of must and decay. The librarians of Muscud were virtual literary pirates, and they had been stealing, looting and tricking their way into books for as long as the library had stood, erected by Tithanus Marl, said to be a disenfranchised royal back in the Imperial Age—which had just ended fifty-odd years ago with the Revolution—and he had intended on bringing the sophistication of the mutants up to a more refined level. Tavlin thought the cause righteous but doomed. Nevertheless modern librarians carried on the tradition, stealing and reappropriating books whenever possible. They would even send raiding parties into the world above to bring back tomes.

The current librarian slouched behind the counter. He was a hulking creature with webbed hands, no nose, and covered in dark striations like tribal tattoos. He looked up when Tavlin entered, blinked, and then, in what seemed like a gesture he had used very little in his life, smiled. His teeth were white and shiny and sharp.

"Two-bit!"

Tavlin shook the man's hand, careful not to let the fellow see him wipe his palm on his pants as he dropped his hand to his side. "Guyan! How are you?"

"Good, good. Business is slow."

"There never were many readers here."

"It's worse than that. It's the . . ." He paused. Sudden wariness entered his eyes, and he looked Tavlin over carefully. Gradually he seemed to find what he was hoping for. In a lower voice, he added, "It's fucking Magoth. Or its worshippers, take your pick."

Tavlin had finished his bowl, and now he tapped it out into the misshapen clay ashtray on the counter. "Not big into reading, are they?"

"Not unless it's their damned bible."

"They have a bible now? Interesting."

"If you say so. Anyway, I shouldn't be talking like this."

"You afraid of them?"

Guyan shrugged his broad shoulders. "There have been some . . . disappearances. People that speak out against them don't speak out for long, if you get me. And they're spreading like fungus. I thought they'd be satisfied when they had their own church. Not only were they unsatisfied, but they've taken over several other churches since then. Remember the House of the Laug? Theirs. The Laugians vanished overnight, killed or driven off, no one knows which. Same with the Satherists. *And* the Church of the Vygun-Iss."

"Might be time for you to set up shop elsewhere."

"And abandon the sacred trust? No. I'm in Muscud for the long haul." Darkly, he added, "One way or another. Anyway, it's good to see a friendly face. Been awhile since you've been around this kink of the Stink. Heard you were topside."

"I'm only back temporarily."

"You know, we could use you. You brought some color to this place."

"It's colorful enough."

"What happened to you, anyway? You don't look the same. You're not still . . ." Tavlin just watched him, and Guyan dropped his gaze. "Oh."

"Listen, I was hoping to look through the public records, see who owns a particular piece of property."

Guyan made a face. "You know how sketchy the records are, but I'll do what I can. Which property?" Tavlin gave him the address, and Guyan yanked out a ledger and thumbed through it, dust pluming upward as he cracked the pages. His eyes scanned a page, then another. Finally he slammed the book closed—triggering an explosion of dust—and looked up. "Do you know anything about the public property records, Two-Bit?"

"Can't say I do."

"Well, we didn't used to have any, but as the city grew, over time parts of it would shift, break away from other parts. Much of it was made of trash and cast-offs, and it wasn't meant to last. Whole sections would sink, or break away into little islets. Finally we elected a mayor and got some organization, and properties had to be approved before they could be built, and more of them were built of stone and wood, and pillars were sunk into the lake bed. Well, it's been hundreds of years since then and the mayors aren't what they used to be. Mayor Jensen, well . . ."

"Yeah." Jensen was deep in the pocket of the mob; Boss Vassas had done quite a bit of business with him.

"You have to get his permission to build or renovate, but he gives permission out of his wallet, if you know what I mean, and the more money's exchanged the less likely he is to report the sale."

"So someone paid him off."

"Must be, because it's not here."

Tavlin nodded slowly. "Well, at least I know where to start looking."

"Don't expect Boss Vassas to tell on the mayor. People at that level know how to keep their lips sealed, at least about others at the same level."

"We'll see."

"Is there anything else I can help you with? I just got a new series by Marcus Synn. Wasn't he one of your favorite writers? This one's about that detective in the tropics. And only slight damage to the pages."

"Actually, I'm looking for more information on one of the old races. Pre-human."

"Which race?"

"The Iuss'ha."

Guyan indicated with his chin. "Upstairs in the far corner. You'll find them in the Arcane History section."

Tavlin climbed up the creaking, peeling ladder to the platform that encompassed the upper half of the building, lined by thick, sagging bookshelves exuding the stink of mold, age and, yes, there it was, sewage. Tavlin donned a pair of gloves to read by, a common practice down here, and selected a volume that was so crumbly he feared it would disintegrate in his hands. The tome covered a span of years long before man had evolved, back during the age of the Iuss'ha.

Tavlin sat down at a listing table, swept the dust from it with a brush of his hand and commenced to read.

Little was known of the strange race. They had lived millions of years ago and few of their writings had survived. It was known that they had been highly advanced technologically, and that some of their technology had been quite otherworldly, unlike anything men knew. Nothing was known of the reasons behind their disappearance, though other races of the same time had left bas-reliefs of some awful cataclysm. Early man had worshipped in the ruins of the Iuss'ha, thinking whatever race had left them must be gods, but they were not unique in this. Beyond that nothing was known, at least in the volume Tavlin had before him.

There was certainly no mention of the jewels Boss Vassas and Madam Elana claimed came from them. Nor was there mention of mysterious ghost women.

Tavlin tried several more books, found nothing of any further use, then spoke with Guyan.

"Perhaps another library," Guyan suggested.

"This is the only one in Muscud."

"Try the one in Urst, or Hadmar. There's more than just this one. You don't remember the raids the Urstian librarians pulled a few years back? We're just now recovering from them. Had to replenish the entire letter H."

"Well, I'm off."

Tavlin left the library and set out for the Wide-Mouth, and Boss Vassas. He had a few questions to ask of his old employer.

* * *

"The mayor won't say jack," Boss Vassas said. "Not because he's tight-lipped—shit, he's as loose as Jasmine downstairs—but because he's scared shitless. Those boys in that factory aren't your usual renters."

Tavlin was stuffing his pipe. He raised his eyebrows without looking up and said, "How so?" They sat in Boss Vassas's study, which was part of the suite that had been attacked last night, though this room had seen no violence. Rich rugs covered the floor and murky oil paintings of mutant heroes and battle scenes covered the walls. A fire crackled in the fireplace, and the whole room smelled of smoke. Tavlin knew the smoke from the chimneys of Muscud gathered at the apex of the cistern chamber, where a vent with a fan in it drew the smoke out; every now and then the motor running the fan would break down and the whole town would fill with an acrid cloud. Fortunately that was a rare occurrence.

Boss Vassas stared out the window overlooking the city. Turning, he said, with a half smile on his face, "Because they're not. Remember, I own a good chunk of those warehouses and factories. The boys in that particular one came to me first, looking for a place to rent, but I didn't have any vacancies, so I directed them to the mayor, who owns a couple himself, and one I knew happened to be empty."

"Who are they?"

"Hell if I know, my friend. But I'll tell you one thing. This one day, after they'd been comin' round for a while, tryin' to build up trust, I guess, 'cause they were from outta town, well one day they asked to use my phone. There ain't many in Muscud and they were willin' to pay for it, so I said alright. I even left the room for 'em." His face was hard. "I listened at the keyhole."

Tavlin lit his pipe and sucked in the first mouthful. He swirled it around his tongue, then breathed it out. Seeing that Boss Vassas needed prompting, he said, "Yeah? And?"

Firelight crackled in Vassas's eyes. "They spoke with an Octunggen accent."

A shudder coursed up Tavlin's spine. Perhaps the chill came from the open window. It was certainly hot enough in here. "A lot of people have Octunggen accents," he said. "Octung used to control a bunch of countries, you know."

"Yeah, but they didn't speak with any accent when they were in front of me. Only when they were by themselves, when they didn't think anyone was listening. And then only a little, like it just slipped out."

Tavlin frowned. "So what do you think they're up to?"

"I don't know, but I got a bad vibe from them, and so did Jensen. He wouldn't have rented to them if he thought they'd let him say no. Those bastards seem to get what they want, every time, and they have connections outside, I don't know where, but more of 'em would arrive, and then more. I don't even know how many are in that damned factory, but they seem to live there, most of 'em."

"What could they be doing there? And why would they need jewelry from some race who've been fossils for gods know how long?"

Boss Vassas rubbed his heavy jowls. "And why would they kill high-profile targets to get them? You'd think they'd at least have enough sense to not piss off people like me."

"Does that mean you'll hit them?"

Boss Vassas looked at Tavlin, then turned his gaze to the flames. After a long moment, he said, "I don't know."

Tavlin studied him. "You don't know how strong they are."

"And I don't know what resources they have. They have weapons that can turn people into . . . well, whatever. Nothing human-looking. White mush." His face twitched, and Tavlin knew he must be thinking about Nancy, about what his beloved had been turned into. "Maybe that makes sense if they're Octunggen. They say Octung has been developing extradimensional weapons for a long time in preparation for their war. Maybe the boys in the factory have more than just the one weapon." He grunted, as if something had just occurred to him. "Maybe that's why they used it, to scare people like me off, if we should find out who did it."

"So what then? Sit and let them continue doing whatever they're doing, right in your own backyard? That doesn't sound like the Boss Vassas I know."

Vassas's expression darkened, and when his eyes swiveled to Tavlin, they were sharp as knives. All of a sudden Tavlin remembered whom he was speaking with.

"What was that?" Vassas said, his voice eerily neutral.

Tavlin made himself swallow. “Nothing, Boss.” He busied himself with renewing the flame on his pipe, which had gone out.

Vassas cracked his knuckles and paced back and forth before the fire. He had asked to speak with Tavlin alone, but now Tavlin half-wished someone else were in the room. If nothing else, it would give the Boss someone else to focus on if he got mad.

“I need to know more about them,” Vassas said. He opened his mouth to say something more, but just then gunshots pierced the night.

As one, Tavlin and Vassas ran for the door.

They dashed downstairs to the first floor, then made their way through the chaos toward the front entrance. Most everyone else was rushing *away* from it. Vassas’s men had moved toward the front, and from that direction more gunshots rang out. Vassas pulled out a pistol and Tavlin pulled out his stolen piece as they reached the entrance, and they stepped out into the street.

A dozen motorcycles roared off spitting black smoke. Each one had a sidecar, and gunmen in the sidecars turned and fired back at the men who stood before the Wide-Mouth. Tavlin hit the ground shooting. Several of Vassas’s other men hunkered low, as well, and the cracks of their guns popped like fireworks. When Tavlin glanced back, he saw Vassas standing tall and indomitable, eyes narrowed, smoke curling up from his large, oiled revolver as fire spat from its barrel.

The motorcyclists swerved out of sight and the gunfire stopped.

Several men were down, and Vassas and his people knelt over them and gave what help they could. Someone called the house doctor. Tavlin assisted in staunching wounds and tying tourniquets. His head spun, and his heart performed a mad jig in his chest. Four men had been shot, and one was clearly dead, his brains leaking on the sidewalk, shards of skull flecking the puddle.

Another body lay twisted in the street further from the Wide-Mouth's entrance than the others. When the wounded were seen to, Vassas, with Frankie beside him, made his way to the body and stared down at it. Tavlin joined them. The corpse was that of a man, naked, beaten and mutilated. His scrotum had been removed, leaving a bloody wound, and it had been stuffed between the man's jaws. Ragged bits of flesh stuck out between cracked teeth.

"Fuck," said Frankie, "it's Serat."

Vassas placed a hand to his forehead, as if a headache had come on him all of a sudden. "Damn it all." He swayed for a moment, then shook his head. For a long time he said nothing, and Tavlin became aware of the sounds of the doctor moving patients into his little office in the back of the building next to the kitchens.

"Who was he?" Tavlin asked, realizing that the motorcyclists must have dropped the body off.

Vassas didn't answer, but Frankie did: "One of our boys. Came after your time. Boss sent him to negotiate Peter's return—that's the fellow we, ah, questioned last night. We couldn't just give him back to his gang, that would look weak, you know how it is, but we were gonna ransom him back and let them off with a good bargain."

"This is Grund's crew you're talking about, right, the ones you thought committed the murders?"

"Yeah. Grund likes motorcycles. Don't know where he got the cash for them all, though. That happened real recent." Frankie looked down at Serat's body, grimaced, and turned away. "Anyway, Serat was our envoy. No one touches envoys, not for a long time."

"Looks like Grund wants a fight."

Boss Vassas grunted, and when Tavlin peered at him he saw that the Boss had changed. The mob chieftain was harder, grimmer, and there was a strange light behind his eyes only hinted at by his unnaturally calm demeanor. "No," he said. "It's war he wants. And by the gods, it's war I'll give him."

Chapter 4

Water lapped at the pilings, and Tavlin felt the skin between his shoulder blades draw tight. This really wasn't a good idea, he told himself for the hundredth time. Yet Boss Vassas had been so distracted organizing for battle that he hadn't been willing to give Tavlin the assistance he'd requested, which left Tavlin no choice if he wanted something to get done about the murders and the missing jewels. Now, however, as he rowed his boat beneath the raised pier of the warehouse district, draped in shadow and all too close to the water, he wondered if he had a choice after all.

It wasn't as if he *had* to be here. No one was making him. Sure, Boss Vassas was paying him, and the girls at the Twirling Skirt expected it of him, but who was he to do this sort of thing? He was a gambler, a former junkie and thief, a member of the mob, a lousy bastard all around. Did he think this bit of skull-duggery was going to make up for a lifetime of misspent energy? It was absurd. And yet, as if despite the rest of him, his arms continued rowing the boat forward.

He made for the factory where the man who had killed Madam Elana had gone. 4302 Eversly. It was late at night, as the inhabitants of Muscud reckoned night, and few sounds filtered through the boards and cement overhead, and what few sounds did leak through were mostly soaked up by the vapor exuded by the water. Tavlin tried not to think of the slimy things that lived just below him, things that might regard an untainted human as a tasty snack.

Rowing forward, he began to hear faint sounds. The vapor created a fog of sorts, a nasty, acrid exudation that constantly made him spit, but it was thin at the moment, and concentrated only in pockets, so that he could see, from time to time, a boat crew make an overnight delivery or drop-off at the trapdoor entrances to certain factories and warehouses. There weren't many such crews about, but they were in evidence.

The trapdoors were marked with addresses so that the boat crews could find them. At the dormant doors, Tavlin rowed close to find out where along Eversly Blvd. he was. The numbers reassured him that he went in the proper direction. At last he came within sight of the trapdoor to what must be 4302. He did not venture near enough to check the address, but he verified the adjacent properties' numbers and they left no doubt that he had found the right one.

He stopped rowing when the boat reached a pillar, and in the shadow of the column—overgrown with barnacle-like encrustations about which hopped things that might have once been frogs—he sat and waited. The temptation to light a bowl came on him, but he kept it at bay. The light and the smell might alert his enemies, if enemies they were, and it was hard to imagine them as anything but. They were likely from Octung, the dreaded Lightning Crown, and they had killed Madam Elana and five of Boss Vassas's people, several of which Tavlin had known. Nancy had been a close friend of Sophia.

The trapdoor to 4302 was still. No traffic in or out. Yet he could hear sounds in the factory above, the creaking of boards, the groan of machinery, and he knew from his vigil earlier that this trapdoor was used frequently. He still wasn't sure what his plan was, if he had one. He had entertained some vague notion of sneaking up through the trapdoor, but there was no lock on this side. Someone would have to let him in, and he didn't like his chances of forcing his way up and through the factory.

He decided he would wait to see if there was a delivery. Perhaps he would be able to sneak up then. At least he might be able to see what was being delivered.

Impatiently, he bided his time. The sounds coming from above grew louder, and he became convinced that the factory was busier than usual, perhaps quite a bit busier. Was there something major going on? It would make sense, if the Octunggen had committed at least two sets of murders last night, had stolen at least two jewels, where no one had heard of any such thing happening over the last few months. Presumably they had stolen other jewels and committed other murders, as well, last night or at least recently, but no one Tavlin had talked to seemed to know about them, and people went missing with alarming frequency in Muscud, so such a disappearance might not be remarked upon. At any rate, whatever activity the Octunggen were about, it was heating up. Might tonight be a climax of some sort?

A dark shape drifted in out of the dark. Tavlin tensed. Fog curled around the bow of a boat, a somewhat heavier, larger boat than the one Tavlin had rented for the evening. Like his, it had a motor, but, unlike his, this boat's motor was revved and purring loudly. The fog had muted it, but as it drew close Tavlin found the motor's grumble and chug disorienting after so much silence.

The boat aimed for the trapdoor, and when it was close the engine shut off and the dark figures aboard rowed it right up under the trap. Tavlin squinted, made out perhaps half a dozen figures aboard, two carrying flashlights, which they played over the ancient, stained wood of the door. Someone rapped it with an oar, three knocks, then two, then three more knocks. A heavy metallic sound issued from above, the door buckled, then was drawn up, revealing a rectangle of amber light that shone full upon the occupants of the boat: mutants in ragged clothes. Various scars and tattoos marked them as the rough sort that often worked shady jobs along the docks.

The largest one, a hulking man whose wide shoulders sloped down to thick, fish-scaled arms, visible because his shirtsleeves were rolled up past his elbow, called to the people above, and the factory people called back. Tavlin was too far away to hear exactly what was said.

Those inside threw a ladder down, and a tall man descended into the boat. He was not obviously infected and wore a dark, waxed overcoat that sort of glistened in a sick, insectile manner. He wore a gas mask around his neck but had not placed it over his mouth. The mutants seemed to defer to him. Once settled, he raised his face to the opening and stretched out his hands as if to receive something. People above, seen by Tavlin as only hands and arms, passed down a suitcase. The tall man accepted it carefully, inspected it, then turned to the mutant leader and nodded. The leader barked an order and the boat set off into the fog, motor purring once more. The tall man stood in the center, suitcase at his side, staring off into the mist.

Tavlin rowed toward the trapdoor. The unseen people above slammed the door down before he came close, though, and the sound of a bolt sliding across rusty metal signaled the end of that plan.

"Shit," he muttered.

Suddenly, he felt very alone out here. To reassure himself, he patted the revolver snugged in its shoulder holster, a gift of Boss Vassas. *I hope it doesn't come to that.*

The commotion in the factory above him continued, but it shifted into a new phase—it started to *lessen.* As if whatever the activity's purpose was had been accomplished. Had it been to prepare whatever was in the briefcase? If so, then now that the briefcase was en route to its destination, wherever that was, the factory workers need only close up shop. Tavlin frowned into the darkness where the boat was disappearing, a dark mark surrounded by yellow-white vapor.

With deep misgivings, he grabbed the oars and began rowing after it.

He followed the ever-changing hole in the mist caused by the boat's passage, and as the mist surrounded him he couldn't resist a shudder. Nothing but cloying, foul, roiling fog, the gaseous secretions of the water. He spat out the bitter taste, reminding himself to take double the amount of pollution pills later on. He hated to be out on the open water. These channels linked to the Atomic Sea; one fall overboard could infect him. He would die of a lingering disease or else become mutated like so many others, forever relegated to the fringes of society. And that was if something didn't eat him.

He rowed carefully.

The sound of the motor began to fade ahead, and he realized he would have to use his own engine—dangerous, but he saw no choice. He revved the outboard with a jerk of his arm, grabbed the steering rod and aimed the boat after his quarry. The other boat's motor was larger and more powerful. He could hear it, just faintly, over the roar of his own. Hopefully that meant they couldn't hear him.

The larger boat, containing the man with the briefcase—could he be Octunggen, as Boss Vassas had surmised?—set off over the open water between Muscud and the walls of the cistern chamber, then vanished into a high passage, with flails sucking on the walls.

Tavlin followed. The sound of the larger boat's motor echoed loudly off the tight stone walls. The boat wound through the dark, empty passageways, traveling down one canal, then another, and Tavlin pursued. Soon he wasn't sure in which direction he had come from, or how to find his way back. They seemed far from Muscud now, and he remembered how large the network of sewer tunnels really was. Occasionally he stopped his motor and pricked his ears to decipher where to go next.

Where could the man with the briefcase be journeying to, anyway? Was he simply a courier, delivering the contents of the case?

Tavlin came across them sooner than he had expected.

The boat with the Octunggen man (if that's what he was) had rounded a bend and slowed to a stop, its motor cut off. Tavlin, lagging behind, just saw it vanish around the corner, and as soon as he heard the chug of the motor winding down he quickly shut off his own engine.

The engine rattled to silence several seconds after his quarry's. His whole body tensed, and he felt his skin prickle along his arms. His scrotum contracted. If the occupants of the boat had heard his engine . . .

He waited. Teeth clenched, he waited. Slowly, he removed his gun and held it before him, aiming at the passage the boat had vanished into. Mist, fainter here in the small canals, drifted slowly over the water.

The boat did not emerge. Sounds did, however. He heard the swish of oars in water, the voices of mutants speaking softly to each other, as if in fear or respect.

Tavlin placed his pistol on the bench before him, took hold of the oars and eased the boat forward. Carefully, he moved beyond the lip of the corner and stared down the passageway. He readied himself to lunge for the gun, but the occupants of the boat were not lying in wait for him but rowing ahead, down the canal, as mist swirled about their hull, and dark, mound-like shapes protruded from the surface of the water all around them.

Tavlin blinked, then swore silently. The mounds broke the surface of the water like disgusting, over-large human brains, gray and slick with slime, and he knew that thick, rubbery tentacles tangled below them, filled with venom. These were slugmines, the slug equivalent of jellyfish, and they made boat passage through the sewers more dangerous than it was already. When startled, they could emit a black cloud of poisonous gas that could make a person suffocate until he died, and then they would jet off into the labyrinth, squid-like. Suddenly Tavlin realized why the man with the briefcase had brought a gas-mask.

Indeed, Tavlin thought the man had donned it, though it was hard to tell with the fellow twenty yards ahead and facing the other way. Tavlin thought he saw straps around the back of his head.

With great care, the mutants rowed the boat through the water between slugmines, not even speaking unless they needed to for fear of rousing the creatures.

Gathering his courage, Tavlin rowed into the passageway. He neared the first of the slugmines, saw the great eye in its side, filmy and covered by a mucus-y membrane, and veered wide around it. The membrane did not open, the eye did not see him. Tavlin breathed shallow.

Forward, slowly now, around the next slugmine, then the next. Oh, shit, there was one coming up on his left, its tip just breaching the surface. He had almost missed seeing it. No, he told himself, don't use the oar to shove it away, just brake with the flat of the blade, turn with the other . . . yes, like that . . . now forward . . . slowly, very slowly . . . hope the bastards in the boat ahead don't look back . . .

The mist was thin here, though it still clung to the corners and edges of the canal and swirled gently over the waters, helping mask the dangerous mounds, and it would be quite easy for the occupants of the boat to see Tavlin if they were to glance back. Surely they would, he thought. Any second . . .

The boat ahead, wider than his own, made its way through the minefield more slowly than his. Thus, without quite realizing it until it happened, so focused was he on evading the slugmines, he approached his quarry sooner than he had prepared for.

One of his oars must have made too loud a gurgle, for suddenly the tall man in his waxy, glistening overcoat spun around.

Saw him.

The man's face was covered in the black gas mask with its jutting air purifier, making him look even more like some alien, insectile thing, but Tavlin still saw his eyes, dark and glaring, through the plastic sheen of the mask.

The man called out, a short, sharp bark.

The mutants wheeled. The fish-scaled leader's eyes grew round, and he reached for a gun on the floor of the boat. He rose clutching a bulbous submachine gun. Others reached for their own weapons.

Tavlin had snatched up his gun as soon as the tall man turned. He fired at the fish-scaled leader, missed, fired again, hitting the leader square in the chest. The man pitched backward, knocking into two others. Another loosed a burst at Tavlin, but the shooter had been bumped aside and the bullets skittered off the wall not far from Tavlin's boat. Shards of stone flew out. Something nicked his ear.

Tavlin aimed at a black mass next to the mutants' boat. Holding his breath, he fired.

A strange shriek filled the air. Black gas jetted from an orifice in the mound's side. The dark cloud engulfed the boat and its occupants, and mutants screamed in horror. Out of control, the boat plowed forward, striking another slugmine, and another. More smoke billowed up.

Tavlin, far away enough to escape the direct blast of the poison, still tasted the bitterness on the air, and something felt like it was biting his tongue, his nostrils, the insides of his mouth. His eyes watered.

All the while, he fired his gun into the black cloud, unable to see the mutants and their passenger but hoping to get lucky. When his gun clicked empty, he reloaded with bullets he had bought that afternoon, fired again until he was out, then once more. By then the cloud was dispersing, and the boat had come to rest against the canal wall.

Warily, Tavlin rowed forward. His heart thumped. Sweat stung his eyes. Blackness, though thinner, still hid much of the boat. He held his breath as he drew close, then let the boat drift forward while he reached for his gun.

His vessel struck the hull of the other. Rocked.

A shape lurched out of the darkness. It spilled over the gunwale into his boat. A long, glistening insectile form reached for him. A knife glittered in one fist. The blade flashed at Tavlin's gut.

Tavlin fired into the Octunggen man's outstretched hand, then shoulder, then twice through the chest.

Gasping, bleeding—he had already been shot, Tavlin saw—the man collapsed against the gunwale, still shuddering. Tavlin wrenched the knife away, shoved it in a pocket, then ripped off the man's gas mask and strapped it about his own head. He sucked in a deep inhalation, frustrated at how the filter slowed his breaths when his lungs were demanding rapid action to remove the spots from his vision.

Chest heaving, he clambered over the side into the other boat and rooted around amongst the bodies, some of which still moved.

There! He beat away grasping hands, heaved a body aside, kicked the face of a certain moribund mutant reaching for a gun, then grabbed the briefcase by its handle and returned to his boat, where the tall man had crawled to the engine and was trying to rev it, to strand Tavlin there.

Tavlin struck him over the head and pulled him away.

"No," the man said, "no . . ."

"What's in this?" Tavlin asked, indicating the briefcase. "Money?" Even as he said it, he knew that was wrong.

"*Du*," the man said, an Octunggen word, Tavlin thought. Probably *No*, maybe *Idiot*. "They will come for you. They were . . . to meet us . . . close by . . ."

"Who?" Tavlin shook him. "Who's coming for me?"

The man glared up at him, an arrogant expression stamped on his pale, weary features. Then the light faded from his eyes, and he sagged. Tavlin watched him for a long moment, then studied the boat laden with mutants that he himself had killed. Abruptly he felt nauseous. He'd never killed anyone before, not in his entire life. He'd been around violence, yes, he'd seen people die, he'd even helped Boss Vassas fight off attackers before. And of course, there were gamblers who had lost everything and resented him that would take a swing at him or worse, and there were people he'd had to stick in duels, people who had lived, but nothing like this . . .

I was gone, he thought. *I was out. Now I'm back a day and I've committed mass murder, plus prompted the death of a Suulmite. Damn you, Vassas . . .*

Tavlin wanted to throw up but didn't dare in his mask, and he didn't trust that the air had cleared enough to remove it. He held the sick in.

With shocking speed, the air changed. Lights filled it. Tavlin's eardrums shook. Light strobed the walls, making the water seem to dance. Energy flickered out, arcs of blue-white fire from wall to wall, from water to ceiling, like a great electric spider web. The buzzing sound increased, and Tavlin felt the shaking in his bones. What the hell was going on?

That was when it happened.

She appeared. The girl in white.

She popped up out of nowhere. One moment there was nothing, then he blinked, and when he opened his eyes she was right there, coming straight at him, that otherworldly ghost-witch or whatever she was, beautiful, ethereal, all of white save for shifting gray shadows, her eyes lances of illumination out of the most perfect face he had ever seen, her lips full and parted, her body ripe and slender.

She flew toward him shrieking, *"You took it! You bastard, why did you take it!"*

He leapt to the outboard, fired up the motor with trembling fingers and shot off down the corridor. He rammed against one slugmine, then another, and black poison squirted into the air behind him, but, gas-mask firmly in place, he didn't care. He rocketed off into the sewers, hairs lifted in the base of his neck, too frightened even to look back.

* * *

Tavlin began to hear sounds. He had been wandering around the sewer system for some time, long enough to have admitted to himself that he was lost. Still shaking, he rowed and rowed, sometimes using his motor, sometimes not. He didn't think he had much gasoline left. He had long ago torn off the gas mask, and he took great gulping breaths of air. It was metallic and rancid, but delicious. He was alive. The woman-thing did not seem to be chasing him, but he could still hear the echo of her scream in his mind. What *was* she?

It was in one of the periods of rowing, when the motor was silent, that he heard them.

At first it was just a dull, muted throbbing, but then it grew louder—and louder. He realized with a sense of alarm that it was the sound of engines. Boats were out. He wondered if he was close to Muscud or some other Undertown but knew that even if he were it was still too early for there to be much traffic about. Even mutants needed sleep.

They will be coming for you. Shivering, Tavlin fired up his engine. It might alert the boats to his presence, but he had to risk it. He aimed his outboard in the direction he had been headed—he could only hope it was the right one—and motored off.

The engines throbbed louder behind him.

"Shit."

If he could still hear them over his own, that meant their engines were the more powerful. They might not be able to hear him, but if they found him they could catch him, kill him and take back whatever was in the briefcase. He itched to open it, but that would have to wait.

The tunnel opened up ahead. He found himself in a large corridor, traveling toward a likewise large opening. And beyond the opening . . . far beyond . . . lights. They were few and far, concealed in mist and darkness that seemed almost opaque, as if the air was as grimy as the walls, but there were lights. He couldn't tell if it was Muscud, but it seemed to be another massive cistern chamber, and in it there was definitely civilization or some likeness thereof. Heart soaring, he raced toward it.

Gunshots snapped behind him.

He jerked his head back to see a boat zooming around a corner. A lumpy figure stood on the bow, arm raised, something metallic clutched in its fist. Fire flashed from the muzzle, and a hole punched through Tavlin's hull right near the motor. Splinters flew.

The gun flashed again, its roar hardly noticeable above the sounds of the engines.

Tavlin hunkered down before his motor, using it as a shield. He glanced back to the front. *Off course.* His hull scraped against the wall of the tunnel. The boat shook. He felt the rattling in his bones. Cursing, he aimed for the lights.

When he looked back, he saw that the boat in pursuit had closed half the gap between them. *Shitshitshit.*

Tavlin wanted to reach for his gun, but it was empty. *I should've looted the dead for their weapons, damnit. The old Tavlin wouldn't have hesitated.*

The opening grew large ahead. Another gunshot snapped, then another. The bullets whizzed overhead.

Tavlin breasted the tunnel mouth and ventured out onto the open water, speeding toward the illumination. It spread before him, a few pinpricks of radiance here and there, as if he headed into an underdeveloped galaxy. Mist oozed up from the waters, thick and foul. He plowed into the fog, hoping it would hide him from his pursuers. Another gunshot rang out, but he didn't know where the round went. The sound of the other boat's engine grew even louder, a beehive screaming in his ears.

Through the fog a cluster of lights materialized. He aimed for it.

The lights drew closer, closer . . .

A dark shape ahead. He saw a boat, figures hunched over the gunwales, lines leading into the water. Early risers. Fishermen eager for a nighttime haul, when the big fish were about. Such creatures were dangerous, but lucrative. Even as Tavlin watched, one of the mutants cried out, his line jerked, and the two others in the boat leapt to assist him before his catch could drag him overboard.

Despite the severity of their situation, they glanced up in startlement as Tavlin roared in out of the fog, and he could only imagine the taut expression on his face.

Another gunshot cracked behind him. Fire lanced up his left arm, and he thought he cried out but wasn't sure.

Ignoring the pain, he steered around the fishermen who were directly in his path.

Still watching him, they clung onto the hooked line, but at the sound of another gunshot one of them dove down and came up with a shotgun, probably used as a last resort to subdue any catch that threatened to eat them or capsize them. Tavlin ducked even further down, but the fisherman didn't aim at him but at the boat that must be behind him, just an approaching shadow in the fog.

Tavlin raced toward the docks, which he could see now, a line of shabby wooden peers and juts, boats bobbing in the vague swells, mist coiling between them. Alchemical lamps of glowing red helped drive back the stink of the sewers. A few guards strolled along the docks, paid by the city to prevent boat-theft. Something about the city beyond told Tavlin this wasn't Muscud. Its towers were too tall, too thick. Lights strung from them stretched all the way up to the cistern ceiling, nestled between stalactites limned in red light.

Tavlin reached the docks just as the shotgun roared behind him. More gunshots split the silence. The shotgun boomed again. He heard cursing, a grunt, a splash, more shots, then silence save for the motor of the boat growing louder. *Damn.*

He clambered onto the docks, blood cascading down his arm. Rotten wood groaned under his heel. One of the guards rushed over clutching at his sidearm. He was a stocky, thick-chested fellow with a crest on his head and gills on his neck.

"Hold there! *Hold*!"

Tavlin ignored him and bent over the boat to retrieve the suitcase. When he came up, the guard was pointing a gun at his chest, perhaps fearing he'd gone for a weapon.

"Stop right there!"

Tavlin stabbed a finger toward the open water with the hand not holding the briefcase. At the motion, the guard flinched, and Tavlin half-thought he would shoot him, but the blast didn't come.

"Hear that?" Tavlin said, meaning the sound of the approaching boat.

The guard cocked an ear. The other three guards were rushing over, too. Likely they had all heard the gunshots.

"They're armed," Tavlin said. "They tried to mug me in the passages. I came here from Muscud."

The guard glanced him over, suddenly realizing he wasn't a mutant. "You live Muscud-way?"

Time to use his ace in the hole. "I work for Boss Vassas. He'll vouch for me. Listen, there's no time. Those bastards just killed three of your fishermen, and they're coming for me next."

But, as soon as he said it, he realized it wasn't true. The sound of the engine was fading now, not growing.

"They must have seen you," he said, to the congregation of guards. The first guard exchanged glances with the others.

"Boss Vassas, huh?" said one.

"That's right."

"Three?" said another. He appeared pained.

"That's right." Tavlin wished he'd had the presence of mind to throw his gun overboard. When they searched the boat they would find it, and it might not be too dissimilar from the one that killed the fishermen, if they were really dead, and he didn't see how they couldn't be if they'd been firing on his attackers but his attackers were still alive. He'd heard other guns, though. Maybe the people aboard the pursuing boat had opened up with types of guns different from his own.

The guards' thinking was going along different lines, however.

"Might be we never saw you," mused the first one. He eyed the briefcase speculatively.

Tavlin fingered the blood trickling down his arm. He didn't have time for this. Already he felt dizzy. "I don't have any money. This—" he rattled the briefcase "—there's nothing of value here to anyone but me." He shook his head. Spots were starting to form in his vision.

"Maybe Boss Vassas is willing to fork something over," said the second guard.

"Yeah," said another, then added, "If this hume isn't full of shit." He peered out into the mist. "Hud and Wally were out there. Wally took his son. If they're all dead …"

"Shit," said the third one. He removed his cap and placed it over his heart. To Tavlin, he said, "If you killed Wally, I ain't takin' no bribe."

"*I* didn't," Tavlin said. "The muggers did. But just to clear up any suspicion, Boss Vassas will donate something to your favorite local charity. He'll even give you the money with the understanding that you turn it to over to them yourself, if you see what I mean. I'm sorry about the fishermen—maybe some of them made it. You should send a patrol out to hunt the ones who did this." He swayed. "Listen, I need a doctor. Let's work this out later."

They exchanged more glances. The first one said, "I'll take 'im to Doc Sarn and put 'im up somewhere. In the morning I'll send someone over Muscud-way and see what we can see about Boss Vassas. If 'e's game, 'e's game."

The others nodded. One added, "And if's not, we'll have to start thinkin' about pressin' charges."

Another grunted. "Guess we'd better take a look at the bodies. Maybe someone's still alive."

* * *

The first guard showed Tavlin through town toward the doctor's.

"Welcome to Taluush," he said. "I'm Sergeant Wales. Of the Night Watch."

Tavlin nodded. "There's no Night Watch in Muscud. Different sectors hire their own, ah, guards." He'd been about to say goons. "We only have one police officer."

"Yeah. Mirely. I know 'im." He spat. "Straight as a hunchback."

"Yes. Very different from here, I'm sure."

Sgt. Wales raised a hairless eyebrow. One corner of his lips hooked upward, and a glint of amusement shone in his eye. "*Quite* different," was all he said.

They passed into the town, and Tavlin beheld strange dwellings he'd never seen the like of before. They appeared as if they had been secreted or drooled by some insect. They comprised most of the ground level, and he felt as though he were walking through some massive hive. They were round, yellow-gray lumpen things with no visible apertures. Thick black hoses sprouted from their sides, and he could hear the chugging of generators. Taluush was a vertical city, and Tavlin saw that more normal, *human* habitations comprised the upper levels, with a sort of buffer of shops and hanging plazas separating this lower level from the sections above.

Sgt. Wales saw his amazement. "You've never been to Taluush before? No? Surely you've heard about it."

"Just rumors. Something about one of the old races, but I never thought . . ."

Sgt. Wales gestured expansively to the hive-like structures that occupied the first level. They were clustered along wide canals, and they glistened in the red light like giant cocoons. "We're right on top of the Rifts, y'know? Whoever built this section of the sewer used a natural system of underground rivers, and some of them have chasms that plunge all the way down to some underground sea or lake or somesuch, I don't know. Well, the G'zai lived down there. Still do. In some black ocean, can you imagine? One of the pre-human races. Never had much doings with us. There usedta be a bunch of disappearances, people said they caused them, but who knows?"

"What are they doing up here, then?"

Tavlin and the sergeant were passing over a bridge between concentrations of the cocoon-like dwellings, making for a ramp that spiraled toward the upper levels. Though weak, Tavlin couldn't help but look over the side of the bridge into the water, imagining the bed of the cistern chamber, a natural lake bed if the sergeant wasn't bullshitting him, and the black rift that led down gods knew how deep to some prehistoric sea. Ancient seas linking up with sewer systems linking up with the strange energies of the Atomic Sea . . . it would all make for a heady brew. He didn't want to imagine the creatures that might live in it, that might have developed a *culture* in it.

"We trade with 'em," Sgt. Wales added.

"*Trade*? What could you possibly have to trade? Do they even have hands?"

"Oh, you'll see them, you stay here long enough. They come out sometimes. But yeah, we trade. They have certain chemicals our alchemists use. Maybe they secrete them, or spit them, or, well, I don't know and not sure I want to. Our alchemists grow all sorts of weird plants in our gardens. You've heard of the Gardens of Taluush? Well, the G'zai trade for our blooms and fruits. Maybe they eat 'em, use 'em in their rituals, whatever. We use their chems, they use our greens, we try not to kill each other." He rolled his shoulders. "Been this way for a long time."

"We have something similar in Muscud, with the Ualissi, but they stay in their own quarter. They're part aquatic, too, but they're from some chain of islands near the equator—or they were. The islands vanished long ago, destroyed by some enemies of the Ualissi, I've heard, and the Ualissi scattered to all corners of the globe, always seeking out the darkest corners they could find—in hiding from whoever did it, I suppose."

"I've heard of the Ualissi. The G'zai don't like them. Old foes of some sort, though not likely the one that sank their islands."

"You get along with the G'zai?"

"We try. They're not like us. There's always some in town, though—their ambassadors or merchants. Workers. You'll see."

Wales showed Tavlin up the spiraling ramp, which led up a thick tower constructed of scrap metal, wood, debris and lots and lots of wire. Rooms like caverns opened from it. The towers of Taluush rose up to the ceiling, all connected by swaying bridges and ropes and chains. Some ropes and chains held aloft large platforms upon which people congregated, but for the main part Tavlin saw activity in the shops and taverns. Actual dwellings seemed to be clustered higher above, as far as the human and human-like inhabitants of Taluush could get from the G'zai. Looking down, Tavlin saw that there were doorways mounted in the top of the G'zai's hive structures, and the sergeant informed him that the hives were filled with water; the pipes and hoses Tavlin had seen created a suction that pulled up the water from the cistern lake; other pipes purified it. The G'zai came and went via entrances in the hives' bases and tops. Tavlin looked for the G'zai themselves but saw nothing but mutants and the occasional uninfected human ambling about the city.

Traffic was slow this early in the morning, but it was starting to pick up. Lamp-lighters brightened the lamps already lit and sparked others of whiter hue, bringing an illumination not unlike dawn to Taluush. Music crackled from cobbled-together radios, the signal poor through so many layers of concrete. Tavlin knew Muscud boasted a radio station, a little one-room affair, but he didn't hear the familiar tones of Raging Marv, so maybe the signal didn't reach.

He clutched his wound with his right hand, feeling blood seep between his fingers. Meanwhile the fingers of his left hand, which held the suitcase, steadily grew numb. He supposed he was leaving a trail of blood behind him.

"Here we are."

Sgt. Wales showed him into one of the yawning openings on the tower, under a sign that blinked on and off: CL NIC, one of the letters burned out. It smelled of mold and antiseptic, and the light in here seemed a sort of green, the walls an unpleasant greenish-yellow. A fly buzzed about the ceiling lamp.

A receptionist with fish-lips and seaweed hair looked up from her dime romance. "First one of the day."

"Is Doc Sarn in?" Wales asked.

"This early? But there's a nurse."

She rang a bell. A figure stepped out of the back room and Tavlin felt warm, firm hands guiding him forwards. He was distinctly faint now, and everything seemed faded, washed-out. Sgt. Wales's voice seemed to come from miles away.

Tavlin was shoved onto a bed, and the nurse rolled up his sleeve. When that didn't get the sleeve up far enough, she produced a pair of scissors, but Tavlin waved them away. He only had one set of clothes on him. Reluctantly, she helped him out of his leather jacket, then his shirt.

It was as she bent to analyze his wound that he was able to focus long enough to get a look at her, and when he did he thought he had passed out for sure.

It can't be . . .

She was far away, in one of the distant cities Maya had mentioned. She was gone, far gone, and there was no getting her back. And . . . a nurse?

She crystallized before him, becoming real.

Their eyes met.

His heart stopped. Then, slowly, started. His head swam.

"Sophia . . ."

"Yes, it's me, you son of a bitch. Now what have you done to yourself?"

Chapter 5

"Easy, now." He winced as she sewed up his arm. He had lost a good deal of blood—the bullet had nicked a vessel—but she had sewn it up without Doctor Sarn's help, for apparently he was sleeping off a drunk somewhere, and she was closing up the wound herself. With a little too much relish, he thought. "Go in a straight line, for Gam's sake. That's crooked as a con."

"You're drunk."

It was true. She had no anesthetic except for a bottle of cheap vodka, and he drank with his free arm while she operated. His head reeled, and he felt nauseous.

"Who, me?" He blinked. "Where's the sergeant?"

"You didn't notice? He left awhile ago. Said he had to go check on your story."

Tavlin burped. "Let him. I've got nothing to hide."

She raised her eyebrows, and as he looked once more into her face he was reminded how beautiful she was. She had been even more beautiful in her prime, back when he had met her and courted her, but she was still lovely now, after years of whoring, addiction, recovery, one disastrous marriage, and Jameson . . . She had blue-green eyes, dark red hair that normally fell in curls to her shoulders but which was tied up behind her head at the moment, wide full lips and a slightly upturned, impish nose. Her cheekbones were high, bold, her neck long and slender. She had strong hands and a strong, slender, womanly body, now covered in a stained nurses' uniform that was covered in patches and scratches and looked handed-down.

Her eyes were steady. "If you've got nothing to hide, what's in the briefcase?"

He smiled, feeling the vodka. "My laundry."

She sniffed, went back to sewing. "Stolen money, probably. Or your gambling proceeds, not that there's any difference these days. I've heard about what you've been up to."

"What have you heard?" Except it came out *Whaddaoo 'eard?*

She didn't look up, but he felt a sharp tug. "You've been cheating the uppers. Getting kicked out of club after club." She gave another sharp tug, and he tried to resist a wince.

He downed another sip, but slowly this time.

"Well?" she said. "You don't have some smart answer to that?"

He said nothing.

She sighed. One more sharp, painful tug, and then she rose and rinsed off her hands. The doctor's office used a heavy filter for its water, and it was actually clear enough to see through, though Tavlin still wouldn't touch the stuff.

"Well?" she demanded with her back turned to him. "What are you doing here, shot up and with some mysterious laundry case?"

"The usual. Favor for Boss Vassas."

"So you're back in the racket, then?"

"I didn't say that."

"What did you say?" she said.

"Favor. As in temporary."

"It's gonna be permanent, you catch another bullet."

"I'll remember that."

He mounted to his feet, feeling the shaking in his legs. How far could he go? "Thanks for the treatment. I'll come back when I can pay you."

"I don't want your money. I never did."

"I guess not. You coulda made much more if you hadn't married me and started giving it away for free."

She turned her head to him. "Maybe I should start collecting back-payments on that. It was never a real marriage anyway."

That stung. As if aware of it, she looked away. He grunted, knocked back one last swig and set the vodka down. "Tell Sgt. Wales I'll find him."

With that, he staggered from the clinic. She didn't stop him, didn't say a word. Outside it seemed colder than it had before, even with the added press of people and the brighter lights. Her words echoed in his ears, and he felt something clench deep inside.

How could she say that?

He tried to shrug it off. Briefcase in hand, he marched away from the clinic, but it came out as more of a prolonged stumble. People eyed him with distaste as he passed them. Even down here, it was too early to be drunk. The briefcase seemed heavy. He thought his curiosity was making it even heavier, the weight of all his expectations. Although in truth he didn't know what to expect. The Octunggen, if that's what they'd been, had stolen strange, ancient jewelry, maybe other things, and they had done something to them at the factory in Muscud. If the contents of the briefcase represented the fruit of their labors, it could be very valuable indeed.

Tavlin decided he would catch up with Sgt. Wales later. If word didn't arrive from Boss Vassas, Tavlin would have to chew the slug and pay the cops himself, if they really demanded it (and since there was no one else to be held accountable for the murders and he was partially responsible, they might), and the doctor's office, too. He still had half his gambling proceeds. The other half rested in the lockbox in his room at the Twirling Skirt . . . along with one other, very important item. At any rate, he'd prefer not to use his own money if he could help it.

He'd need to use a little, though.

He lurched into a hotel, which comprised a section of one of the twisted scrap-heap towers, like functional junk art—about five floors, from what he could tell, with windows and terraces jutting out irregularly from it and a blazing neon sign that proclaimed THE LAVISH. With high hopes based on the name, Tavlin entered only to find a rundown, seedy dive, albeit with colorful if tacky trimmings. Pink chairs, gold-leaf-framed mirrors, once-expensive carpets that should be burned for public health, a chandelier sporting more cracked crystals than whole ones. The man at the counter snored loudly, a big fat hairy fellow with bristling sideburns. A light spattering of wine-colored spots on his cheek was his only visible mutation. He jerked awake when Tavlin rang the bell.

"Gods be cornholed!" he said, eyes popping open.

Tavlin grinned what he hoped was an appropriately seedy grin. "Room for the night."

"Bit early, innit?"

"You complaining?"

The man eyed him up and down. "You can pay?"

Tavlin always separated his cash into different pockets in case they got picked, and now he reached into one and flicked a few coins on the desk. They made satisfyingly loud noises as they rolled and plinked.

The desk jockey watched them as if they were alien things. "Surface money."

"You won't take it?"

A slightly cagey look entered the man's face. "Oh. Well. I suppose . . . just this once . . ." He scooped the coins off the counter and counted them, seeming to savor every chink and rasp. He glanced up with guarded interest. "Just the one night?"

"We'll see."

For the first time, the man smiled. He leapt to his feet, snatched a key off the wall behind him, and said, "Right this way, sir." He showed Tavlin up a flight of stairs, which was tight and winding. The boards trembled underfoot, and the air stank of rot. The deskman showed him to a room on the third story. The door swung into a small, somewhat crooked chamber whose window frame actually crooked in the opposite direction from the rest of the room. Fleshy, peeling wallpaper adorned the walls, and the heart-shaped bed took up most of the room.

"It vibrates," the man leered.

"I'm sure." Tavlin tipped him, and the man grinned wider.

"Let me know if there's anything you need. A girlie, maybe. Or a boy. And we got things inbetween and others, too. There's this bearded squid-thing, and I mean to say—"

"Thank you."

The man frowned, shrugged and left. Tavlin closed the door after him. Then, with no further ado, he locked the door and flung the briefcase on the bed.

"Now, let's see about you."

A thief before a gambler, he tackled the lock with skill. It had been made sturdily but not sturdily enough to resist an experienced burglar. Tavlin unlocked it in minutes, and then, barely containing his excitement, pried it open. The briefcase yawned like a great mouth, shadow falling away only slowly to reveal what was inside.

Within lay a canister of gun-metal gray, gleaming dully, strapped to the bottom to prevent it from shaking. In shape it resembled a thermos, but larger. It looked heavy. Industrial. Tavlin frowned at it. What had the factory men put in there? It was obviously something of great import to them. Curious, he reached a hand toward it . . .

At first all he felt was coldness, radiating out from the canister. Later, he was unsure of what happened next exactly, but he thought he remembered touching the canister's surface, and the burning cold sensation that flowed up his fingers, through his hand. What happened after that was completely a blur, but through the blur he distinctly remembered an overwhelming sensation of fear and horror, and senseless images wheeled through his head. He left his right mind for some time. He came to himself gibbering and clutching at himself on the floor, knees drawn up to his chest, in the corner. Spittle sprayed from his trembling lips. He stared rigidly at the canister, which he could just barely see over the lip of the briefcase. Gooseflesh prickled his arms, and his scrotum had contracted so far up into him that it was painful. His teeth chattered, and his stomach spasmed. If he'd had anything in it, he would have retched.

Knocking from the door. He started, heart racing.

More knocking. His eyes swiveled to the door. The banging on it grew indignant, and he could hear swearing from the other side, a jingle of keys.

Collecting himself, he stood—shakily—and crossed to the door. He swept his hair back, took a deep breath, and opened it.

The deskman, holding a set of keys, glared at him. "Neighbor a' yours said you woke him screaming."

"Wh—? Oh. Uh . . ."

"Whatcha doin'?" The man's eyes left Tavlin, and he scanned the room suspiciously, his gaze lingering on the briefcase and the canister, narrowing, then moving on, at last returning to Tavlin, irritated and mistrustful.

By then Tavlin had collected himself, more or less. “B-burned myself on the coffee. In the thermos. Sorry I screamed.”

The man stared. Tavlin imagined his haggard appearance, circles under his eyes, hair unwashed, fingers shaking, skin whiter than bone, pores clearly visible. He would look like a junkie.

He said what a junkie would say: “It won’t happen again.”

The man grunted, but he seemed relieved at the answer, as if he’d been able to pigeonhole Tavlin at last. “Better not.” Still he lingered for a moment.

Tavlin sighed and handed him another few coins. The man nodded without a word and left. Shaking, Tavlin closed the door after him, then rested against the door.

He turned and stared at the briefcase.

What are you, now?

He breathed deep, closed his eyes and counted to ten. Then, opening his eyes, he marched to the case, snapped it shut, removed it from the bed, and shoved pillows under the sheets to make a form resembling a sleeping man.

Satisfied, he crossed to the tilted porthole-like window, which opened under his touch, and breathed in the heady reek of Taluush: spices and sewage, rust and oil, sex and musk. It seemed like a long way to the ground, even though it was only a few stories. Tavlin told himself to man up, then swung himself outside and scaled down the façade of the hotel, ignoring the stares of pedestrians below. He clutched the briefcase between the thumb and forefinger of his left hand. The bullet wound ached when he moved his arm, but it was bearable. The effects of the vodka were beginning to make his head throb.

He lit on the sidewalk, glanced around—several mutants stared openly at him, but the majority were oblivious; this was the underworld, after all—and made his way through the streets. It was important that the deskman not see him go. That way he could tell whoever came for Tavlin that he was in his room, where he should be. When he was some distance away, Tavlin bought himself a sandwich—his spasming stomach almost heaved it up—and popped a pollution pill just to be sure, even though the meat was supposed to be mutton, which should be safe.

He searched for a whorehouse. He tried four before he found one that would take him in. It was located on a branching outgrowth of one of the junkheap towers, suspended by cables and chains from the cistern ceiling—so close to the ceiling that queer stalactites drooped past it, flails sucking on them, armies of bats just visible as dripping black fruit from the grime-encrusted surface. Scaffolding supported the sidewalks of the branch, which was known as the Singh-Hiss, he learned, and mutants kept up a steady traffic on both avenues that ran along either side, though the sidewalks were too uneven and fragile for motorcycles, and the branch was not strictly horizontal even though it joined the tower it sprouted from perpendicularly.

Tavlin entered the whorehouse from the sidewalk entrance, under a sign which ran PLE SURE GA DEN!!! GI LS AND MOR !!! and into a lounge of trashy red hell—dusty red plastic chairs, couches and red-painted walls. Perhaps it was supposed to look opulent or kitschy, but instead it resembled an abattoir. At this hour, only two young women lounged on the couches, and they snored loudly. The madam was actually a skinny, nervous-looking man with an equally skinny, nervous mustache that continually twitched back and forth like a rabbit's whiskers. He wore an albino alligator-skin jacket (the alligator caught down here, surely) over a black shirt tucked into blood-red jeans which matched the walls. It was an ugly outfit that was supposed to be showy, and the poor man looked awkward in it. He looked just plain awkward, actually, and he jumped at every sound. His eyes flicked back and forth as Tavlin asked him for a room, but when he saw the color of Tavlin's cash the eyes steadied, and he smiled widely, revealing jagged yellow teeth, and said, "Why, yes, actually we have the perfect room—if you don't mind a little noise."

Tavlin, dead on his feet, just blinked slowly at him. "I wouldn't mind a hurricane."

Five minutes later saw him in a small room with a view overlooking the towers and occasionally interlocked stalactites of the city. The sounds of the first john of the day enjoying a morning toff from a room directly above did not affect his sleep in the slightest, though he did have to deal with the briefcase first, and his dreams were anything but pleasant.

* * *

He woke with a screaming head and more screaming coming from overhead. The ceiling banged with the rhythms of a rocking bed frame, and moans and grunts and yells filtered down through the layers of junkyard construction—and it really did look as if the pieces had come from a junkyard. Numerous hubcaps glittered from the walls and ceiling by the light of the alchemical lantern, and Tavlin saw rods of steel and car doors sewn into the fabric of the walls, along with things that might have been rusted engine blocks, the mashed frame of a sofa, two-by-fours stolen from a construction site and a chipped gargoyle. Here there was a broken radio, there half a fan. All mashed together and bound by wire and luck, like most cities of the underworld. With the noises of what seemed like a rowdy three- or foursome overhead, Tavlin got himself together and made plans for the day.

First he visited a pay washroom down the street—you had to pay for clean water down here, even if it was stolen through hijacked plumbing from the world above. Afterwards he ate an egg sandwich with another pollution pill and smoked a large bowl on a coffee shop terrace that looked out over the city. Activity of all sorts stirred below, and he saw by the clock tower—carved out of a down-dripping stalactite, with an ornate stained-glass façade, lit by alchemy within and inset with wrought-iron numbers and clock hands—that it was late afternoon. Good. He wondered if the people hunting him had found his pillow-self yet. Were they even now combing the streets for him? Safest to assume so.

Traffic buzzed around him in the café, mutants going about their daily lives, and he found himself scanning the faces with suspicion. The smells of their foods, coffees and smokes helped mask their sometimes fishy odors and the musky fragrance of the alchemical lamps designed to drive back the worse reek of sewage, and he welcomed them.

The briefcase by his leg seemed to throb, and with each pulse his headache flared anew. The container was wrong, its contents somehow abominable. He could feel its presence by the shrinking of his skin, by the bitterness on his tongue. Its nearness made him nervous, his palms clammy, his mouth dry. He had only been able to sleep at the whorehouse by moving the briefcase into the closet and barricading the door with a chair.

He loathed it. He *feared* it. He knew he had to get rid of it.

There was no way he could tolerate being in constant contact with it, or near-contact. Also, the risk of his enemies taking it off of him was too great. Part of him wanted to unscrew the container's cap and pour its contents into the sewer, but somehow he sensed that would be a mistake. It might kill everything in the under-cities, or worse. Gods knew what the container actually held. Octunggen technology and engineering was said to be absolutely otherworldly. If they had devised whatever was in the container with their skill, coupled with the stolen jewelry—and alchemy—from some lost pre-human civilization . . .

He found himself staring at the briefcase, fascinated, repulsed. He realized he had drawn his body as far away from it as he could get without leaving his chair.

"Enough," he said, not caring if anyone heard.

He rose, paid the waitress, took the briefcase (with a shudder) and made his way through the city streets, hunting for the police station. He stopped and asked for directions, then continued on his way, pressing down through the levels toward the mid-point of the vertical city. He had yet to see any of the non-human G'zai, though in truth it was hard to tell, with everyone being so inhuman already.

He stopped when he saw a group of people congregating around a certain café. It seemed as if all the traffic on the block had ceased, and everyone had gathered to the eatery, all pressed together. In fact, Tavlin couldn't even hear any city noises any more, or at least very few of them. It was as if the entire town had shut down.

Curious, alarmed, he made for the press of people. "What's—?" he started, but a lobster-like individual hissed him to quietude, accentuating his request with a snap of a barnacled pincer. Others turned to glare at Tavlin.

He realized he was hearing a crackling voice coming from ahead, from within the press of people. It was a voice from a radio, straining to receive signals from the world above. It was this voice that everyone was trying to hear. Frowning, he listened in.

" . . . and now action. The Minister's comments . . . wait. I am just getting an update." The clipped, crisp voice of the announcer paused, then: "Yes, we have confirmation from correspondents at the *Nythril Star*, backing up what the government of Sorvelle has just confirmed. The army of Octung has indeed invaded Vrusk, the critical Orzafan border city along the Rulehain. Reports claim that bombers first took out the military base in the Edrid region, accompanied by a strange bombing run on both military and civilian centers that appears, and this is according to numerous eyewitnesses who have only seen the event from afar—and yet appear to be factual—*the bombs seem to have suspended time in the affected districts.* That's right, folks, those in the areas hit by the bombs are now in the grip of some sort of *suspended animation*, stuck in the middle of doing whatever they were about when the bombs dropped. They sit helpless and immobile as the tanks and soldiers and military apparatuses of Octung sweep down upon them. Octunggen technology has long been rumored to . . ."

Numb, Tavlin staggered back, feeling suddenly sick. He barely heard the announcer continue detailing the events of the attack until he finished and said, "Here is a clip from the press announcement by our own Prime Minister Denaris just fifteen minutes ago." A woman's cool, methodical voice crackled over the radio: "Octung has declared war on Orzaf, and with the eminent fall of Vrusk I anticipate hearing news of Orzaf's surrender shortly. This is unlikely to be the end of hostilities, however. Brace yourselves, fellow citizens. Even now Octunggen forces are mobilizing along the Saenth and Murascan borders. This is the news we have long waited for—and dreaded. Octung has finally launched its war."

* * *

Shaking, Tavlin lit another pipe and continued through the city, seeking the police station. He was still trembling when he came upon it. The cops were all huddled around their desk wrestling with a radio when he entered, and as he approached them the police officer with the screwdriver stepped back from the radio, and the same announcer's voice rang out, crackly and hissing but audible: " . . . 'epeat, confirmation has just arrived that the Premier of Orzaf has suspended all defensive measures against Octung, and an Orzafan envoy has been dispatched to treat with the Octunggen generals. The centuries-old and stalwart army of Orzaf, famed throughout Urslin for its cavalry, is, it seems, unable to stand against the overwhelming military might and sophisticated technology of the Lightning Crown. Meanwhile I have just received word, unconfirmed as yet, that hostilities have began in Saen."

The announcer continued, but the man fiddling with the radio turned down the volume in disgust. "Fuck this. Fuck it all."

A large, round-bellied figure appeared through a doorway—Sgt. Wales. "Hey, I was listening to that! Turn it back on."

The cop with the screwdriver grumbled but complied. The announcer's grim voice filled the room once more. Before Wales could become absorbed in his litany of doom, however, Tavlin approached the sergeant and said, "Have you made contact with Boss Vassas?"

Sgt. Wales blinked, as if trying to remember what the subject had been, then glanced Tavlin over, ran his eyes to the briefcase and nodded. "Aye, it's all sorted out."

"Good." That would save Tavlin some money, at least.

Sgt. Wales frowned at him, then clapped him on the shoulder and drew him aside, conspiratorially. Tavlin feared the sergeant would try to extract more consideration from him and mentally tightened his purse-strings.

"Yes?" He tried not to sound impatient.

"That girl o' yours. What'd you do to her?"

"Girl?" For a wild moment he thought Wales referred to the ghostly figure last seen chasing him through the sewers. But he instantly realized that couldn't be right. "You mean … Sophia? I didn't do anything."

"Yeah? Well, I tried to pay her fer fixin' you up an' all. Only she wouldn't take it. When was the last time you heard of a dollie like that turnin' down money?"

"She's a nurse, not a dollie."

"They're all the same. Me, I like nurses. I like them short skirts. An' I like a girl with access to drugs, if y'know what I mean. Medicinal, o' course. But that ain't the point."

"What's the point?"

"I looked her in the eye, like I'm lookin' at you now, and she's starin' back at me, just like you are, and you know what she says?"

Tavlin waited, then said, "What did she say?"

"She says, 'I wouldn't take his money if grabbing it were the only thing keeping me from falling on a bed of rusty nails.' I say, well, it ain't his money, it came from Boss Vassas, and if you don't want it that's fine, more for me, and she says, 'Keep it and choke on it.' Now, not too many people can say that t' Sgt. Wales, but I let it pass because she's got knockers that could put your eye out—and wouldn't that be a good way to go blind?—but I think you'd better call on her. Taluush needs a good doctor. It don't have one, or if it does he's at the bottom of a bottle most nights. She's the best we got, medicine-wise, an' I want her in top working order. Only whatever you said to her last night's got her all riled up, you know how women are."

"I wish I did."

"Just call on her."

Tavlin changed the subject. "Did any of those fishermen live?"

Wales let out a long breath. "Little Wally lasted awhile, but . . . no. All of 'em dead. I just came back from calling on Big Wally's widow. She didn't take it well. Husband and son gone in one swoop like that. Horch didn't have no family, no one to call on. No one'll be at his service. Somehow I think that's even sadder."

"I'm sorry," Tavlin said honestly. "Did you catch the killers?"

Wale's face darkened. "Never did. By the way . . ." He produced a gun from his coat and passed it to Tavlin, who tensed before recognizing it as his own. "Might want this back. We tested it. Wasn't the gun killed Horch and the Wallys."

"Would it have mattered? I mean, with the money from Boss Vassas?" Tavlin was genuinely curious.

Sgt. Wales gave him a wounded look. "I'm liable to take offense at that."

"Yeah, you're a regular humanitarian."

* * *

Tavlin left the police station and purchased bullets at a nearby gun store. Everywhere he went people huddled around radios, if they could get them to work, or congregated in city squares or shops where runners relayed the latest news if they couldn't. Tavlin wondered what Octung's designs were. They had launched their war at the same time their agents—if agents they were—reached some sort of critical phase at the factory in Muscud, culminating in the contents of the container. Or so Tavlin reasoned it. Were the two connected? Was the Octunggen presence in Ghenisa part of a larger plan?

In any case, he had to do something about the briefcase. He couldn't keep carrying it around with him; it was too easily stolen, and, besides, he couldn't bear to have it near him. Thus he picked his way down to the docks, which were not as extensive as those of Muscud. Taluushians might trade with the denizens of the Rift, but evidently they did not trade much with other under-cities. Nevertheless Tavlin was able to buy a length of chain with an anchor attached—a rusty, pitted thing that looked ready to break apart if breathed on too hard—and rented a boat with an outboard motor. It looked suspiciously like the one he had brought here, including a fresh plank where the bullet had struck. Sgt. Wales had likely not donated it, either. Crime did pay.

Tavlin revved up the motor and took the boat out into the tunnels. He ventured so far out he wasn't entirely sure if he remembered the way back. At a conspicuous cross-roads, he tied the length of chain about the briefcase and dropped the anchor overboard. Chain rattled against wood, there came a *plop*, and the heavy metal dragged the briefcase under. Tavlin stared at the ripples with satisfaction, feeling lighter already. The ripples faded, he revved up the engine once more, marked the intersection in his mind, and headed back toward Taluush, hoping he remembered where it was. He thought of returning to Muscud, but for some reason he didn't. He told himself that the enemy's presence was stronger in Muscud—gods knew how many Octunggen bastards resided at that factory—but the truth was he knew better.

Still, after he docked the boat and paid the second half of the rental fee, he did not set off for the doctor's office but instead returned to the coffee bar. More news filtered in regarding the fighting, and he listened to it tensely, side by side with the others. Gasps ran through the crowd with each new revelation. Tavlin added liquor to his coffee and drank it interspersed with puffs on his pipe, slowly chewing a bagel. When he'd had a belly-full of caffeine, carbs and bad news, he set off toward the Pleasure Garden. To reach it from this point he had to pass the Lavish, the first hotel he had stopped at.

As he approached the area, he heard flames and the cries of many people. He smelled smoke.

He rushed forward, rounded a bend and saw the Lavish caught in a bright conflagration. Black, foul smoke curled upwards toward the stalactites of the cistern ceiling, and a crowd had gathered before the rearing hotel. A rudimentary fire department blasted fluid from hoses onto the fire. Other firemen manned the pumps: the hoses ran down to the lake and pumped nasty water onto the flames … which only made the smoke fouler.

It seemed to work, though. As Tavlin watched, the fire began to diminish.

"How did it happen?" he asked one of the passers-by who had stopped to gape.

"No one knows."

"Was anybody hurt?"

She shrugged, but a man nearby said, "I saw them wheel several bodies away, and they said there were more trapped in the upper floors still alive."

The woman looked pale. "They're not trapped anymore."

The man grimaced. "No. I suppose not."

Tavlin stared for a long time, feeling cold despite the flames. Those people had died because of him. He had led the killers here, had even set up a decoy for them. *I didn't know they'd burn the whole fucking thing down!* he told himself. *I thought they'd just go after the decoy!* Still, people had died because of his actions.

Sudden concern for the working girls and the nervous man at the Pleasure Garden flooded him. He hurried up one ramp, then another, finally reaching the Singh-Hiss, that horizontal junkheap structure suspended from the ceiling between two vertical spires. Sweat popped out on his forehead as he neared the brothel, and as he scrambled over the scaffolding he knew what he would find. Still, as he came within sight of the whorehouse entrance, he saw no flames, no crowd. Perhaps there was time yet to warn the employees.

Hairs lifted along his neck as he entered the whorehouse. His eyes scanned the abattoir-like lobby, with all its garish red trappings. It was substantially more like an abattoir now, with dead bodies sprawled across the floor, blood pooling in thick puddles. Whores and johns, all tangled together, flies settling on eyelids, on protruding tongues. Some of the victims had been shot, some stabbed. Most were gagged. One prostitute had been stripped, tied up, then had the flesh on the left half of her face peeled away. Another had had an eye gouged out. The nervous man had been nailed to the wall and tortured, with grisly results, perhaps while the killers sliced up his girls in front of him. For information on Tavlin, it must be. Others must have guarded the doorway to prevent guests from leaving or prospective ones from entering.

Noise in the hallway. Shadows flung on the wall, marching toward the lobby. Footsteps.

Tavlin froze. The killers had completed their search of the whorehouse, finished killing and torturing everyone they could find. Now they would burn the place down to remove any evidence.

Tavlin reached for his gun, knowing even as he did that a shootout against such men—and, possibly, women—could only end one way. These weren't thugs like the men on the boat. They were trained killers. Agents of Octung. Deadly, ruthless spies of the Lightning Crown, which had just declared war, if not in so many words, on the world.

The bootsteps came closer. The shadows on the walls grew larger. Tavlin saw an arm, a foot, a gloved hand gripping a heavy revolver with a silencer on the end of it. Blood dripped from the muzzle.

Tavlin ran.

He fled back outside, weaving through the scaffolding. There was little traffic on the sidewalks in this seedy section of the city at this time of day, but he scattered the few people in front of him. "Run!" he shouted. "Get away! They're after me!" Panicked, several followed him. Others disappeared into holes in the structure. Tavlin was tempted to join them, but he wanted to put as much distance between him and his pursuers as he could.

A bit of scaffolding exploded by his cheek. Shards flew. He whipped his head back to see three figures racing toward him from the brothel entrance. The lead one had a gun outstretched. As Tavlin watched, a flash appeared at its silenced muzzle. Tavlin threw himself to the ground. Something shattered overhead. He hefted himself back up. Ran.

Sweat burned his eyes, but he was hardly aware of it. He realized he was still gripping his gun in a shaking fist. He rounded a corner and pressed himself flat against the wall. Swiveled and fired back the other way. The three figures crouched. Flame spat from their guns. Tavlin felt a sting against his ribs, another at his thigh.

He staggered back, nearly dropping the gun. He ran on, limping, bleeding. *Shit shit shit.* He was leaving a trail of blood for them to follow.

Various lifts led from the dock level to the upper levels of the city, though Tavlin had never taken one before. He didn't like the feeling of being caged. He was desperate, though, and he couldn't walk far, so when he put the Singh-Hiss behind him he found the nearest lift, bodily hurled the two people that were on it off of it, stabbed the button and descended just as the three figures ran toward him.

They raised their guns, but then he was below their level. They beat the bars and cursed above him. One squeezed off a shot, but the angle was wrong. The bullet went wide. The people that had been on the lift ran.

Panting, Tavlin sagged against a wall and analyzed his wounds. He was bleeding, not copiously, but not a little either. He needed a doctor. Or a nurse.

No, he thought. *I can't involve her. It's not fair. I've put her through enough.*

He was feeling weaker by the moment, though. At the level just above the G'zai Zone, at the buffer level, he lurched out of the lift, shoved his gun away—it would only alarm people—and found a public plaza. There people wandered the shops and crowded around radios. Tavlin found a young boy smoking a cigarette and hawking watches that were surely stolen. "Bring me the nurse Sophia," Tavlin told him, shoving a wad of money into the boy's hands. The boy's eyes lit up, and Tavlin added, "There will be more when she gets here. Tell her to bring her kit. Oh, and tell her it's Tavlin." The boy nodded and ran off. Tavlin slumped against an alley wall, wondering where his hunters were.

He was beginning to think the boy had taken off with his money and not bothered about Sophia, but at last he saw the lad leading her out to the area where Tavlin had engaged his services. The two scanned the shops, benches and crowds looking for him, and Tavlin whistled. Sophia glanced up, and their eyes met. Some indefinable emotion washed though him.

When the two came over, he paid the boy the promised money. "Would you like a watch?" the boy asked. Tavlin raised an eyebrow, and the boy shrugged, as if to say, *You never know.* "You could time the pumping of your blood," the boy suggested.

"Just clear off," Tavlin told him. Then, as an afterthought, he added, "You should steer clear from this area for a few days. There's bad people out looking for me. They won't reward you for information, so don't get your hopes up. They *will* carve off your bits and pieces until you tell them everything you know about me, though." He thought of the nervous man at the Pleasure Garden and shuddered.

The boy stared at him. When Tavlin made shooing motions, the lad shot him an obscene gesture, which Tavlin didn't blame him for, and left.

"You do have a way with people," Sophia said.

"I try," Tavlin said.

She looked him over, then dug into her kit. "Why not the doctor's office?"

"I didn't want to lead them to you."

"And who are 'they' exactly? Enemies of Boss Vassas?"

"Not exactly." He grimaced as she tore away his shirt and inspected the first wound. A bullet had grazed his ribs at the level of his elbow, and blood leaked out in a trickle.

Apparently satisfied that the injury was not life-threatening, she had him pull down his pants, and she inspected the wound on his inner right thigh. This one bled more freely, but her expression did not change, which reassured him.

"A grimy alley isn't the best place to do this," she said. "Let me take you somewhere moderately sterile, at least."

"Where?"

She peered up at him, her expression neutral. "My place isn't far."

"Your place …"

She misread his surprise. "Don't worry, I remember how to make sure I'm not followed."

He swallowed. "These guys are good, Sophia. Better than some crook that might want to rip off the card-player's wife."

"Do you want to die of bacterial infection?"

"No."

"Then come."

Chapter 6

"Ouch!"

"Is that all you can say?" She pulled another suture tight, cinching closed more of the wound along his ribs. His shirt and pants were off and he lay on her kitchen floor atop a towel that, while clean, had seen better days. He wore only his boxers and socks. With the hand not propping himself up he drank from a bottle of Urzan whiskey: thick like honey but with a smoky, almost clove-like flavor.

"That's not even a straight line," he said, eyeing the stitching.

She started to sew another stitch, tugged on it. When he gasped, she smiled, "Now might not be the best time to complain."

"Afterward will be too late. I thought *I* was the one that was drunk."

"Not my fault you can't pace yourself."

"It damn well is." He glanced at the ragged wound on his thigh, which she had already stitched up. Blood caked the towel underneath. "I wouldn't drink so much if you could sew straight."

"Maybe I like seeing you drunk."

"So you admit it! You're sewing crooked on *purpose*."

"Got to take life's pleasures where we can."

"I knew it!"

For a moment their eyes met, and he was uncomfortably aware of her body bending over him, of her firm breasts straining against the fabric of her white uniform just inches before his face. He could smell her, over the antiseptic and alcohol, a sort of rose scent. Then she placed a hand on his chest, which was tacky with sweat, and pushed him down. Her fingers were very warm.

"Two more," she said.

He drank. Her apartment was small and tidy. A neon sign flashed through the window, illuminating the rooms in strobes of red.

She scanned his torso, and he saw her eyes linger on his new scars, on the tattoo over his right breast, a serpentine lion coiled around a flaming sword.

"What have you been up to the last few years?" she said.

"I thought you knew all about it."

"Only the cheating and the getting kicked out of clubs. I used to think you were intentionally getting kicked out of clubs up top so you would be forced to return down here. But you never showed up. You kept finding ways to remain up there, gambling in taverns, rooftop gardens."

"Yeah, well, I had to balance things out. You were upwardly mobile, I had to be downwardly."

She started on the last stitch. "So where's your laundry case?"

"At the dry cleaner's, where else?"

She tugged the stitch tight, using more force than she had to, and he hissed through clenched teeth. Instead of tying it off or snipping it, she pulled tighter. "I'm going to ask you something, Two-Bit, and I want an honest answer."

"If I have strength left."

"Those sirens earlier, the fire at the Lavish, and the police rushing up to the Singh-Hiss on our way here—that was you, wasn't it? Whatever you're involved in?"

"What, no—"

She tugged the stitch tight, and he groaned. Blood leaked down from the wound.

"Yes, all right, yes."

She released the pressure, but did not snip the line. "What's it all about, then?"

"You wouldn't believe me if I told you."

"Try me."

He started to say something, closed his mouth. Finally, he said, "There's Octunggen spies doing something at a factory in Muscud. I stole whatever they were working on and now they're out to get me. And they don't seem concerned with keeping it low-key, either."

"Why did you steal it?"

"Because they killed a bunch of people in order to make whatever it is, and I had to figure whatever was in that case was meant to kill a whole lot more." He decided to tell her about Nancy later. "Now it's where it can't hurt anybody."

"But they can. And you know where it is."

"Yeah." He glanced away. "They might . . . they might come for you. Even if they didn't follow us here, they might figure it out in time."

"I was just working that out for myself, but thanks for your concern."

"They killed everyone at the hotel. At the whorehouse. Everywhere I've been."

Angrily, she snipped the line and leaned back. He was aware of the rose-scent of her diminishing, and he realized he missed it. She inhaled a breath, and he realized something had changed in her. No longer was she feistily mad. Now she was *pissed.*

"Damn you, Tavlin Metzler. Do you know how long it took me to get here?"

"Soph . . ." He felt a sinking feeling.

"Shut up. To start with, nursing school while whoring wasn't fun. Three *years* of that. Three long, slow, horrible years of whoring during the nights and studying during the days, of changing sheets and finding veins. Then I had to look all over for a position. Not many doctors want ex-whores as nurses, surprisingly enough, even down here. Finally I found a job, just six months ago. The asshole doctor made me give him favors till I proved myself, and I don't mean taking out the trash. Lately he's come to rely on me so much I've been able to stop. That was like *three weeks* ago." She swore. "I was just settling in here—*just settling in*—and now I'm going to have to leave it, aren't I? Just because I stitched *you* up. I'm going to have to go on the run—from fucking Octunggen spies! Shit!" Tears hovered at the edges of her eyes, and her lips trembled. "Fuck you, Tavlin Two-Bit. I hope the Octs take you. I should have let you bleed to death in that alley."

He stared at her. His head reeled from the vodka, but somehow her words had burned away the buzz. "I . . . I'm . . ."

"Don't you dare apologize."

He backed away in irritation and tried to stand. His head may have been clearing, but his body was still soaked with booze, and he fell back down, gasping. Angrily, he spun back to her and said, "Then what do you want me to do? I did what I had to. I'm not sorry about it."

"Yeah, you never are. You're never sorry for anything. You're Tavlin Two-Bit Fucking Metzler, famous gambler and rogue. There's never been a rule made that you can't break, a law you can't talk your way around."

He ground his teeth. Her anger was sparking his own, and he felt deep wounds unknitting. "What are you so angry for? What gives you the right?"

"You ruined my life!" she said.

That did it. The wounds opened. He sucked down a breath, and then he said something there was no taking back. He looked her in the eyes and said, "*I'm* not the one that killed our son."

Her eyes went wide, and she looked as if she'd been slapped. Then her face grew red, and she stood shakily. "Get . . . out. Get out right now or so help me . . ."

He wished he could retrieve the last few seconds, but he couldn't. He tried to stand again, but he collapsed. She stepped forward and tried to lift him up bodily, to hurl him from her apartment, but he shoved her away. They both fell in ungainly heaps, glaring daggers at each other.

"I ought to tell the Octs you're here and let them take you," she said. "They'd probably spare me if I did."

He wiped at the blood on his ribs; with all the activity, the wound had started to bleed again. "Do it," he said. "You always were good at looking after yourself."

"Fuck you. I was a good mother."

He started to say something, then stopped. "Yeah," he said, "maybe you were. But you were a lousy wife."

"Oh, sure. Blame me for trying to provide. What was I supposed to do? After you quit Boss Vassas, we didn't have enough for Jamie's pills."

"You could've earned money some other way than on your back. And don't you dare use leaving Boss Vassas against me. You *wanted* me to leave."

"I didn't want Jamie raised in the fucking mob! If you were half a good father, you'd have realized that."

"That's why I quit!" Shaking, he gripped the kitchen countertop and hauled himself to his feet.

In her corner, she did likewise. Tears coursed down her face, but she looked furious more than she looked sad, though she appeared sad also. A deep pain burned in her eyes. "We needed money. When Jamie got sick—"

He waved her to silence, tugging on his clothes. "Your son died without his mother by his side *because you were off whoring.*"

She stood so rigidly he thought something had gone wrong in her head, maybe a stroke, but then she lifted her arm and pointed at the door. "GET—THE FUCK—OUT."

He lurched toward the door, still yanking up his pants. The world seemed to spin around him. He staggered, nearly fell, but she did not offer to help. He remained upright, barely, as he reached the portal, then sagged against it for support. He snapped a button closed on his pants.

Without turning to look at her, he said, "The last thing he said in this world was, 'Where's Mommy?'"

He heard a choking gasp behind him, but he didn't dare turn around. He fumbled at the doorknob.

A plate broke by his head. Shards of porcelain sliced his cheek. Another smashed between his shoulder blades.

"Damn you!" he said. He wrenched the door open.

"Damn *you*!"

Another plate caught the side of his head, ricocheted and cracked against the doorframe.

He stumbled through the door, down the stairs. She followed, hurling plates after him. She must have shoved some under an arm.

He fled down the stairs and through the tight, winding halls of the tenement. They smelled of mold, fungus and alchemical lamps, not to mention the myriad smells of mutant cooking, cabbage and sulfur and unprocessed fish. Radios blasted newscasts of the war. Plates shattered about him as he ran. Sophia cursed him vilely.

He made it to the front entrance, slammed the door behind him and staggered down the road. She didn't follow. He heard her crying through the door.

*   *   *

He skulked through the streets. Hating himself, he buttoned his shirt as he went and drew his jacket tight. It was cold—cold, and late. He didn't know what time it was exactly, but he was exhausted. And hungry.

Shaking, he wasn't sure why, he found a streetside café that advertised "safe" food and ordered a plate of spiced meat and flatbread. After he'd eaten, he smoked a bowl and sat there, staring out over the little city, trying to calm his mind. He knew he had gone too far, had cut too deep. He hadn't wanted to. But the bitterness, the pain he had felt since that day, since his little boy had died in his arms crying for his mother, and Tavlin had had to tell him lies to prevent Jameson from knowing the truth about where his mother really was—lies, even as Jameson shuddered and trembled and his eyes rolled up into his head, and the last thing Tavlin had ever said to him in this world was a lie . . .

He had never forgiven her for that. He didn't think he ever could.

But he shouldn't have said that she had killed him. That had been wrong. Jameson had been their miracle—in many ways. For one, they had always used protection to prevent Tavlin from becoming infected. Somehow, someway, Sophia had gotten pregnant anyway. Second, Jameson had survived the pregnancy itself. All the doctors had agreed that he probably wouldn't, that they shouldn't get their hopes up, the progeny of infected and non-infected rarely survived. But then, somehow, he had. He had been born, and he had survived his first year, and his second, and his third. Tavlin and Sophia had dared to hope, each day a battle against despair. Jameson was normal, healthy, non-infected. All the doctors warned them. A non-infected child would surely bear the seeds of infection somewhere inside him, passed on to him by his mother. But Jameson had survived his fourth year, and his fifth, and his sixth. During the seventh year, Tavlin had done something foolish. He'd allowed himself to believe. He thought Sophia had, too. Tavlin had quit working for Vassas and started gambling professionally to support them. That had been enough. Until the inevitable.

When Jameson grew sick at last, Sophia had supplemented their income against Tavlin's wishes to afford Jameson's medicine. Another year had passed, and then another. Finally, though, Jameson's frail little body could take it no longer.

When he succumbed to the infection at last, Tavlin thought he himself would die. He'd wanted to. He took to drinking and cheating at cards. He had cheated dangerous men. Only chance and the lingering favor of Boss Vassas had spared him. Meanwhile Sophia had continued to whore, as she had done when he'd first met her, before he had fallen in love, asked her to marry him and gotten her to quit. Grief and bitterness on both sides had split them apart as surely as rot can break an oak.

Tavlin had always blamed her for not being there, for making him lie, and somewhere in the back of his mind he had blamed her for passing on the infection in the first place, and she blamed him for not making enough to buy the expensive pills Jameson had required, and blamed him for his drinking and self-destructiveness later. Yet what could he do? His son was dead and his wife was once again a whore, and they hated each other. He thought she had almost been relieved when he had left her, when he had abandoned the under-cities and returned to the upper world. His world. A place she could never feel comfortable in again.

He stared out over Taluush now, at its lights, the boats coming and going on the water. There was little traffic out now, but there was enough. He supposed the Octunggen were out looking for him still. Where were they? Were they combing the streets and alleys? He supposed he had better be off. Back to Muscud. Sophia knew she needed to leave, she would be fine. He was sorry he had screwed things up for her here. That would just be one more thing she could hate him for. Give her something to do, some reason to go on. In a way, he was almost doing her a service. A real humanitarian, like Sgt. Wales.

He sighed, finished his bowl and settled up. Then he lurched off through the city streets, receiving strange looks from people about him, and he realized he was bleeding again. He had torn his sutures with all the activity. He was a bloody, ragged-looking non-infected man in a city of mutants; he would stand out like a preacher in a whorehouse—or, knowing several preachers, maybe moreso. His pursuers would find him easily.

Yes, it was time to leave. He made his way toward the docks. He descended ramp after ramp, finally descending into the buffer zone between the upper levels and the territory of the G'zai. The activity of a plaza surrounded him. It was nighttime, and the nightlife of Taluush teemed, riotous. One three-breasted woman with conical funnels sticking up from her head in a straight line instead of hair sold glowing vials to shady-looking characters. A loud nightclub blared with noise, and Tavlin saw thumping, leaping, gyrating shapes in the smoky darkness, lit by neon strips and cigarettes. A male prostitute in tight pants and an unbuttoned snakeskin shirt lounged against a streetlamp, smoking a cigar suggestively, while moths flapped about the light over his head, sometimes covering the light completely and throwing him into darkness, sometimes illuminating him fully, as if he had his own personal strobe light.

A boy in ragged clothes sold stolen watches. His eyes widened when Tavlin grabbed him by the back of the neck. "Hey! Lay off! What're you about?"

"I told you to clear out," Tavlin hissed. "Lay low for a couple of days."

He released the boy, who thrashed like a wet dog, then glared up at him. "Who are you to tell me what to do?"

"Someone who's trying to look after you."

"Fuck off."

The boy started to walk away, but Tavlin spun him back around. He wasn't sure how he could convince the boy to take him seriously, but he was determined to try.

Before he could give it a go, however, something behind the boy drew Tavlin's attention, and he stood riveted, eyes fixed on the sight.

Dripping wet, the great monstrosity oozed up from the level below, towering over the infected men and women around it. Tavlin stared at it, trying to make sense of it. It wasn't quite shaped like a maggot, nor a centipede, nor a shrimp, but it shared attributes of all three. Its head was vaguely shrimp-like, and white shrimp-flesh covered the whole of it, shot through with pink veins. Writhing cilia. Chittering mouth-parts. A profusion of whip-like tendrils. It carried itself erect, walking on a bed of cilia, but Tavlin sensed it could also walk horizontally, crawling like a fat centipede. Black, glistening eyes stared out at the world from its head—alien, insectile, unblinking, of different sizes. Maybe six or eight of them, maybe more, it was hard to tell with the jutting pincers, the stalks of antennae that sliced the air overhead. As it moved through the crowd, people fell away from it on all sides, giving it space.

Tavlin stared, mouth open.

The boy took the opportunity to wriggle loose of his grasp and back away. "Never seen a G'zai, huh, mister?"

"No. Never."

The white horror moved closer, towering perhaps two or three feet over the heads of the mutants, its antennae whipping several feet even higher. Tavlin could hear the cutting noises they made. *Whup whup whup.*

"Don't worry, mister, they're harmless," the boy said.

"Are you sure? It looks dangerous."

"I'm sure. See, I'll—"

Two whip-like cords shot out from the G'zai and lassoed a man about the middle. It was an uninfected man, Tavlin saw, of medium height and build. Likely an upper coming down into the sewers to enjoy a night of depravity on the cheap. The man screamed and was dragged off his feet toward the abomination. Energy like green fire passed through the tendrils into the man, and his screams turned into howls of agony.

Two constables, who had been loitering in the shadows watching for people to extort money from, rushed forward, drawing their pistols. A gun cracked, then another. Tavlin saw bursts of flesh erupt on the G'zai, and a viscous white substance ran from the wounds, but the creature didn't seem to register any pain.

Others appeared.

Tavlin hadn't noticed them, so focused was he on the first one, but more G'zai, perhaps a dozen or so, had wormed their way up from their cocoon-like lairs and now cut through the crowd on the platform. Tavlin heard a scream and spun to see three more of the chittering white abominations slice and whip the crowd about them. Green fire erupted among the mutants, spreading from one to another. Tavlin saw one of the G'zai lift an appendage with an opening at the end. The appendage rippled in a muscular fashion, like an elephant's trunk or a throbbing phallus, and then some sort of energy passed out of the dripping orifice—the air rippled around it, though the energy was invisible—and the blast struck the nearest constable. He exploded into a thousand wet pieces.

A second G'zai whipped its tendrils at the other constable, and the tendrils tore through him as if he were butter and the tendrils superheated knives. He collapsed into even chunks revealing perfect cross-sections of flesh and bone and fat on the floor, like a selection at a butcher shop, each chunk wrapped in a decorative layer of skin and uniform.

People ran, screaming. Where they ventured too close to a G'zai, tendrils whipped them to shreds, or green fire burned them into strange charred shapes, reducing them to flaming lumps that still seemed to scream, or else were blown apart by dripping orifices on the end of certain limbs. The G'zai butchered the infected with no mercy or seeming motive. Tavlin saw the uninfected man they had dragged down surrounded by two more G'zai, who wrapped their own tendrils around him. His screams grew so hoarse he could no longer scream. He simply juddered and writhed on the ground, foam frothing his lips. Strangely, they did not kill him.

The G'zai took down another non-infected man, and the same thing began to happen to him.

Some fleeing person smashed into Tavlin, knocking him over. Boots stampeded his abdomen. Someone kicked the side of his head.

The boy grabbed his arm and helped haul him to his feet. "Run, you idiot!"

The boy fled into the chaos, toward a ramp leading up. Tavlin pelted after him, wondering if perhaps he should take a ramp down, toward the docks, but as soon as the thought occurred to him he shrank in horror from it. The G'zai occupied the bottom level. To go down was to die. Even as he found the boy and started up a ramp, he saw the towering, white, chittering shapes flow up a ramp from below and swarm the plaza, cutting bloody swathes through the crowd.

They're after me. They had captured two uninfected men of his general height and description. They could only be looking for him.

He cut through the crowd following the boy. The youth vanished into a pool hall on the next level, and Tavlin pushed his way in through the opening after him. It was darker in here than out, and the press of people blocked many of the lights. It stank of stale cigarette smoke, mold and body odor. Fighting through the press, Tavlin mounted a pool table and scanned the crowd until he saw a small form slipping through the packed shapes toward the rear of the hall. Tavlin jumped down and elbowed his way through them, after the boy. Mutants around him were breaking pool cues into jagged-tipped sticks to use as weapons or pulling out their own guns and knives. The employees of the pool hall gathered behind the bar, the apparent owner checking to make sure his shotgun was loaded.

With practiced ease, the boy slipped through a doorway and into a back room, and Tavlin followed.

"Don't follow me, asshole!" the boy shouted over his shoulder as he ran up a narrow stairway.

Tavlin ignored him and plunged upward.

Screaming erupted in the pool hall behind him. He heard the shotgun roar, then the cracks of smaller weapons. The screams pitched higher and higher.

The pool hall occupied one level of a tower, and the boy was leading up into the rest of it, which stretched out like a junkheap honeycomb on all sides. License plates stuck out from the walls between bicycle wheels and sheets of metal. People vanished into their warrens, blocking the doors behind them. One shouted to the boy, who cursed him and ran on. Breathless, heart smashing against his ribs, Tavlin followed.

The boy pounded up another stairway, then another.

Screams filtered up from below. More gunshots. Tavlin felt sick in the pit of his stomach. *What have I done now?*

The boy led on, and Tavlin began to wonder if he had any destination at all or if he were just putting distance between himself and the G'zai. At last the boy reached the highest level of the tower and sprinted through an exit, across a ramp toward a platform.

Running beside him, Tavlin panted out, "Is there a way out of town that doesn't involve going down to the docks?"

The boy hesitated, as if not sure he wanted to reveal his secrets even then. He started to open his mouth to reply, but just then a pair of G'zai appeared from a connecting rampway. People screamed and divided all around them.

The tall white things cut through the press of mutants, smoke pouring around them. A gang of townspeople very close to Tavlin and the boy, armed with homemade weapons, rushed toward the creatures. One G'zai lifted a dripping tentacle, then another. Two separate blasts hit the mutants. Tavlin, wondering if they did in fact mean to take him alive, threw himself to the floor even as the G'zai released the pulses. He dragged the boy down with him.

The lad screamed. There came an awful *splat* sound, and then something wet covered them both from head to foot. Tavlin tried to turn his mind off to it as he pulled the boy up the ramp and away from the G'zai.

"Well?" Tavlin demanded. "Is there another way out of the city?"

Around him the people they passed were staring at them, and it wasn't until Tavlin had to wipe blood and oozing flesh out of his eyes that he realized why. He and the boy were absolutely soaked in viscera. The boy was trembling and crying, much of the brave townspeople that had just died now coated onto him like glue, but at the moment he looked livid enough to put his grief aside.

"Yes," he said. "There's a way."

The two emerged onto a plaza that was full of smoke and screams, where Tavlin and the boy paused to gasp for breath and wipe gore from their hair.

"Well?" Tavlin pressed.

"There's tunnels up above, through the rock of the ceiling. Smugglers used to use them." With a crooked grin, the boy added, "Still do."

Tavlin didn't know what the boy and his people smuggled and didn't care. "Then let's be going."

More screams filtered up from below.

"This way," the boy said, and led them up a ramp. Bodies littered the ground around them, as well as signs of great destruction, as though a hurricane had swept through, but hopefully the creatures that had done this had already passed on.

Tavlin started to go with the boy, then paused.

"What're you waiting for?" the boy said, as he ushered the others up the ramp.

"I have to go back for somebody."

The boy looked at him as though he were mad—worse, as though he were one of the walking dead. "Change your mind, I'll be at the end of the Ale-Maru." Tavlin knew this was another hanging section like the Singh-Hiss, the one that terminated in the clock.

Tavlin nodded, then turned away. The boy and the others vanished up the ramp, into the chaos. Tavlin wished them well, but he had something he had to do.

Sophia, be ready.

Chapter 7

Tavlin picked his way through the rubble, trying to keep to the shadows along the walls. Green fire ate at several of the buildings and he was forced to take wide detours. Groups of survivors huddled in hiding spots, which were not very good if he could spot them. Some motioned for him to join them, some made threatening gestures when he came too close, others just studied his gore-coated body. His shirt and pants were both sticking to him, and he smelled something foul. He thought dissolved bits of flesh had gone up his nostrils. Some had definitely clogged his ears. He constantly spat out what tasted like blood, and chewier bits caught in his teeth and under his tongue.

At last he reached Sophia's tenement. Warily, he entered the smoking doorway, past the sagging, half-melted doors. Screams and fumes already issued from a lower floor than the one he had entered on, but if his orientation was right Sophia lived on the level above. Not daring to hope, he mounted quickly and found her door. Knocked hard. Then again. No one answered.

"Shit."

He began kicking down the door, calling her name as he did. The door splintered open and he stumbled in, blinking his eyes in the darkness. She had doused all the lights.

"Sophia!"

No one answered.

He found her in the bedroom. She had crawled under the bed and clutched a ridiculously large pistol in her hands. He thought she was going to take his head off with it when he got on his hands and knees to look under the bed. He could barely see her face around the enormity of the barrel.

"It's me," he said.

"I know. Why do you think I'm pointing a gun at you?"

"The G'zai are on the floor below. They'll be here soon. We need to leave."

"Why?"

"Because they'll kill us."

"No," she said. "Why are they *here*?"

"Because they're pre-human monsters with no human motivation."

"Bullshit. They're doing this because of you, aren't they? I don't know how, or why, but I know it's you."

"Soph . . ."

"If I shot you now and left you for them, would they be satisfied? Or perhaps I need to hand you over to them alive." The blackness inside the barrel looked very dark. He could just see one of Sophia's eyes glimmer slightly around one side of the bulging bullet chambers.

"We don't have time for this," he said.

The gun continued to point straight at him. "They want your briefcase, don't they? That's what all this is about. But you've hidden it somewhere. So if I shoot you, they won't get it, and I can only think that would be a good thing for the world."

The same thought had occurred to him. "They're underwater creatures, Soph. I hid it underwater. Finding me will probably hurry up them getting it, but they'll get it one way or another. But if I live, maybe I can think of something to *do* about all this. Some way to *stop* them."

The destruction on the floor below grew louder.

"Sophia," he said, almost growling.

She sighed. He heard a click and realized she was shoving the hammer back. She had actually drawn the hammer!

"Well, it was a thought," she said. She crawled out from under the bed, and he stepped back. She glanced him over, wrinkling her nose. "What the hell happened to you?"

He grabbed her free hand and pulled her from the room. She shook loose of him and said, "They're in league with the Octs, aren't they—the G'zai?"

"Less talk, more running."

He stuck his head through the splintered front door, looked one way, then the other. He stepped through, his own gun drawn and ready. Motioned for her to follow. The smell of smoke was very strong now. The vibration of the tower beneath them trembled up through the soles of his feet.

He and Sophia ran up a flight of stairs, then another. He didn't know this tenement well, but he assumed it would have exits onto all of the major platforms it abutted. All around him he heard the sounds of residents barricading their doors and sealing up any windows onto the hallways. A few realized the tower was doomed and were fleeing upwards, the same as he and Sophia. They encountered more and more deserters as they rose.

"You have a plan?" Sophia said, as they mounted one tight, smoke-filled stairway.

"Go up."

"Fire rises, and there's no escape."

"There might be. Just follow me."

"You'd like that, wouldn't you? Why shouldn't I go off on my own?"

They emerged from the stairway, coughing and rubbing their eyes. Tavlin saw the stream of people headed in a certain direction and knew that must be the way out. Before following them, he turned to Sophia and said, "We used to say we were in it together, remember?"

She watched him, cold and furious at the same time. "We're not in it together anymore."

"Maybe for just a little while."

The tower shuddered.

"Maybe," she said "For just a very small while." Then: "This better work."

With more conviction than he felt, he said, "It will."

He pushed his way through the crowd, and Sophia followed—perhaps reluctantly, but she followed. They emerged, coughing from the fumes, onto a hanging bridge that shook and trembled under the weight of so many people. Clearly it was not meant to support the number that currently trampled across it, trying to escape the burning, G'zai-infested tenement. Tavlin winced at the sounds of snapping cables around him. With each twang and pop, the bridge trembled. *Please hold, please hold.*

They made it across. Judging by the sounds of pounding feet and heavy breathing behind him, the bridge did not immediately collapse behind them. That was good. Of course, it also meant the G'zai could follow them over it.

The press of people led into a series of plazas, bridges and ramps. This was the busy metropolitan area of Taluush, and platforms mounted by all manner of shops, restaurants and bars arced through the thick junkheap towers like mushroom tops, or perhaps lily pads, each one higher than the next and connected by bridges and walkways, even rope swings. From below came the glow of green fire.

It all stank of smoke and panic. The air was filled with the sounds of rending metal, crackling flames and screams. To Tavlin's left a gang of mutants looted a clothing shop. To his right another group barricaded their own shop.

A great, unanimous scream issued from behind, and Sophia clutched Tavlin's hand. "The bridge fell," she whispered. She realized she was gripping his hand and dropped it.

"This way," he said and ran toward a particular ramp, then into a tower.

Sometimes he had to push and shove his way through the crowd, but at last they stepped from an upper level onto the high, vertigo-inducing walkways of the Ale-Maru, a large, tubular section that, like the Singh-Hiss, hung suspended horizontally from the cistern cavern ceiling. The Ale-Maru sprouted from the tower Tavlin and Sophia had just left and merged with a great, dripping stalactite, coated in slime and ash, on its far end—a thick stalactite that must drop to its point seventy feet or so below the ceiling. Flails flew around it, their undersides lit by the weird green glow of the fires. It was the stalactite the great town clock was set into, and the clock faces—all three of them, at equidistant points all around—blazed the time, with the second hand ticking down the fate of the city, as if to say, *The end is coming.*

Wind tore at Tavlin's clothes and hair, a breeze spurred by the flames. Few people occupied the scaffolding that supported the walkways, and he knew that most would be barricading their doors within. He and Sophia passed darkened shops and dives, all seedy and depressed-looking. This had obviously not been a thriving area of the city. The ground looked very far away, and the many towers, platforms and flames between this hanging branch and the water level gave the perspective a certain franticness that made Tavlin feel queasy.

He and Sophia picked their way toward the far end of the Ale-Maru, where it was pressed into the giant clock stalactite, just as the whole structure began to shake violently. He glanced back to see that the tower it sprouted from was crumbling. Green flames licked most of the way up its length, climbing higher by the second. Soon it would reach the Ale-Maru and begin eating into it as well. Tavlin wondered if the Ale-Maru could stay intact if the tower collapsed. Many thin wires, and a few thick ones, held it up, and they were bolted securely into the stone and metal of the cistern ceiling. But *how* securely?

"Where are we going, damnit?" Sophia asked.

"The boy said to meet him at the end of the Ale-Maru. He must've meant where it joins the clock face."

"There are chambers in it, I know that much. People work there, in the clockwork."

"I guess there must be a secret passage from the machinery rooms into smugglers' tunnels."

He pressed on, heart pounding, sweat weeping from every pore, keeping the blood that caked him from solidifying. His eyes scanned the way ahead for signs of the boy.

Nothing.

That was when events took an unexpected turn.

Suddenly, Tavlin heard a peculiar hiss, as of waves breaking along a shore—a strange shore, as if formed of some unfathomable material, and a strange sea, as if the water moved too slowly, too thickly, and the sound only heard over a radio broadcast, full of metallic crackling. At the same time, the lighting changed. Green-white illumination pulsed off the walls and scaffolding around him. Shocked, Tavlin drew back, nearly tumbling off the walkway into the oblivion to the left of him. Sophia grabbed him. Her eyes were wide, too.

"What is it?" she said.

Tavlin opened his mouth to answer but could only fumble for words. *No, not her, not now . . .*

The air crackled behind them, a great hissing vortex of energy. Tavlin and Sophia spun. Out of the vortex flowed a form, all of white, phantasmagorical vapor spilling everywhere, taking strange shapes. The vapor drifted forward, tall and roiling, then it parted in the middle like some alien, ghostly flower, and the girl appeared—the witch-girl, the girl in white—beautiful, naked, otherworldly. Light shone from her eyes.

A finger stabbed at Tavlin. *"You took it. Why, oh why did you take it?"*

Her voice seemed to come from far away, and it had an odd echo to it. The way she said the words almost sounded as though she cared for Tavlin, as if by taking "it" he had betrayed her in some way.

Tavlin backed away, Sophia at his side. "I—I—"

Sophia raised her gun. Fired. The bullet punched through the ghost-girl as if she were made of air, and perhaps she was, or nothing more solid at any rate. Sophia fired again, and again, to the same result.

Behind the ghost-girl, green fire consumed the tower. Leaping flames began to eat into the Ale-Maru, silhouetting the girl in surreal tones. The flames could just vaguely be seen through her luminous form.

"Where is it?" she said. *"Where did you take it?"*

Tavlin backed way, careful not to tumble off the edge. "Y-you should know," he said. "You seem able to follow me anywhere. What *are* you?"

The phantom threw back her head and screamed, *"Here! Here he is! Take him!"*

The G'zai must have heard her, for Tavlin saw them pour out of the tower, tall and white, their tendrils whipping the air about them, black eyes unblinking. The young ghost woman drifted forward, but even as her fingers locked about Tavlin's neck—with him thrashing and throwing himself backward—she dissipated into white smoke, then not even that.

The G'zai took her place, scuttling forward through the scaffolding, both awkward-looking and amazingly limber. And *fast.* They closed the distance with horrifying speed.

People within the structure fired at them—Tavlin saw the flashes through shop windows—and the G'zai responded. Tendrils dipped inside cavities of the Ale-Maru and dragged out screaming, thrashing victims, who were promptly engulfed in flames or ripped apart in bloody showers.

Sophia raised her gun to fire at them. Tavlin let loose, too. The G'zai drove on, not even pausing.

Tavlin shoved the gun away. Still one bullet left.

"Run!" he said.

He scrambled toward the clock face. Cursing, Sophia followed. The hissing and chittering of the G'zai grew louder. Closer. The scaffolding thumped and shook as they climbed. The roar of fire grew louder. Tavlin heard a loud snap and spun to see that one of the four main strands of cables that held the Ale-Maru up had torn.

The Ale-Maru vibrated underfoot. People screamed inside.

A great squeal and a terrible roar sounded behind him. He craned his head to see the tower the Ale-Maru was connected to collapse, slowly, in stages, sagging away while flames gushed up from it. Bits of metal and debris plumed out in gunmetal clouds that glittered where chunks caught the light. The tower struck a platform, then another, and kept listing, falling away, taking out more and more of the city with it, until finally the dust of its passage obscured it from sight. Surprisingly, it didn't drag the Ale-Maru with it as Tavlin had feared, but it tried; the Ale-Maru extended wide out to the side, pulled by the tower, and then the links broke in loud pops, hardly distinguishable over the other noises, and after that the tower fell, and the Ale-Maru, flexing and bending, swayed back the other way, its endpoint, anchoring the structure into the great stalactite, crumpling hideously.

Stomach lurching, Tavlin grabbed on tight. Beside him, Sophia did likewise.

As the Ale-Maru mashed against the clock stalactite, the wires holding it up broke, one by one, unable to support its weight without the tower. Now only the cluster of wires at the far end, near the clock, held any part of it up.

As if swung on a pivot, the Ale-Maru fell, and Tavlin and Sophia flattened themselves and hung on as the horizontal branch now became a vertical one. Metal screamed, as did hundreds of people still trapped within the structure. Tavlin glanced back to see that several of the G'zai had been thrown off and were even then falling away into the madness of the city, their pale-white forms writhing against the green glow.

Nauseous with vertigo, Tavlin climbed upward, toward the stalactite. Only one strand of wires held the Ale-Maru up.

"Hurry!" he said. They had to reach the clockwork passages before the wires snapped.

Movement in the stalactite. A shadow appeared, and he realized it was some sort of opening, just below one of the great clock faces. A figure in it beckoned to him. The boy! It must be the boy. Clicking gears arced behind him, ticking down to the end, etched in the red glow of an alchemical lamp. Tavlin climbed toward him. Sophia followed. The figure gestured them on.

A pall of smoke shifted. Tavlin saw who it was in the cave mouth, what must be the entrance to the maintenance shafts of the town clock. It was not the boy. It was a man, a tall man in a dark overcoat, framed against the clicking doomsday gears. He had a face carved of granite, square of head and jaw, completely bald. He had had some sort of pox as a youth, and scars pitted his face. The coldest, clearest blue eyes that Tavlin had ever seen shone out of that ravaged visage. Above them hunched shaggy white eyebrows, almost grandfatherly. Betraying no emotion, he said, "Hurry! You can still make it!"

Bodies lay at his feet. Tavlin could not see if the boy's was among them, but surely it must be. The bald man had murdered them all, all the survivors of the boy's little smuggler clan, or whatever it was. Other figures stood behind the bald man, impossible to see in the dimness.

"Come!" he shouted. "If you don't, you'll die!"

Tavlin hesitated. The structure swayed like an out of control pendulum beneath him. People screamed in terror inside it. Green fires licked up from its lower end, and, silhouetted against them, the nightmare shapes of the G'zai crawled closer. They were so close now Tavlin could smell them, all ammonia and brine.

Tavlin aimed. The bald man showed no fear. Tavlin fired. He only had one shot left in his gun, but it fired true. He struck the last strand of cable holding the Ale-Maru up, and the structure fell away. His stomach dropped, and he nearly went spinning out into the abyss. He just barely managed to grab on in time. The Ale-Maru dropped, and dropped, metal squealing, wind shrieking. Sophia cursed him so loudly he could hear it. The Ale-Maru smashed into one platform, then another, and another. With each jolt Tavlin thought he would be flung off into space, but each time he just barely managed to cling to the structure's surface. His hands bled from the grip.

At last the Ale-Maru smashed onto a tangle of debris that had already fallen, including the former tower, and rolled down the rough incline created by this mound to plough into the cistern lake with a loud hiss. Steam rose from the impact. It bobbed once, then again, and with each bob Tavlin nearly vomited.

Still gripping the structure, he glanced up to see that Sophia was already standing and surveying the scene about them. There was no sign of the G'zai. Carried by the force of its impact, the Ale-Maru, buoyed up by the large air pockets of its many shops and dwellings, drifted farther out into the lake, away from the city. If it sank, it would sink very slowly.

The city burned. Tears stung Tavlin's eyes as he watched it go, as he saw the green flames dancing on the cistern water. Around him the occupants of the Ale-Maru began to crawl out, dazed and sore, from their burrows. Some clutched broken arms or bleeding heads. Doubtless some had worse injuries, or had not made it at all. But most of them lived. If they had not fallen, they would have all died.

"We're stuck," Tavlin said.

Indeed, they were marooned on the Ale-Maru.

"Speak for yourself," Sophia said. "*I* can survive the water."

"You wouldn't . . . The water, it's …"

She smiled at him. Without another word, she dove off the side and into the so-called water, vanishing into its murky depths. He stared after her for several minutes, not quite believing it. After all that, and she had left him without a word goodbye. Well, he should have figured as much. She could bear him no love. Not after everything he'd said. He deserved to be marooned.

He was surprised when he heard the sound of a small motor a few minutes later and looked up to see Sophia approaching the drifting Ale-Maru on a boat presumably liberated from the Taluushan docks.

"Climb on," she said.

He did, saying nothing about her smell. The other survivors watched them, but none asked to leave with them. They were too busy watching the city burn.

"Where to?" Sophia asked.

"Away," Tavlin said.

As they motored off, he turned back one last time and stared as green fire engulfed the towers of Taluush. Even as he watched, another tower collapsed, and strange green sparks flashed high into the air, frying the flail nests plastered against the distant cistern ceiling.

Chapter 8

For a long time, Tavlin didn't know how long, they drifted, aimless, through the high, dark halls of the sewers, guided only by the steadily fading lamp that had been in the boat. Tavlin shone the lamp while Sophia steered. They didn't speak, just put physical and mental distance between themselves and the ruins of Taluush. The boat's motor sounded very loud in the stillness, but Tavlin barely heard it over the beating of his heart and the preoccupation of his brain. He could still hear the roar and grind of the town collapsing. The sounds seemed to chase him.

At last she said, "It's hard to believe all those people died just because the G'zai wanted the location of the briefcase."

He nodded guardedly. "They wanted me. The Octunggen couldn't find me and they didn't want to waste any more time trying, so they contacted the G'zai."

"That's what I don't understand. Why would the G'zai have anything to do with them? They don't like uninfected humans. They only deal with us because we've been touched by the Atomic Sea. They think we've transcended humanity."

Tavlin shrugged. "The Octunggen seem able to befriend the old races. I remember in Muscud, at the factory, they had Suulm working with them."

"Suulm! Here?"

"One tried to kill me."

"It's going around." She cast him a glance as if to say she might have caught it.

"So," he said, "the way it must have gone down, they contacted the G'zai and asked them to find the uninfected humans of my general description—that's if we're not all the same to them—and not to worry about any collateral damage. Maybe the Octunggen promised to give them a hundred-year supply of the chemicals the Taluushians were feeding them, or maybe it was a religious decision—the Octunggen are supposed to worship strange gods; maybe it's the same as the G'zai—who knows? Anyway, the G'zai agreed to serve Octung, or at least work with them."

She studied him, and there was a long silence broken only by the chug of the motor. Tavlin wondered how much gasoline was left. Finally she said, "They tore the whole town apart, killed countless people, to find you. Whatever you know, it might be more dangerous—for the *enemies* of Octung—for you to be alive than dead."

"You still saying it would've been better if I'd died?"

In a small voice, she said, "Prove me wrong."

Again they lapsed into silence for a time, until finally she asked, "Who was that . . . woman, if that's what she was? Girl, really. That *thing*?"

He whistled. "Hell if I know, darlin'. I'm kind of glad you saw her."

"You're alone there."

"I'd begun to think I was imagining her. I don't know who she is, or where she comes from. She just appears, generally at an inconvenient moment, and takes ten years off my life every time. Thank the gods for alcohol, or I wouldn't have slept a wink the last couple days. Which reminds me, I'm about due for a nap." His blood was still racing too fast though, and he knew he wouldn't be able to sleep. Perhaps some booze . . .

"What's that?" Sophia had cocked her head.

"What's what?" He didn't hear anything.

"Listen."

He strained his ears. Still nothing. He picked out some of the bits and pieces that had stuck in his ear canal and flicked them over the side. Either because of that or the closing of the distance, he began to hear noises. At first he wasn't sure what they were exactly. They sounded ominous, yet sweet, harmonious … grand . . .

"Singing," he whispered. "Music."

She nodded, said nothing, and he realized he had the desire to be silent, too, as if the only thing he wanted to do in this world was to listen to that wonderful, unearthly singing. Perhaps unconsciously, Sophia steered the boat toward the sounds, and they grew louder, magnified by the tight, slime-grown corridors all around them. Some of the mutated lichen, which could absorb and emit sounds, provided a chilling counter-note.

Sophia shut off the motor and grabbed an oar. Tavlin rowed from the other side, wood rasping into his torn hands, but he barely felt it. The music consumed him. Together he and Sophia rowed toward it in silence, down one hall and then another.

Soon they entered a corridor filled with slugmines. Tavlin came to himself enough to recognize the place where he had stolen the briefcase, where he had killed those men. And yes, there was the boat, still resting against the stone wall where he had left it. Little was left of the mutants he had killed except bones, he saw, and there weren't many of those. The creatures of the sewer, their situation notwithstanding, wasted nothing. A few blood-red crab-things, overgrown with green, luminescent barnacles, scrambled amongst a ribcage. A black, oily eel slithered out of one eye socket and into the other. That was it.

"They said someone was coming to meet them," Tavlin said, as he and Sophia carefully rowed around the bone-filled boat and even more carefully avoided contact with the dark, slimy mounds of the slugmines.

"Who?" Sophia asked, also in a whisper. She spoke as if in a dream. In the distance, the singing continued.

"The thugs the Octunggen had hired. The briefcase, the container, they were taking it somewhere, I don't know where. One of the Octunggen went with them. He's who I took the briefcase from." Something occurred to him. "I think I know the way back from here. Back to Muscud . . ."

She nodded, sleepily. "Yes, we'll go to Muscud . . . but first . . ."

He nodded, feeling a pleasant numbness. "The singing . . ."

They rowed forward, through the tunnel of the slugmines, then into a wider thoroughfare. All the while the singing increased in volume, bouncing around the thick walls of the underworld with mighty echoes that seemed staggered somehow, complimented by the slapping of the waves against the boat's hull. At last Tavlin and Sophia rowed past a high archway and into a massive chamber, and Tavlin's entire world changed.

The chamber was grand, as grand or grander than the one Taluush occupied, but it was not filled with the junkheap bulks of an undercity but something far more lovely, far more unexpected. It was, and there could be no mistake, a *temple*. A great, soaring temple, all of white, with graceful, bone-thin columns that soared up and up, through the high spaces of the cavern chamber, to a great dome overhead. It was construction on a scale that beggared belief, something that almost looked as if it had come from the ancient L'ohen Empire, noted for its awesome buildings, many of which still stood today. But the architecture here had a different quality. It was more subtle. More unearthly. Ghostly, even. And the angles and facets of wall and column seemed somehow *wrong*. They made Tavlin's eyes itch to look at. And yet he couldn't tear his gaze away.

At the sight, he gasped, and beside him he heard Sophia suck in a breath as well. Unthinking, they clutched hands. Tavlin felt something rise inside him, something sweet and pure—something *longing*. He rowed toward the temple with an almost painful urgency.

Ahead of him, the structure glowed.

Luminous, shining, its columns emitted a pale white light, as if carved from mutated fungi, but they were clearly not fungi. They were strong as granite, maybe steel. And the dome they supported glowed as well. But it was what lay *within* the temple that threw radiant white light across the water and drove back the hovering blackness. Something huge and white and splendid loomed beyond the pillars, within the temple's walls, and its light shone from the many great doorways, windows and balconies, seeming even to glow from the walls themselves. It looked as if there were pools, areas where worshippers could come and go from the water, and of course there was a boat dock, but even this was beautiful, if rudimentary—but eclipsing all of it, every bit, was the huge glowing brightness that emanated from the center of the temple, not visible, exactly, but still felt.

The light sort of glimmered, shifted. One moment it shone as bright as day, the next barely dusk. When it faded, Tavlin felt the breath suck from his lungs, and the sweet pureness welling up inside him dwindled. Then, gloriously, it would return.

And all the while, the singing. It crashed from wall to wall, throbbing in Tavlin's ears like a second heartbeat—like a first. He glanced to the side to see the sheen of the glorious light hitting Sophia's face, making her eyes sparkle, making all the years and all the stress fall away from her. She looked in that moment as she had when he'd first met her, turning men's heads at the Twirling Skirt all those years ago, the light of the night, the fire in his brain. She was lovely. He squeezed her hand, and she turned to look at him. Their gazes caught, and they allowed their eyes to linger on each other. Her smile grew smaller, but somehow deeper. She said something, he couldn't hear it, but he knew it was *Tavlin*. He said her name back.

They renewed rowing, toward the light, toward the life. The singing continued, pulsing in waves from up ahead. From the temple. Tavlin began to see shapes, small but many: the temple's worshippers. They congregated in organized groups on the platforms and balconies, all gazing toward the inner workings of the temple, at the splendor of the shining light. Tavlin thought he recognized one of them from the docks of Muscud. Others worked on the temple itself, some sort of construction. They clambered about on the pillars up high, making their way along scaffolding that Tavlin was just beginning to see. They appeared to be installing windows of unusual design between the pillars in neat rows. Where the light shone through it, it turned slightly greenish, but still beautiful, an amazing green-white flood of holy illumination.

Tavlin and Sophia rowed closer. Singing filled Tavlin's mind. He found himself wanting to run across the water toward it. Wanted to bask in the light. *Soon*, he thought. *Soon*. Then he and Sophia would be one with the light. One with the light . . . one with . . . one . . . they would be one . . . one . . .

He shook his head. Something was wrong.

The singing electrified him. It filled him, pulsed through him, inside him. He *was* the music.

The light inside the temple faded, as it had been doing, sort of flickered—although softer than a flicker, more a pulse—and he was able to shake himself loose of the dream, just for an instant. Frantically, he began rowing again, this time paddling the water in reverse. Combined with the forward motion of Sophia's oar, this movement swung the boat around to face the opposite way.

Sophia looked at him as if he were mad. She was facing the other way now, and the light only picked out a highlight here and there, the gleam off one eye, off her high, full cheek, off one perfect set of gills. But he could tell from her tone what she felt.

"What . . . are you *doing*?"

He gunned the motor. His motions were fear-fueled. At any moment the brightness would return, and the singing would fill him once more. He didn't think he would have the strength to resist a second time.

The motor roared, and he shot off toward the halls that led away from the temple chamber.

"No!" Sophia said. "You're . . . you're . . . leaving it!" She lifted her oar out of the water, rose and turned toward him, where he crouched over the motor. She raised her oar as if to strike him with it.

He tensed, trying to decide whether he should duck or busy his attention with aiming the boat away from the wall it was currently barreling toward. He and Sophia locked eyes. Water dripped from her oar.

The light filled her face again now that she was turned, and he saw the anguish there, the pain, the confusion. Then something rippled, and the old Sophia returned: tough, stubborn, obstinate. She staggered back. The oar dropped to the floor. She glared—*glared*; it was rage she felt now, he could tell, and felt a swell of pride—over Tavlin's shoulder, toward the temple. He heard her gasp as she sank down beside him.

The light pulsed strong again.

Tavlin guided the boat into a tunnel, and darkness, wonderful, beautiful darkness, swallowed them once more.

Clutching his arm, Sophia whispered in a small, horrified voice, "What would have happened if we had gone *into* the light?"

* * *

They set off toward Muscud. For a long time, they said little that was sensible, just fear-filled mutterings of awe and fear. Both trembled. Tavlin retched over the side, but Sophia, staring blankly, didn't seem to notice. From time to time they clutched at each other for comfort, but they were hardly aware of this either.

At last, as the sound of boats ahead, the sign of civilization, came to his ears, Tavlin was able to master his own mind enough to think straight. He wished he had his pipe, but it had fallen out of his pockets during the collapse of the Ale-Maru, along with his gun. He could really use a puff now, damn it.

Positioned at the bow at the moment, holding the lantern and searching for obstacles, Sophia turned back to him, and he marveled at how composed she appeared, despite the coating of tainted water, despite the terror and horror of the last few hours. By the light of the lantern, she was pale and her face set, but there was no trembling, no stuttering, nothing to indicate what she surely felt inside—what *he* felt, anyway.

"Do you know what it was?" she asked.

He didn't hesitate. "It was the cult of Magoth. It had to be. I recognized one of those guys on the docks—it was the preacher spreading the word of Magoth in Muscud."

She considered. "When I left Muscud, the cult of Magoth was just rising, and since I've been away I've heard rumors of it growing like crazy. I knew there were many chapels to it, not just in Muscud but other undercities, too—but I never imagined its followers would build . . . *could* build . . . something like that."

"Maybe they didn't. Maybe they found it. Restored it. They were working on it, remember. Installing the windows. Also, I think I saw some other construction."

"Yes, maybe."

"What worries me more than their remodeling project is the fact of that singing. That light. Could it really be … *Magoth itself?*" He blinked his eyes fast, trying to calm the pounding of his heart. "I thought it was just a bogeyman."

She sort of smiled, and the gesture contained a hint of her old mischievousness. "You should know better than that. Down here there are no *just* bogeymen."

He tried to laugh. It came out more of a whinny. "Well, we'd better get our story straight. Word is going to go around that Taluush burned and the G'zai rose up, and some will know we were there."

She rolled a shoulder. "We're refugees—like many others, surely. Well, I am. You were just visiting."

"Why was I visiting?"

"Coming to see me, I guess." She smiled ruefully. "*Some* will believe that."

"We'll have to keep a low profile. Remember, the Octunggen have a presence in Muscud: the factory. So does the Church of Magoth. We're going into the lair of our enemies."

"Are the people of Magoth really our enemies? I mean, the singing, it was so … lovely . . ." She shook herself. "Maybe their religion is their own affair."

"Look, I don't know what they were worshipping—call it what you like, what the hell *was* that light coming from, anyway?—but it's no coincidence it was close to the tunnel of the slugmines, where the boat was."

"I don't get you."

"Remember, the Octunggen agent was delivering the briefcase to someone. He said they would meet him nearby. Who else could it be than worshippers of Magoth?"

"So . . . the Magothians and the Octunggen, in league together on the eve of war. You know, Two-Bit, I think it might be time to consider a move."

* * *

They came into wider, more traveled halls. Here the fog exuded by the sewer water was beginning to break up. The boats Tavlin spied kept their distance when they could and, when they came close, much playing of flashlights and lantern-lights was needed to put both sides at ease, a sort of code. The tunnels of the underworld were notorious for thievery and murder, but also stranger, more otherworldly dangers.

Soon they came into the great cistern chamber of Muscud, and Tavlin couldn't help but breathe a sigh of relief at the sight of the so-called city sprawled across the lake, thousands of lights twinkling eerily through the fog, like rheumy yellow eyes. It was early morning, and the city was just beginning to rouse for the day. He saw cranes loading and unloading things from larger boats along the docks, saw fisherpeople casting nets over the sides of their small boats out in the harbor, fog still coiling around their hulls. Few paid Tavlin and Sophia much attention, and he was glad they weren't close enough to see any details.

The two docked and paid a marina official too much to put the boat up for the day. It was necessary. Tavlin was drenched in crusted blood from head to foot. Even in Muscud keeping that quiet cost a little extra. Sophia went ahead and found a bathhouse that advertised "safe" water, and Tavlin crept his way toward it, keeping out of sight as much as possible. Two feral bagriths, a species of batkin, fighting over what looked like a human thigh bone growled at him as he passed a certain alley, and he didn't linger.

The bathhouse had three wings, one for men, one for women, and one for both. Sophia vanished into the women's side, and Tavlin, reluctantly, chose the men's. He was in no mood or condition to fool around in the common area. The bath was the best thing he'd ever felt in his life, steaming hot water pouring over his tired, aching, filthy body, washing away the grime, the despair, the horror. Steam surrounded him, and all he could hear was the slap of water and the echoing laughter of other men. In the dressing room one of them let him bum a hand-rolled cigarette, and he smoked it down to his fingers, relishing every inhalation. He did miss his pipe, though.

The bathhouse employees did what they could for his clothes, but they were ruined and he knew he needed something new to put on. He found Sophia lounging in the courtyard that comprised the middle of the building, in the midst of spreading fronds and cobbled walkways. Incense burned from a golden lion's head, and she drank something out of a coffee mug—coffee, maybe, but likely with something a little stronger in it, too. She looked refreshed and healthy. Pink bloomed in her cheeks, and her lips were very red. Her eyes seemed tired, but calm, and they sparkled just a bit as he emerged, dressed in his ruined, stained clothes. A grin twisted her full lips. She was dressed in a white bathrobe, and her wet red hair hung down past her shoulders.

Glancing him up and down, she said, "I think we need to go shopping."

They set out from the bathhouse, both dressed in their soiled attire, and toured the nearest cosmopolitan district on Aimes Street, where hunched brick buildings with large warped-glass displays and patios piled with chipped flowerpots and stolen sculptures did a brisk business, even this early in the day, and the two eagerly whittled away what money Tavlin still had on him. Just the same, he felt much better when, an hour later, he and Sophia took breakfast at a café overlooking the Ulong Canal, which cut through the heart of Muscud, both wearing their new clothes. The Ulong was a busy commercial artery, and Tavlin enjoyed the sight of small barges and motorboats plying its thick dark waters.

"I miss the nurse's uniform," Tavlin said, of Sophia's new knit top and jeans.

She pursed her lips but said nothing. Perhaps she was trying to figure out if he was flirting or not, and how she should take it if he were. As for himself, he too wondered where they stood with each other. Maybe if he said nothing they could pretend like the harsh words of yesterday had never happened.

"I'm bushed," she said. "The coffee's worn off, and, I can't believe I'm saying this, but so has the fear."

"Yeah. It's past time for me to crash, too. I have a room at the Skirt."

She visibly tried to repress a certain pain. "You are a *good* customer."

"Not like that. I was hiding out. We're been very visible this morning. We need to go there, lay low, and not come out for awhile. I'm hoping the Octunggen won't be looking for us here, but they will, sooner or later. Probably sooner."

"I don't know how I feel about staying at the Skirt . . ." She rubbed her upper arm nervously, for a moment looking very young. She gulped down a deep breath. "But hell, I guess I spent ten years there. One more night won't kill—" She stopped. "Well, we'll see."

They navigated back roads into the Jasmine Quarter, where the Twirling Skirt stood sandwiched between two other buildings. There was already a john waiting in the parlor smoking a cigar on a chaise lounge, while a couple of yawning young women in negligees kept him company. He presumably waited for some girl in particular.

A pretty woman in her middle years approached; she wore an exotic silk robe of turquoise-and-amber cinched with a red belt, and her hair fell in ringlets down the back of her neck. Tavlin didn't recognize her, but Sophia did.

"Abigail!" Sophia rushed forward and they embraced, carefully, so as not to ruin Abigail's make-up.

"Soph, don't tell me you're *back*."

"What? I—"

"I mean, your old room's always open to you, you know that, but I heard you were a *nurse* now." She seemed disappointed somehow, as if she had taken comfort in the thought of a working girl made good.

"No, no, I'm with Two-Bit here. Well, not *with* him. He had a room here."

"Oh." Abigail looked at Tavlin, nodded, "Yes, of course. I remember you. I didn't make your acquaintance the other day. I'm the new madam now, by the way. The ladies voted on it."

"*Madam*," Sophia said. "Well, congratulations."

"Is my room still available?" Tavlin asked.

"You paid through the week, so yes," Abigail said. "Now, that was a special accommodation, and it wasn't made with me, but I'll honor it. I can't promise I'll renew it, though. Some things are going to change around here."

"I understand."

One of the girls accompanied them upstairs to the room, though Tavlin remembered quite well where it was; he suspected Abigail didn't want him patrolling the hallways unescorted, and she evidently didn't trust Sophia to keep a tight enough rein on him.

"Not much," Tavlin said when he opened the door to reveal the narrow, cramped room. "But it's home."

The girl that had accompanied them had left, and Sophia gave an inscrutable look first at Tavlin, then at the room. "There's only one bed."

"I'll take the floor." He waited for her to suggest otherwise, but she didn't. It didn't matter. He was so exhausted he figured he could sleep anywhere.

She made him turn around while she undressed and slipped under the covers, and he made a show of hiding his body from her view as he undressed. He thought she looked amused but couldn't tell by the light of the single candle; she had drawn the threadbare drapes, and it was very dark, almost oil-dark, despite the day-lit lamps throughout the city. It smelled of old wood and mildew, and the air was thick with humidity. A misshapen moth flapped about the candle.

Tavlin found an extra blanket to throw over himself and used a shoe for a pillow. The boards of the floor dug into his back, and he tossed and turned, trying to get comfortable. True, he was exhausted, but he couldn't stop thinking about a naked Sophia just a few short feet away, all clean and pink, long and lean and ripe like the ripest melon, maybe even a little overripe. The sounds of Skirt business from an upstairs bedroom didn't help any.

He wondered what would happen if he should try to make a move on her. Maybe he should. Maybe she would make a move on him. Why not? She was an independent woman. They could forget the past, let bygones be whatever the hell bygones were.

Or maybe she would welcome his attentions. Yes, almost certainly. She was probably waiting for him right now. He need only turn around and arch his eyebrows suggestively, and she would draw back the sheet, revealing a long, naked leg, then let the sheet fall away from a naked shoulder, then pull it lower, revealing the top of a large firm breast . . . then she would pull it a little lower, and a sharp, red nipple would just out, slightly erect in the cool room . . . and then . . .

He couldn't take it anymore. He rolled over and reached out for her.

Stopped.

A low, groaning snore came from her recumbent shape. Then another.

He drew back his hand. Grunted. He rolled over and tried to sleep. The sound of banging, gasping and moaning continued above. He plugged his fingers in his ears.

* * *

They ate and coffeed in the women's kitchen area downstairs. The Twirling Skirt was in full swing, and there was much music and laughter trickling in from the front rooms. All the lights blazed, and the air smelled of cooking biscuits, seafood and cayenne pepper. Tavlin couldn't help share frequent looks with Sophia as he dined, but they didn't talk much. For some reason, he felt very warm.

"I wish I could visit with the girls," Sophia said, wiping her lips. She had just finished her fish and biscuits and had inclined her head, listening to the sounds of the parlor.

"I know," he said. "I'd like to take a crack at the piano. It's out of tune, but I could make do." He loved musical instruments, especially the trombone and the piano. Many a night back in his old life, he had played with the band, either here or at the Wide-Mouth. He remembered when he had first started courting Sophia, he would play the trombone for her while she circled through the gathering, ostensibly to find a john for the hour but really to keep her eyes and ears on him. He remembered how their eyes would lock through the smoky gloom, softened by all the gleams of light on brass and aged wood, and the music would pour out of him into the trombone, and into the air, into her . . .

Then, inevitably, she would steal off with a john after Madam Saraja gave her a sharp look, and Tavlin would feel that same old bitter pain. He would start drinking more heavily, and he would move to the piano. In later days he would simply start buying Sophia for an entire evening, and still he would serenade her; it might cost him several days' pay, but he was a man in love. And she would sit on the sofa watching him all evening, ignoring every john that came close.

He sighed now and shook his head. "There's too many people out there, and the Octunggen are bound to be looking for us in Muscud by now. We can't show ourselves."

"But we can't just stay holed up."

"You stay here. I'll have one of the girls bring you some books to read."

"You're going *out*?"

"I have to meet with Boss Vassas," he said. "Don't worry, I'll stay hidden."

"You get to go out and I don't?"

"This isn't a game."

She groaned. "Fine. But be careful."

He escorted her back to their apartment. The other rooms in the Skirt were thumping and pounding, groaning and gasping. It was like walking through a zoo. Tavlin could even feel the rocking beds through the floorboards. He could *smell* the sex, all around him.

When they reached the room, he stopped her at the doorway by taking her hand. Surprised, she turned back to him.

He started to say something, couldn't figure out the words, and closed his mouth. Embarrassed, he glanced away.

He opened his mouth to start over again, but she placed a finger to his lips and he shut up.

"Don't say anything," she told him. She sounded sad, as if the words pained her. "I . . . think I know what you want to say."

"You do?"

She nodded. "And you can never say it. It . . ." She sighed. "It's over, Two-Bit." Her voice sort of cracked as she said it, and he felt something brittle inside him begin to break. "We had it once, but it's gone."

"We . . ." He swallowed. "We could try to get it back."

She shook her head. "Some things that are broken just can't be fixed."

"Maybe. But …"

"Yes?"

"Maybe this isn't one of those things."

Very slowly, she shut the door in his face.

Chapter 9

With a lowered head, he made his way back downstairs, where he asked Abigail's permission (through an intermediary, as she was in the parlor) to root through the lost-and-found. Johns were always leaving clothes behind. He found a suitably ragged trench coat and hat and donned them. He also found a cane with a dented brass handle and decided to take it along, just in case he had need of a blunt object.

Draped in his trench coat, with his hat pulled low over his face, he left the Twirling Skirt through the rear entrance and picked his way down the alley. This alley connected with another one, and this to another. He navigated through the back ways of Muscud with all senses cocked. Dark figures eyed him, but his shabby coat and dented cane did not entice them. One asked him if he had any *gunsai* on him, but he replied that he was dry.

Inwardly, he sneered. *Gunsai.* One of the many alchemical drugs popular in Ghenisa at the moment. It was a sad thing that drug use was so prevalent among the mutant population, but Tavlin supposed it was understandable. He hadn't had nearly as good an excuse back in his druggie days.

He shambled down streets and across rooftops, making for the Wide-Mouth by the least visible route. As he drew closer to Boss Vassas's territory, he noticed a certain stillness, an unnatural calm. Few people were out and about, and those that were kept to the shadows and stared out with watchful, grim expressions. People hid in their homes, in their shops. Many kept their hands on bulges in their pockets. Tavlin found one passed-out drunk with a newspaper over his face—the *Muscud Statesman*—and plucked it off. A quick scan showed that the entire front page was devoted to the mob war between Boss Vassas and Boss Grund. Apparently there had been several shootings, and two confirmed bombings, since Tavlin had been away. The death tally was over twenty now, and a handful of these were regular civilians caught in the crossfire.

Tavlin approached the Wide-Mouth via rooftop. Just as he was passing a water tower, someone grabbed him from behind. The assailant's arms pinned Tavlin's own arms against his side and squeezed the air from his lungs before he could shout.

Another shape appeared before him. A knife pressed against his throat—he could feel the touch of steel—before a short, squat figure shoved a gun against his belly.

"It—it's me!" Tavlin gasped.

There was a pause, then a flashlight blinded him. A chuckle came, and another. The knife retreated.

"Get that damned thing off me," Tavlin said, shoving the flashlight to the side. Blinking, he glared at Frankie, who was replacing the gun in its shoulder holster.

Frankie, a dim, toad-like form with spots dancing all about him, said, "Sorry about that, Two-Bit. We've got all avenues covered. Nobody's gettin' to the Mouth without our leave."

Tavlin brushed himself off. "This war's really gotten going, then."

"Yeah. Boss thought Grund would back down if we showed some force, so we bombed one of his storehouses and mowed down some of his men. The prick's just pissed off now, and the fuck of it is he's stronger than we thought he was. We don't know where he's getting his gear—his guns, his motorcycles. Could be a real problem." The spots started to fade, and Frankie swam into focus. "Well, you're back. Where the hell you been?"

"Never mind. I need to talk to the Boss."

"You'll need to hurry. He's just leavin'."

"Leaving?"

"You'll see. Sam, show Two-Bit through. Don't want him getting waylaid again." He laughed. "Shoulda seen the look on your face!"

Following Sam, Tavlin made his way down a crumbling fire escape, up a final alley and then onto Ilusthane Avenue. The Wide-Mouth stood there, proud and tall, made of stone, its batwing doors aglow with light. Windows blazed above, shining through the unnaturally foggy night, and here and there lamps glowed in the murk, spreading a creeping sort of illumination, making the vapor phosphorescent. Moths battered the lamps, a thousand soft furry thuds in the stillness. Tavlin half-expected tall dark shapes to emerge from the fog at any moment, teeth gleaming, eyes alight. Or maybe shrimp-like antennae.

He sensed forms on the rooftops: snipers. Even now crosshairs would be centering on his back. He felt himself hunch his shoulders and tried to stop it, with limited success.

Sam pushed before him into the Wide-Mouth, which was as dead as Tavlin had ever seen it, only a few desultory drinkers at the bar, a few gamblers tossing dice or staring at each other over their cards. As soon as Sam and Tavlin entered, all eyes swiveled to them, and everyone tensed. They relaxed when they saw who it was, but not altogether.

Sam led Tavlin through into the back rooms, where Tavlin expected to find Boss Vassas beating the shit out of another of Grund's goons. Instead he found Vassas's own goons strapping on shoulder holsters, shoving ammunition into shotguns and even a few submachine guns. Most smoked cigarettes anxiously.

Boss Vassas himself smoked a foul-smelling cigar and called out to someone through the trapdoor below, apparently to a boat. "Closer, you idiot! And tie that thing up!" He turned to the first group of men. "It's ready, boys. Let's get in and get crackin'."

Led by Galesh, Vassas's lieutenant, the group descended through the trapdoor and out of sight.

When Vassas noticed Tavlin, his eyebrows climbed his forehead. "Well, look who decided to show up. Good timing."

"Yeah," Tavlin said. "Glad I caught you before you—"

"Grab a gun." Vassas directed the next group down into a waiting boat.

"What, no, I just came to report in—"

"Shoot first, report later."

"No, really, I—"

Someone shoved a shotgun into Tavlin's hands, and another propelled him toward the trapdoor. Despite Tavlin's protestations, when the next group went down the hole, Tavlin was carried with them. Half cajoled, half forced, he found himself crouching in a boat on the water beneath the Wide-Mouth, with several other boats around him—there was more than he'd thought, maybe five, no, an even half dozen. Above, Vassas stood framed in the slow amber light, directing the last teams into their boats. The Boss himself dropped into the final boat, still smoking his foul-smelling cigar, and the other vessels gathered around him. When the trapdoor slammed shut, Vassas's cigar was the only light in darkness, a glowing red ember that made his black eyes glimmer. All that could be heard was the slap of water on rotting hulls, and the fast breathing of the men.

"Well, this is it, lads," Vassas said. "We're goin' to hit Grund so hard he'll wish he'd wedged himself in his mamma's fun tube and never come out. We're gonna end this fuckin' war right now, and when we come out the other side of this I'm gonna mount Grund's head over the bar *and use it for fucking target practice!*" This was greeted by rough cheers, and Vassas's teeth gleamed briefly in something that was not quite a smile. *"To war!"*

Boss Vassas revved his engine personally, and as his boat blasted off into the darkness with him at the bow, still smoking, submachine gun clenched in his meaty fists, it seemed as if the breath of everyone nearby was let out in a great rush—even Tavlin's—and then, one by one, the boats stormed off after him, six boats laden with cursing, heavily armed men and a few women.

"Where are we off to?" Tavlin asked Harry Scraggs, a man he used to drink with back in the day.

"One o' Grund's strongholds." Scraggs was a big man, heavily bearded, with wartstar encrusting his arms. "A warehouse where he stores drugs he sells. Nasty shit, like *gunsai*. All alchemical."

Tavlin knew Vassas turned his nose up at dealing drugs, especially the alchemical kind. Grund must smuggle them in somehow, because Vassas actively discouraged such industry in Muscud.

"Will this really end the war?" Tavlin asked.

Harry Scraggs rolled his lumpy shoulders. "Depends on what resources Grund has, I guess. At any rate, we can't just sit back and let him gore us up the ass like he's been doin'. Let *him* sit scared for awhile."

As they motored through the blackness, Tavlin tried to control the rapid beating of his heart. He realized he was sweating and trembling. *Can't believe I'm fucking doing this.* The last thing he needed was to get involved in a gang war, of all things. He'd been half hoping he could simply tell Vassas the situation, the location of the briefcase, what the Octunggen were after, and let him deal with it while Tavlin went back up to the surface world. There was nothing here for Tavlin anymore, especially not after what Sophia had said. And as far as Tavlin was concerned, he'd already cocked things up enough. Vassas couldn't do any worse. But now here he was, a gun in his hand and likely a bullet in his future.

Thanks, Boss.

The boats plowed on, stinking and smoking. All too soon they entered the Infested Quarter, where Grund made his lair. Vassas sent two boats ahead with their engines cut, presumably to deal with any sentries Grund might have placed on the water—he was expecting attack, evidently—and they came back with their blades bloody. Vassas had all the boats cut their motors, and as a small, grim armada they rolled forward.

They came up to a small dock with a ladder leading up to a trapdoor, and Vassas whispered, "Here it goes, boys. Remember the war plan."

"Plan?" Tavlin whispered. "I didn't . . ."

Three goons fired their shotguns up into the trapdoor, obliterating it. While they fell back to reload, others scrambled up into the warehouse interior. Guns roared. First the occupants of one boat, then Vassas's boat, then, Tavlin's boat. Suddenly he found himself propelled up the ladder, and he was climbing, awkwardly holding his shotgun at the same time, trying not to blow anyone's head off, trying not to think, and then he was hurled up in the warehouse itself. Goons swarmed around him.

Guns cracked. Boomed. One man's head exploded right beside Tavlin, throwing bits of brain matter and skull onto his right arm.

Tavlin threw himself to the side, beside a crate. Chips flew from it. Dark shapes fired at him from around a corner. He shoved the shotgun stock against his shoulder and fired back. Then again. The gun rocked him. One of the shapes ahead reeled back, but he wasn't sure if it was from his blast or another. Guns were shaking the hallways, and bodies were toppling everywhere. The smell of gun smoke pervaded everything.

A bullet whizzed by Tavlin's cheek. He scurried to the corner, where he breached the barrel of the shotgun and hastily reloaded—his fingers barely trembled, he noted with bemusement—using shells Harry Scraggs had given to him. He snapped the barrel shut. Looked up.

A man was training his submachine gun's sights on Tavlin from about twenty feet away. Tavlin fired. The shotgun was double-barreled, and he fired first one barrel, then the second when another shape replaced the first. He wasn't sure if he shot either of them, but they both dropped out of sight. More targets appeared.

The warehouse wasn't what Tavlin had expected. The room he hunkered in was actually fairly small, made of lichen-covered stone, the ceiling low and spanned by cobwebs. Many hallways snaked off from this chamber, the loading chamber. Shapes that must be Grund's people vanished into them, and other shapes that must be Vassas's people followed.

Someone slapped Tavlin on the back. "After them!" The shape—Galesh—vanished with two others down a hallway in pursuit of a group of Grund's men.

Gathering his courage, Tavlin followed. Galesh and the other two fired at something up ahead, then pressed themselves against the walls. Tavlin saw why instantly. A broad figure up ahead let loose with a machine gun, and sparks split the darkness as rounds filled the hallway faster than Tavlin could count.

Ducking out of the way, he plunged into a doorway and saw a shape wheel to face him, gun raised. Tavlin fired. The man toppled backward. Another man stood in the far doorway. He had been headed out, likely leading the first man, and at the sound of the gunshot, he turned and raised his own gun.

He and Tavlin fired at the same time. A bullet whizzed by Tavlin's neck; he felt its heat. The man in the doorway stumbled, clutching his gun arm. With a glare at Tavlin, he spun about and darted off.

Tavlin gave chase. The halls twisted and turned, and he realized that the warehouse was actually assembled out of a collection of preexisting buildings, some smaller, some larger, some with high ceilings, some with ceilings so low he had to stoop. It all stank of mold and chemicals. Gunshots crashed from the battle all around. The halls had begun to stink of gun smoke.

Tavlin followed his quarry up a flight of crumbling cement stairs to a second story. There the man turned and fired. Tavlin dodged out of the way, but when he glanced up the man was gone. Gritting his teeth, Tavlin rushed forward. He rounded a bend, swiveled and turned, gun raised and ready. Nothing.

A sound came from a side-room.

Hairs raised on the back of his neck, Tavlin leapt inside. It was dim, and he had to strain to see. Conscious that he might be visible silhouetted against the doorway, he moved aside, rotating this way and that to find his quarry. Nothing but shadows. It was a dark, crowded room full of shelves laden with what looked like technical equipment—plenty of hiding spots. Below, gunshots rang. Men yelled.

A small, dirty window admitted a scant amount of light, and by this radiance Tavlin searched the room, finding nothing but shadows and equipment. Just as he was about to give up, he heard a noise behind him.

He spun.

A man—not the man he'd been chasing, but one he recognized nonetheless—stepped out from the shadows. The man struck the shotgun from Tavlin's hands with one hand and with the other raised a gun of his own.

By the faint glow of the window, Tavlin saw a polished pistol of foreign manufacture aimed at his head. And holding it, bald head gleaming greenly in the light, was the man who had offered his hand to Tavlin in Taluush.

Chapter 10

"We meet again," said the bald man. He spoke with a thick brogue, and though he sounded like a well-traveled sort—his voice showing flecks of various accents—there was nothing in that voice to indicate nationality.

"Maybe this time we can chat," Tavlin said. It seemed an appropriate comment, as the other option was less amenable. Before the man could either answer or shoot him, Tavlin added, "It was you that conspired with the G'zai, wasn't it—to destroy Taluush?"

The man showed no reaction, save a vague hardening of his craggy, pocked face. "You destroyed Taluush, Tavlin Metzler," he said. "You destroyed it by not cooperating with us. Do you want the same thing to happen to Muscud?"

"You didn't give me much chance to cooperate, did you? Anyway, you're Octunggen, aren't you? That's how you communicated with the G'zai. Octunggen can deal with the old races."

The man didn't deny it. "You know what we want. You know how to get it."

"What are you doing here? Why are you with Grund's men?"

Gunshots crashed from below, and there came an explosion. The floor jumped beneath Tavlin's feet, and dust rained down from the ceiling. He leapt for the bald man's gun. The man lunged aside with astonishing speed and clubbed Tavlin on the head with the butt of his pistol.

Tavlin collapsed. A hand went to his head, and he felt wetness there. The world gyrated around him.

The dark shape of the bald man remained steady, though. He seemed older than Tavlin had thought, his face heavily lined, his bushy white brows showing many curling, wiry hairs. The pox that had ravaged his face had not made him ugly, strangely, but somehow only more distinguished. The scars drank up the light, creating numerous dark wells all over his wide, heavy face. His eyes glared like arctic blue ice.

"Tell me where the canister is," he said.

Tavlin spat. "No."

"You don't even know what it is."

Tavlin's right hand skittered over the floor surreptitiously, feeling . . .

"What, then?" he asked.

"It could end the war."

"Some weapon, I suppose."

"You say that unthinkingly. Weapons end wars. It is their purpose."

"Or start them. And it would be used against my own people," Tavlin reminded him.

"Are they yours? Look around you, Tavlin Two-Bit. You're in a *sewer*. Is this where you would be if your people gave a shit about you?" The man sighed. "If you care about your friends down here, though, you will agree. Or we will do to Muscud what we did to Taluush."

Tavlin's hand found what it was looking for. He flipped his wrist, and a stone, shaken loose from the ceiling, sailed through the air. The stone struck the bald man's pistol, and the gun spun away. Tavlin threw himself at the shotgun, grabbed it and turned about.

The door burst open. Galesh and another man charged into the room, guns firing. Glass shattered, and Tavlin glanced at the window to see the shape of the bald man squeeze through it and vanish.

Galesh fired after him, then stood there, panting. Gun smoke curled around him.

"It's over," he huffed. "The fight's over."

Dusting off his pants, Tavlin climbed to his feet. "No," he said. "I think it's just begun."

* * *

Tavlin's words were more accurate than he knew. Before Boss Vassas and his men could trigger the small explosive devises they had planted throughout the warehouse—larger ones might destabilize the surrounding structures, which would bring Vassas no end of hell from the mayor and the consortium of businesses that supported him, all of which had their own goons—the sound of motorcycles filled the air. At the head of a fleet of motorcycles, Grund stormed in. Before Boss Vassas could even organize a defense, Grund's enforcers burst in and drove Vassas and the rest back toward the loading room. Tavlin fired and ducked, and he had to squint to see in the gunsmoke-filled hallways. Grund's men had come in large numbers, and they proved too numerous and well-armed for Vassas's people to repel. Grund drove Vassas's faction through the trapdoor and onto the water.

Tavlin fired his shotgun at the shapes on the dock even as his boat shot off into the darkness in the churning wake of Galesh's boat until at last the invaders were safely away. Tavlin's limbs trembled, and sweat drenched his hair and stung his eyes. His stomach quivered. *Please don't puke.*

Harry Scraggs, who had received a bullet in the gut and was slouched against the gunwale, grinned a bloody grin at him. "Fun, wasn't it?"

Tavlin felt a swell of dismay. "What happened?"

"Whattaya think?"

Blood pooled around Harry, pumping fast from the wound on his abdomen. His face looked very pale, even in the faint light filtering down through the floorboards above. Other men gathered around him. One squeezed his hand. Tavlin found a flask and gave Harry a sip, then another. Harry took his last sip before they reached the Wide-Mouth. Tavlin closed his eyes when he passed.

* * *

Tavlin got good and drunk with the others. Together they toasted each other and the dead long into the night. Toward dawn, Tavlin saw Galesh whispering to Vassas in the corner, their eyes on him. Soon Vassas sent for Tavlin.

"Galesh says you were talking with Havictus," Vassas said.

"Havictus?"

"The Octunggen bastard. I met with him before, remember. He was the leader of the ones looking for a factory to rent. That's what he called himself, anyway. Gods know what his real name is. Right Bad Bastard, I shouldn't wonder."

"Talking with him's just the start of it," Tavlin said. "I've got a lot to tell you." He was slurring his words a bit by then, but not enough to be unintelligible. Adrenaline still buzzed through him, and grief too.

"Come with me," Vassas said.

He showed Tavlin up into his study on the top floor, and there they shared an expensive bottle of wine. Laughter and toasts still drifted up from the ground floor, but the sounds were muted and somehow strange. Moths battered the streaked window, which was lit by gas-lights below, illuminating the stains and algae that coated the glass and filtered the light. The effect was a sort of green hue, which complimented the eeriness of the muted cheers below. In this light, sipping the fine wine, Tavlin told Vassas most of what had happened over the last two days, and he watched Vassas grow grayer and more ashen with every word. Finally, as they were slurping the dregs of the thick red wine, Tavlin finished.

Vassas gazed at him with red-rimmed eyes. "Taluush is gone? All of it? Are you sure?"

"It's a pile of rubbish, although maybe something could be rebuilt from it. I'm sure you'll see some refugees from it over the coming days. Where the G'zai went I don't know."

"Back to their black, watery hole, I'd guess." Vassas stood and stretched. Pacing back and forth before the green-streaming window, he said, "So the Octs want the briefcase, or what's in it—this canister of yours. The one that gave you nightmares."

"Havictus said it was some sort of weapon. Maybe it's alchemical, but if so it's like no alchemy we know. They needed those ancient jewels to make it, remember, wrought by some pre-human means."

"But why were they delivering it to this church? The Temple of Magoth, if that's what it was."

"Good question. They must be working together, the worshippers of Magoth and the Octunggen. And Octung is also working with Grund, too, it seems; that's why Havictus was in Grund's warehouse. Maybe Havictus is the one who's been supplying him with guns and motorcycles, maybe even money to pay for mercenary soldiers. Havictus is using them all—toward what end, who knows, but we have to stop him. It can't be good, whatever it is. And it has to be us. No one else will do it or even believe us."

"Shit, I'm not sure if *I* believe us."

Tavlin paused. "You don't doubt me, do you, Boss?"

Vassas returned his stare, gray and ill-looking. His eyes looked very red. At last he said, "No. No, I guess not. Still, what can we do about it?"

"You just launched a raid on Grund. Launch a raid on the Octunggen factory. Smash their equipment to bits so they can't make any more of this weapon, and we'll work to hide what *was* made. Maybe destroy it."

Vassas stopped pacing. He stood framed in the green window so that a dark shadow flung before him and green light bathed the air to both sides. "You just saw what happened to us, Two-Bit. We lost some good men tonight, and that was against enemies we *know*. The Octs have weird weapons. Powerful weapons. Shit, you saw what they did to Nancy and my people, and that was in the *next room*. You would have us make war on them?" He shook his head. "We're not fucking with the Octunggen."

"Then they'll find me—or you, now—torture us for the location of the briefcase, retrieve it and use it on Ghenisa."

"Ghenisa is responsible for us living in a sewer."

"Yes, but it's a sewer *of Ghenisa*. You really think the Octunggen will let you stay down here once they overrun the country? Besides, Ghenisa's not so bad. It's a good country, maybe one of the best in all of Urslin. The best food, at least that appeals to me. The best art. Hell, prostitution's even legal in some counties."

Vassas scratched his ear, looking agitated. "What do you want me to do, huh, Tavlin? I can't take on Octung."

Tavlin sucked in a deep breath. "I'm working on that. Meanwhile, I need to lay low. And Sophia, too. She's staying at the Twirling Skirt."

"I know."

"You do?"

"Yeah. She just sent a runner little while ago. Forgot to tell you. Wanted to know where you were. I told the runner to tell her you were with me, and you were fine."

"Good. Thanks." Then Tavlin sat up straight.

"What is it?"

Tavlin felt cold all over. "Havictus, he knows I'm working for you. He knows now if he didn't before. He'll know I'm here, and he would have had people watching the Wide-Mouth. They would have followed the runner back to the Skirt!"

He lunged out of the chair and made for the door. Vassas stopped him with a hand on his shoulder.

"Let me give you a ride."

* * *

Wind tore through Tavlin's hair, and his eyes misted under the air pressure. His heart beat like an out of control engine. To each side roared the motorcycles of Vassas's men. Tavlin himself sat in the side-car of Vassas's motorcycle, and the Boss hunched big as life on his mount, leading the armada through the streets. He would have taken Tavlin alone, Tavlin knew, but what with the war it wasn't safe for Vassas to be out without protection.

People scattered out of the way of the motorcycle fleet, but they didn't run once they hit the sidewalks. Many waved or saluted. Vassas would occasionally indulge in a nod back to them. At least in this one quarter of the city, he was a beloved figure. He had brought peace and stability in an age of warring bosses. Of course, now there was war all over again, and the Octunggen were helping the other side. Tavlin couldn't quite get his mind around it.

At the moment, he didn't try. All his thought was bent on Sophia. *You'd better be all right, you'd better be all right, you'd better be all right.*

The armada pulled up to a stop in front of the Twirling Skirt, and Tavlin coughed at the sudden swirl of diesel exhaust and gravel. The Skirt loomed above him, light blazing out from beneath its peaked gables. A large hunter-snail slithered across its peeling facade and vanished around a crenellation, leaving a trail of slime in its wake. People gathered on the veranda, talking and socializing like always. Music flooded out through the open doors.

Part of Tavlin sighed in relief to see the Skirt still standing. He had half-expected it to be razed or in flames, like the hotel in Taluush, or to see its halls running with blood, like the whorehouse there.

But he didn't see Sophia. She was not on the veranda, nor hanging out a window waving to him. He would not relax until he saw her, until he held her in his arm—however reluctantly on her part.

He climbed out of the side-car as the men around him cut their engines. The people on the veranda were staring at them expectantly, perhaps a touch nervously. Tavlin started to step away from Vassas's motorcycle, toward the Skirt, when he heard a voice behind him.

"Want us to go in with you?" Vassas said.

"No. I'll do it alone."

He marched up the stairs. People made way for him, their expressions curious or worried. He didn't explain but pushed the doors open and moved into the parlor. Here the music had drowned out some of the sounds of the motorcycle fleet, but only some, and the people closest to the windows had gathered around the glass panes to watch, and others had noticed and were gravitating in that direction, too. Several raised eyebrows at Tavlin.

Madam Abigail approached him. "What is it? Is there something wrong?"

"Sophia. Where is she?"

"Why, in her room, I suppose."

"You've seen her?"

"Only a little while ago. What's all the fuss?"

Tavlin found a narrow staircase and climbed upstairs. His breaths came short and shallow. He vaguely heard someone calling to him, but the sound seemed distant. Everything seemed distant, lost. Everything but his goal.

He reached the room he shared with Sophia and wrenched the door open. He paused outside, breathing hard, trying to get his mind straight, then stepped inside.

It was a small room, and the cracked window shone strange pale light across the narrow bed and aged boards.

The room was empty.

A note lay on the pillow. Tavlin snatched it up. Written in a firm, masculine hand, it read: AN EXCHANGE. YOU FOR HER. COME TO THE FACTORY BY NOON TOMORROW OR SHE DIES. SLOWLY.

Tavlin was hardly aware of Boss Vassas and Frankie helping him down through the halls, out to the waiting motorcycles. He was even less aware as Vassas shoved him in the side-car and the fleet roared off again. He clutched the note tightly, and it was only around the time they returned to the Wide-Mouth that his fist began to unclench.

Vassas forced him up to the study again, and there they sat drinking some more while Vassas, Frankie and Galesh read the note.

Tavlin smoked a pipe with trembling hands. When he wasn't smoking, he drank. The drink seemed to steady him, but it wasn't enough. It could never be enough.

"The bastards," he said, over and over again. "The fucking bastards!"

At last, either because of the alcohol or because enough time had passed, he felt the shock drain away, replaced by clear, cold sobriety. Despite the whiskey, he felt as sober as he ever had.

"I have to do something," he said.

Vassas and the others watched him.

"You back?" Vassas said. They had been talking amongst themselves, Tavlin realized.

He nodded. "I'm back. And I have to do something."

"What can you do? You can't give the fucks what they want. Whatever weapon they're trying to build, you can't just hand it over to 'em."

"Fuckin' aye," said Frankie.

Tavlin eyed Frankie and Galesh. "How much did you tell them, Boss?"

"Enough," Vassas said.

Tavlin sighed and nodded. Some of the tension was draining away, but strangely it wasn't replaced by relaxation, only more tension. A different sort. The kind that endured and existed under everything, until the source of the tension was gone.

"They want you to show 'em where the briefcase is," Frankie said. "That's why they want you. Well, whatever the fuck is in it, you can't let 'em have it. You can't go."

"He's right," Galesh said, leaning back against a wall and smoking a foul-smelling cigarette. "The Octunggen can't be allowed to complete their mission. It's obviously part of the war effort, something designed to cripple and destroy Ghenisa, maybe beyond. Somehow the people of Magoth have been helping. Maybe they have ancient knowledge, passed on to them by religious writings or even the old races who once bowed to Magoth."

Tavlin thought about it. "That makes sense, I suppose. But the worshippers of Magoth wouldn't be helping the Octs out of good will—at least, I don't think so. They must be getting something in return."

"What?" Vassas snorted. "Listen, we can figure all that shit out later. Right now we need to come up with a plan."

"Maybe we can break Sophia out," said Frankie.

Vassas glared at him. "Did you see what the Octs did *in the next room*? And that was just one of the bastards, with one weapon. No way are we attacking their stronghold."

"Boss is right," Galesh said, predictably. "We can't attack them at their factory. But maybe we can attack them outside of it. Wait them out."

"If we wait, Sophia dies," Tavlin said. He drew down a long pull on his pipe, and thoughts started to take shape in his head. "But maybe we can *coax* them out."

"Coax?" Frankie said skeptically.

"You don't coax Octunggen," Vassas agreed.

Tavlin looked him in the eye. "I have a plan."

Chapter 11

Mist swirled around Tavlin as he approached the factory, and he spat at the acrid taste. *This is not a good idea.* Of course, he had no one else to blame for it. The idea was his. Gritting his teeth, he stepped nearer the factory. It had no windows, only a solid bank wall of stone and mortar, poorly laid, with a thick metal door set within it. The setting was rough, and Tavlin could see rugged stone glistening in the mist around the door. The door itself was thick and heavy, coated with brilliant verdigris.

He rapped on it experimentally.

There came a pause, then pops as locks were thrown, and at last the great metal door ground open, and amber light spilled out from the interior. Shapes stood silhouetted against the light. The lead one was bald and square-shouldered.

"You made it," issued the deep voice. "I was beginning to worry. For her sake, of course."

"Of course," Tavlin said.

He removed a gun from his pocket. The bald man—Havictus—did not move. In one motion, Tavlin pointed the gun at his own head and pressed it to his temple.

"Release her or I spatter the coordinates of the canister all over the ground."

"I don't think any of us want that," Havictus said, his voice without inflection. He drew back, and the other shadows pulled back with him. "Please, come in."

Gathering his resolve, Tavlin stepped through the entrance and into a sort of receiving room. The walls were irregularly-spaced stone overgrown by lichen. Slugs sucked and slithered all around. One glowed with a pink-red light. Lamps hung down, illuminating the cold stone halls. Tavlin received the impression of large rooms adjacent to this one, huge dark spaces filled with strange machinery just barely hinted at by the faint light coming from this room. A dozen men occupied the chamber with him, and they gave him plenty of space.

They did not look particularly Octunggen. A few boasted the black hair and gray eyes of the Octunggen ideal, but many had brown hair, or blond, and there was even a man with bushy red hair and beard. They were a hard-looking lot, anyway, and Tavlin wouldn't want to cross any of them.

They all seemed to defer to Havictus. "Welcome to our humble home," the bald man said.

Tavlin stepped into the center of the room, gun still pressed to his head. He was all too conscious of the cold metal digging into the flesh of his temple.

"Where's Sophia?" he said.

"You will see her only when you have shown us where the canister is."

"I can draw you a map right now."

Havictus shook his large head, once. His full lips pursed and he said, "No, that will not do. We must have the canister in our hands before your woman is released."

"What assurance do I have that you'll do as you say?"

"Well, there is that gun."

"You want me to actually take you *to* the canister?"

"But of course." Havictus spread his hands. "When that is done, your woman and you will be released."

"To feed the fish-things, I suppose."

"You will have to trust us. It is the best I can do."

Tavlin nodded. He had expected as much, but he didn't want to let on. "Then let's get this over with. And don't anyone try to get too close."

"You're not afraid your arm will tire?"

Tavlin smiled grimly. "Not at all." The truth was that his gun arm was already beginning to grow weary. Oh well. *Sophia had better appreciate this.*

Havictus and the other Octunggen showed Tavlin down a hall to a large room whose lights were off. The beam of light from the hallway illuminated the trapdoor. One of the men opened it, and others descended the ladder to ready the boats below. Soon Tavlin heard motors chugging, and then he was motioned toward the trapdoor. He made the Octunggen back off several yards—he would have to use both hands on the ladder—then climbed down to the docks. A boat waited for him, and he stepped into it, feeling the rocking movement below his feet, smelling the brine and stink of the lake. It was warmer down here. Sultry.

He placed the muzzle back to his temple.

Havictus and the others scaled the ladder and stepped into their own boats. At last a hooded and bound figure was forced down the ladder and into a boat—far from Tavlin.

"Sophia!"

She cried something back at him, but her voice was muffled by some gag. Nevertheless, he recognized her voice. Some part of him relaxed, but only barely. *She's alive.* He held onto this thought with fixed determination.

Havictus took up position at the bow of Tavlin's boat. The engine idled, and smoke curled out.

"Where to?" Havictus said.

Tavlin pointed. "That way."

Havictus nodded at the boatman, who manned the motor, and the boat sped off in the indicated direction. The others trailed along behind, Sophia's boat at the rear. The stink of the sewers enveloped Tavlin as the alchemical lanterns that subdued the stench faded behind. Some of the men broke out nosegays, but none offered him one and he wished had had thought to bring one along. The old ways of the sewers had really left him, it seemed.

He pointed down a certain hallway, and the boatman took it. He pointed down another and another. Soon he felt disoriented. He only knew certain routes down here, and in his haste he had left them. He asked the boatman to travel down a particular channel, and from there it was easier. The motors roared loudly off the tight stone walls, and when they moved through the larger spaces flails would whip around them, dripping mucus and slime. Occasionally some white thing breached the dark waters, expelling vapor or tainted fluid.

Tavlin's gun arm grew even heavier, and he had to alternate hands. Sometimes he would sit down on the boat's bench, propping his elbow on his knee and shoving the gun up under his chin. Havictus sometimes glanced at him worriedly when the boat took an especially sharp corner, and he would give the boatman stern looks. After that the boat would move more smoothly for a time.

Frequently a man in the second boat called the others to a halt. He would stand up, cradling a device with several complicated-looking antennae sticking up from it. It beeped and buzzed, and he would shake his head or nod.

"He can tell when we're getting closer," Havictus explained. "We've been combing the sewers for days without finding it, but we'll know if you're leading us wrong."

"It never crossed my mind," Tavlin said. Actually, it had, but he had been afraid—rightly, apparently—that they would know if he lied.

The convoy resumed moving, and Tavlin continued giving directions. At one point, he shouted over the roar of the engines, "What *is* it? What is *in* the damned canister?"

Havictus turned from facing front to look back at him. The bald man's bushy eyebrows rose, but there was no humor in his icy blue eyes. "Death," he said. "Only death."

"What does that mean?"

Havictus hesitated, then sort of shrugged, and Tavlin could guess his thoughts; Havictus was already planning to kill Tavlin anyway, so why not pass the time by talking?

"It's a formula," Havictus said.

Tavlin screwed up his face. "A … *formula*? Like in math or science?"

"I guess."

"But it's a container for a liquid!"

"It's like no formula you've ever heard of, Tavlin Two-Bit, or could conceive of. But it will destroy all you know."

Tavlin smacked his lips. His mouth had gone dry. "And the worshippers of Magoth are helping you, what, develop it?"

"Oh, no. The people of Magoth have lost the technology, the resources, to develop the formula, but we have them. But only Magoth itself can activate it."

"*Magoth* …" Tavlin shook his head. Havictus spoke as if the god were real. "Why are you giving cultists some formula?"

"Their gods and ours are allies. No more talking."

"Don't want to waste any more words on a dead man?"

Havictus gave him a look, and it was so cold that Tavlin shuddered. In that moment he knew he was right, that the Octunggen had no plans to release him and Sophia. Not alive, at any rate. This came as no surprise.

"Just point the way," Havictus said, and his voice could have withered a rose.

Tavlin pointed. The beeping of the machine grew louder, but it often hissed and fizzed, and sometimes the beeps would become warbles, and sometimes they would fade altogether. The machine clearly was encountering interference from something, or perhaps it simply didn't work very well. Nonetheless, if one listened closely, one could hear it steadily marking the proximity of the canister. Tavlin supposed it could sense the canister's extradimensional signature or some such thing.

Tavlin guided the fleet forward until at last he reached the intersection he'd been looking for.

"This is it," he called to Havictus over the roar of the engines.

Havictus made cutting motions to the other boats. The Octunggen stopped their engines, and the boats idled forward into the intersection. Mist rolled slowly away from the boats, the whitish swirls illuminated only by feeble lamps. The whole place stank of ammonia and waste, and something unnatural breached the surface of the water fifty feet away, hooted, then went under again. Tavlin received the impression of many stalks and fins, and eyes where there should be no eyes.

"We're here," he said. "It should be right below us."

Havictus raised a bushy eyebrow at the man with the divining machine, who analyzed his gadget and said, "I think he's telling the truth."

Havictus ordered the others to begin the search. Several lifted long metal poles with hooks on the end of them and dredged the water, hoping to snare the handle of the briefcase, while others swept the area with nets. Tavlin tensed in the stern of the boat, shooting frequent looks at Sophia. She was still and quiet, and too far away for his liking.

At last an Octunggen hauled up a dripping, reeking briefcase, and the rest let out cheers. A broad smile spread across Havictus's pocked face, and he turned shining eyes on Tavlin.

"Now," Tavlin said. "Release Sophia."

Havictus raised a pistol and pointed it at Tavlin's face. He started to squeeze the trigger.

Tavlin, who had expected this, knocked the gun wide and in the same motion brought his own gun up. Havictus chopped the wrist of Tavlin's gun hand with a stiff-fingered motion, and Tavlin's gun whirled away. Tavlin sprang forward and tackled the other man to the deck of the boat.

Around him, battle broke out.

Boss Vassas and his men had waited, lurking in the darkness beyond the intersection just as Tavlin had instructed, and now they burst out of the shadows, their boats shoved by oars, men and women standing in the bows firing long bursts into the Octunggen with rattling machine guns. Arcing shells ejected into the water. Several Octunggen pitched over the sides, blood spurting from their wounds. One of these was the man holding the dredged-up briefcase. When he fell into the channel, he dropped the briefcase and it vanished back into the water.

The Octunggen leapt toward their weapons and fired back. Gunfire echoed off the tight stone walls, and the intersection quickly filled with gun smoke to mix with the exhaust of the engines.

Tavlin wrestled with Havictus. He kneed the bald man in the groin. Clubbed him on the head. Havictus elbowed him in the face and punched him in the throat. If Tavlin hadn't drawn back at the last second, the blow would have crushed his larynx.

Each man grabbed the gun and tried to shove it toward the other. Tavlin grunted and strained, feeling every muscle tense in his body, feeling sweat ooze from every pore. He could smell the beef and cabbage that Havictus had had for lunch.

Finally Tavlin bit into Havictus's gun-hand wrist as hard as he could. He sank his teeth into Havictus until he could feel his teeth clamping bone, until pain filled his jaw and blood flooded his mouth.

Havictus arched his head back and screamed. The hand loosened. The gun flew over the edge of the boat into the water. With pain-fueled strength, Havictus struck Tavlin across the face with his left elbow, launching Tavlin backwards. Havictus rose to his feet, glaring wildly around, clutching his bleeding wrist. Blood pumped through his fingers.

Tavlin searched for a weapon. The Octunggen manning the engine had been shot, and he had crumpled over, bleeding to death. Tavlin rooted through the man's jacket for his gun.

Havictus whistled and gestured, and a boat roared over to him. He scrambled aboard and barked orders in Octunggen. Even as the boat jettisoned off into the darkness, he wrested a submachine gun away from one of his people and turned to fire at Tavlin, even as Tavlin fired at him with his liberated pistol. Havictus fired first, and his rounds tore stitching through the boat. Gouts of water shot up from the holes. Tavlin flung himself to the side. His shot went wild.

When he glanced back up, his gun trained in the direction Havictus had been, the bald man was gone into the gloom.

Water began to fill Tavlin's vessel through the bullet holes.

Sweating, knowing that he would be infected if he became submerged, Tavlin started the engine of the sinking craft and aimed it at a nearby boat. It struck, knocking one Octunggen overboard and sending the other two to their knees. Tavlin shot one in the chest and dodged a blast from the other. One of Vassas's men, or perhaps even Vassas himself, finished off the surviving gunman, and the man toppled over the side with a shattered skull even as Tavlin leapt into his boat. The boat he'd been on sank with a pop and a gurgle.

Tavlin piloted his boat toward the one Sophia occupied, barreling toward her even as bullets tore the air around him. Some smacked into the boat or dotted the water, while others ricocheted off the walls, and Tavlin felt more than one whiz by his head.

Too late, the two men in Sophia's boat saw him coming and adjusted their guns to fire on him. He shot one through the face—the man flew backward and vanished—and the other collapsed when Tavlin rammed his boat. Tavlin shot him point-blank through the chest before he could reorient himself.

Sophia had thrown herself to the floor, and as Tavlin hunkered over her, fumbling at her ropes, she thrashed and cursed through her gag. Soon he had her hands free, and she tore off her hood herself and spat out the gag. Her eyes were wild, her hair in disarray, and someone had given her a black eye. Nonetheless, she was the most wonderful sight Tavlin had ever seen. Even as she swore at him and struggled against him, he took her in his arms and kissed her.

She didn't exactly melt, but her struggles turned less aggressive. Then she pulled away and slapped his face.

"Don't," she said.

"But—"

Her voice softened. "Thank you, Tav. I *do* appreciate you saving me. But … no."

By the time he'd started the motor and glanced around, several of the other Octunggen boats had taken off in the same direction as Havictus, and one more was just vanishing. The Octunggen that had stayed behind were quickly dying, and bodies littered the small boats or bobbed in the water between them, water which was now slicked with blood. As Tavlin watched, some thing below the surface dragged one of the corpses down with a sudden sharp movement. Bubbles frothed the surface filled with pink and red, and the body did not reappear.

Boss Vassas's men pushed their boats forward, even as Tavlin did, and Tavlin met Vassas in the middle of the intersection. All the Octunggen had fled or perished. Vassas appeared hard and winded, his face red, a submachine gun clutched in a meaty fist. A bullet had grazed one of his arms, and blood trickled freely from the wound. He didn't seem to notice.

"You got her," he said, nodding once at Sophia, who nodded back. "Good. And I saw the briefcase go back under. Now let's lam it."

"No," Tavlin said. "We've got the bastards on the run. Now it's time to finish them off. But have one of your men take Sophia back."

"I'm not going anywhere, except after *them*," she said.

"Fine," said Vassas, and there was a gleam in his eyes. "Let's end this."

They roared after the Octunggen. Tavlin allowed Vassas to take the lead before his men, but Tavlin and Sophia occupied the next space in line. They tore down dark halls, slowing only enough to let their lantern-light show them the way; Sophia knelt in the bow, holding a lantern out over the water. When it shone off a moss-covered wall that threatened to crack their boat to splinters, they curved sharply off. At times they lost the Octunggen only to see one of their boats vanishing around a bend ahead.

At last Tavlin and Sophia burst out in a large chamber, huge and high and cavernous. The boats of the Octunggen flew across the black water before them . . . right toward the Temple of Magoth.

Tavlin swore.

So did Sophia. "Not this again," she said.

The Temple blazed ahead, massive and phosphorescent, a shining, glowing beacon in the dark. Its graceful columns proudly held up the great canopy, and the work being done on it was even more advanced than last time, the strange angles and facets even more pronounced. The whole thing shone a ghostly pearl-white. The brightest light came from the interior, flooding out from windows and doorways. The illumination bathed the surface of the cistern lake, throwing light far out into the great chamber. And, just as before, the sound of singing carried across the waters.

The boats of Vassas's men slowed momentarily. Vassas's eyes bulged, and his mouth hung open. The singing washed over them.

Tavlin clamped his hands over his ears, and Sophia did likewise.

"Back!" Tavlin shouted to Vassas. "Go back! Cover your ears! Don't listen. *GO BACK!*"

Instead, one boat at a time, Vassas's men revved their boats' motors and started forward, though whether toward the Octunggen or the Temple Tavlin couldn't say. He wasn't sure if they knew, either. Vassas started to motor toward the Temple, as well.

"Hells," Tavlin said.

He aimed his own boat toward Vassas's and gritted his teeth.

"Hang on," he told Sophia.

They struck with such suddenness that Vassas was knocked to his knees, and the other man in the boat with him nearly went overboard. Shock passed across Vassas's face, but then a look of dazzlement replaced it—as the singing drove reason from his brain—and Tavlin saw Vassas start to look around for a means of continuing toward the Temple.

His eyes settled on Tavlin's boat.

Vassas rushed him. Tavlin hit him on the head, hard, with an oar. Vassas toppled like a sack of spuds, and Tavlin wrestled him aboard the vessel. Vassas's man tried to tackle them, but Sophia shot at him. Startled, he leapt back. She blasted out the engine, leaving him stranded. He cursed them as they moved away. Tavlin wanted to believe this might have saved the man, but he thought he knew better. The cultists would round him up soon enough, or maybe the Octunggen would.

Tavlin sat Vassas down as gently as he could, then returned to the motor. Plugging one ear with a finger and trying to press the other to his shoulder, he piloted the boat out of the Temple chamber and into the halls beyond. He looked back over his shoulder once to see the other boats vanishing into the white glow emitted by the Temple. Among the men in the boats was Galesh, whom Tavlin had known for many years and liked a good deal. *Dear gods,* Tavlin thought. *What will happen to them now?* Anguish rose in him, and he wished there was something he could do to stop the men from going to their dooms—for what else could it be?—but there was nothing he could think of, nothing that could turn them back. They were lost. The singing was all around them, somehow both crashing and mellifluous at the same time, beautiful and terrible, and completely overwhelming.

Feeling his eyes burn, Tavlin turned back around and continued piloting the boat further from the chamber of the Temple. The sound of the singing lessened with each yard. At last the sound became too faint to master Tavlin, and he unstopped his ears. Breathing heavily, he shared a look with Sophia.

"They're all gone," he gasped. "All Vassas's men. Or at least the ones he took with him."

She looked as shaken as he felt. "I wonder what the people at the Temple will do with them."

Tavlin continued on, and soon Vassas stirred and cracked an eye. He groaned, sat up, and Tavlin braced himself for any sudden movements. Vassas was fine, though—or as fine as he could be. He swore and vomited over the side, then rubbed his head.

"What'd you bastards do to me?"

"Tavlin saved your life," Sophia said.

Vassas glared around him. "Where's … my boys?"

When Tavlin told him, Vassas was inconsolable. He raged and screamed, kicking at the gunwales. He shouted so loudly Tavlin had to remind him some of the enemy might still be out here, hunting them. After that Vassas grew very quiet, and he picked up a submachine gun and clenched it tightly, peering all around them at the darkness.

At last he said through clenched teeth, "They'll pay for this, the sons of bitches. See if they won't."

Tavlin nodded but didn't reply. Soon he saw a familiar-looking passage. The pattern of water reflected off the arching stone ceiling, slapping up against the stone columns. A half dozen boats bobbed there, their gunwales eaten away by gunfire. Bodies lay over their sides, and blood slicked the scummy surface. It stank of gunpowder and split intestines. Sophia placed a hand over her nose, and Tavlin tried not to breathe in.

"What are we doing here?" Vassas said, training the gun all about them.

"We have to retrieve the briefcase," Tavlin said. "They may have dropped it when you attacked, but they know where it is now, and they'll be back for it."

"We shouldn't waste time. We need to get back to the Wide-Mouth and regroup."

"Tavlin's right," Sophia said, sounding reluctant. "We have to move that damned thing. It's too dangerous."

"Havictus said it contained some sort of formula," Tavlin said, "but that doesn't make any sense to me. To me, a formula means math or chemistry or something. Maybe baby food. *He* was talking about the end of the world … and gods. And the formula is in a container for a *fluid*."

"And he's giving it to the worshippers of Magoth?" Vassas said.

"That's right. Apparently Octung is using them for some purpose. Havictus wants the formula activated, whatever that means, although it sounds like if that happens … well, he said it would be the end of all I know."

"Damn."

"He also said only Magoth could activate it."

"Magoth . . ." Vassas looked pale. "Havictus spoke of the god as if it existed?"

Tavlin nodded. "At any rate, I suppose Octung needs the cultists just like the cultists need Octung, since only Octung can *provide* the formula, at least that we know."

"I wonder if this has anything to do with the construction that's going on at the Temple," Sophia said.

"You noticed that too?"

She nodded.

He found a long pole the Octunggen had been using to dredge the water and began hunting for the briefcase. He searched right below the boat whose crew had found the object. Sure enough, it wasn't long before he encountered an obstruction and brought it up, and he almost laughed to see the dripping, seaweed-entangled briefcase. He shook it off and reeled it into the boat.

Sophia backed away from it. "I can *feel* it."

"Yeah," Vassas grunted. "Me too."

Tavlin noticed it, also—the same sensation he'd felt before, or at least a small drop of it, when he'd touched the side of the container in Taluush. It was an uncomfortable throbbing in his skull. Something bitter grew on his tongue. He tried to push it away.

"Just ignore it," he said. "Don't let it get into your mind."

"What does that even *mean*?" Vassas's voice was ragged.

Tavlin lowered the briefcase to the deck, then threw a blanket over it. He didn't answer the question, but he remembered the missing hours from the last time and the dim recollection of awful nightmares.

"What can we do with it?" Sophia said. "I mean, if it is some weapon of Octung, or the cult of Magoth? Can we *destroy* it?"

"I've been giving that a lot of thought," Tavlin said.

"And?" Vassas said.

Tavlin scratched his cheek. "I learned in Taluush that the G'zai are enemies of the Ualissi—the pre-humans that live in Muscud."

"I do business with them sometimes," Vassas said, nodding.

"Well, if the G'zai are helping Octung because they share the same gods, then that might mean the Ualissi are opposed to those gods, maybe even that they worship gods who regard Octung's gods as their enemies. A religious dispute between fanatical peoples. Anyway, they might know more about all this than we do—what the contents of that canister mean and how to counteract it. I say that when we get back to Muscud we look them up."

"They have strange technology," Sophia nodded. "Maybe they really *could* do something about it, or help *us* figure out how to do something."

"We'll do it," Vassas said. "That thing … it makes my skin crawl."

"Mine, too," Sophia admitted, her voice small.

Tavlin bent over the engine, planning to pilot them back to Muscud, but, before he could even open the engine up, *she* appeared.

The girl in white.

"Oh, no …"

Ghostly and phosphorescent, she materialized from around a bend. She was as beautiful as before—lovely, shimmering, floating across the water on a bed of white vapor that curled around her, enfolding her slender, naked body in phantasmagorical clouds. Her hair stirred to the currents of some sea or wind that Tavlin could not fathom, and her luminous eyes gazed straight at him, searing his soul with their power.

"No no no," he said. His voice came out in a choke. "You . . . you *do* see her?"

"Yes," said Sophia, her voice a throaty rasp. "I see her."

"Who is she?" said Vassas. "What is she?"

As the girl drifted closer, her eyes drank in Tavlin and the briefcase.

"You," she said. "You took it!"

He opened and closed his mouth. "Yes, of c-course I did. You said that last time."

"Why? Why did you take it?" It was as if he had committed some grievous wrong, a personal affront to her. As she spoke, the anger visibly built up in her.

"I-I—"

Suddenly the anger overwhelmed her and she shot forward. One of her hands wrapped around Tavlin's throat. Her touch was like ice, but it burned, and he screamed as she wrenched him upward. He flailed and beat at her. Below, Vassas shot the girl, or rather through her, trying to aim around Tavlin, while Sophia struck at her with an oar. The oar passed right through.

"Why did you take it?" the girl screamed, staring straight into Tavlin's eyes, his soul. As she spoke, she continued to choke him, shaking him like a dog would shake a bird

Tavlin started to lose consciousness. His grip on the briefcase loosened, but he retained enough awareness to keep hold of it. He was dimly aware of Sophia and Vassas fighting the girl, trying to get him back, but she was apparently immune to their efforts, and their blows just passed through her. Tavlin gagged, unable to breathe, feeling his skull pound.

Behind the girl, boats appeared, lantern-light winking through the mist. Vaguely Tavlin saw mutants in robes crowding the vessels, many of them armed. When they saw the ghost-girl, their eyes filled with reverence—but not surprise, or at least not *complete* surprise; something about this was strange to them, but she at least was known somehow. Had they been following her? Had she led them here? In any case, they saw Tavlin and the others, and immediately they lifted their guns toward Sophia and Vassas.

"Run!" Tavlin choked. "Run!"

"We can't leave you!" Sophia said. She grabbed Vassas's gun and fired a burst at the mutants. They ducked down as bullets whizzed over their heads.

Vassas was more pragmatic. "We'll come back for you," he said as he started the motor. "We'll get these bastards, see if we don't."

"No," Sophia said. "We can't leave him, you bastard."

"Take this," Tavlin wheezed, and hurled the briefcase to them. He almost missed. Sophia had to stretch herself out to catch it, and even so she almost tumbled into the filthy channel.

Vassas opened the motor, and the boat sped away, Sophia righting herself as they went. The newly arrived mutants fired at them, and bullets struck the wall behind them, sending fragments everywhere. Enraged, Sophia fired back. Tavlin saw her out of the corner of his vision, her eyes aflame, standing on the pitching deck of the boat firing the submachine gun even as bullets kicked the water around her and flashed off the pillars behind her—then she was gone. Vassas piloted the boat down a tunnel and out of sight.

The robed people gave chase, howling as they roared down the hall after the two. Tavlin heard gunshots. Some of the infected people, however, gathered around Tavlin and the girl.

He had stopped flailing and fighting. All the strength had left him, and he felt himself beginning to fade. Helplessly, he stared into the face of the girl.

The rage seemed to have left her, leaving her full of pity. She was very beautiful, like an angel, almost. She set him down in one of the boats.

As darkness came over him, Tavlin heard one of the infected people ask, "What shall we do with him, Lady?"

"To the Temple," she said, her voice seeming to come from far away. "Take him to the Temple."

Chapter 12

When Tavlin was little, his mother used to take him down to this church near the docks. It had been a modest establishment, but with a high, proud steeple, and though the paint on the outside was peeling and stained, the parishioners had placed flower garlands and wreaths all over it, and vines with beautiful blooms grew in the cracks. It had been a popular, bustling church, frequented by a surprising number of infected people, who sat in the back. It had also been the church of many sailors and whalers—rough, scarred men who would entertain Tavlin with stories for hours when his mother let them. He idolized them. He had especially looked up to one, a huge, burly, black-bearded whaler named Horgst, who chewed tobacco constantly, even during service, and was always quick with a ribald joke or a hearty laugh. He had scoured the waters of the Atomic Sea and had stories to tell of every port.

But what Tavlin most remembered was the preacher. He, one Aaron Sambol, had been youngish, maybe thirty, full of energy, and had astonished the crowds with his passionate sermons, while lightning flickered up from the sea behind him, visible through the great window beyond the pulpit, constantly framing him in the electric furnace of the Atomic

Sea. But he wasn't just known for his passion. Oh, no. Before each service, he would inject himself with a certain alchemical compound that *made him glow.*

By the time he stepped onto the podium, he would be burning like a candle, shining with a bright but somehow soft white light; the light would pulse against the walls and the faces of the parishioners, growing louder and louder as the preacher's voice and passion rose, a blazing candle against the churning, boiling madness of the sea.

But when he sang . . .

Tavlin remembered, and he smiled. When Aaron Sambol sang, strange colors would light up in the air before him, hovering over the congregation, changing from red to yellow to purple to green to orange, a borealis of shifting, kaleidoscopic color. It would throb to the rhythm of the song and take fantastic shapes. The whole congregation would sing along, and the light would only grow louder over their heads. Tavlin had never been very religious, but in those moments, filled with song and awe, he had *believed.*

That's how he felt now, curled up in one corner of a white room, flooded with singing, steeped in the energies emanating from the Temple of Magoth. He shoved his fingers in his ears, he screamed, he bashed his head against the walls, but it made no difference. The singing from the great room beyond—how far beyond he didn't know; he'd only been half-conscious when they dragged him in here—pummeled him, suffused him. All he knew was that one glorious, shimmering cascade of sound, like the tinkling of silver bells, like the quiver of water after it plunged from a fall, like a wellspring of peace and serenity and power.

Tavlin raged against it. He slashed himself with his fingernails. He tried to choke himself into unconsciousness. Nothing worked. The sound assaulted him . . . *became* him. Soon the song was all he could hear. It filled his head. It wanted to issue from his lips, but he managed, painfully, to suppress it.

Then *she* came.

Lovely, beautiful, the most splendid creature he had ever seen, the ghost-witch appeared in the room before him. Only she wasn't a ghost anymore, or at least she didn't seem to be. Of apparently solid flesh and blood, she stood tall, clothed only in a shimmering silver-white dress.

Her voice, when it came, seemed to come from a thousand miles away: "You are well met, Tavlin Metzler."

He tried to curse her, but the effort proved beyond him. He collapsed sputtering to the floor.

She drifted closer, pausing above him. "Are you enjoying the Song? Isn't it magnificent?" Love and reverence filled her voice.

He wanted to slap it out of her. "I . . . I . . ."

She smiled. "Don't try to speak. It's all right. I know you feel it in your heart. I can sense it in you. Some of my children wanted to deliver you unto death, but I decided you would be better used as an example. If even one of our greatest adversaries could be shown the way, surely there is hope for everyone."

"You . . ."

She stroked his cheek, and her touch was both ice and fire. "You may call me Esril. I am the High Priestess of Magoth in this Order. Some call me simply the Lady."

"Lady … yes, I think I knew … When I saw you for the first time . . . on the docks of Muscud, I called you 'Lady'…"

She frowned. "Yes. About that—"

From somewhere he found strength. "And you're flesh now! I don't understand. Whenever I've seen you before, you've always been transparent, like a phantom." Experimentally, he poked her arm with a finger. Her flesh yielded, and he jerked his hand back. "I don't understand."

"I'm afraid I don't either. My people told me about the … *me* that apprehended you. That held you till they arrived."

"There are *two* of you?"

"I …" She shook her head. "There was only one that I knew of until just now—me." She smiled. "I know as little about this matter as you do, and I don't pretend to understand what it signifies. Only that …"

"Yes?"

She drew in a breath. "I am Lord Magoth's voice here in this plane, and I humbly lead this order in Its honor."

"*Its.*"

"It is neither male nor female, but both—and neither. It is beyond such limitations, although it is sometimes more convenient to give It a gender. Such as 'Lord'. There is no asexual version of 'Lord' that I know of. And sometimes we call It Him. Magoth most certainly embodies a certain aggressiveness that is more male than female. At any rate, It has changed me. Granted me powers, abilities. In my experiments to understand the limits of my power, I've discovered that some of them are temporal in nature."

"Temporal—as in time?"

"That's right." She paused. "It's possible that some event occurs in the future; it's definitely not the past, or I'd remember. Somehow I … well, *bond* with you, I suppose." She cleared her throat. "And that bond fuses a part of me to you, but, because of the temporal nature of my abilities and my inability to control them, it sends that fragment of me back along your own timeline."

He drew his brows together, thinking. "You really believe that's what she is—the ghost-witch?"

"That's what you call her? Well, I can't think of any other explanation, Tavlin Metzler." She reached down and took him under the arm. "Come. I am to bring you before It. There you will understand more fully."

She hefted him up, and he gasped at how strong she was. Once on his feet, he wobbled and nearly collapsed, but she stabilized him. Panting, he stood before her, powerless to do anything more than keep his feet.

"Tell me," he wheezed, and spots danced in his vision for the effort. "The Octunggen . . ."

"Yes, they are proud people, are they not? And quite knowledgeable. We are fortunate their gods have not forgotten the ancient arts. But don't trouble yourself about that at the moment. Just think, in mere minutes you will meet the Glory!"

She helped him from the room, and servants manning the door bowed to her as she passed. Tavlin waited for one of them to take over the job of escorting him, but instead she continued half-carrying him forward. Her smell, like burning metal mixed with rose petals, filled his nose. The singing grew louder and louder around him, filling him, smashing against him. The walls, composed of some pearl-white material, glowed and pulsed in time to the song, just like the lights of that preacher long ago.

"We're almost there," she whispered. "Just a little more . . ."

They rounded a corner and came into the main room, what he would later learn was called simply the Great Chamber. It truly was a great, cavernous room, more than a hundred feet high and more than that wide, but what transfixed Tavlin's attention was what occupied the space in its center.

It could be nothing other than Magoth.

Tavlin saw it, and his mind reeled. He nearly fell, but Esril caught him, laughing gently.

"Marvelous, isn't It?" she said.

Tavlin hardly heard her. He stared . . .

Then he felt It turn Its attention to him, or part of Its attention, and all thought and reason was driven from his mind.

He wasn't sure how long it lasted, but when he came to he was on his knees before it, weeping, tears coursing down his cheeks and staining his shirtfront below.

He heard himself saying, over and over again, "It's beautiful. It's beautiful . . ."

When he glanced up, Esril was smiling down at him, almost motherly.

"Yes," she said, and it was almost a sigh. "It is, isn't it? Now see how we honor It."

She motioned to the rear, and several of her followers ushered ragged figures from the same hallway Esril had taken him from. With a start, Tavlin recognized Vassas's men and women, the same ones who had been drawn to the singing. They marched between the people of Magoth, their eyes aglow with wonder as they beheld the great being.

Tavlin and Esril moved aside. He realized that they had stood on a sort of platform jutting out into the vast space Magoth occupied.

Now one of Magoth's many limbs moved, in a slow, majestic arc, coming to rest directly before the platform. Its end was blunt and deeply creased, like an orifice closed tight. As Tavlin watched, the orifice opened, and a strong white light, stronger than any other, flooded the platform, seeming to come directly from the interior of Magoth's being.

The worshippers of Magoth muttered in awe, then ushered forward the first of Vassas's people. The man stepped into the orifice without pause or qualm, transfixed by the singing. He was silhouetted for an instant against the whiteness, and then he was gone. Something snapped in Tavlin, and as the second man was ushered forward—it was Galesh, Vassas's second-in-command, a man Tavlin knew very well indeed, even considered a friend; he had attended Galesh's daughter's wedding—he tried to lurch forward, to shove Galesh away. The singing overcame him, though, and he fell to his knees screaming.

With a smile on his face, Galesh marched into the glow.

Tavlin felt a hand on his shoulder, and he looked up into the concerned but gentle face of Esril. He couldn't believe this sweet creature had been the nightmarish thing haunting him the past few days. She was so . . .

Her voice was kind. "Fear not, Tavlin Metzler. They feel no pain. Magoth feeds on energy. It is a being of pure lifeforce, and that is what it feeds on, like a flower feeds on the sun."

Tavlin wanted to say it was monstrous, *evil*, but the singing overcame him again, and for a time there was nothing else but the Song.

It was beautiful.

* * *

That night he received his tattoo. He was vaguely aware of being led into a large open space in the upper reaches of the Temple—whose rooms existed almost like an elegant beehive surrounding the vastness of Magoth—with many people all around. He and Esril, known as the Lady, occupied the center of the room, and Tavlin knelt before her, hardly able to stand at any rate, while she spoke. He didn't hear the words.

Then he laid his hand on a gleaming white pedestal, and one of the men brought forward some equipment. It was the Lady herself, though, that wielded the needle. He screamed as she carved into his flesh, but the pain was only part of it. The ink *glowed.* It burned palely against his flesh, like an echo of Magoth itself, like that preacher from long ago. The ink was evidently alchemical, or perhaps the cultists transformed it in one of their rituals, Tavlin didn't know, but it filled him with fire and heat, as if he'd downed a liter of vodka in one long gulp.

When he was done, each member of the cult stepped forward and pressed their own tattooed palms against his, squeezing his hand. He groaned in pain, and blood dripped with each handshake, but that seemed to be part of the ritual. Each one bore the same tattoo. They pressed their tattoo against his. They were a large and disparate group, he had learned, hailing from many cities of the underworld, some even from the upper world, most of them here only on temporary errands before returning to their hometown chapels, where they were the priests and leaders. It was an honor to come here, to dwell here. Many of the cult's members made pilgrimages to the Temple, to bask in the glory of their god, but they did not stay long. Only the so-called exalted received that privilege.

After the ceremony, they gathered about Magoth and sang, joining their voices to the Great Song. This actually issued from Magoth itself. Tavlin saw no human-like mouths capable of singing on the leviathanic being, but nevertheless . . . it sang. It sang without words, at least not any that Tavlin knew, but he could feel the spirit wash over him with the sound, enter him, and compel him to lift his own voice in worship; it would guide him in what to say.

He tried to resist, but it was all a blur, and soon it was lost in all the whiteness.

* * *

"Snap out of it!"

He felt someone kick him and glanced upwards groggily. A bleary shape stood before him. He rubbed his eyes. Sophia materialized from the fog. All around him the Song pounded, relentless and beautiful. He was in his cell. He didn't know what time it was, or even how long he had been at the Temple. Days, maybe. Years, even. All was whiteness.

And the Song.

Sophia was not part of the Song.

"You . . ." he said, trying to stand. "You . . ."

She bent over him, shoved something into his ears. Immediately he felt the Song recede. Angrily, missing it like a physical pain, he raised his hands to remove the plugs, but she slapped them away.

"Leave those alone!" she snapped, her voice muted by the plugs but loud enough to hear. "Now come on, I don't have all day."

Someone stuck his head through the doorway and said, "Hurry! I think I hear movement!"

Urgency filled Sophia's face. She removed a syringe from a pocket, checked it—something spurted from the tip—and, before Tavlin could stop her, she jabbed him in the upper right arm, through his shirt, and pressed the plunger.

He ripped it out of his arm, but too late; it was nearly empty.

"What did you do to me?"

She grabbed him under the arm. "Woke your ass up, I hope. Now let's get out of here before it's too late."

She marched him to the door. He felt a burning sensation begin to course through his veins. What had she given him? At the door one of Vassas's men waited, fear and awe in his face. It must be his first time to the Temple. He must have beheld Magoth on his way here and been stricken by the sight of it. Stricken by the lovely sight … the lovely …

"This way," Sophia said and led the way out. She and the lookout supported Tavlin on either side. He resisted, but weakly. He tried again to tear out the earplugs, but once more Sophia slapped his hands away.

"Leave those."

This time, when she moved her hand to slap at him, he saw something on her palm.

"You're tattooed," he said.

She grimaced and eyed the glowing symbol of Magoth that adorned her hand. Out of the corner of her mouth, she muttered, "Don't I know it."

They passed down one hall, then another. Tavlin saw three bodies lying on the ground, blood pooling around them. He recognized them as members of the Temple. How many had Sophia and her people killed? Part of him ached. *My brothers and sisters . . .*

They ushered him outside, onto the docks. There a boat waited with several people already in it. One was Frankie. All gestured urgently to Tavlin's party.

"Hurry, damn it," Frankie said. "We need to get going."

Sophia and the lookout loaded Tavlin onto the boat. Fear rose in him. "No," he said, shaking his head. "No no no . . ." They were going *to take him away.* A spike of pain lanced his heart.

"Damn, look at you," said Frankie, eyeing him. "What the fuck?"

"You can't take me," Tavlin said. He tried to climb out, but hands restrained him. "You bastards can't *do* this . . ."

Someone revved the motor, and the boat started away, bubbles churning the water behind it. Tavlin tried to jump in the lake, but they stopped him. He screamed and shouted at them. He stared at the Temple as its lights began to fade, feeling wretched, feeling empty. He could still hear, very faintly, the Song of Magoth, but it had lost its power over him. That hurt, in and of itself. He *ached* to let it wash over him again, to let it fill him with its brilliance.

Suddenly, there was activity on the docks. Temple members flooded them, swarming the boats.

"You took care of them, right?" Frankie demanded of two of his men.

"We got most of 'em," one man said. "We didn't have time for all of 'em."

"Damn it."

"Don't worry," Sophia said. "The plan will work."

Frankie didn't look so certain. "It better, darlin'. If it don't—"

"I know, I know."

"What—plan?" Tavlin asked.

They ignored him.

Behind, several boats raced across the water toward them, the lights of the Temple throwing shadows before them, like black blades stretching across the lake. The rest of the cultists remained on the docks, cursing their sabotaged boats.

The racing boats drew closer, closer . . .

"Move over," Frankie told the man who steered the vessel, then hunkered over the engine himself and throttled it to full speed.

The boat fishtailed down a tunnel, leaving the chamber of the Temple. Tavlin screamed at them and struggled against them, but they pinned him down. The burning sensation that had begun to course through his veins filled him with fire, and he felt himself start to shake. Sweat oozed from his pores.

Gunfire ripped the night around him. Sparks flashed off the sewer walls.

Frankie's men fired back.

The pursuing boats chased Tavlin's vessel down one hall, then another, firing their guns whenever they got a clean shot. Once they struck one of Vassas's men and he pitched overboard. Another was struck in the gut and sank back while others took his position, firing at the pursuers. The cultists gained on those fleeing, and at one point Tavlin flinched as one of the pursuing boats rammed the one he was on. A shotgun roared and one of the mobsters was flung into the water.

Then *she* was bending over Tavlin. It was Esril, the Lady, the High Priestess of Magoth. She was of flesh and blood still, but he thought she glowed faintly; she was filled with power.

"Bring it back to us, Tavlin," she said. "Bring it back."

The formula, he thought. *She means the formula.* She had come along with her fighters to send Tavlin off, but with a mission. To return what was hers.

"I …" he started to say, then realized he didn't know how to respond. Part of him wanted to say, *I'll do it, Lady. Anything for you.* But vaguely he realized that wasn't him speaking, that was something else. That was …

The Song. It's the fucking song.

"You stole it," she said, almost chiding him, while the others fought.

One of the mobsters trained his gun on her, but a hole appeared in the man's forehead and he toppled forward.

"You stole it," Esril said, ignoring the violence all around, as if she existed in a calm bubble, a sphere of peace, and maybe she did. Maybe she was exerting her power to protect herself. "It's only right that you bring it back."

". . . bring it back," Tavlin managed.

She smiled. "That's right. Bring it back to me."

From somewhere he found strength. "… no."

Her face ticced. *"What?"*

"No." He tried to punch her but missed clumsily.

Enraged, the Lady wrapped her hands about Tavlin's throat and squeezed. All around him was chaos, but the only things he could see in the entire world were her eyes. They *blazed.* Her whole being shook—not a physical shaking, but somehow an extraplanar shaking. Magoth had gifted her with strange powers, and now they were vibrating inside her, thrown into a frenzy by her anger.

"You took it!" she shouted. "I let you live *even though you took it!*" She screamed wordlessly and shook him, and he felt her fingers turn hot. Her whole being vibrated, and something from her passed into him.

This is it, he was able to think, believing it would be his last flicker of consciousness before oblivion claimed him. *This is how the ghost-her gets into me.*

Anger rose in him. He grabbed the dead man's revolver and clubbed the Lady over the side of the head with it; there was no time to aim. She shrieked and flew backward, and Frankie gunned the engine. Tavlin's boat shot away from the Lady's, leaving her rage far behind.

At last Frankie turned them into a certain corridor, wider than the others, and Tavlin saw two other boats lying in wait. At first he thought they were about to be ambushed, but then Frankie called to them.

Wire cages hung over the sides of the boats, and some form of animal occupied each one. Tavlin realized they were slugmines, dark and glistening, bobbing in the water but restrained. Now the men in the boats opened the cage doors and the slugmines swam away, tentacles stirring the water around them. They moved slowly and languidly, and Tavlin knew the men who had been caging them must have known how to manipulate them. When spooked, the slugmines would release their deadly gasses.

The creatures filled the water behind the boats, creating an effective blockade, and Frankie's men cheered.

Without wasting a moment, all three boats roared off, just as the Temple's boats turned the corner and entered the hall of the slugmines. The first boat didn't recognize their peril and struck one of the animals. Instantly the surrounding slugmines squirted their black gas into the air, and a weird, watery shriek filled the hall.

Tavlin was far away by then, and he still had his plugs in, but even so he could hear the screams of the people from the Temple as the gas ate into their lungs. Was the Lady with them?

"You . . . you killed them . . ."

Sophia knelt over him, her face all business. "How do you feel?"

He was breathless and jittery. "F-fine. What did you do to me?" The burning sensation had left him, and he felt strange. Clearer.

"Gave you something to help with the withdrawal."

"Withdrawal?"

She nodded. "From the Song. It won't cure you, they told me, but it'll help." Gently, she reached up and removed his plugs. She had already removed hers. Pity showed in her face, but also something else. "I'm glad you're back, Two-Bit. We need you."

He stared about them, at the grim and frantic men and women that occupied the boat. "Is that why you came for me?"

"We didn't come for *you*," she said.

She picked up a strange bag—not canvas, but something thicker, that lay in the bottom of the boat. The others around her glanced at her and the bag warily. Tavlin felt his hairs prickle. Something was not right. Now that he was starting to calm down, he noticed a general sort of . . . greasiness . . . to the air. A rancid, bitter greasiness. And a thrum. A grating vibration, just barely noticeable. What had they done?

Visibly steeling herself, Sophia opened the bag. Tavlin, wondering what he was about to see, peered inside. Lying in the bottom of the bag was purple metallic-looking rod with strange bumps at its top. It looked thoroughly . . . alien.

"Dear gods," Tavlin said. "What is it?"

"The Ualissi made it," Sophia said. "Just for this purpose. They needed what they called an extradimensional reading from inside the Temple. Only with that can they combat the Formula. We just took the reading before we grabbed you."

"The Ualissi ..."

"We followed your advice, Tav," Frankie said. "We went to them and brought them the canister containing the Formula. Asked them to help us. That device is the result. Now let's get a move on. We can explain the rest later."

Chapter 13

"You're mad, all of you," Tavlin said as they entered Muscud once more. He was glad to see the familiar surroundings: the fishermen plying the waters, the docks teeming with activity, strange fish flopping on wet boards, mutants squelching and calling to each other, mist coiling and uncoiling across the water and the little city that sat atop it. Lights from the many squat towers winked out at him blearily.

"You shouldn't have come for me," he said. "You shouldn't have come for *it*--whatever that rod measured. You could have all been killed."

"Well, we did," Frankie said over the roar of the motor. "And you'd better be damned glad we did. They say if you'd spent any longer in that fucking place you'd have become another damned zombie like the rest of them. There would've been no coming back for you. You can thank your girl here for that."

He glanced at Sophia questioningly, but she broke eye contact.

"Who's this 'they'?" Tavlin asked. "The Ualissi?"

Frankie grunted, seeming a little pale. "You'll see."

Tavlin scratched at his tattoo; it still itched. Seeing the motion, Sophia said, "You'd better have that burned off right away."

"We'll get ours removed together. It will be romantic."

Apparently that was the wrong thing to say. She refused to look at him.

The boats did not dock at any of the main harbors but instead circled around the city until they neared one of the slums. Tavlin wanted to ask why but supposed he would find out soon enough. The boats docked at a half-collapsed pier overgrown with slime-mold and colorful fungi, and the men and women of the boats climbed out, Frankie carrying the satchel. Several people kept their guns at the ready, scanning the windows and streets all about them. The buildings sagged, slouching like drunks across the narrow, winding roads, and, as Tavlin entered the ghetto's maze, he became aware of the wilting buildings looming over his head, of all that brick and stone and debris ready to collapse on him at any moment.

Moths with too many wings beat around the few gas-lamps that worked, but everything else was plunged into darkness with only occasional lights from within the buildings revealing any sign of occupation. Tavlin felt cold. He wasn't familiar with this area of town—a pre-human slum, the Ualissi Quarter normally excluded outsiders—and he didn't relish being here.

Frankie rapped on a door whose paint had peeled long ago. Tavlin guessed the occupants of the area didn't care about things like home decoration.

When the door opened, a dim form moved backward as if beckoning them inside. Alert, guns drawn, Vassas's people entered, Sophia and Tavlin with them, to find that the inside was poorly lit, with a few lanterns throwing vague illumination throughout the room, the light seeming to strive through layers of soot and shadow.

But what occupied Tavlin's attention was the thing that had opened the door. It stood, if stood was the right word, in the center of the room, squelching and undulating, pulsing and glowing. Tavlin, who had never received a good look at one of the prehistoric things before—they always wore trench coats or muumuus when outside of their quarter—couldn't help but gape. The creature resembled something like a jellyfish if a jellyfish could move upright and had a crest of glowing spines along what should be its back. Composed of various sacs of gel and air, all fringed with lacy cilia, and sporting a myriad of long, graceful flagella—that, Tavlin was aware, could sting a man to death in seconds—it was completely inhuman-looking, lacking even any visible eyes, mouth or ears. But it was, strangely, beautiful. It pulsed with bioluminescence, as many undersea creatures did. Gentle pink flushed one bulging sac, then spread to another. A bloom of vermillion flared up from a lower extremity and crept throughout the being, fading like the burst of a firework, only to be replaced by another. Subtle lights constantly strobed up and down its flagella and spines. The creature's bioluminescence provided most of the light in the room, pulsing off the walls. And when it moved, it was graceful and balletic, almost as if it were underwater, seeming to defy all known laws of gravity. It bobbed along, its sacs almost weightless, the feather touch of its flagella helping propel it.

Sophia watched Tavlin's face and squeezed his hand. "Lovely, aren't they?"

He nodded, wordless.

"The Ualissi have been helping us, ever since Vassas was driven from the Wide-Mouth," she told him. Strange light played off her face.

Tavlin shook himself. "Vassas was *driven out* of the Wide-Mouth?"

Sophia nodded, and Frankie, having heard them, said, "Hell of a thing, ain't it? Never thought I'd see the day."

Shock washed over Tavlin, and he felt nauseous and weak. It was all he could do to keep upright. The Wide-Mouth was one of his bedrocks. He had worked there for a decade, had considered it not just a fixture in his life but in all the underworld.

"How?" he asked.

"Later," Frankie said. To the Ualissi, he said, "Can we go down?"

The creature bobbed, and its colors flashed, starting in the middle and rippling outward, a brilliant electric green, quickly followed by purple.

Frankie frowned at it. "I'm gonna take that as a yes."

He showed the way to a door, and the Ualissi moved aside, almost floating across the aged floorboards. Frankie shoved the door open and clattered down a set of half-rotted stairs, and the others followed, one at a time, Tavlin and Sophia last. They descended into a dank, wet basement that must breach the waterline—indeed, Tavlin could see the waterline as a stain against the wooden walls, brown and gunky below and yellowish above. A trapdoor was set into the floor and Tavlin guessed that normally this basement was flooded and kept open for the Ualissi to come and go from the water. The whole place stank of rot and mildew.

A few cots and folding tables cluttered the room, and Boss Vassas and some of his men had apparently been playing a game of cards. They all leapt up as Frankie and the others trooped down, and when Vassas saw the satchel his eyes widened.

"Did you get it?" he said. When Frankie nodded, Vassas embraced him. "I was beginning to get worried."

Frankie nodded to the men who'd come with him. "We were all part of it, Boss."

"Of course. Here, celebrate, all of you. Have some beer." Vassas kicked a keg that rested on the floor. "I was ready to mourn or rejoice, depending."

Two of the men hauled the keg onto a table, which creaked under the weight, and the group began to drink and talk, toasting the fallen. The man who had been wounded was seen to. Vassas embraced Tavlin and offered him a mug of ale. Tavlin declined.

"I haven't been right in the head for awhile, it seems," he said. "Let me get clear before I get muddy again."

"It's good to see you're back," Vassas said. "We were all worried for you."

"Glad to *be* back."

Tavlin wasn't really in the mood to talk, and Vassas seemed to sense this and moved on, talking with those he had sent into battle. Someone turned on a radio. Dancing broke out, though mostly it was men dancing solemn beer dances while others clapped and stomped their feet. The few women present were fighters, not good-time girls, and they didn't seem to want to confuse the issue by taking part other than to clap or stomp. Water seeped through the walls, and the wood groaned.

Still shaky and overwhelmed, Tavlin collapsed on a bunk and tried to get himself together. Everything had changed so much. His entire world had shifted. Added to it, he still felt the craving in him for the Song of Magoth. The need for it made him ache, made his stomach tight and his mouth dry.

He started when he felt a weight in the cot beside him and opened his eyes to find Sophia there. She stared down at him with an unreadable expression.

"Feeling okay?" she said.

"Never better."

"Liar."

"You know me."

She actually smiled a bit at that, but it was a sad smile. “I did, once.”

“What does that mean?”

“The Tavlin I knew never would have risked his life against Octunggen spies, or against the people of Magoth.”

“Maybe you never knew the real Tavlin, then. The truth is I never meant to risk my life at all. It just sort of happened.” He nodded at the room. “I’m surprised they threw themselves into it as deeply as they did. How long was I at the Temple?”

“Three weeks.”

He tasted something bitter in the back of his throat. “Well . . . then what happened in the last three weeks to change the world?”

Her hand was resting on his chest. She sort of moved it, making him aware of it again, but she didn’t take it away.

“You,” she said.

“Me?”

“You’re the one that started this ball rolling. You convinced both me and Boss Vassas how important the canister was, and you’re the one who suggested going to the Ualissi to find some way to counteract what was in it. We did, and the Ualissi were only too happy to help. The Formula terrifies them, and they hate and fear the G’zai. Then Grund hit Vassas hard, all across the board.”

Tavlin could hear the capital F in 'Formula'. “It was Havictus, wasn’t it?” he said.

“Yes. At least, I think so. The Octunggen were helping Grund, giving him some of their technology. I was at the Wide-Mouth one day when there were shots. It was just a ruse, but a bunch of Vassas’s folk rushed outside—just in time for Grund’s people to throw a light-grenade. It erupted, and everyone that laid eyes on it when it blew turned ill.”

“Ill?”

"Some sort of plague. Boils and vomiting, skin peeling off, muscles liquefying. It was horrible. The Wide-Mouth became a triage. Over twenty people had seen the bomb go off, and they all grew sick. Grund's men must have taken some sort of pill to resist the effects, but there was no hope for the people hit by it. They died within two days. Only about half of them were Vassas's men and women; the rest were just civilians at the wrong place at the wrong time. Luckily it wasn't contagious. Grund must want to take Muscud whole, not inherit a city of corpses."

"A light-bomb . . ." Tavlin shook his head.

"More of a grenade, I think. Anyway, I was staying in one of Vassas's whorehouses—not working; he'd just put me up there to be out of the way—when I heard that Grund's people had struck the Wide-Mouth. By then so many of Vassas's toughs had been killed, one way or another, that he couldn't hold out, not even in his stronghold. He and these people, a dozen or so, managed to escape, and that's it. They made it to a dock and took to the water. I think Grund's still hunting for them out there." She gestured vaguely, taking in the halls of the sewer. "Little did he know that Vassas had contacts in the Ualissi ghetto; he just circled back around through the tunnels and entered town again. Now he's waiting for his chance to strike back."

"And meanwhile the Ualissi were studying the formula. The *Formula*," he corrected himself.

"Exactly. Well, about a week ago they told us that they were missing something, some critical information, about how to combat the contents of the canister. They needed critical diagnostic information on Magoth, if you will. If you're going to kill something, you have to know what makes it tick. So they built that thing we used to record the data, the extradimensional frequency of Magoth, or as close to it as they could come. If they had that data, they could defeat it. The Formula."

"What *is* it?"

"I don't know," she said. "Not exactly."

"And some, ah, agent has to be manufactured to destroy it? I guess lighting it on fire won't do the trick."

"No. Acting against it in any way other than the correct method will end in disaster, the Ualissi say. It could crack open space and time and spill this planet into some howling dimension that will warp us like hot plastic. It can't be watered down, it can't be frozen. Only by some very specific method can it be rendered inert."

"And the Ualissi believe that device of theirs, the one that, ah, took Magoth's temperature, contains the key."

"Something like that. With that data they can finalize the toxin."

"So now all we have to do is wait for them to read the device?"

"That's about it."

He watched her. "You all went through a lot of trouble. The tattoos . . ."

Sophia scratched her palm; it must still itch. "It was the only way to get into the Temple. Luckily the Ualissi know how to duplicate the tattoos. They've been helping us quite a bit. They hate Magoth, fear it, and will do anything to stop its designs."

"Which are . . . ?"

She smiled again, but it was fleeting and rueful. "No one knows. Except maybe the Octunggen or the Order of Magoth, and they aren't talking." She patted his chest. "Just get some rest. We'll fill you in on everything else tomorrow."

He was feeling tired. The music—someone had turned on a gramophone—and the celebrants were quite loud, but he was more exhausted than they were raucous, and to the sounds of toasts and of groaning wood, as water squeezed the sides of the basement, he drifted off to sleep.

* * *

"I appreciate you breaking me out," Tavlin told Vassas. They were on a rooftop garden not far from the building whose basement part of the band was using; others were bunking in other buildings. A whole network of Ualissi was aiding them. Around Tavlin strange fungus and white, lichenous plants waved in the gentle, gaseous wind. The Ualissi cared little for gardening, but apparently they extracted various chemicals and drugs from the plants. Half-leaning against the railing, Tavlin smoked a bowl and stared out over the lights of the city. His palm still ached from having the tattoo removed, but he was glad it was done. The cult's hold over him was leaving, if gradually. He could still hear the Song, though.

"We didn't do it for you, you know," Vassas said. He stood nearby, smoking a cigar and swilling wine. The two of them were alone.

"I know."

"Don't get me wrong, when Sophia insisted, I went along with it well enough, even though it might have jeopardized the operation. We owe you, Two-Bit." In a lower voice, he added, "*I* owe you."

Tavlin blew out a fragrant cloud of smoke. "We're even now."

Vassas grunted but said nothing. In the distance, gunfire rattled.

"That Grund?" Tavlin asked.

"Yep. He's cleaning up any opposition. I wasn't the only one who didn't like him taking over. When Mayor Jensen backed me over Grund, Grund sacked the Mayor's Mansion. That's where he's making his lair now, ruling over the city."

"Shit."

"Godsdamned Octunggen. Why are they helping him like this? Without their weapons he'd be back to square one."

"They want the town locked up so there aren't people like us fighting them." Tavlin drew in the spicy smoke, playing it over his tongue. "They picked Grund because he was your enemy, and you were the biggest man in town. Remember, you wouldn't even rent them a building for their factory."

"They must have sensed I didn't care for 'em. Whatever. It's not like I'd want to be in Grund's shoes—well, if he had shoes. Or feet. Then again, it would be a damn sight better than being in mine right now. Hiding out in an alien ghetto in my own fucking town . . ."

"You'll get it back." Tavlin said this with more conviction than he felt. He let a beat go by, then added, "What about the canister? The Formula? Now that the Ualissi have had all this time to analyze it, can you tell me any more about it?"

Vassas ran a hand across his unshaven face, looking dispirited. "Apparently the Octunggen had the recipe for this 'Formula', and they gathered the ingredients and assembled it, but it has to be brought to the Temple in order to bring it to life or what-have-you."

"Yes. Havictus said only Magoth could 'activate' the Formula. And the Octunggen were bringing it to the Temple when I intercepted it."

"It can't be any coincidence that it happened when it did, too. Right on the eve of them launching their damned war. They meant for this plan of theirs to be implemented as soon as the war started. That has to be why they risked stealing the jewels from my place and Madam Saraja's when they were occupied instead of just waiting. They needed those jewels to make that Formula before the war kicked into gear." His eyes blazed hate. "*That's* why Nancy died."

Tavlin grimaced. "We're talking about something that could win the war for Octung, aren't we?"

"Probably."

"It … could be worse than that, you know. Havictus seemed to be talking about something … well, apocalyptic."

A long, grim silence passed, interrupted only when someone cleared a throat behind them, and the two men turned to see Frankie stepping into the garden. "Boss, the jellies are done studying it—the measuring device, I mean."

"Well?" said Vassas. "What do they say?"

Frankie fidgeted. "Apparently only a certain mix of compounds can nullify the Formula —kill it, I mean. The Ualissi say they can get most of the materials themselves—get them, make them, secrete them, whatever. But there's one thing they don't have, and that's a kind of mineral fashioned by a lost race of gods known as the Ygrith."

"Where can we find this mineral?" Vassas said.

Frankie shifted again, clearly uncomfortable. "That's the thing. It's rare. Any direct artifact left by the Ygrith is rare, apparently. The Ualissi say that this mineral, inaja, is sometimes gathered in black jewels and used on staffs to give them power. Like magic wands or something, but tapped into the user's mind."

"A jewel," Vassas mused. "Like my gemstone?"

"Maybe. But black."

Vassas tapped his chin. "You know, the vendor that sold that stone to me, he sold several others around the Stink."

"He sold one to Madam Saraja," Tavlin said. "That must be how she got hers. I suppose Havictus murdered the other buyers, too. That is, if he couldn't steal the jewels outright."

"There was one jewel the vendor offered me that was black," Vassas said thoughtfully. "They were all very expensive, and he claimed to have retrieved them from the body of some inhuman thing he found in a dead city far from here. Well, the black one was shiny, and I could feel a kind of power in it, but the red one was prettier, so I took it. I think, though …"

Tavlin leaned forward. "Yes?"

"I think the Mayor took the black one."

Tavlin and Frankie exchanged a glance.

"You mean to say the key to ending this whole thing is at the Mayor's Mansion?" Tavlin said. "Which is currently occupied by Grund and his gang?"

Vassas shook his head. "I don't have enough strength to assault the Mansion."

"It *can't* end here," Frankie said. "The black jewel is so close …" He stared out toward the Mayor's Mansion, its peaked roof just visible in the far distance, as if he could see the black jewel itself through the mansion's brick walls.

"It won't," Tavlin assured him. "Just let me think on it awhile. There has to be a way into the Mansion without launching a full-on assault."

"There better be," Vassas said. "Because it's an assault we can't win."

They spent some time on the rooftop garden, staring out over the city, talking quietly, then went down to rejoin the others. The days passed, slowly yet frantically. Tavlin spent a week with them, then two, and each day they planned and plotted, schemed and fretted. On the one hand, he felt frightened and tense, worried that Octunggen spies, Grund or the cultists might find them, ferret them out and destroy them. Surely they were looking. Surely the Octunggen had psychics out trying to seek the location of the canister and its contents. Surely they would come across them at any time. But on the other hand, he felt good. He felt relaxed and at ease, for the first time in a long while. Finally, he was with friends once more. Compatriots. He relished the company of Frankie and Vassas and the others, but mostly he enjoyed the company of Sophia. She kept her distance from him, but always there was something there . . .

Maybe it wasn't dead, he thought, whatever was between them. Maybe she'd been wrong.

One day, when inquiring about her whereabouts, they told him she had gone out.

"You let her go alone?" Tavlin asked. "That's dangerous! She could be recognized."

"It's alright," Frankie told him. "She wears the same disguise every time, and she's never had any trouble."

"Every time?" Tavlin was confused.

Frankie gave him a strange look. "Yes. Every time." He chewed his thick, frog-like lip for a moment, then said, "If we hurry, I can help disguise you, too. You can catch up with her before she arrives."

"Arrives where?"

Frankie didn't answer, just beckoned to one of his men to get out the make-up and box of outfits. Tavlin, impatient and strangely nervous, submitted to their ministrations, sitting in a chair mutely while they dabbed make-up on him, arranged his hair, then draped him in a ceremonial robe. At last it was done. Frankie gave him the route Sophia would have taken, and something about it made Tavlin frown, but he wasn't sure why. He didn't dwell on it but hurried after her, shuffling down the streets in his robe, careful not to go too fast. They had dressed him as an Izcai priest (as he was passing near the Izcain quarter of town), in metallic-gold robes and white face-paint, wearing sandals on his feet.

The city seemed quieter than usual about him and the moisture dripping from above heavier, almost as though it were raining. The buildings stretched strange shadows toward him, and he found himself trying to walk around them. He left the pre-human ghetto and entered another slum, a human one, then another. Strange faces peered out at him from cracked windows. Buildings hunched over him, some listing and leaning over the road. He smelled roasting corn and sulfur and cayenne drifting from the kitchens.

Finally he saw her. Sophia walked ahead of him, tall and elegant. Something about her stride was sad, her head lowered. She was completely unaware of him, and he overtook her swiftly.

She was a vision. She wore the same metallic-gold robes as he, embossed with red designs, and her face was covered in white face-paint, with an oversized red tear below her left eye, and her hair fell behind her back in an elaborate queue ringed by gold bands. Her brown eyes glistened with moisture, and he thought she might be crying in earnest.

Then she saw him. She straightened and cleared her throat, but said nothing, just watched him come closer.

He found that his own throat had constricted. "Sophia."

"Two-Bit."

"You don't have to call me that, you know."

She said nothing, and they fell into step beside each other. The only sounds were their footfalls, sandals on stone, and the battering of soft furry bodies against the lamp-posts.

"So where are we going?"

She gave him an odd look, the same one Frankie had, and it was then that he noticed the single white rose she carried, holding it delicately, almost reverently, in both hands. She didn't answer him, but in that moment he knew. He felt his stomach drop, and something behind his eyes burned. He found himself slowing his gait, dreading what lay ahead.

All too soon they reached it. The black wrought-iron gate towered over them, encrusted with age and tragedy, and they passed through it with wariness, conscious of the maze before them. Then around them. Great, listing banks of marble and stone and iron and concrete loomed in all directions, gargoyles peering around corners, chipped statues of angels littering the intersections. Everywhere were names carved into stone. Names and dates. Two dates, usually, where both were known, but sometimes not even one. Some didn't even have names. This was the cemetery of Muscud, where the dead waited out eternity. There was no ground to be buried in. Bodies were cremated and stored in urns, urns which in turn were placed in small vaults. Banks of the vaults stretched high overhead, so high in places that Tavlin could barely see the ceiling, and in twisting avenues all around. A strange, unearthly mist coiled between the lanes, and somewhere Tavlin heard crying. The labyrinth of the dead was supposed to be haunted, Tavlin knew, and many people avoided the cemetery altogether.

Together, he and Sophia walked slowly through the aisles, not in any hurry, almost afraid of their destination. They didn't speak.

They arrived at a certain bank and had to mount a cracked cement stairway to ascend to the walkway that ran before the proper section. At last they came to a stop. Tavlin stared at the name, at his son's name, Jameson Gorun Metzler, and those two dates, horribly, cruelly close together, and he couldn't stop the tears that came to his eyes, and the hitches that racked his chest. Beside him, Sophia wept, too. She knelt to place the single white rose at the foot of the vault beside similar flowers and an alchemical lantern that had been left burning next to two wax figures. A man and a woman. When Tavlin saw that, he felt a heat inside him. Sophia had not forgotten him. She had wanted Jamie to know that both his father and his mother would look after him in the afterlife.

Tavlin was surprised to feel the pressure on his hand, and glanced down to see that Sophia had gripped him tightly. They knelt before the vault, crying silently, and in the background the baritone wail of a foghorn rolled across the town.

At last Sophia took her hand away. Reluctantly, he let her.

"You've been coming here everyday," he said, counting the flowers. As he spoke, he heard the rasp in his voice.

Sophia nodded, wiping a tear away. The tears had cut channels through the white cake on her face, through the symbolic red tear and down to her lips and chin, making her look ragged and ghostly, but very, very beautiful. Her lips trembled as she said, "I couldn't stand being away from him. In Taluush I thought of him every day."

He started to say something, but couldn't, and the words died in his throat.

"He should have lived, Tavlin," she said. *"He should have lived."* Her face screwed up in anger and grief, and for a moment she seemed as if she would go over the edge once more into despair, but at the last instant she reined herself in. She mashed her eyes shut.

This time he reached out and took her hand in his. She resisted at first, but she let him. He squeezed both her hands and said, "Yes. He should have. You did everything you could, Soph. I know. I know I've said some things . . . I've blamed you when I shouldn't have . . . I was just so angry. But I know better. In here." He tapped his chest over his heart.

She opened her eyes and stared at him for a long moment. He thought she might wrench her hands away, but she didn't.

Finally she nodded. Another tear spilled down her cheek. "I blamed you, too. And the things I said to you . . . I know it wasn't your fault. I want you to know that I'm sorry."

She pressed his hands, and he pressed back. He almost, *almost* leaned forward to kiss her, but he waited, unsure if it was the right thing to do or not, or if she would even let him, and the moment passed.

She climbed to her feet. "Come on. Let's get back."

He looked up at her, sighed, and stood to go.

* * *

The ghost-witch appeared. The Lady. Or her twin, anyway, if that's what she was.

Tavlin and Sophia had been walking back to the pre-human ghetto, silently but less awkwardly than usual, when Tavlin suddenly noticed a white shadow trailing along beside him. Startled, he spun about and raised his fists in front of him. Sophia jumped back.

The Lady, wreathed in mists and radiating light and beauty, stared at them.

"You took it," she whispered. "How could you take it?"

Tavlin squinted at her. "You keep saying that. Whenever you appear like this. Is it . . . is it really *you*?"

Instead of answering, she said, "You took it." She sounded as if by taking it he had wounded her personally and irrevocably, and also as if he had disappointed her. "You shouldn't have taken it. But you have only delayed the inevitable."

"And what is that?" Sophia said.

"Why, the Great Change, of course. The Opening, when all boundaries collapse, and we are as one."

"What does that mean?" Tavlin said. "Open what?"

She smiled, somewhat sadly, somewhat serenely. "I cannot say, and you cannot know. You hear the Song within your heart, but you do not answer. You can only know the truth when you answer."

"What do you want?" Sophia said.

The Lady drifted closer, her mists swirling about her, half hiding, half revealing her slender, naked body. Though she was called "Lady", her body was little more than that of a girl, her breasts small and firm and high, her legs long and coltish. She raised a finger to trace Tavlin's jaw. Conscious of Sophia, he backed away. The Lady's eyes registered interest.

"I only want to awaken the Song," she said, and drew back.

Tavlin and Sophia peppered her with questions as they resumed their walk, but she just stared at them, sad but wise, trusting in their better natures to redeem themselves and aid her cause. She would reveal no answers, no great truths. She merely drifted along, a mute ghost on their journey back to the Ualissi Quarter. Tavlin found himself taking a circuitous route so that she would not be led back to Vassas's hiding spot. Not that he thought it really mattered, of course. This version of the Lady wasn't really *her*. At least he didn't think so. But still.

"What *is* she?" Sophia asked Tavlin, speaking as if the ghostly figure weren't there.

"Damned if I know," he said. "Some echo, maybe. Imprinted on me when she touched me that day, when you brought me out of the Temple. She was mad at me then for taking the briefcase, and whenever she appears like this there's always an echo of that anger, like she's stuck in some sort of loop or something. But somehow, because of her power—the *real* Lady's power, anyway—well, the part of her that fused with me, or became attached to me, was thrown back in time, or at least back along my own timeline. She herself told me this would happen back at the Temple, only … well, I think she thought we would bond in some *other* way than her trying to kill me." He coughed. "Anyway, she appeared to me like this … like a ghost … long before I even knew the real Lady existed. But *this* one is different somehow. The real Lady is more imperious and somehow older. This one is just angry and confused."

"So she's, what, *haunting* you?"

He frowned. "For lack of a better word, yes, I suppose."

They moved on, sometimes sneaking sidelong glances at the ghostly figure, who simply glided along beside them, sometimes humming to herself. Tavlin thought he recognized parts of the Great Song. The sound stimulated a sort of burning inside him, not unpleasant. It wanted to take over, and he realized he was unsteady on his feet. He had to struggle to suppress the feeling. It was so *beautiful* …

"Do you think she's evil?" Sophia asked. She said it quietly, as if not wanting the apparition to hear.

Tavlin shook himself, clearing his head. "I don't know. I don't even know what the cultists are up to, really, and I was there."

"You can't remember *anything*? You were there for weeks."

"It's all . . . cloudy. Like I was in a haze the whole time. I don't know, it's hard to explain, but I don't think I was in my right mind. The Song . . . it overwhelmed me. *Became* me."

"And she wants it to overwhelm you again."

His eyes moved to the ghost, or whatever she was, still mute at his side. "Yes, I suppose. So that I'll steal the canister and bring it back to her. The real her."

"Do you think . . . do you think you might?" Quickly, Sophia added, "I mean, do you think the Song is strong enough to take you over again?"

"I . . ." He wanted to say *Of course not.* He wanted to say he could fight it. Instead he sighed and answered truthfully: "I don't know." Again he studied the apparition. "We need something to call her. At the Temple, they called the other-her 'the Lady'. Her real name was Esril, or at least that's what she called herself." To the ghost, he said, "Is that what we should call you?"

The girl stared off into the night, and at first he didn't think she was going to answer. Then, as if seeming to come to herself, she spoke, but her voice sounded as if it came from far away. "I was called … in another life … Millicent …"

"It's nice to meet you, Millicent. I'm Tavlin. This is Sophia."

"I know who *you* are," Millicent told Tavlin.

"I suppose you do."

"Are you self-aware?" Sophia said. "Is that the word?" She swore, half under her breath. "What am I doing? You can't ask a ghost if she's self-aware, can you? And could you trust the answer?"

"I am … me," said Millicent. Her pretty face was frowning, just slightly, as if puzzling over something. "I am not … what I was. What I came from. Like an acorn from a tree. Or perhaps a carving from a flowering plant. Yes. Yes, that seems more like it."

"I'm surprised you know what a flower is," Tavlin said, half ironically. "There are so few of them down here."

"I am not from here. Or at least she isn't. The Lady. The real Lady. I, of course, was born down here, in that one moment of her rage, just as you said. But I remember …"

"Yes?" said Sophia. "What do you remember?"

"I remember sun, and rain, and wind. I remember her life, but it's unclear. Out of focus."

"You're not infected," Tavlin said. "How did you come to be down here—or how did *she* come to be down here?"

"A preacher on the surface world. They have them, you know—the people of Lord Magoth. They have people that spread the word even up there. She came to a meeting, then another. She was very young, a runaway, but she had passion. She began to speak at the meetings, to gain a following. She moved up in the levels of the church … then down, if you take my meaning. Closer to the Temple. That's when she renamed herself Esril. A caterpillar becoming a butterfly."

Tavlin nodded. He was about to ask another question when noises came to him from around a bend—the sound of motorcycles, perhaps ten or more. Their motors slowed, and there came curses, then a grunt.

"What's this?" he said.

He started to investigate, but Sophia pulled him back. "Don't. It's Grund's men. He's been sending them out to patrol the town. They go out every day. Sometimes they rough people up that aren't showing the proper pro-Grund spirit. Sometimes they drag them away to the Mayor's Mansion. Those don't usually come back."

"Can't believe Vassas allows this."

"What choice does he have? Grund's men are numerous, and heavily armed. Besides, he's what Grund's people are really hunting for. Grund seems to believe that Vassas abandoned town, but he can't help a suspicion that the Boss might still be around somewhere, hiding and waiting for his moment to strike."

The sounds grew louder.

"Quick," Sophia said, "we'd better hide."

They slipped down an alley and hid behind a bank of trashcans. Millicent's lambent shadow surrounded them, shining on the broken jags of windows and bathing the bricks in pale light.

"Can't you shut that off?" Sophia snapped.

"I …" Millicent seemed to be concentrating. "I glow," she said, and it was as if the notion surprised her, as if she hadn't given it any thought before now, and perhaps she hadn't. In any case, it was a poor time for self realization. "I can't make myself not glow …"

"Then make yourself *go*, already!"

The motorcycles were turning onto the street they had just left. In moments they would pass the alley.

"I can't," Millicent said. She sounded miserable.

"You can't vanish?" Tavlin said, hearing a note of desperation in his voice even as he had to pitch that voice over the sound of the motorcycles' engines. "Can't go back inside me or whatever it is you do?"

She shook her head. Tears glimmered in her eyes.

"Shit," said Sophia.

The motorcycles' headlights pierced the dark road, beaming back off the walls of buildings and the cement and stone and asphalt of the road. Shattered glass gleamed like fangs. The motorcycles burst into visibility, a long line of them. Tavlin guessed that his original estimation had been off and that there were closer to fifteen of them than ten. In any case, one was probably too many. The vehicles, passing the alley, began to slow.

"They've seen us," Tavlin hissed. "Come on, hurry!"

He started up the alley and the others followed. He cut down the first cross-alley he came to, dark and rancid. Things squelched beneath his feet. Flails, feasting on something ahead, made shrieking noises and rose in a cloud around him, then up, spraying mucus as they went. Darkness draped the alley so thickly he could barely see at all, but Millicent's radiance lit up the gloom like a faint flashlight, and he felt the blood drain from his face at what it revealed.

"A dead end," Sophia moaned.

They stopped before the brick wall that sealed off the alley, then swiveled to face the only outlet, back the way they'd come.

"Maybe they didn't see us," said Millicent.

But Tavlin could hear motorcycle engines idling.

"They saw us," he said. "Or Millicent, anyway. They're stopped along the road."

Indeed, he could hear footsteps approaching up the first alley. In just seconds they would reach the cross-alley. The dead end. *It had better not be OUR dead end*, he thought, and resolved that it wouldn't be.

"Look!" Millicent said.

Tavlin turned back to see her sticking her head through a small plywood planking plastered against one corner of the dead end wall.

She pulled her head out and said, "There's nothing on the other side!"

Quickly Sophia moved to the plywood panel and jerked it aside. "It's a false wall," she said. "A way through. Hurry!"

She started to duck through, but Tavlin hesitated.

"What is it?" Sophia said.

He made a decision. "You go on. I'm staying."

"You *can't*. They'll *kill* you."

"You don't know that. But this might be my only chance to get access to the Mayor's Mansion ... and the black jewel."

"You're mad!"

"Listen to her," Millicent said. "Don't do this."

Tavlin straightened his back. "I'm staying. But, Sophia, please go. I'm willing to risk my life, but not yours."

The footsteps were getting louder.

Sophia paused in the tunnel entrance. Then, with deliberation, she stepped out and replaced the plywood panel. "If you're staying, I am, too."

His heart sank. "No, Sophia—"

As if it were the punch line to some cosmic joke, Millicent flickered several times, then vanished from sight. She'd gone back into Tavlin, if that's the way it worked, although he couldn't feel her in any way.

"Just great," Sophia said. "Just fucking great."

The shadows of the bikers flung across the pavement of the main alley, hurled by the beams of the bikes, and then the bikers themselves, about seven or eight of them, stepped into the mouth of the dead end alley. Four played flashlights while the others played guns.

A flashlight beam lanced Tavlin in the eyes, then another. Trying to conceal a flinch, he stepped forward, smiling widely. "What's the problem, boys? We were just about our own business. Say, those are nice rides. I can tell by the engine noise that—"

"What was that light?" one snapped. They were just silhouettes to Tavlin, but he could see this one had crests sprouting from his head, one along the top and one running along either side. They would have made it impossible for him to wear a helmet. He casually aimed a sawed-off shotgun in Tavlin's general direction.

"Just my flashlight," Tavlin said.

"Bullshit."

"It's alchemical."

"Where is it?"

Tavlin patted his pockets. "I seem to have lost it. Lacy, do you have it?"

Sophia, playing along, gamely inspected her person. "No, Rennie, I don't. You must have dropped it. It's not the first time."

"There you go, boys," Tavlin said, then made a show of wincing as a beam stabbed his eyes again. "Maybe you couldn't shine that in my face? There you go, lads. Well, if that's it—"

"Why'd you run?" said another biker. He was short and spindly, with pulsing sacs along his neck.

"Wouldn't you, with a pack of bikers gunning down the street?"

"You're not some Vassas loyalist, are you?"

"Of course not!" Tavlin laughed. He might want to get taken, but he couldn't *act* like he wanted to get taken. But just how was he going to make them suspicious without being too obvious?

Another figure stepped forward, bigger than the others. One of his arms had mutated into a terrible, pasty-white, boneless appendage with milky blind eyes blinking from its sides and its fingers fused together; it had also grown considerably in length, becoming one of the more gruesome tentacles Tavlin had ever seen, and he had seen too many. The awful limb snaked forward, curled around Tavlin's torso and wrenched him off the ground. Immediately Tavlin felt warm stickiness all around him. He issued a shriek, then managed to wheeze out (as the tentacle was squeezing air from his lungs), "Let me go!"

"This one's Tavlin Two-Bit Metzler," the figure said. "I recognize him from the old days. He's a crony of Vassas and no mistake." He shook Tavlin roughly. "What you doin' back in town, Two-Bit?"

"Just . . . seeing the sights."

"You lied," the one with the crests on his head said. "And you." He poked a scaly finger at Sophia. "You did, too. You called him Rennie."

"They're up to something," said another.

"Some business of Vassas, I reckon," said the one holding Tavlin up.

Sophia was starting to edge backward, perhaps meaning to try for the secret passage. She was either putting on an act to make this more convincing or else she'd come to her senses. Tavlin prayed she made it through the passage.

Three of the bikers lunged forward and half-surrounded her, forcing her back against one wall.

"Don't hurt her," Tavlin wheezed.

The one with the tentacle drew him close to its face, and now Tavlin could see that it was grinning. "Oh, we won't," it said. "Boss Grund reserves first right of all fillies. But afterward … oh, yes, afterward …" He laughed, and so did the others.

The three cornering Sophia grabbed her and flung her to the ground. She screamed and struggled, but one punched her on the jaw, hard, and she sagged. They bound her hands behind her back with a length of cord possibly brought along for just this purpose. Tavlin beat at the tentacle, but its owner cracked him over the side of the head with a pistol butt, and the world plunged into darkness. When it came back on, Tavlin was in the side car of a motorcycle and approaching downtown Muscud.

Right toward the Mayor's Mansion. Right toward the black jewel.

Chapter 14

Tavlin's head rang with the pain of the blow, and he tasted blood in his mouth. The sound of the motorcycles' engines filled his world, as did their throbbing and the jounce of the side-car's wheels over the uneven wooden planks and periodic asphalt and concrete. He tried to find Sophia, but the world spun around him and he sagged back in defeat, unable even to lift his head.

The fleet of motorcycles drew to a halt in the half-circle drive before what had been the Mayor's Mansion, a huge cobbled-together affair with thick stone walls overgrown with slime mold and cultivated glowing moss. The thick, warped-glass mirrors reflected the sheen of the motorcycles' headlights, gleaming like eyes in a ravaged face. The biker whom Tavlin was riding beside (it wasn't the fellow with the tentacle) kicked the stand, propping the bike up, then grabbed Tavlin and hauled him to his feet. Tavlin wobbled and started to fall, but the man slapped him hard across the face and somehow he managed to keep his feet. The world still twisted about him.

"Sophia," he tried to say, but the word came out thick and garbled. "Sophia …"

He saw her as they dragged him up the stairs toward the mansion. She was being carried along just like he was, but toward the back; she didn't look like she'd been struck over the head, or anywhere else for that matter, which was a blessing. But fear shone in her eyes. It welled up from the tenseness in her posture and by the set of her mouth; she was trying bravely not to scream.

They'd better not hurt her, Tavlin thought. *If my plan gets her harmed ...*

The bikers were met at the head of the stairs by a stout woman in a suit, and they nodded deferentially to her. Scarlet fish scales covered half her face, and they were doing something Tavlin had seen before, but rarely—molting. They were flaking off her face, presumably being replaced by new ones. By the irritation in her eyes, Tavlin knew it must itch. He didn't feel sorry for her, though. *Tough titties, bitch*, was his first uncharitable thought as he was brought before her, and he didn't recant the thought when her cold eyes fell on him.

"One of Boss Vassas's old chums," said the lead biker, the one with the tentacle for an arm. He flicked that limb, indicating Sophia. "And his girl."

"Interesting," the woman said. Tavlin presumed she was some lieutenant of Grund's. "Bring them in."

She brought them into the foyer, then into a large open space where a marble stairway curled up to the second floor. Tavlin thought that stairway might be heavy enough to justify its own pillar going down to the lakebed. Armed men and women stood about in alcoves and landings. Some seemed to be coming and going from various errands.

The female lieutenant consulted with the bikers, then gestured to the left, and three of the toughs dragged Sophia in that direction. Tavlin called out to her, or tried to. As soon as the first syllable left his throat, someone punched him in the gut and he doubled over, the taste of bile once more in his mouth. Sophia turned back to watch him sadly, perhaps to say goodbye, then was jerked around a bend and was gone from sight.

"The Boss will want to see him," the female lieutenant said, meaning Tavlin. "Take him to the second room."

Apparently she didn't need to say *what* room, exactly. It was merely *the* room. The second one. Tavlin had a bad feeling about what that meant, not helped by the bikers grinning hard grins at each other.

"I'd handcuff him first," said the fellow who had recognized Tavlin, although Tavlin didn't recognize him back. "He's a wily one, if I recall."

"Do it," she said.

One of the men produced a set of cuffs, jerked Tavlin's arms behind his back and snapped the links on, squeezing them painfully tight about his wrists. Tavlin grimaced despite himself. *Show no pain.*

"Take him up," the woman said.

The man who had cuffed him, along with two others—they were taking no chances—hauled him up the heavy marble stairs to the second floor, then down a richly carpeted hall still decorated with bloodstains from the ousting of the mayor and his family. Tavlin wondered if any of them still lived. *The girls*, he thought. Mayor Jensen had had two young daughters. They would still be alive, Tavlin was sure of it, but in what condition he didn't want to speculate.

A scream drifted from down a side hall, but it wasn't feminine. Tavlin supposed that sound must have come from the *first* room. If he was going to some sort of interrogation chamber, it was only one of a number, apparently. Well, at least two. It wasn't surprising, really. Vassas had several backrooms at the Wide-Mouth that served the same function, although rarely did he use one, let alone two at the same time. Grund had his own way of doing things, it seemed.

Tavlin made sure to brush up against the fellow who had cuffed him before they reached the solid oak door of the torture chamber; it was flanked by two goons. Tavlin wasn't sure if they were permanently stationed there or if they had just been dispatched here because of his arrival. If so, he was honored. He was also glad to note that his old thieving skills hadn't deserted him. He only prayed it would take some time for the fellow to notice.

At a particular door they were passing Tavlin's ears perked up. Two men were talking on the other side of it. One voice Tavlin didn't recognize, but the other he most surely did. By its bass grumble and international inflections, it could only be the spy Havictus. *Interesting.*

His jailors tossed him in what had once been a bedroom, to judge from its size and position, but the bed and everything else in it had been removed and bars had been hastily and crudely mounted over the window.

"Enjoy," said one of the bikers, or at least that's what Tavlin thought he said. The poor fellow's lips had become those of a fish, hard and thin, and it was difficult for him to enunciate. *Enjoy* sounded like *E'oy.* "Boss'll be here to see you soon," he added, but it came out *Oss'l ee ou oon.*

They slammed the door shut, leaving Tavlin alone. He stared at the door, the window. No way out. He wondered what they were doing with Sophia, then forced the thought away. *Keep it cool, Two-Bit. I need my wits about me like I never have before.* He stomped the floorboards, seeking a weakness. Sewer construction was notoriously shoddy and most buildings could be broken out of if you could find a weak or rotten board. This was the mayor's mansion, though, and this bedroom might have been that of one of his daughters (*Don't think about them*, Tavlin told himself. *You can't help them now*); it had been built regrettably solid.

"Millicent, are you there?"

He waited.

Nothing.

"Millicent, damn you, if you're there, if you're … in me … now's the time to come out. I could really use your help right about now. So could Sophia."

Nothing happened. He could feel nothing, either, no glow, heat or anything else—no sign that Millicent was in fact inside him, if that's what she was. He was beginning to think that was wrong, that that was not the right way to look at it. Whatever she was, she wasn't *inside* him, not really, not floating around in his guts or clogging up his arteries, but bound to him. Tied to him on some other plane, only able to cross at certain times. Perhaps she had to be strong enough, or the stars had to be in a certain position, or Tavlin himself had to be in a certain receptive mood. Or maybe none of those things. At any rate, she wasn't coming. Not now.

"Damn it all."

Tavlin began to pace. There had to be a way. There *had* to. The room was lit only by the vague lights coming in from the window and from under the door, but soon his eyes adjusted. Through the bars he watched flails flutter and swoop through the air over Muscud, a town under a terrible shadow, one that might have finally come to devour him, too. *I should never have followed Frankie that night.* Then again, if he hadn't, the Octunggen and the worshippers of Magoth would still have the canister. The Formula. And they would have activated it by now, surely.

At last, after what might have been an hour, the door opened, throwing light into the room, and Tavlin squinted into it. A silhouette crouched on the threshold, and behind it loomed two large figures. The shape between them, Tavlin knew, must be Grund. The man, surprisingly, was in a wheelchair, though Tavlin could see few other details about him. Tavlin knew little about the man, personally, other than that he was an upstart pretender to the underworld throne of Muscud and perhaps beyond—and that he had allied himself with Octunggen. That was enough by itself to get him a high place on Tavlin's shit list.

Gripping the wheels of his chair with surprisingly strong hands, Grund rolled himself across the threshold and into the room, and the two men followed. Tavlin edged back.

"Well well, look what we have here," said Grund. His hands moved in the darkness, and then light burst from them, making his hands seem to glow for an instant. He passed the alchemical lantern to one of his assistants, who accepted it without comment; though pulsing with waves of slowly moving light, the globe didn't seem to produce any heat and he didn't wince at the contact. "A foe of my good friend Havictus."

Tavlin tried to conceal the surprise he felt at seeing Grund's condition: the man's infection had more than simply fused his legs together and covered them with scales, it had given him a flipper, too. His lower half was a silver-scaled fish tail, but he was no mermaid, at least not one Tavlin had ever hoped to see. His upper half was that of an emaciated old man, withered and covered in barnacle-like growths. His skull was misshapen, one side of it transformed into a clam-like shell, or at least one face of the shell. His eyes blazed out of his ruined face, fierce and green, and Tavlin was impressed at the force of personality there.

"You know Havictus?" Tavlin said, but of course he had heard them speaking together not long ago. He didn't want Grund to know that, though.

"Oh, indeed. And when my second reported your arrival, Havictus grew quite interested. He had simply been visiting, as he sometimes does, as we have things that need coordination between our two parties, but I'm glad he was. He was able to tell me just whom I had caught in my net."

"I'm no one. Just someone who used to run a casino. Came back into town for a visit."

Grund smiled. "Don't be coy, Mister Metzler. I know that you've been quite the spirited nemesis of my good friend from Octung."

"What if I have? Kill me and be done with it. Only let the woman I was with go. She's done you no harm."

Grund fell silent. Tavlin waited impatiently. He found the way that the light played on Grund's face especially eerie. The alchemical globe, being held to one side of the man's head, threw shadows from the clamshell ridges across his ravaged, barnacle-covered face, so that his eyes appeared and then disappeared as the alchemical fluid ebbed and flowed, flared and faded.

Finally, Grund hunched forward, as if to peer more closely at Tavlin. "So: Vassas never left, did he?" Grund seemed to be speaking as much to himself as to Tavlin.

"I don't know what you're talking about."

"Well, I'll spell it out for you. An old associate of Vassas is found in town, near a bad quarter where most normal folk don't go. An *inhuman* quarter. Where only those who traffic in the strange substances grown by the Ualissi go, and what they offer in return I don't want to know. The Ualissi worship terrible gods, I understand. Strange and terrible. Oh, yes."

"More strange and terrible than Magoth?"

"Magoth is a Herald of even greater powers than itself, young man, and some of those powers are rivals of those worshipped by the Ualissi. *That* is why they aid you. Oh, don't deny it. You were seen near their quarter. Which must mean that's where Vassas is holed up. He wanted me to believe he was gone when all along he was gathering his forces here, waiting and plotting, readying himself to pounce."

"You're wrong. I was merely visiting the cemetery. My ... I have family there."

"Don't we all? But no, that's not why. That's not all of it. *Vassas* is here." Grund tapped his bony chin. "But if you don't return, he'll know I know, and he'll either slip away for real or else he'll dig in for a fight. I could win it, oh yes, even with his pet monstrosities. But I don't want a fight, not at this time. The time of Magoth's ascension is so close ... All we need is the Formula. And I would rather acquire it by stealth than force. I would not weaken myself right before the good part happens. I must go into this new world strong, a true force to be reckoned with."

Tavlin shifted uneasily. "You won't get anything out of me."

Grund grinned, and again it was mirthless, or if there was any humor in it, it was especially grim. He beckoned toward the floor, and the man holding the lantern bent forward. At first Tavlin didn't know what they were trying to show him, but then he saw it and had to suppress a gasp. Blood stains *covered* the floor. From one side to the other, and in many groupings, some fresh, some old, they decorated the floorboards as far as Tavlin could see.

"You've been busy," he said, shocked at how steady his voice was.

"Indeed," said Grund, and there was a certain satisfaction in the word. "And in my time of, as you say, busyness—in that time, do you know how often I've heard some version of *You won't get anything out of me*?" He grinned, widely, and this time there was humor in it. But when it reached his eyes, it was transformed into something hideous. "As many times as there are bloodstains."

Tavlin tried to speak but couldn't. An iceberg of fear lodged in his brain and blocked out all rational thought.

Slowly, Grund said, "I think we can avoid that now. You have no information I need. Vassas is here. He can't have many men with him, but he has allies, and he's had weeks to fortify his position, assuming he hasn't escaped Muscud and then returned, which I do assume. No, he's been here the whole time, hasn't he? And … he's expecting you back."

Tavlin made himself swallow. "You plan to release me?"

Grund's scaly eyebrows rose. "*Release* is an interesting word, but perhaps not accurate. *Unleash* might be better."

Tavlin made himself stand firm. "I won't betray Vassas." Instantly he winced; he'd just revealed that the Boss was in fact in Muscud.

As if understanding this, Grund smiled, but it was his thinnest yet. His face bunched like wet paper when it moved, sliding over fragile, twisted bone. Tavlin half feared it might catch on a snag and rip, and he half hoped it would happen. The bastard deserved it.

"You value the girl's life," Grund said. "Or woman, I should say. And her continued wellbeing." He paused again, allowing Tavlin to digest his exact meaning; it wasn't rocket science. "Well, I have something you want, and you can get access to something I want."

"The canister." Tavlin nodded. "Did Havictus put you up to this?"

"Oh, we plotted it out together, rest assured. We're partners in this venture, along with the Church of Magoth. To use an Octunggen analogy, we're the three prongs of a trident. But that doesn't matter now. What matters is retrieving the canister. As you're the one who stole it originally, or rather massacred a bunch of people to lay your grubby hands on it, you should be the one to bring it back to us."

"And then you'll let Sophia go?"

"Is that her name? Then yes."

"How can I trust you?"

Grund spread his hands, oddly large and muscular for his shrunken form. But then his arms would be strong, too, and his chest. He liked to wheel himself about, disdaining help from his lackeys. He was no invalid, but merely different, likely more at home in the water than on land. "What choice have you? And know that I would have no motive for hurting her, not if I didn't need to. And if I reneged on the bargain, it would look bad in front of my people." He nodded to his men. "*They're* your insurance, Tavlin Two-Bit. I'll let her go so my word is still good for my men."

Tavlin wanted to run a hand through his sweaty hair, but his hands were still bound. He had kept them that way on purpose.

"Well?" Grund demanded. "What do you say? Will you do it?"

Tavlin forced himself to look the old man in the eye. This had to look convincing. "And what about me? Afterward? Will you just let me go, too?"

"Havictus would like to get his hands on you, I have no doubt. You killed several of his people and have made life unduly difficult for him by stealing that briefcase. I believe he was uneasy when you were with the worshippers of Magoth—he wanted the Lady to give you up to him. She refused. She said you were one of *them* now." He snorted. "More fool her. Havictus should have killed you long ago. But if I told you that I would give you to him afterward, that wouldn't provide much motivation for you, would it? And we've already established that if I promise something, I must deliver. And I'm sure he would much rather have the Formula than you. So … yes. Very well, you cunning little thing. Once the canister is in my possession, I will release you and your woman, and I will wish you well on your way." His voice hardened. His eyes gleamed. "So? What is your decision?"

Chapter 15

Shortly after Grund left, two men came for Tavlin, almost as large as those who'd been escorting the boss, and one said, "Come on, then, you. We're to escort you to the Ualissi quarter."

"Thoughtful of you," Tavlin said, and leapt up sprightly from where he had been reclining against the wall, or as sprightly as he could with his hands behind his back. "I was in the mood for a stroll."

"Check his cuffs," the first one said, and the other tugged at the silver links encircling Tavlin's wrists. Satisfied, he grunted. The first one led the way out while the second shoved Tavlin forward, across the threshold and down the corridor.

"Where we goin'?" the one in back asked. "This isn't the way to the main entrance."

"Boss said to take him out the side. In case Vassas's got people watching."

"Smart. He probably does."

For a wild moment, Tavlin panicked. If the dumb bastard stayed directly behind him, there was no way he could employ the cuff key he'd liberated earlier. He wouldn't be able to escape and all would be lost. *Do something*, he thought. *Fix it.* Once upon a time he'd been Vassas's fix-it man, and it seemed he still was after a fashion. He could do this. His years of desperate and self-destructive living in the surface world hadn't completely dulled him. Had it?

Feeling sweat bead his hair, he slowed his pace.

"Faster, damn you," the man behind him grumbled, shoving him forward.

Tavlin feigned a limp. "I'm sorry, but I've hurt my leg. This is as fast as I can—"

The goon was having none of it. Coming abreast of Tavlin, he grabbed Tavlin by the arm and hauled him forward. Tavlin pretended to trip and stumble, just to maintain the ruse, but the man dragged him along, keeping him up by main strength. As the man's jacket flapped open, Tavlin saw a large knife and a revolver at his waist. Each rested in a separate leather sheath. The man himself was fish-like, with gray stubble trying to force its way out between the scales on his face.

Tavlin shook the key out of his sleeve and into his palm. He jammed it into the hole and twisted. One cuff snapped open.

His first instinct was to pounce, *now*, while he could, but there was too much activity here. People regularly passed them coming the other way. *Wait*, he cautioned himself.

They descended a stairway, then made their way down a deserted-looking hallway. Now. It had to be now. The first goon was still in the lead, with the second one jerking Tavlin along, the man's jacket flapping open as they walked.

Tavlin's hand whipped out, lightning-quick. Cheating at cards for the last few years had done nothing to diminish his skills. A leather strap anchored by a silver button bound the knife's crosspiece to the sheath. Tavlin flicked the button, wrenched the knife loose and plunged it into the man's kidney. The man cried out and slumped against the wall, clawing at his back. Blood cascaded down his legs.

The first man wheeled about, one hand flying to the butt of his own revolver. Tavlin stabbed him in the belly. The hand stopped, held rigid by pain.

Tavlin started to yank the blade loose and slash the fellow's throat with it, but he hesitated. Too much blood would attract attention. Instead he removed the man's revolver, avoiding the dying fellow's clumsily groping hands, and struck him over the head with its butt. The man sank to his knees but didn't pass out. Tavlin hit him again. The man fell backward, eyes closing.

"Fucker," hissed the second man.

Tavlin spun. The man had his gun out, but his hand—only one hand; the other was pressed over the knife wound along his back—shook too badly for him to aim.

Tavlin shoved the gun's barrel to the side. Before it could roar, he smashed the man over the head with the by-now bloody gun butt. The man groaned and crumpled, either dead or unconscious. Blood dripped from the gun butt, hair matted to it.

Tavlin gasped, drawing in deep breaths. Sweat burned his eyes. He glanced both ways down the corridor. Clear.

He found an unlocked door, poked his head inside to make sure the room on the other side was empty, then dragged one thug in, then another, trying to avoid leaving trails of blood.

"I'm so sorry," he said to the men once they were in the room and lying lifelessly on the floor, blood pooling around them. "You were bastards, but I wish there had been another way."

He removed the holster belt from the first man, put it around his own waist, then shoved the knife and pistol through it, wiping off the knife first.

He quit the room, locking it behind him, and surveyed the scene of combat. There was a little blood from the first thrust, but most of it had fallen on the man's clothes or spurted onto the back inside of his jacket when the knife had come out. No one would be likely to notice a little smear of blood, especially not in this building, not now, and so what if they did? By that time, Tavlin would be well away, and with Sophia.

Which direction had they taken her? He tried to recall which way Grund's female lieutenant had indicated, but Tavlin had been turned this way and that since arriving here, and he wasn't a hundred percent certain.

That way, he thought. *I think she said that way.*

He found a cross-hall that led in the general desired direction and started down it. His heart hammered thunderously beneath his ribs, and sweat ran in molten rivers from his armpits. He thought he must reek of it—that and fear. His legs trembled, and so did his fingers, just as they sometimes did before pulling a card switch. They always straightened out in time, though—at least, that's what he told himself.

He tried to ignore all the times he'd gotten caught. But that hadn't been entirely by accident now, had it?

No. Sophia had been right about that much.

That me is over, he thought as he pushed down another corridor. *I'm a new man.* And it was true. If anything positive could be said to have happened over the last few weeks, it was this: he had learned to love life again. Life, in all its tangible, dirty, gritty, squelchy, oozy, wonderfulness. He *loved* it. He could wrap it in his hands and squeeze it like mud his whole life through and never get sick of it. He was on *fire* with living.

Which is why, he was sure, the rug was about to be pulled out from under him. It was the way these things always worked. At least for him.

But not Sophia.

She, he vowed, would come out of this thing alive, even if he had to die to see it done.

Several men and one woman came down the hall in his direction. He wanted to flinch down a side hall, but that would look suspicious. He continued forward, keeping his face slightly down, and the group passed on his left. He waited for one to call out, *Hey, you, stop!,* but none did, and when he came to the next intersection he turned right, out of their line of sight. Immediately he turned left again.

He found himself in the mansion's lobby. People moved in all directions, coming up the stairway and down, from one of the halls or out through the grand front doors. Tavlin paused. What now? He had no way of knowing where Sophia had been headed, only that she had been taken into the opposite wing. He didn't even know on what floor she was on. If he could find someone who could tell him where she was, that would be most helpful. His gaze landed on the female lieutenant, now occupying the stairway landing like it was some sort of throne with its view out over the room and giving orders to one person, or small group, at a time. She was a matronly woman in her forties covered by brilliant striations, shading from purple to green to orange, like a fish glinting in a coral reef. For that alone, she was beautiful, even if she was molting.

Face down, Tavlin picked his way up the carpeted stairway to her. Two men stomped past him, going down, and he avoided eye contact. He reached the landing and paused. The lieutenant was in conversation with two women. When the pair nodded and moved off, leaving the lieutenant unoccupied for a brief moment, Tavlin knew he didn't have much time. He started forward immediately.

Her eyes met his and widened. "You—"

He shoved the gun against his pocket so that she could see it. To prove it wasn't his finger, he cocked it, and the click was audible even over the noise of the room.

Her eyes narrowed. "You dare do this *here*?"

"You're coming with me."

"*Idiot.* You should have let be done what would have been done. It would have gone easier for you."

"You're to lead me to Sophia, the woman I was brought here with."

The lieutenant paused. She had heavy jowls and wore thick-rimmed glasses, but still she was beautiful. "You have more character than I suspected. Still, I cannot take you to her."

"Then die right here. No, don't say it. I'll die, too. I know. But I'm prepared for that." He let her examine his eyes to see if he was telling the truth, and when he saw that she saw it, he added, "Are you?"

"Very well. Come this way."

She marched up the stairs, then turned left down the wing Tavlin had remembered Sophia going in. A man detached himself from the wall to follow her—a bodyguard, apparently—but she waved him off. She and Tavlin passed into the corridor alone. He swiveled his head once to see if anyone else was following them, but when he glanced forward he could see the woman tensing her body for a strike—or perhaps she had a gun stashed away—and he said, "Don't even think about it."

"You won't get away with this."

"We'll see."

"Boss Grund will destroy Vassas, and all who oppose him will suffer. You're only damning yourself by this foolishness. Surrender now and I can make it so that this never happened."

And the two men I killed? Can you undo their deaths? "Just keep going."

She moved down the length of the wing, turning once at a cross-hall. As she turned, two men passed going the other way, and they nodded respectfully to her. She nodded back. She started to speak, caught Tavlin's eye and kept going.

At the end of the hall she opened the door with a key. As it swung inward, she said, "I'll leave you now."

Tavlin half smiled. "I don't think so."

"You don't think I'd really step foot inside that room, do you? I might never step back out again."

There was no one coming. Tavlin removed the pistol so that she could see the blackness of the barrel pointed straight at her belly—a slow, painful death. "If you don't go in, you'll never step anywhere again."

Her face ticced in rage. With deliberate slowness, she stepped across the threshold, then paused.

"Keep going," he said.

She obeyed, and he followed her into the room, kicking the door shut behind him. Just as he did, she spun. One hand knocked the gun away while the other dove inside her jacket and started to pull out a snub-nosed revolver. Before it could, he grabbed her wrist with his left arm and seized it. She punched him across the jaw with her free hand, and he crashed against the door. Sparks flared in his vision.

He started to bring the gun back around, half blind, but she grabbed that wrist and forced the hand back. He'd let go of her wrist, and now she did pull out the gun. Before she could aim it, he batted her arm aside. She punched him again, right on the jaw, and his head popped against the door. He tasted blood in his mouth. She was strong.

He kneed her in the crotch. She grunted.

When she had punched him, she'd had to let go of his gun hand, and now both their guns swiveled around to point at each other's heads. Panting, they glared at each other.

"Bastard," she said.

"Bitch." He spat blood from his mouth.

He stepped forward. She stepped back. Nervously, she glanced over her shoulder, probably expecting Sophia to leap at her back. Tavlin used her distraction to wrench her pistol out of her hand with his free hand and then to club her over the side of the head with his gun butt. She tottered, then fell sideways to the floor. He stuffed both guns in his jacket and stepped over her unconscious form to the large bed, where Sophia was handcuffed to one of the four posts. The lieutenant had been right to be afraid. Sophia had stretched herself to her limit in an effort to be able to use her legs against the woman, but the lieutenant had been too far away for her to do any good.

"Tavlin!" Tears sprang to Sophia's eyes.

He wrapped her in his arms and kissed her. Almost to his surprise, she kissed back.

"You're alive," he said. "I was so worried."

"Please, Tav, get me out of here."

He removed the cuff key and freed her in a moment. They had removed her make-up and Izcai priest get-up, and she was dressed in only a silken shift, which she tore off without seeming embarrassment. Nude, she crossed to a cabinet, pulled out the clothes she'd been brought in with and yanked them on. Tavlin dutifully turned away while she worked, but he could see her reflection in the metallic frame of a painting. She looked as good as he remembered.

"You can look now," she said.

He turned. "Why were you dressed that way? They didn't . . . ?"

"No, but they were going to." Angrily, she kicked the lower back of the lieutenant, who didn't stir. "*She* told me so herself. Three men were going to have me at once. I thought it was them coming when I heard the door."

"That means Grund never meant to uphold his promise at all."

"I don't know what sort of deal you made with him, but no, I'd guess not. What sort of deal *was* it?" Her tone was almost accusing.

"Don't worry. I double-crossed him first. But if there are three men coming, we'd better be on our way. I don't think I could take on all three without some gunfire, and if I have to use one of these things—" he tapped the guns "—we're dead."

"Speaking of which." She held out a hand expectantly.

He passed her one of the weapons, and she promptly made it disappear.

"Remember," he said. "Don't—"

"I know, I know. Only in an emergency. Now let's get out of here. Oh, but first ..."

They dragged the lieutenant to the bed, handcuffed her hands to either side of a post and gagged her with a pillowcase, then moved to the door.

"Serves her right if they take her instead of me," Sophia said. Then her face fell, and he saw the anger go out of it, replaced by fear. He was just about to open the door when she swung him back and, to his surprise, kissed him again on the lips. The hairs rose on the back of his neck.

"Thank you," she whispered.

"You're ..." He blinked. "You're welcome."

They moved out into the hall. Noises came from around them. Tavlin had been so preoccupied on the way here he'd barely noticed them, but now he recognized grunts and groans, the creaks of beds, and, once, the crack of a whip. He ground his teeth and saw Sophia tensing beside him.

Tavlin constantly expected three men to pass them going the other way, but so far so good. Once a solitary man did pass them, but Tavlin and Sophia kept their faces lowered and the man was too excited about the pleasures ahead of him to examine the two.

When they reached a cross-hall, Sophia said, "This way. There's a stairway going down, and a side door leads out. I saw it coming up."

"You can go that way if you want. In fact, you probably should. But I've got other business."

"The black jewel?" She swore. "After all this, I'd kind of hoped you'd forgotten about that. I was almost *raped*, Tavlin." The faintest suggestion of tears touched her eyes again, and for the first time he realized how ragged she looked, how on edge.

He released a breath. "I know. I know, Soph. I'm so sorry. Please, go on. I never wanted you to endanger yourself by coming in the first place."

"I'm coming with you."

"Please, don't."

"Are you going to stand here arguing with me or are you going to get the damned jewel?"

He saw by the set of her face that there was no point in arguing. Either because she didn't trust him to do it himself or because she wanted to keep him safe, she was coming.

"Fine, damnit," he said.

They continued on, coming to the grand foyer with its huge, heavy staircase. There seemed to be some slight commotion going on, with Grund's people buzzing about, going in and out of the various halls, often stopping to talk to each other.

"They're looking for her," Sophia whispered, meaning the lieutenant.

Heads lowered, the two made their way back across the upper level of the foyer and into the opposite wing once more. They made a turn, coming upon a quieter stretch of the mansion, and Tavlin recognized the door he'd earlier heard the voices from. There were no guards in front of it now, which meant it must be unoccupied.

"This is the study, I think," he whispered. "It's where the Mayor would've kept the jewel, I'm sure, to show it off for his visitors."

He knelt beside the lock and proceeded to pick it with the hair pin he'd lifted off the lieutenant. At one point a pack of Grund's men rounded the bend and Sophia whispered a warning. Tavlin was able to straighten up in time, and he and Sophia marched down the corridor, heads lowered, passing the enforcers, then doubled back when the men were gone.

"Whew," Tavlin said, kneeling before the lock again. "I'm glad you came along after all."

"Don't forget it." But her words were not spoken in the cavalier manner she no doubt intended. They came out tight and clipped, tinged with fear. He felt it too, a sick ball twisting in his gut. This could all go wrong, horribly wrong, any moment. He remembered the blood stains on the floor of the interrogation room. And that was what happened to people who *hadn't* pissed Grund off. And if Havictus became involved in the torture …

The lock clicked, and Tavlin pushed the door open. He and Sophia slipped inside just as another patrol rounded the bend coming from the direction of the foyer. Sophia closed the door gently behind them.

The footsteps of Grund's men sounded louder, increased … increased, coming closer …

Tavlin and Sophia held hands and didn't breathe.

The enemy drew abreast of the door, seemed to pause, and Tavlin thought his heart would stop, but that was probably his imagination. The footsteps continued, then faded. The men were gone.

Tavlin breathed out. Sophia disengaged her hand from his, but she didn't do it swiftly, as if his touch were distasteful, and that encouraged him.

"I really am glad you're here," he said, quietly.

"I'm not."

"I mean, with me."

She returned his gaze, and he was heartened by what he saw there. Softly, she said, "Let's just get this over with, Tav."

He nodded. The study wasn't so much one room as a small suite of rooms, complete with a small office for a secretary, then a storage room for various files, then the opulent study proper, with a huge desk and many bookshelves lined by precious trophies, with a small private bathroom off to the side. The lights were off, and Tavlin stubbed his toe and barked his shin as he searched, but there was enough light coming in from the large window behind the desk and the smaller one in the bathroom that he and Sophia could see by, if barely. They groped and fumbled, searching Mayor Jensen's desk and various shelves. He had many knickknacks, most of which seemed expensive.

"Here," she said. She was standing before one of the bookshelves. Before her was a large, rugged black jewel glimmering with odd highlights and mounted on a mahogany stand apparently carved just for it.

Tavlin joined her. "It's …"

"I know.

He could feel the thing's power, a sort of hum. It emanated from the jewel in slow, steady waves. How could Jensen sit behind the desk, *right across* from it, and not feel the thing's unwholesome, pulsing energy?

Tavlin reached out a hand for it, felt his skin prickle when it drew close, then found a cigar box, dumped out the cigars (regretting the necessity of it; they seemed like fine specimens) and scooped up the jewel into the box. That done, he stuffed it into his jacket pocket.

"Okay, let's—" he began, but cut off when more footsteps sounded.

The door jingled as a key was inserted. He and Sophia tensed. The doorknob turned.

"Quickly," she whispered, and drew Tavlin into the Mayor's private bathroom. He closed the door behind them.

"… and if he gets the canister, you'll get it," came Havictus's bass rumble.

Grund responded, his voice testy: "Damn you, I'd better get that shipment *today.* I need those weapons, you bastard. You've been promising them to me for too long. That one light-bomb was not enough. I've got Vassas here in town now plotting to unseat me. With those toys of yours—"

"Yes, and you'll *get* them." Havictus's voice was hard. Tavlin glanced to Sophia. Her face had drawn tight and was as pale as a moon.

Gently, she eased open the bathroom window, directly above the sink. The motion caught Tavlin by surprise, but he recovered. *She's fast on her feet.* Again he was glad she'd come along. He gestured for Sophia to climb onto the sink and ease herself out first, and she nodded, accepting his graciousness.

Havictus was saying, "… only after you deliver the canister."

"And if Vassas catches on? If he nails that Two-Bit character before he can get the canister back for you, you'll just let me hang? I'm telling you, you jackbooted son of a bitch, if you betray me—"

Havictus's voice was a snarl: "Fine. You want the weapons, you can have them."

Sophia swung herself out of the window, hanging on to its lip with her fingertips. Tavlin, wincing at the slight noise it made, climbed onto the sink, having to duck his head or else knock it against the ceiling, a potentially fatal mistake. He stuck a leg out the window, crouching to take his weight, then shimmied out. Sophia moved aside, giving him room.

"I'll present them to you tomorrow, canister or no canister," came Havictus's voice from the other side of the door. "But if do that, it means you must *use* them. You must hit Vassas yourself, tomorrow, as soon as you've taken possession of the arms. And if you don't have the canister by that time, you will retrieve it from his corpse. Do we have a deal?"

There was a long pause. "We have a deal. Now about . . ."

Tavlin and Sophia climbed down the ivy-overgrown mansion, using the many vines and loose bricks as handholds, and finally dropped to the floor, directly before one of the doors.

A pair of sentries armed with submachine guns stared at them.

"Just having a little fun," Tavlin told them.

The sentries exchanged a glance. Tavlin frowned when he saw that one of them looked familiar—it was one of the two goons who'd originally taken him to the interrogation room. He only relaxed slightly when the man's expression didn't change.

"Have a good night," the man said, as if people climbing about on buildings was not uncommon, and perhaps for him it wasn't.

Tavlin and Sophia were moving up the street when a shout sounded behind them. Tavlin whirled to see the guards sprinting toward them, guns swinging around.

"It's him!" the guard said. "It's that card-player, I recognize him."

"Great," sighed Sophia.

"Stop right there, you bastards! Stop or die!"

"Run!" Tavlin said.

Chapter 16

They ran.

Gunfire cracked the night behind them, and scavenger flails shrieked and spun above, spraying mucus. Bullets punched out a window right beside Tavlin, and shards of glass sliced his right arm through his jacket. On his left, Sophia cried out and ducked against him. They ran on, coming to an intersection and darting down an alley.

"Stop!" came the cry of the guard again. "Stop, you fuck!"

Tavlin turned, pulling his gun and loosing one round at the pursuers, then two more. The guards crouched but remained standing, and the bullets didn't appear to discomfit them. One guard's gun cracked, and a searing pain came from the side of Tavlin's leg. Something hummed by his ear. Beside him Sophia fired behind them, but he wasn't sure if she struck anything.

They ducked down an alley. Before the metal hail could resume, they took the next turn and then the next. The alleys grew strange and exotic around them, and lilting music flooded the narrow passageways, which were bright with gold and purple glimmering under the light of red alchemical lanterns. Images of brightly colored lizards decorated many shop fronts, and before the rear entrances of some lounged the grand lizards themselves, a few more than ten feet long, and all bound by chains set in iron hoops beside the doorsteps of their shops. Two guards manned each of these entrances, occasionally feeding the huge lizards, which were kept against the walls. People in bright orange and teal clothes bustled through the networks redolent with garlic and strange spices.

"The Izcai Quarter," Tavlin said, needlessly. "I used to have friends here."

"Do you still?"

"No, they were gone years ago. But …"

"Yes?"

"On the other side of this quarter is the library, and I have a friend there."

"Will he be happy to see us?"

The pain in his leg was diminishing; the bullet had only grazed him. "I guess we'll have to see. They could be on us again at any moment."

She seemed to sense he was holding something back. "Is that the only reason you want to go there?"

"No," he admitted. "I want answers. I went to the library before all this started, but back then I didn't know what to look for. Now that I know to investigate the gods of the G'zai, I've got a starting point. A thread to unravel. Maybe Guyan will have some other ideas if I let him in on the truth."

The two pressed through the bright throng, still bustling even at this hour. Red alchemical lamps blazed from the street corners, painting all the gold crimson, a sunset splendor that came alive to the sound of the reedy, melodious music. Alchemical smoke teased at Tavlin's nose, and he longed for his pipe. Finally they passed out of this quarter and into a quieter section, in the center of which was Lovell Blvd., where the library was. No one responded to Tavlin's knocking, so he opened the door and stepped inside, then immediately recoiled when a gun fired and a bullet punched into the wooden wall over his head, showering splinters. Something hot ran down his neck.

"Stop right there!" a voice cried.

Tavlin squinted through the darkened air of the library—the lights had been doused—to see a hulking form behind the main counter, rifle gripped in hand.

"Guyan?" he said.

There came a pause. "Two-Bit, is that you? Come in, you crazy bastard!"

"Can you put the gun down first?"

"What? Oh—" Guyan set the rifle down on the counter.

Tavlin beckoned for Sophia to come inside, and, hesitantly, she did so, her eyes wide. The chamber still smelled of gun smoke.

"What's all this about?" Tavlin said. He threaded his way between piles of books as he made his way toward the counter, and as he did he could see guns and ammunition behind the piles, as if they were fortifications in some war. A pair of mutants hunkered behind one mound, apparently friends or employees of Guyan. Both gripped weapons, one a beaten-up looking pistol and one a sawed-off shotgun. Tavlin was glad that one wasn't the nervous type.

"It's the damned cultists," Guyan said. "The worshippers of Magoth. They came in last week demanding that I hand over certain books about their god. I'd forgotten there was even mention of the thing in some of my tomes, but apparently a few of my former patrons, now converts, had found those passages some time ago and remembered them. They told their new masters about them, and the faithful didn't like me havin' books about Magoth that weren't worshipful. Afraid I might spread discontent or something. Well, you know I don't take that shit lightly."

Indeed, Tavlin remembered Guyan telling him about little wars fought between the libraries down here. In the sewers, information was precious and hard won, and there were some, like Guyan, who would die to defend it—and others who would kill for it.

"Did anyone die?" he said.

"Two on their side, none on ours. They didn't think I'd fight back. Fools. But next time I expect it will go harder for us, so I've prepared, as best I can. And until it's over, one way or the other, I've closed up shop."

Tavlin surveyed the dark room with its papery barricades and three stalwart defenders. "You can't hold out against them, you know," he said. "Not for long."

"Not to mention," Sophia said, "that any battle you fight here will only damage the books you're fighting for."

"You think that hasn't occurred to me?" Guyan said, sounding testy. "But what choice is there—let the bastards run me over? Run the *truth* over? Hide and bury it and twist it?"

Tavlin tilted his head. "What *is* the truth? Guyan, have you discovered some insight into Magoth? That's one reason I came here—to find out what it *is*."

Guyan shared a look with one of his compatriots, and that fellow glanced away, appearing troubled and unhappy. Guyan passed a web-fingered hand across his face.

"Maybe," he said. "There's references to it in a few places, all in the books I have on religions of the pre-human races."

"I'd like to know, if you'll share."

"I will. It's why I'm doing this, to keep that knowledge available. But some of it …" Guyan looked pale. "Some of it might drive a person mad."

"You don't look mad."

Guyan's eyes were dead. "It's eatin' at me, Tavlin. It's …" One of his hands fluttered at the back of his skull. "It's rattling around. *Burrowing*. I'm trying to fight it, to not think about it, but … it's difficult, Two-Bit."

"I'll take my chances. First things first, though." Tavlin moved to one of the windows. They'd all been painted over, but he could still see out the corner of one. There was no sign of their pursuers or of anyone else in the House of Grund that may have been roused to the hunt.

"Anything?" Sophia said. She'd half-raised her gun to aim at the door. When Tavlin shook his head, she lowered it, but not all the way. Still, she approached him and hugged him with one arm. "We're safe," she breathed into his ear.

He wanted to believe the intimacy meant something more than mere relief, but he knew it didn't. "For now," he said.

"I guess you two didn't come just to check out a book," Guyan said. "You said there was another reason."

"Yeah. Grund's after us. I don't think they tracked us this far, but I won't lie to you—it's possible. We need a place to lie low until the heat's died down, then—well." He didn't want to mention Vassas's presence, since that seemed disloyal, but Grund already knew, so the proverbial cat was out of the bag. "Then we can return to Vassas."

"He's still in town? He's crazier than I thought."

"Maybe. But if we can reach him, I think I can see a way to end this whole mess—stop both Octung's agenda here and Grund."

Sophia's voice contained a strange note: "I want to know more about Magoth. Its worshippers might be the real enemy."

Tavlin nodded. "Guyan, do you mind telling us what you know?"

The librarian let out a weary sigh, but it was not exhaustion that made the sound quaver. He pointed to the rickety upstairs portion of the library. "That's where the books in question are, under lock and key. One of you, come with me. That place will only support the weight of two. Tavlin, you're the one I know. I'd rather it be you."

"That's fine," Sophia said. "I'll stand watch down here." She knelt behind a pile of books as far from the entrance as she could and took up the rifle leaning there. She hadn't known much about guns when she and Tavlin had been together, and he was surprised to see her check the loading chamber with the competence of an expert. In a more subdued voice, she said, "I can listen from here, anyway."

* * *

Guyan blew off a plume of dust and creaked one of the volumes open. It was an ancient affair bound in what Tavlin hoped was leather, and the librarian had just removed it from the small safe beside the listing table around which the two sat. An alchemical lantern set on low cast an undulating orange glow on the age-darkened and toothed pages.

"'A History of the Pre-Human Races in Urslin After the Disappearance of the Ygrith'," Guyan read, then thumbed through the pages carefully. "There are only a few copies of this book left, and few are in better condition. Its contents were partially compiled from histories left by the pre-human races themselves, some of whom are extinct or otherwise vanished, like the fabled Ygrith, worshipped by many races—the Iuss'ha, for example—as terrible gods themselves. Perhaps they were. All evidence indicates that they were powerful beings beyond our ability to understand—that or they never existed at all and are mere mythology of the old races."

"What about Magoth?" Tavlin said. Once more he itched for his new pipe and alchemically enhanced tobacco.

"Patience," Guyan said.

From outside came the lilting music of the Izcain; they were gearing up for one of their exotic revels. It seemed like once a month their little community would buzz with excitement and activity, at least back when Tavlin lived here, and several times a year that excitement would spill over into greater Muscud, and parades and floats would follow. Tavlin pictured Grund's minions slipping their way through the confusion outside, drawing ever closer to the library. Would they be able to find Tavlin and Sophia here? Would they search the library?

"I'm short on patience at the moment," Tavlin said regretfully.

Guyan nodded understanding. He delicately lifted another page, then said, "Here it is. An account of the Vitriculus—that's as close as I can come to pronouncing it. Most of this book is written in Ancient L'ohen. I can parse it, but it takes a moment for the old gears to catch, if you know what I mean. Anyway, the Vitriculus are all gone now, but they were among those on this world who worship or worshipped a subset of a greater pantheon. The greater pantheon are the deities known as the Outer Lords, dread and terrible titans who wallow in abysses that plunge into greater abysses, deep labyrinths woven into the cosmos, and their merest twinge can rattle an entire galaxy like the thread of a spider's web. Calling them titans does them a disservice, since they're like nothing we could comprehend, but it gets across their vastness, at least in part. They exist across dimensions and various planes of existence."

Tavlin felt his mouth go dry. "You … believe in these things?"

Slowly, Guyan nodded. "Honestly, I'd forgotten I had these books until the cultists reminded me. But it's all come back to me now. I read them long, long ago, and I must have purposefully blocked them from my memory. I can remember it now, though, becoming obsessed with these passages, with tracking down pieces of lore, even artifacts, mentioned here and there in the manuscripts. Some of the tomes were written by pre-humans and are like nothing you've ever seen before. I scoured them and the like for information on the Outer Lords. I'm not sure if I wanted to confirm their existence or find proof, to save my sanity, that they *don't* exist. In the end I found just enough to indicate that they did exist. After that I stopped looking and tried to forget it. I didn't want that indication to turn into actual proof."

The music grew louder outside—perhaps a parade was beginning—but to Tavlin it seemed to come as from another world. "So … you were saying."

Guyan had thoughtfully brought along two bottles of ale, and he popped the top of his and downed a long sip. Tavlin did the same.

"The Vitriculus worshipped a subset of the Outer Lords, a subset whose unholy, loathsome matriarch is the arch-goddess Metiphrosis, whose notorious diadem bears jewels fashioned of poisoned nebulas. The Vitriculus did not dare worship Metiphrosis directly, so they worshipped her chief Herald, so feared by the priests of the Gaddi that they severed their own tongues lest he hear their prayers, so feared by the whore queen of Istagranth that she blinded herself lest her eyes befall his graven image in her husband's chapel. The Herald has many names, or none. Oft times he is simply referred to as Magoth."

"Gods."

"Indeed, he is worshipped as a god by many, and may in fact be one. When dealing with actual beings, how does one define 'god'? I confess I don't know. At any rate, the Vitriculus' writings contain many mentions of other worlds and times, and some scholars believe they actually came from another planet. That's certainly what this history suggests." Guyan scanned the page, then turned it and read another. "This passage describes how their civilization spanned many worlds, and at every world they conquered they brought the worship of Magoth. Always their priests and scientists—the two are interchangeable, apparently, at least to my understanding—worked on ways to reach Magoth, to open this cosmos to him. He was separated from it by a barrier of some sort, and they could pass things through to him—sacrifices, prayers, songs, what have you—but he could not reach out to them. And they longed for it."

Guyan slapped his hand on the page, and more dust drifted up. "I've been reading this book and others the last week, and it's clear *how* they longed for it, them and others that paid homage to the dread entity known as Magoth. They were desperate to make real contact with their god and for him, or it, to enfold them in his or its awesome might. But our reality operates by different physical laws than the ones he—I'm going to call it 'he'—hails from, thank all that's good, and he couldn't exist here."

Tavlin absorbed this, then took a long sip. "I sense a *but* coming."

Gravely, Guyan nodded. "But it's possible he could—exist here, that is—if the right spells or science was concocted. And so the Vitriculus tried. And tried. For eons they tried. Until finally the happy day came, and their priests or sorcerers developed the proper equations … or spells … whatever. They had it. They just had to use their new formula to construct a temple using certain materials, configured at just the right angles—crazy, unfathomable angles—and when it was done the space within that temple could correspond to space on another plane … occupied by Magoth."

Tavlin felt the blood drain from his face. "The Formula … *that's* what it is … And the Temple . . . that's what they're trying to do, to bring Magoth over." He knocked back his ale. "I remember . . ."

Guyan leaned forward. "Yes?"

"I tried to tell myself it wasn't a real memory, but . . ."

Sophia was looking up from downstairs. "What is it, Tavlin?"

He swallowed. "In their Great Chamber, there was this . . . thing . . . great and strange, but not entirely connected to our world, not yet . . . They said it was Magoth, or at least some part of him."

Guyan swayed backward. "You *saw* Magoth?"

Tavlin took a long pull on the ale. "Maybe. If that wasn't a delusion."

"You never told me," Sophia said. She spoke softly, but her voice carried.

He only shook his head. "I guess I was trying not to remember. To tell you the truth, I don't remember much, just bits and pieces. Some of it's starting to come back, but others … I can't recall Magoth. I can't picture what he, or it or whatever, looked like. I'm not sure I want to."

Guyan let a long moment pass, then turned another page. "This passage describes the great chaos that befell the Vitriculus once their breakthrough was known to the other races in their quarter of the galaxy, some of them their slave races. When the other races realized that Magoth might be able to cross over, they panicked. If Magoth were to ever touch our plane, he would warp the laws that govern it beyond our ability to survive—at least as we are."

"I don't want to imagine."

"No. You don't." Guyan turned another page. "This passage describes how the other races rose against the Vitriculus and slaughtered them in the millions, in the billions. How they drove that proud race to the edge of extinction. Only a few, concealing their true selves, found refuge on this world. But the Formula that would allow them to bring Magoth over, or part of it, or at least open this plane to him, was gone. Lost."

"Thank the gods … Well, other gods."

Guyan let his gaze bore into Tavlin's. "So the question is, Who is giving them the Formula?"

"'Them'? You mean, the Vitriculus?"

"No, they were finally caught and slaughtered some ten thousand years ago, but they managed to pass their faith on to others already here—that is, if you believe the story that they came from another world in the first place. Many don't."

"But you do."

"Better believe it. Anyway, that faith managed to survive in the darker corners of the world, so it shouldn't be surprising that the sewers are one such bastion."

"I always thought Magoth was just a boogeyman," Tavlin said. "Some thing hiding out there in the darkness between towns."

"Oh, there are things out there, Tavlin, and some of them aren't to be condescended to, but Magoth is of another order of entity entirely. But you're right, its worshippers on this world posed no threat, not until recently." Guyan lit a cigarette but didn't offer one to Tavlin; his supply must be limited. "I've heard that Octung has been exploring archeological sites they believe to possess Ygrithan relics or information about the Ygrith."

"The lost race of gods? So?"

"So the Ygrith and Magoth are, in a roundabout way, allies. They belong to that same subset of the Outer Lords."

"You think the Octunggen believe in Magoth?"

"Damn it, Tavlin, you *saw* Magoth. And if he was visible to the naked eye, that must mean he's very close to crossing over. So no, I don't think *belief* enters into it. It's either a known thing or it's not. And the Octunggen know about this stuff. You don't even want to hear about the rumors I've learned regarding the Collossum, the gods *they* worship."

"And somehow they got their hands on the Formula …"

"That's what it looks like. Either because of their gods, their technology, or their friendship with the old races, it looks like they either developed or secured the lost Formula of the Vitriculus."

"I think they must have developed it. Made it. They had to steal all those jewels first, and their factory …" Tavlin slumped back. "Is this as bad as I think it is?"

Guyan took a drag on his cigarette, then stared at the tip blazing in the dimness of the chamber. "If the worshippers of Magoth finish that temple, our world will end."

"And *that's* what was in the canister—the Formula to finish it?" Tavlin felt ill. "No wonder it gave me nightmares."

Guyan's brow furrowed. "It gets stranger. According to these texts, the Formula, if concocted, will be *alive*."

Slowly, Tavlin said, "So you're telling us, what, that if you poured it into the sewers, it would stay together?"

"Not only that, but it might attack you."

Tavlin suppressed a wave of hysterical laughter. "Attack me?"

Guyan was serious. "Yes."

From the first floor, Sophia spoke up. "Tavlin, they let me take a look at it."

He started. "You saw the Formula?"

"Yes."

"Why not me? *I'm* the one that found it. Or stole it, anyway."

"I asked," she said simply.

He nodded. The truth was that he hadn't wanted to look. But now curiosity filled him. "Well? What did you see?"

A strange light entered her eyes. "It was like … quicksilver. Mercury. And it moved."

Tavlin bit the inside of his lip. "So the Formula's intelligent?"

"I don't know." Her expression was grave. "All I know is it's dangerous. Definitely not something to be let loose. They'll keep it in that canister until it can be killed."

Tavlin patted his pocket over the cigar box containing what he hoped was the salvation of the world. Possibly it was the first time a cigar box had ever been so important.

"It won't be dangerous for much longer," he said. "Not once we get back."

Chapter 17

"We've gotta get out of here," Tavlin said, checking his gun. Three bullets left. He was once more on floor level, Sophia beside him, and they were moving toward the door.

"How do you propose we do it?" she said. "Grund's people are after us, and they know where we're going. They'll have cordoned off the section of the city between the Mayor's Mansion and the Ualissi Quarter by now. By the way—" she spun to Guyan, who was once more taking up his rifle behind the main counter "—the Ualissi. How do they fit into all this? You said they worshipped different gods."

"They worship a subset of the Outer Lords opposed to Metiphrosis and all her brood," Guyan said.

"But the gods of Octung are allies of the Temple of Magoth?"

"Apparently," said Tavlin. "So it's the Octs and the Temple against the Ualissi. The Ualissi aren't actually on our side as much as they are against the people of the Temple. But what about the G'zai?"

Guyan seemed to think. "If I remember correctly, the G'zai worshipped, and perhaps still worship, the Ygrith, making them allies of Octung and the faith of Magoth."

Sophia turned to Tavlin. “We’re just pawns of gods, is that it? This is bullshit. All of it. I don’t care what’s in those books, they can’t be right. Just because some ancient peoples worshipped a thing doesn’t make it real.”

"What I saw in the Great Chamber . . ."

"You were delirious. You don’t even remember it."

"Yes, but what *made* me delirious? Sophia, how else do you explain the Temple and what went on there, other than the existence of Magoth? How do you explain the singing?” He could still hear it, distantly in the background, falling over his eardrums like a silver waterfall, filling him with joy.

“That is no song,” Guyan said. “Not as we understand. He is not *singing* to you.”

“Then what is it?”

“The vibration of reality itself as he grows closer to breaching this sphere—and, yes, it is probably a psychic echo of his thoughts, too, or a resulting manifestation from them.”

Sophia glanced away. “I don’t know what it means. All I know is I don’t *want* to believe. It’s too horrible. If I allow myself to believe in it, I’ll never sleep again. Anyway, how are we going to get out of here? And should we bother? Maybe we should wait till Grund gives up the hunt like we’d originally planned.”

“And what if that’s not till tomorrow or later?” Tavlin said. “By then Havictus will have given him the Octunggen weapons and Grund will have wiped out Boss Vassas and all his men. If Vassas’s people die, so does all hope of stopping the completion of the Temple, because we'll need their strength and numbers to do it. Also, we need Vassas alive to deal with the Ualissi; he does business with them, and they cooperate with him—with us, I don’t know. But we have to get the black jewel to them, and I think it would be better if it were Vassas who handed it over. We have to act tonight.

Now. If we act fast enough, maybe we can slip through Grund's net before it draws too tight."

"I'm afraid he's more cunning than you give him credit for," Guyan said. "He knows how to seize advantage of an opportunity—and how to exploit the weaknesses of his enemies."

"What, then?"

Sophia gestured beyond the door. "The festival. We use the festival to escape. Do you know any Izcain?"

Tavlin shook his head, then raised his eyebrows at Guyan, who let out a reluctant breath.

"I know a few," the librarian admitted.

"Send for them. Ask them for help. You know how urgent it is."

Guyan conferred with one of his confederates in terse whispers, and the man slipped out through the door and was gone. The rest waited, tensely, jumping at blares of Izcain horns outside and swaying, unconsciously, to the sound of the very human, and very lovely, singing being conducted in their parades. Tavlin realized he'd missed the Izcain parades of Muscud. He'd *missed* Muscud. He wouldn't have thought it was possible, but it was true. But the current Muscud wasn't his Muscud. Only when Grund was removed and the church of Magoth burnt and its blackened foundation salted would this be his Muscud again.

Finally, after an hour, the library assistant returned, saying, "He wasn't home, sir. He was participating in the event. But one of his sisters was home, and she knew how to find him."

"And did you?"

"I told him the situation, and he said he would help—for a price." The man named a figure, and Tavlin whistled.

"I hope he doesn't want that in cash."

"You would think saving the world so he could continue to live in it would be enough," Sophia muttered, but the assistant seemed to hear her.

"I didn't get into all that," he said. "He wouldn't have believed it. Anyway, he'll take the assignment on Guyan's word of honor that the amount will be met."

"I don't have that kind of money," the librarian said. "Don't look at me."

Tavlin thought of the riches to be looted from the Mayor's Mansion. "We'll get him his price. What next?"

"I'm to take you to him," said the assistant. "He's in charge of one of the floats, and I think he plans to sneak you under one. When it gets close to the Ualissi Quarter, you slip out and none's the wiser."

"Let's not waste any more time talking about it," Sophia said.

They said farewell to Guyan and followed the library assistant out into the surprisingly crowded streets of Muscud. Others had come out to celebrate, not just the Izcain, drawn by the music and merriness, but there were far fewer of them than there should have been. Colorful if small floats oozed down the narrow streets, drawn by huge, brilliantly mottled lizards by chains aflutter with colored ribbons, and a gay throng pressed in all around, cheering and dancing and drinking the strong spice liquor favored in Izcai. The Izcain (shorter and darker than most Ghenisans) wore their most ostentatious garments, silken robes of gold and turquoise, garlands of golden scales in their hair. Of course, all were infected by the Atomic Sea, but even their mutations were ornamented, with golden baubles trailing from tentacles or jade rings encircling mandibles. Upon the floats beautiful Izcain women sang and strummed lur-harps. Genuine Izcain priests, dressed almost exactly like Sophia and Tavlin had been dressed earlier (Tavlin still sported the robe, though sweat had made most of the make-up run from his face) tossed paper flower petals with religious symbols embossed on them to the crowd, and believers snatched them up eagerly before they hit the ground, where they would lose their luck.

Tavlin and Sophia ducked to avoid being seen by the crowd. He feared every moment that a cry would go up and Grund's men would close on them, but so far so good. After one block, the assistant brought them to a man striding beside a certain float featuring a horned slug head made of clay and painted in garish colors. The man saw the library assistant and, without expression, twitched aside the flap hanging down from the float. As if it was all part of the show, Tavlin and Sophia ducked inside, and immediately Tavlin began to sweat in the close heat. The flap closed behind him.

Tavlin and Sophia glanced at each other, moving to keep pace with the float being drawn by gaily-painted reptiles. The two were now alone.

"Think this will work?" she said.

He gave her a smile with more assurance than he felt. "Sure it will."

The float made a turn, and another, but Tavlin couldn't tell which way they were facing now. The library assistant was long gone, and the float boss presumably still strolled to the side, waving at the crowd and throwing occasional liquor-flavored candy. Tavlin remembered it fondly.

Sweat stung his eyes and pasted his shirt to the small of his back. He realized his arm was brushing against Sophia's. Almost nervously, he glanced sideways to see if she had noticed. She was *just* noticing, evidently, and turning to look at him. Their eyes fixed on each other and held.

They glanced away, but Tavlin could feel a flush creep over his face despite everything. Around them sounded the noises of celebration, but they seemed to come from a million miles away. In here, right now, was a bubble of silence in which he could only hear Sophia's breaths and his own heartbeat. They could have been the only two people in the entire world.

"Sophia," he said, hearing the hitch in his voice.

She didn't answer. Not at first. Finally she said, "Tavlin."

It wasn't much, but it was something.

"That kiss," he said, his mind spinning. "Back at the mansion—"

"It didn't mean anything, Tav."

He winced. "Are you sure?"

She hesitated, and his heart leapt. Just as she opened her mouth to respond, the float boss tapped on the drape. Tavlin and Sophia cautiously looked out to see him waving urgently, and emerged. He pointed down an alley and gave Tavlin a stern look as he edged by—*Don't forget what you owe me*—and then Tavlin was fleeing beside Sophia down the alley. They turned a corner and ran. When there seemed to be no pursuit, they pressed their backs to the grimy wall and panted. Sweat streamed down Tavlin's face. It had been hot in the float, but it was hotter now.

"Are we in the Ualissi Quarter?" he asked.

"I think so. It's quiet."

Indeed, the celebration had not entered this area, and the only territory in the town that would forgo that tradition had to be that of the Ualissi. Tavlin glanced around, noticing the alien construction of the buildings for the first time. Foul fog slithered through the alleys, and through it a strange, gelatinous form drifted. Tavlin and Sophia gasped, but the shape merely slouched across the street and away on its own business.

"I'll never get used to this place," he said. "Come on, let's find Boss Vassas."

They found him in his watery basement lair, asleep at this hour. His guards took a risk and roused him, and he overcame his initial grumpiness to be overjoyed at Tavlin's and Sophia's return. "I didn't think you'd make it back," he said. "I have scouts out looking for you."

"Recall them," Tavlin said. "Oh, and we have a little something to cheer you up."

With no small amount of pride, and a little showmanship, Tavlin withdrew the cigar box from his jacket pocket and placed it on the desk before the Boss. Vassas looked from it to Tavlin, then to Sophia.

Slowly, Vassas said, "You brought me some cigars? I am low."

Tavlin smiled. With a flourish, he opened the box, revealing the glimmering black jewel. Vassas's eyes grew round.

"Is that … ?"

"It is," Tavlin said. "Or at least it had better be. You'd best deliver it to the Ualissi as soon as you can and get them working on creating that compound that can destroy the Formula."

With all due amount of reverence, Vassas lifted the box and gazed at the jewel. Its otherworldly energies, just faintly filtering through its opaque facets, lit his face with an eerie light.

"I will," he said, his voice far away. "I'll get right on it …"

"There's one other thing," Sophia said.

"Yeah?"

To Tavlin, she said, "Tell him."

"We weren't late because we took the scenic route, Boss," Tavlin said. "Grund caught us. We got away free, but we overheard something you should know. The spy Havictus is going to arm Grund with Octunggen weapons sometime tomorrow—and they know you're here. No, I didn't tell them, Grund figured it out himself."

Vassas nodded. "I'm glad you made it out. If they get those weapons, I'm toast. I …" He glared at Tavlin.

"You've been trying to get me to attack the Octunggen factory since you got here. How do I know this isn't some trick to get me to do it now?"

"He's telling the truth," Sophia said. "Grund and Havictus have a deal. I heard them talk."

Vassas studied her, but she didn't give an inch, and he sucked in a breath. "Very well. Then either we flee or attack. There's no third choice."

"We can't flee, Boss," Tavlin said.

"You don't give the orders around here, Tavlin Two-Bit."

"I know, sir. I only meant … if you flee, Grund will grow too strong. You'll never stop running from him. But if you strike now, before he gets those weapons, you can still get your old position back, and he'll be history. Don't you see? You can use the Octunggen weapons *against* him."

"*That* would a lovely thing. Yes, that would be very lovely indeed. Alright, I'm game. But a frontal assault on the factory would be suicide. And I only have a handful of men left against a well-fortified enemy with otherworldly weapons."

"Set the factory on fire," suggested Sophia. "Force the Octunggen outside. I'm sure they'll bring their most valuable items with them, like their strange weapons, and hopefully they'll be too disoriented to use them. Then your people just ambush them like before, in the tunnels."

"Won't work. The factory is stone."

"What if … ?" Tavlin gestured around them. "Well, the Ualissi are beings just as at home, or more at home, in the water, right? And they're our allies."

"So?"

"Well, if the factory is stone, that must mean it has stout pillars holding it up from the cistern floor. Have the Ualissi pull out one of the pillars. The factory will tremble, possibly crack in places. That might be enough to force the

Octunggen out, or it might take another pillar—whatever. Either way, they'll have no choice but to evacuate that factory, and Sophia's right, they'll bring their weapons with them ... right into our hands. Then we use those weapons against Grund."

"That's genius, Two-Bit. You, too, Sophia. I'll set it up. It will take a few hours to organize, though. I'll need to coordinate with both my men and the Ualissi. Hopefully they won't be so distracted by all this that they stop working with this black jewel of yours to kill the Formula. We can't lose sight of the big picture. Anyway, why don't you two get some rest? We attack at dawn."

* * *

Tavlin was given a room to sleep in, moldy and reeking of strange, watery substances, and Sophia was given one across and down. The cot that had been shoved in here, beside two other unoccupied ones, was shaky and of poor wood. Tavlin tried to get comfortable but couldn't. At the back of his mind there was always the singing. He wondered if it would go away when the Temple was destroyed. *If I live that long.* For he fully expected the carpet to be yanked out from under him at any time.

I can cheat it, he thought. *I can cheat anything if I put my mind to it, even death.*

Part of him longed to rise from bed and tiptoe down the hall to Sophia's room, then slide in next to her and wrap his arms about her, feeling her softness against him. He *ached* to do it. He even fancied he could smell the faint floral scent of her hair filling his nostrils. An uncomfortable swelling stirred in his briefs, straining against the cotton.

He held himself back. He remembered her looking away from him beneath the float, remembered the haunted look in her eyes. Whatever that final barrier was, pushing her would not dissolve it. She would have to lower it herself.

Sleep came fitfully.

*   *   *

Mist drifted across the water and over the docks, half enshrouding the factory. Tavlin, Frankie and several others in Vassas's organization crowded the lip of a roof on the other side of the street, waiting for the signal. Even then Ualissi would be getting into position below, attaching their acid-explosives (the acid apparently being secreted from one of their numerous flowers) to the pillars underwater. Tavlin prayed the Octunggen didn't have any of their G'zai keeping watch on the factory underneath—or if they did that the Ualissi were up to the challenge. Sophia had wanted to come along on the ambush, but Vassas had forbidden it. He wanted only veteran warriors along on this mission. Tavlin doubted he qualified, but he couldn't very well sit this one out, and Vassas hadn't forbidden his participation. The Boss was a bit old-fashioned in that respect.

"Think this'll really work?" said Frankie.

Before Tavlin could answer, one corner of the dock peninsula that the factory rose from trembled, then sank to a great snapping sound audible even through the water. White foam billowed out. The factory listed in that direction.

"They did it!" Frankie said. "The Ualissi broke the pillar!"

For a long moment, nothing happened. The factory loomed, impregnable. Gargoyles coiled on the ledges, red gemstone eyes shining. Some said that the Octunggen psychic that had come with the espionage crew could see through those eyes. If so, Tavlin wondered what the psychic saw as yet another pillar was dragged out from under the factory, this time at the other corner of the peninsula, and the factory's back fourth dropped, or one side of it, anyway. Water splashed and foul waves spread out, vanishing in the fog. Wood creaked ominously.

Tavlin tensed. *Now*, he thought. It had to be now.

The front door burst open. An organized phalanx of hardened Octunggen agents rushed out, guns blazing. Tavlin and the others on the roof fired at them with rifles, then ducked for cover as the bullets flew above them. Tavlin heard a bullet whine right above his head, then another.

On street level, gunfire came from a new direction, and the Octunggen gunfire paused, then shifted to answer this new threat, which Tavlin knew to come from around the side of another building. Only then did Tavlin and the others lift themselves up and fire back at the Octunggen. Some of the agents lifted their guns, mostly pistols, to return fire at the roof. Tavlin ducked. Shards of stone flew by his cheek. He rose up, snapped off a shot and saw a man in a suit fall to the ground. Blood spread out from the chest.

The Octunggen, unable to push forward, off the peninsula, edged back toward the open door of the factory. Behind them the structure groaned and was listing ever more precipitously. Tavlin saw two boats slipping off into the darkness and knew they had come from the factory's underside. He wasn't worried. Boss Vassas had three boats out, two men or women to a vessel, with the boss himself leading one. They would stop the boats. Indeed, he heard the first cracks of gunfire in that direction.

Another Octunggen pitched to the docks, then another. Over half had fallen and the others could not advance except into a storm of lead. One of them shouted and they threw down their weapons, then dropped to their knees.

"It worked," Tavlin heard himself say. He could hardly believe it.

The team on the street level closed in to disarm them, and Tavlin's group clattered down the jury-rigged fire escape to assist. Tavlin himself snapped handcuffs around the wrists of several of the captured Octunggen. He searched for Havictus among them, but of the bald man he could see no sign.

A triumphant Boss Vassas led his three boats from the water, and when Tavlin asked how things had gone, Vassas said, "They were well armed. Your bald man was in one of the boats."

"Did you get him?"

"No, damnit. The other boat stayed to slow us down. The four men aboard her gave their lives so Havictus and his two comrades could get lost."

"Hell."

Vassas glanced at the captured Octunggen, who were being searched by his people.

"What are you going to do with them?" Tavlin asked.

"What do you think?" came the sharp answer, and Tavlin sensed that Vassas wasn't any happier about this than he was.

"They're hostages," Tavlin said. "It would be a crime to murder them."

"They're spies and assassins plotting to fuck us all up the ass," Vassas said. "They know this sewer network and they have contacts here. We let them go, they'd just return, and if the cult of Magoth is gone by then they'd just find some other puppets."

"But, Boss—"

To Frankie, Vassas said, "Give the order."

"Wait," Tavlin said. "Wait!"

"Fire," Frankie said, and the gangsters facing the captured Octunggen let loose as the ones who had been searching the prisoners scurried out of the way. Blood flew and expressions of shock and pain registered on the Octunggen's faces before they fixed in death.

"What have you done?" Tavlin said, when the shooting was over and gun smoke drifted in a cloud over the corpses.

"What needed to be done," Vassas said. He surveyed the bodies without pity. "Have them thrown in the water. No ceremony. Hopefully something vile will get them. And gather up all their guns. When that's done, do a sweep of the factory. Bring all of their extradimensional weapons out. Now it's Grund's turn."

Tavlin swallowed. Suddenly he remembered why he had gotten away from this life. He vowed to himself that, if somehow he should live through this present crisis, he would never go back to it again, no matter the temptations.

He flinched when he felt pressure on his palm and looked down to see that a feminine hand had gripped it. Sophia stood beside him. He'd been so preoccupied he hadn't noticed her arrival. Her gaze was sad as it lingered on the Octunggen corpses.

"I had to see what would happen," she said. "It was partly my plan, too. I suppose I should have known this would've been the result, if it was successful. Somehow I didn't see this coming, though." She wiped a tear away impatiently. "I don't know why it makes me sad. I *hate* the Octunggen. They want to take over the world. They're actively attempting to bring over some evil alien god-thing. But …"

"I know. I feel it, too. Death in combat is one thing, but this is another."

"Does that make it worse, I wonder? Or does it just *feel* worse?"

He knew what she meant. Perhaps they couldn't afford things like feelings at a time like this. Now was their moment to ensure survival. They could worry about the rest later.

The two drew back as strange shapes rose from the water. It was only the Ualissi, though, gelatinous and pulsing. They emerged from the foul cistern lake in a line and gathered over the bodies of the Octunggen while one of their number consulted with Vassas privately. Then one and all resubmerged in the dark lake, presumably to return to their quarter underwater. When Tavlin asked Frankie what Vassas and the Ualissi had discussed, the frog-man said, "The Ualissi met resistance down there. The G'zai weren't prepared for the Ualissi, though, and the Ualissi sent them fleeing. For now, anyway. The Ualissi will have to be on guard in case they come back. Boss wanted 'em to help fight Grund, but they said that was his look-out. They'd fulfilled their end of the bargain."

"Bargain?" said Sophia.

"Aye. When all's done, the Ualissi won't be confined to their quarter anymore. They'll have the run of town." He snorted. "Kind of ironic, ain't it? We muties were trapped in our quarter up top, that's why we bailed, at least some of us, but soon as we get our own town we lump the outsiders in *their* quarter. Just goes to show, don't it?"

Tavlin didn't ask what it showed. "How goes the work on making the compound?"

"They're on it," Frankie assured him. "They want the Formula destroyed as much as we do. From what I understand, it won't take 'em long now that they have the black jewel. Good job getting it, by the way."

Frankie went back to overseeing the looting of the factory. Before long all the mobsters were armed with the Octunggen weapons and experimenting with their use—which resulted in one man being liquefied and another vanishing altogether, among other things. Soon the men and women seemed to master the strange weapons, though, and were ready to put them to use against the boss's enemies.

The first step was another ambush. As soon as they heard Grund's motorcycle fleet roaring toward the factory—the news of the battle must have reached Grund—Vassas's people slipped into the alleys, climbed onto the rooftops and took aim, using their mundane weapons this time. No sense wasting extradimensional ammunition when regular bullets would do. As soon as the motorcycles came beneath them, the snipers let loose, Tavlin right there with them. In two long sustained volleys, all of the motorcyclists were slain. Their vehicles slid down the road, raising sparks and knocking against buildings. Luckily the bodies softened the blows to the machines, and when Tavlin descended to the road with the others he found that most of the motorcycles were still operable. Good: the next stage of the operation could take place without deviation. To his annoyance, Sophia insisted on being part of it. After nearly being gang-raped at the Mayor's Mansion, she intended to be there when it was taken and Grund thrown down. Vassas didn't object.

There were about as many motorcycles (plus side-cars) as people left under Vassas's command, so they climbed astride the vehicles, stuffed themselves in the side-cars, and drove hard for the Mayor's Mansion. Tavlin tasted the bad air in his teeth and his eyes misted as the mansion came in sight. A rabble of Grund's men had drawn up heaps of junk, likely taken from dismantled homes, before the house and hunkered behind them as if they were siege barricades, and more lined balconies and the multi-leveled roof. They didn't recognize Vassas's men until too late, masked as they were by their vehicles, but when Vassas roared out, "Now!" and the extradimensional weapons blazed and hissed and oozed, Grund's people returned fire, if too late. Tavlin felt a bullet whiz by his cheek. Another sparked off his handlebars.

Sophia, in the side-car, fired with her bulbous Octunggen weapon, and eerie green light whickered out of it, almost liquid-like, and consumed one of the barricades. It began to melt and the men behind it scrambled for cover. Others cut them down.

Vassas's people, armed with their stolen Octunggen arms, quickly overwhelmed the defenders, who either died, fled, or fell back inside the mansion. Vassas's people pursued, Tavlin and Sophia in their midst, but Tavlin remembered little of it afterward. It was a crazy, chaotic battle, fighting room to room, hall to hall. Walls sagged and doors blackened, and Grund's people melted or froze or flickered out of existence when struck by the Octunggen guns. Tavlin was awed and horrified. Just how had Octung *made* such things? They were far beyond any human technology, beyond even the laws of physics as Tavlin knew them.

At last, when the building was secure and the bed slaves freed and given food and clothes, Vassas summoned his available crew to the cavernous living room on the first floor. There they had nailed Grund's palms to the floor and driven more nails through his fish tail. Blood pooled beneath the writhing mobster, and the flesh around his right eye was darkening.

"Bastards!" he said. "You'll burn in the Jade Hell for this!" He fixed Vassas with the eye he could still see out of. "You motherfucking piece of corroded—"

Vassas aimed a sawed-off shotgun at his face. Grund fell silent.

Addressing the crowd, including the liberated rape victims, Vassas said, "Tell this to all who ask, and they *will* ask about this historic moment—tell them that once someone dared to take away what was mine, and in return they lost their head."

Vassas fired, reducing Grund's head to wet lumps against the floor. His headless body jerked and thrashed, the tail tearing loose of its nails, then fell still.

"Parade it through the streets," Vassas commanded. "Let the Muscudities see what becomes of those who oppose me. If the people of Magoth give you any flack, fire off a few pulses from those guns."

And so it was.

Again, Tavlin felt Sophia's hand in his. Surprised, he looked sideways at her.

"It's starting to end," she said. "The nightmare, I mean. This is the first step on the path to healing this madness."

Unfortunately, only the smallest portion of the nightmare was actually ending. The real danger still loomed, and over a much larger area than just Muscud.

Vassas sent Grund's body out to deliver the message to the people of Muscud that Grund and his gang were gone. Slowly, people started emerging into the streets, amazed. They smiled and shook each other's hands. Some lit strings of firecrackers. Others broke out kegs of ale. Tavlin and Sophia watched it all from one of the mansion's balconies. Vassas had appropriated the building for the moment, though he said he planned to restore it to the town council when he was sure the threat had ended.

Tavlin believed him. He knew the Boss was eager to get back to business as usual. The last thing Vassas wanted was the bureaucracy of running Muscud. He had profit to make.

"Did you remember to send the float boss his payment?" Sophia asked, and Tavlin nodded.

"I made him a gift of the Mayor's gilded bookends. Here, let's go somewhere more private."

She hesitated, then nodded.

* * *

"I'm almost tempted to go down and join them," Sophia said, watching the celebrating townspeople from Tavlin's balcony. He had been given a temporary room.

Tavlin touched her arm. "We can if you want."

She didn't answer. "Do you think they're all right?" she said, nodding to the walls, and he knew she referred to the mayor's daughters, recovering and staying a few rooms down. They were to be given to their aunt in Taluush, which apparently was rebuilding. The town council would then begin restoring the mansion and holding elections.

"They will be soon," Tavlin assured her.

"What happened to their father and mother …"

"Don't think of it." They had learned that Grund had turned Mayor Jensen and his wife over to the priests of Magoth for sacrifice, and that the rituals had been especially gruesome. "It's over, and they have to start new lives, in a new place." He glanced at her meaningfully. "We can *all* start new lives."

She avoided his gaze. "Maybe some can. I can't." Delicately she stepped back from him. "I have to find a job as a nurse somewhere and resume my *old* life. The one you disrupted."

He tried to mask his pain. "If that's what you feel is best."

"I do."

She started to walk away, perhaps to retire to her own room, but sudden feeling made him grab her elbow and spin her back around. Her eyes widened.

"What do you mean—"

"Sophia. I love you. I've always loved you, and I know you love me, too. Why don't we begin fresh like everyone else? Jameson was important to us, but he wouldn't want the weight of his passing to drag us down for the rest of our lives. He would want us to start anew, to begin fresh chapters of our lives. Why not?"

She sniffed. "And where would we live? The surface world? I'd be stared at. I won't go."

His heart swelled. She had just agreed in principle to them getting back together! "Then we'll stay here. Right here."

"Muscud? You must be joking. It's in shambles, and Vassas is an asshole."

"But he's an asshole we know. We can trust him to be Vassas. *We* wouldn't have anything to do with him—I'm out of that line."

She studied him for a long time, and her eyes grew wet. At last she shook her head. "I wish I could, but I can't. I won't let the past go. I won't let Jamie go." She clutched her chest over her heart. "I *love* him! He *means* something to me." Tavlin could see the pain in her face. "We're over, Tavlin. I thought … maybe …" She shook her head again. "But we can't. I see that now."

He still held her arm. She pulled it loose.

"Sophia, please, don't say things like that. You can't live in the past forever. At least you shouldn't."

She marched toward the door and opened it. She was *this close* to leaving his life for good, he could feel it. If she left now, there would be no getting her back.

"Wait!" he called.

Almost to his surprise, she paused, still with her back to him. Again his heart swelled. She *wanted* to be sold, he saw that now. He would just have to make this good.

"Wait," he said again, softer this time.

She turned. She was staring at him with her face unmasked, her emotions naked, perhaps for the first time since his return to the underworld. She wanted to stay but couldn't make herself, or allow herself. Whatever had been between them was broken and unfixable; at least that's what she thought. He had to prove her wrong.

He sank to one knee.

Her mouth started to open, started to form words, but she saw his expression and stopped.

With a suddenly trembling hand, he removed the item he kept in the inner pocket of his jacket. The ring gleamed faintly by the lights of the street outside, and the diamond winked almost mischievously.

"I had this on me the night Frankie found me up top," he said. "I stashed it in my room at the Twirling Skirt when I stayed there, and I retrieved it when I came back."

"Is that … ?"

As if against her will, she closed the door and drifted over. With one hand, she cradled the hand holding the ring and lifted it up toward her, giving her a better look at it.

"My wedding ring," she breathed. "That's really it. The last time I saw it …" She laughed. "I was throwing it at your face."

He sort of smiled and put his other hand to his temple, as if still feeling the ache. "It was a good throw."

"You kept the ring." It was as if this was the greatest discovery man had ever made. She couldn't believe that he had done such a thing.

"I don't know what I intended to do with it at first," he admitted. "I wanted to throw it back at you, but I kept it. When I went up top, for awhile I thought about selling it, but I just couldn't quite do it. I always found a reason to keep the ring, even when I was broke, even when I could see every one of my ribs in the mirror."

"Tav, I … don't know what to say." Slowly, gently, she pulled him to his feet. Her hand was still clasping his, her other hand gripping his arm. They stood face to face, touching, gazing into each other's eyes, with only the ring between them.

"Take it," he said. "It's yours. It always was."

"But …"

"*Take* it." He didn't make it a request.

Wonderingly, she accepted it from him, but she didn't immediately move to slip it around her finger. "Are you … Tavlin, are you asking me to marry you?"

"No."

"No?"

He smiled again, easier this time, though he could still feel the tremble in it. "We never divorced, not really. There was no paperwork, anyway. I'm asking you to *stay* married to me."

"I …"

He tilted her chin up and kissed her. He bit her bottom lip, softly, then played his lips over hers. He crushed his lips to hers. Their tongues probed each other, questing. Her breasts shoved against his chest.

"Oh, Tavlin," she said between kisses.

"Sophia … I've wanted this for so long."

She smiled, a little impishly. "I know."

She slid the ring on her finger, but it wasn't her ring finger, he saw with disappointment, it was her pointer finger. She was saving it for later, just making her hands free. At least she hadn't thrown it at him again.

With her now-free hands, she began to unbutton his shirt. He helped, yanking his shirt tails from his waist, then jerking down his pants. His member was already rising, pushing against his briefs. He helped Sophia off with her dress, lifting it over her head, her arms outstretched, then tossing it to the floor. He was so enflamed with lust that he didn't bother unclipping her bra, just yanked it up so that her wonderful breasts spilled free, large and still quite firm, with huge red areolas, the nipples poking out. Well, one of them was red; the other had turned blue after her mutation, and it was even sexier. He sucked on them, teasing his tongue around her nipples but not touching them, then rubbing their hardness with his thumb. She gasped and trembled. Her gills quivered.

"I can't believe we're doing this," she said, pushing him back. The back of his knees hit the bed. She pushed him further, and he sank onto the mattress. She came immediately after, wrapping her long legs about his middle. His member rubbed her red bush, his balls grinding into her wet cleft.

"I can't believe we waited so long," he said, cupping her face with a hand and bringing her in for another lingering kiss.

"I want you inside me," she said.

"I think I can arrange that."

He slipped on the necessary condom (he was prepared), then grabbed her wide hips and shoved her down, impaling her on his hardness. They both gasped. She was very wet, but tight, and he could feel her muscles rippling around his member even as her breaths came fast and shallow. He pumped into her, as well as he could in his position, and then she began grinding against him. She seemed to like being on top, but he couldn't get the leverage to pump very much.

He eased her to the side, then rolled over, getting all of his body onto the bed and pinning her beneath him.

She gasped and shuddered. The bed creaked and the floorboards bucked. Then she was crying out and moaning beneath him, sweat beading her breasts. He couldn't hold out anymore but exploded inside her.

At last, panting, he collapsed to the bed beside her. For a long time they lay like that while sounds of revelry drifted in from outside.

They were silent for a long while, just enjoying each other, but then Sophia said, "Can I ask you something?"

"Anything."

"You cheating at cards up top."

He almost laughed. "This again."

"I don't get it, Tav. Getting kicked out of club after club, getting in fights like the one you were about to get in when Frankie found you. He told me about that. What was that all about?"

He sighed. "You really want to know?"

"Yes."

"I … don't know if I want to talk about it."

"Then I'll start. There can only be one reason for it, and it isn't a pretty one, Tavlin Metzler. You *wanted* to get caught."

He passed a hand across his face. "Okay, fine. We'll talk about this. I guess I wanted to be punished, but it wasn't for the reason you think."

"No?"

"I didn't wanted to *die*. I only wanted to *feel* something again. For too long my life had been a tedium of grayness, if you'll forgive the flowery language. Of despair. I'd been empty—a husk blowing in the wind, if you will. But a sound thrashing after getting caught? *That* made me feel alive again. That, the taste of my own blood and the rattling of my teeth in my gums. At least for a little while. Then I would have to do it all again."

Her voice was filled with emotion when she said, "Damn, Tav. That's terrible. Sooner or later that would have killed you."

"I know." He knew it, as he knew every card he had ever dealt. "But that me is gone now. I'm a new man now. All that I've been through over the last few weeks, it's taught me to love life again. Especially …" His throat constricted. "Especially if I have you to share it with." Their fingers intertwined, and he realized the ring was still on her pointer finger. "Are you going to put that on for real?"

She started to look nervous. "I don't know."

"But … what we just did …"

She smiled and turned to kiss his shoulder. It was a tender gesture, but somehow sad. "We both needed it, Tav. Maybe I needed it more than you, I don't know. It wouldn't have been right to deny ourselves that much, at least. But any more than that …"

He felt exasperated. "But why not?"

A troubled look entered her eyes. "After all we've done, all we've said, all the anger we've harbored inside us …"

"Yes?" he said, and it came out as a whisper. He felt that now, finally, he would learn what that ultimate barrier was, the real reason she was holding herself back.

"After everything," she said, "do we really *deserve* to be happy?"

He stared at her. "Are you serious?"

"Yes. Of course I am." She half sat up. "Why?"

He almost laughed. "Because 'Yes'. Of *course* we deserve to be happy. Why *wouldn't* we?"

"Because … after Jameson … the anger. It became us, Tav. It consumed us." Her voice was small. "*Ruined* us. There can be no coming back from that."

"Nonsense. We lost our boy, and yes, we were angry with each other because of it, but don't you see, Sophia? It wasn't either of our faults. It just happened. Hell, we did everything we could to prevent having Jameson in the first place, precisely because we knew what might happen. But he came anyway, and you know what?"

"What?" She seemed honestly curious.

"I'm glad he did! I wouldn't trade those years for anything."

"Neither would I. Of *course*."

"So don't you see, he brought happiness into our lives, he didn't take it away. *We* took it away, by blaming each other for something neither of us deserved any blame for. But what we took away, we can put back. We can make whole what was broken. I don't hate you anymore, Sophia, and I don't think I ever did. Why else would I have kept the ring? But my pain clouded my feelings, and I think it's clouded yours, too. Push past that, Sophia. Push through that and we can be together, just like Jamie would have wanted."

She blinked again, but this time she was blinking back tears. Shakily, she rose from the bed and started putting on her clothes. Despair filled him. Had he lost her again, pressed her too hard?

"Sophia, please."

She bent down and kissed his cheek, surprising him. "Let me think about it, Tavlin."

"If the ring was too much, forget it. We can start by dating again, if that's what it takes."

She smiled. "No. But I think … maybe you're right, about being married. But my heart is … well, it's like there's a cloud around it, and I can't tell what's inside, through that darkness. Let me see if I can see inside it. Just give me a little while. A few hours, maybe. Okay?"

She didn't give him a chance to agree but slipped quietly out of the door. He stared at it, hoping she would come back through it, but she didn't, and finally he moved to the cupboard and poured himself a drink—he had snagged a bottle of brandy and two cut glasses, just in case—then knocked back a stiff one. His throat burned. He knocked back another.

He drank and watched the rowdiness outside. It must be very late by now, but still they celebrated, only slowly moving back indoors. The noise gradually faded, but Tavlin didn't wait for it to recede altogether. Tipsy from the drink, he climbed into bed—he didn't want to reflect on whose it had been originally—and closed his eyes. Sleep didn't come easily. Strange shapes rose around him, and singing engulfed him. Millicent came out and swirled around him, making him dizzy, her eyes shining through the white mist that seemed to come from her. Terrible forms wheeled overhead, streaming from the horizon. They were vast, and formless, and yet their forms were horrible. *They're coming!* Millicent cried. *They're coming!*

Tavlin woke to a knife at his throat.

Gasping, he stared up into a dark face, broad and striped by a pale streak of light streaming from the window, that was all. Still, it was enough. Tavlin recognized Havictus.

The tall, square-framed Octunggen had straddled him and one hand pinned one of Tavlin's arms down, while at the end of the other glittered the knife. It pressed down into Tavlin's throat, drawing a thin line of blood.

"Oh, good, you're awake," Havictus said. "That makes this much more satisfying."

Tavlin tried to slow the beating of his heart. "You're after the canister, aren't you? The Formula? Well, I won't tell you where it is."

Havictus's dark face moved, and Tavlin caught the gleam of teeth in what might have been a smile. "Oh, I already have it, but thank you." He patted a bulge under his breast pocket.

"But … how?"

The grin, and it was a grin, widened. "The Ualissi don't have very tight security—or didn't. I had to kill a few, I'm afraid." He made tutting sounds. "No, this has nothing to do with that. I just wanted to pay you a visit before I left. You've inconvenienced me a good—"

Tavlin lunged to the right. Havictus compensated. It had been a feint, though. Tavlin rolled hard to the left and sprang up on the other side of the bed. He ripped open the bedstand drawer and pulled out the automatic pistol there. Havictus bounded over the bed, the knife falling away, and grabbed Tavlin's gun wrist. The gun slammed against a wall, as did Tavlin's back. He made a fist and punched Havictus's gut as hard as he could. It barely made a dent. Havictus was tough as stone, though he could have been old enough to be Tavlin's father, almost grandfather.

Havictus punched him across the jaw. Tavlin reeled, and the world listed around him. When he came to, Havictus was just about to land another punch. Tavlin blundered forward, under Havictus's swing, and tackled the Octunggen awkwardly. They fell to the ground, rolling and punching. A blow landed on Tavlin's side. He punched at Havictus's throat. The spy kneed him in the side.

The Octunggen, larger and stronger, edged the gun barrel toward Tavlin's head. Jerking swiftly, Tavlin reached up a hand to the gun, hit a button and ejected the clip. It clattered to the floor. Only one bullet now, in the chamber.

Havictus shoved the barrel toward Tavlin's head. Straining, Tavlin shoved back. The two men glared into each other's eyes.

"You can't win," Havictus snarled. "Even now the Temple is being completed. By tomorrow it will all be over."

He shoved with renewed strength, sweat dripping from his brow onto Tavlin. Desperate, Tavlin pushed back hard.

"You're mad!" he said. "Dealing with the people of the Temple! Their god will kill us all!"

"*My* gods can contain it. It will throw our enemies into chaos, and in that chaos we shall advance."

"Fool!"

"Magoth will come to dwell with the Lords of the Abyss and be revered with the Great Elders. It will have its own temple in Xicor'ogna."

The door opened. Sophia, wearing only a slip, was framed in the doorway. *She decided!* Tavlin realized. *She made up her mind and came back!* And by the smile on her face he knew what her answer must be. Part of him was flooded with joy, but the rest of him shook with horror. How could this be happening? Dear gods, after everything they'd been through, for it to end like this …

No. No, he wouldn't let it.

"Tav?" she said. "What, oh—?"

"Sophia," Tavlin grunted. "Get—out—"

It all seemed to happen in slow motion. Havictus straightened his arm, taking Tavlin's with it, and aimed the weapon at Sophia. Tavlin shoved with all his strength, but Havictus was like a bear. Like a steel fucking bear. Tavlin thought he could have worn the older man down with time, but time was one thing he didn't have.

Before Tavlin could stop him, Havictus pulled the trigger. The gun roared, smoke wreathing up from it.

Sophia—beautiful, intelligent, hard-as-nails Sophia, mother, lover, nurse, warrior and survivor—crumpled to the floor.

Tavlin screamed.

Havictus kneed him again, and Tavlin was too numb to resist when the larger man tore away, which had surely been why he'd done what he had. Havictus rose, having to stumble out the door. It was clear he wanted to be away before the others in the mansion were roused; the gunshot had sounded very loud in the stillness of the great house. He turned back at the door and swung a baleful eye on Tavlin. He started to say something, then seemed to think better of it and vanished from the room. Tavlin snapped the trigger of the gun at him, but no bullets came out. He dropped the gun to the ground and ran to Sophia. Falling to his knees, he pulled her into his arms. She was still warm.

"Sophia!"

Blood pumped on her chest. More blood trickled from the corner of her mouth.

"Tavlin …" Feebly, she groped for his hand.

He grabbed it. Squeezed. "I'm so sorry. So, so sorry. I … Sophia …" He studied her, noting again that she wore only a thin, silken slip, perhaps borrowed from the eldest of the mayor's daughters. He noticed something else: as he'd suspected, she wore her wedding ring on her ring finger.

His throat constricted. "You were going to say yes."

Her eyes glimmered wetly. She tried to answer, and her body trembled. "I … love you, Tavlin Metzler. You're …" She didn't seem able to finish.

"I love you, too. Sophia Metzler."

She trembled one last time, then went limp in his arms, and her eyes stared far away.

For a long time, Tavlin held her. Tears streamed down his cheeks and dripped off his chin, and he held her tight, as if the world would end if he let go. For a long time, he thought it might.

Chapter 18

Boss Vassas's eyes widened slightly as Tavlin approached. Tavlin knew he was still trembling, and his face must be agonizing to look at. The boss hunched behind his desk. After the gunshot, his people had been roused to action and had searched the mansion and grounds, such as they were, for Havictus, finding nothing, while he had repaired to his office—well, the former mayor's—to receive reports and plan for the next day. Tavlin knew the Boss had conferred with the Ualissi and had learned that, indeed, Havictus had murdered several of them at their laboratory and taken off with the Formula in its canister.

"I'm so sorry," Boss Vassas said, not for the first time. A flail feasted on some slime mold growing on the window behind him, but Tavlin was immune to its squirming, teeth-lined sucker smearing mucus all over the pane. Evidently Grund had not bothered to clean as well as the mayor had.

Vassas rose and actually came around the desk to clasp Tavlin's shoulder. His thick fingers sank in deep. "Sophia was a good woman."

Tavlin nodded, not caring that tears still spilled down his cheeks. "That's not why I'm here."

Vassas waited.

"Havictus. He said the Temple would be completed tomorrow." Tavlin had been too racked by emotion to give a full report earlier, only mentioning the part about the Formula.

"The fools," Vassas said. "What do they think they're doing, messing around with such forces?"

"I don't know, but they're not an isolated bunch of crazies. Havictus said his own gods could contain Magoth, which means Octung's bought into it, too."

"They did not *buy into* it, Tavlin," said a voice by his ear, and Tavlin jumped. It was Millicent, of course. She'd leapt into being more silently than usual and now hovered off to the side, her face sad and beautiful and intangible. "It, Magoth, simply *is*," she said. "To be worshipped and feared and to pay homage to. We bask in its Song."

Tavlin wondered if she had been listening when Guyan described its song. Could she see through Tavlin's eyes and hear through his ears even when he couldn't see her? Did she have life in some capacity even when she was inside him, if that was the right way to look at it?

"Anyway, they must be stopped," he said. He let his eyes bore into Vassas. He knew his eyes were red and terrible, like open wounds, and he wasn't surprised to see Vassas cringe, if only a bit. The Boss was a hard man. "If they don't …" Tavlin let the thought hang in the air, unfinished and awful.

Vassas sank back into his appropriated chair. It was smaller and probably less comfortable than his own chair atop the Wide-Mouth, hinting at the true power dynamic in Muscud. Still, the trappings of being the mayor did seem fairly opulent.

"We'll do what we can," Vassas said, sounding reluctant. "To that end, there *is* some good news."

"Yes?"

The Boss let out a breath. "The Ualissi. They completed it."

"The counteragent to the Formula?"

"That's right. They used that jewel you and Sophia got, may her soul rest in peace, along with some other ingredients, and were able to make what they call a nullifier." He reached into a drawer and, with a sense of gravity, held up a small brass-looking container. Waggling it gently, he said, "In this is the power to destroy that Formula, whatever it is."

"We can finally end this, then. A pity they couldn't have finished it before Havictus stole back the canister, though."

"Yes. A shame."

"There's nothing for it, then. We must attack the Temple."

"How?" said Vassas. "It's madness. Assaulting the Temple with its god on the verge of … well …" His gaze flicked to Millicent, then veered away. "That should be the job of the Army, not my boys."

"The *Ghenisan* Army?" Tavlin said. "You've got to be kidding. They'd never believe it. They'd laugh at us if we tried to tell them what was going on."

"They won't be laughing tomorrow," Millicent said, and Tavlin couldn't tell if that was fear or pride in her voice, or if it was both.

"There's no one else," Tavlin plowed on. "It must be us. Boss, you just said you'd do whatever you could, and you accomplished a direct assault on them once before."

"Twice, actually," Vassas said. "The first time I lost a dozen men. The second was an infiltration, not an attack. But we had weeks to prepare, and plenty of time to make those tattoos that got us in—and they do take time. Besides, the cultists will have improved their defenses. Especially now."

"Boss, there's no choice. They have the Formula. If we don't strike, *right now*, all is lost. Not just Muscud, not just the sewers, but the whole world."

Vassas produced a cigar from his pocket and lit it. Thoughtfully, he puffed on it as he swiveled to watch the flail feast on slime mold. Tavlin could hear it now, a nauseating *squelch-squelch, squelch-squelch* through the warped window pane. At last Vassas blew an acrid cloud at the ceiling and said, "Did you learn anything while you were there, Tav? Something that would give us the edge?"

Tavlin started to open his mouth to answer *No*, then reconsidered. "Some memories are coming back to me … I think I remember … Yes, there *is* a passage behind the Temple, it goes into parts of the Underworld I've rarely gone into. The people of Magoth had a couple of guards posted there, but that was it. The channel goes up a series of locks. A whole attack party couldn't pass through them, not effectively. It would take forever. You can only get a couple of boats into those locks at a time."

Vassas tapped ash into a clay tray that looked as if it had been made by one of the mayor's daughters in some class years ago; it was brightly colored and misshapen. "Interesting."

"It does suggest a possibility," Tavlin said.

"Go on."

"I'll have to go in alone—maybe with one other. I don't know how to operate the locks, how to get a boat from one level to another. And, well, honestly I could use a good fighting man at my side. One that can do it quietly."

"If I like the plan, I'll give you Frankie. He knows locks, and he's a good knife and brass-knuckle man. Now about that plan …"

Tavlin leaned forward and began to speak.

* * *

After a time, Boss Vassas called in several leaders of the Ualissi, along with some of his own captains, and together they hashed out the details of the operation. Fortunately, the Ualissi agreed to cooperate, and indeed the gelatinous beings seemed *eager* to die for the cause of opposing their Masters' enemies. They spoke in long, slowly ululating song-like sounds, something like the groan of a whale, and their cilia moved along their bodies as they did. Since he was the person leading the infiltration of the Temple, Tavlin was given the brass vial Vassas had shown him, to be used on the morrow. Inside it was the fate of the world, a serum that could nullify the dreaded Formula. A few drops of the contents of that vial and the Formula would be rendered defunct—*dead*, they said, maintaining the mad notion that the Formula was somehow alive. Finally, Tavlin was allowed to leave them and return to his own room.

For a long time, he stared at the bloodstain on the floor, or what he could see of it. Vassas's people had taken Sophia's body away and mopped up the blood as best they could, but there was still some left, over which they had thrown a dark-colored blanket. Tavlin could still see a few drops of blood, though, glimmering through the black threads. The blood was almost completely hard.

Tavlin lost all strength. He closed the door and sank to his knees. He cried, and his tears moistened the blood beneath him, making it fresh again. *We came so close, damn it,* he thought. *We came so close to happiness. If I hadn't given you that ring, you would still be alive. Damn it all, why did I have to be so selfish? I should have just let you go off on your own, live your own life, be a nurse, be whatever you wanted to be. Why did I have to insert myself back into your existence? I didn't deserve you, Sophia. I never did. Now you're beyond me—in the stars, I hope—beyond my reach forever.*

He was hardly aware when Millicent appeared, but she knelt beside him for a long time, and he thought he saw tears in her eyes, too.

He removed something from his jacket pocket and stared at it. It was the ring. Frankie had ordered it returned to him after Sophia's body was seen to, and Tavlin hadn't had the heart to send it back. Besides, Sophia would be cremated, as everyone was down here. It wasn't as if she could be buried with it. Tavlin stared into its winking facets and imaged he could see Sophia gazing back at him, smiling sadly. Then his vision dissolved into tears, and all the facets ran into one.

Havictus, he thought. *I'm coming for you.*

Chapter 19

Wind roared around Tavlin, and he braced himself against it. Frankie was taking these turns too fast, too recklessly, and the boat was almost scraping off the sides of the narrow channel. Flails feasting on the walls to either side stirred at the passage of the boat. Some flew overhead, showering mucus, or even dive-bombed Tavlin's head. At one point Frankie nearly bumped into a slugmine and had to jerk to the side at the last moment, almost dashing them into the wall, which was brick at this point.

"Watch where you're going!" Tavlin said.

"*You* wanna drive this thing?"

"Yes!"

Frankie swore but didn't offer Tavlin the helm of the small, wooden (and falling apart) outboard motorboat. No more slugmines waited ahead, thank the gods. Tavlin crouched in the bow of the boat, shouting back directions. Their only lights were a lantern gripped by him and one jutting from the floor near Frankie. With their small, shaky lights (shakier when Frankie took a turn too fast), the shadows of the flails flung far across the moss-covered walls. In the middle of the boat was one other source of light, but it was faint—the ghostly form of Millicent. She had never left Tavlin since Sophia died. She said nothing, just stood there jouncing to the rhythm of the boat but seeming quite serene.

Tavlin tried to focus on the task at hand. It was difficult. Part of him was still kneeling on the floor over that bloodstain, tears streaming down his cheeks and Sophia's wedding ring gripped in his hand. *Sophia, I'm so sorry.* He couldn't stop thinking it, couldn't stop seeing her face all around him. He could even see it gazing back at him from the water.

Focus, he told himself. He had to concentrate on the mission. If he didn't, all was lost. Besides, he had a certain Octunggen he had to kill before he could rest and let the world fade away. Revenge would keep him going if nothing else did. Hate would keep him sharp. He must nurture it, let it grow, let it overtake him, let it become him.

"Now!" Tavlin called to Frankie. "Cut the engine."

Frankie obeyed and the boat drifted forward.

"This it?" said Frankie.

"I think so."

"You *think* so?"

"Just a few more bends and there will be the cistern lake with the Temple in it."

"And the guards," said Frankie, going forward to man the oars. He nudged them as they came on a wall too fast, shooing the boat back into the center. Something large and white breached the water to port, let out a watery gurgle that chilled Tavlin to the marrow, then submerged once more with a plume of vile-smelling mist.

Light up ahead. Tavlin doused his lantern and Frankie followed suit.

Millicent shone on, faintly green and translucent. Her eyes stared straight ahead, and Tavlin wondered if she knew where they were. Sometimes it seemed as if she were still on that other plane.

"Stop," Tavlin said to Frankie. "We'll wait here."

Frankie halted the boat, grumbling, "We could have gone further if she weren't here." He turned his bugged-out eyes to her. "Just who are you, lady? *What* are you? I stopped believin' in ghosts weeks ago."

Without turning to look at him, she said, "An extradimensional reverberation of the Lady's psychic imprint. An echo."

He looked at Tavlin. "Can't you make her go away?"

To Millicent, Tavlin said, "Can you … absent yourself?"

"Scram," Frankie clarified.

"We have delicate work ahead," Tavlin added.

"We can't have you shinin' up the joint, honey."

Finally, she turned her gaze, staring straight into Tavlin's eyes. "I am *bound* to you." Her voice came as if from far away. She looked back ahead.

Tavlin and Frankie were silent, until at last the frog-man let out a sigh. Looking Millie up and own, he said, as if reluctantly, "I wouldn't mind having her bound to *me*."

Tavlin was still too full of mourning to smile. "You can't touch her. She may not be a ghost, but she might as well be one."

"That's not true at all," Millicent said.

Gracefully, she held out an arm, and a passing flail alit on it, just like a hawk to a trained handler, and she stroked its slimy, mucus-y hide fondly. Then she bobbed her arm, gently, and the flail took off spraying slime. Her arms were as white and clean as they had been, bearing no visible residue.

"There," she said.

"Okay," Tavlin amended. "*Sometimes* she can touch you. When she wants. Like the time she tried to strangle me, for example."

"I don't get it," said Frankie.

Tavlin didn't either, but they had other business. The boat had come to a stop. "I don't hear any fighting," he said.

"Good. It hasn't come yet. Then I guess ..."

Tavlin nodded. They both knew Frankie had work ahead. Frankie checked the knife in his breast pocket, then nodded farewell to Tavlin, shooting Millie a brief glance, then leapt over the side of the boat and into the foul water. For a long moment, there was silence save for the very gentle lapping of the water and the squelching and rustling of the flails. When Tavlin judged that enough time had gone by for Frankie to get into position, he sparked the lantern again and jerked the cord of the outboard motor. The engine sprang to life. Millicent didn't jump at the loud noise or show any other reaction. She just stared forward, seeming oblivious to everything else.

Suddenly, Tavlin understood. *She sees the Temple. Damn it all, she sees the Temple.* Somehow, someway she could see through the brick and earth and stone to the great alien building beyond. At the thought, Tavlin felt new beads of sweat pop out on his brow.

After the boat had passed a couple of turns, he killed the motor again, knowing that it must have been audible to the two guards posted at the tunnel mouth. Tavlin's memory of his time at the Temple was sketchy, but, like he'd told Vassas, it was starting to return, in fits and starts, and he believed the two guards would be armed only with pistols ... and a radio. If they saw or heard anything unusual, they were to call in, and the Lady would send reinforcements. But they wouldn't want back-up to arrive to find them being menaced by an innocent fishing boat. Tavlin felt certain one of them would go forward to investigate the noise while the other hung back, radio at the ready.

Sure enough, a shadow slipped around a bend, gun clutched in a steady fist. The gun swiveled and fixed first on

Millicent, who was glowing and otherworldly. This would have been the perfect time for Tavlin to have shot the man, but Tavlin wanted no gunshots. He knew what his best weapon was—his mouth, as always.

As the man's gun moved on to Tavlin, still hunched over the now-quiet motor, Tavlin said, "Shit, is that the Temple ahead? *Again?*"

The gunman was just a dark shape on the walkway beside the sewer channel, but Tavlin could read suspicion in his stance. Tavlin's lantern illuminated the man very little, and Millicent's glow just shaded his face a sort of dim green-gray. It was covered in fish scales.

"Who are you?" the man snapped. Then, more to the point: *"What the fuck is she?"*

"Oh, just one of us, you know. A mutant. That's her mutation. Glowing."

"She's not just glowing, pal. I can see right through her."

"Yeah, right. Just like a jellyfish. And some of them glow, too. Maybe that's where she picked it up from. Where her mutation came from."

"That is some serious bullshit, pal."

You have no idea. Tavlin knew he only had to keep the man talking for a little while. Frankie would have taken out the other man, the one with the radio, as soon as the engine noise drew this one away, and would already be on the way to save Tavlin and stick this worshipper of Magoth in the back.

"So just what are you and this fellow mutant doing out here, huh?" said the gunman. "And by the way, I'm not seeing any sign of the Taint on you, pal."

Tavlin kept talking, easy and casual: "It's under my clothes. Kind of private, really. It's my dong, if you want to know. It's shelled like a lobster. Hell of it is, it extends when it gets hard. Like a fucking telescope, believe it or not. Oh, don't mind her. She's heard worse. She hears worse all the time. Don't you, Millie?"

Millicent didn't respond, just continued staring forward. Toward the Temple.

"That doesn't tell me what you two're doing out here," said the gunman.

No, but it ate up some time. "Ah, well, now that's a real long tale, I'm afraid," Tavlin said. "See, we were on a fishing expedition—"

"You ain't got no gear."

"I said it was a long tale. Well, anyway—"

"Hey!" the gunman pulled out a flashlight and shone it right on Millicent's face, even though he hardly needed it and the light fell on nothing save the brick wall on the far side; the beam had passed right through her. "Ain't you the Lady?" The man swore and made sounds of amazement. "How can it be?" Suddenly awe overcame him, and he sank to his knees. "Your Magnificence, forgive my language, and my impertinence to ask, What are you doing out here, with this … man? And why can I see through you? And … that light … ?"

Still she continued to stare forward, toward the unseen Temple. She had never acknowledged the man's existence and she didn't now.

Surreptitiously, Tavlin grabbed an oar and propelled the boat a little closer to the fellow, who alternately bowed and stared at Millicent. He seemed to take no notice of Tavlin.

"I don't understand, Your Grace," the cultist said. "You should be at the Temple. The Final Preparations are underway. I'll escort you back, shall I?"

She said nothing.

Now, finally, doubt crept into the man's face.

"Lady, I must insist. And … wait a minute, I saw you, that is, the Lady, just before shift started, and—"

Tavlin whacked him as hard as he could with the flat of the oar. The man fell like a bag of cement to the walkway, his gun flying into the sewage. Tavlin leapt to the walkway, searched the man, tossed away a knife, then dragged him back.

"What am I supposed to do with you?" he said, but no one answered. Along the walls, flails feasted. "I know what Vassas would do."

Tavlin tugged off the man's shoes, pulled out the laces, then tied the man's wrists to his ankles. It would have to do. Tavlin couldn't stomach killing a defenseless man, so he would just have to hope that that held him until it was too late.

Another shadow edged around the bend. Tavlin jerked up, a hand going to his own pistol at his waist, then eased off when he saw Frankie's familiar hunchbacked shape.

"Took you long enough," Tavlin said.

Frankie snorted. "You weren't quite accurate about how close we were. It was further than you thought. Anyway, that the other guy? He alive? You've gone soft."

"I was always soft. I was the casino guy, not the backroom guy, remember."

"I remember." Frankie's gaze switched to Millicent, then Tavlin. "What now?"

"Let's get in position."

They climbed back in the boat, Frankie strapping his pistol holster around his waist (he hadn't wanted it getting wet before), and resumed rowing toward the mouth of the temple. Rather, Frankie rowed, grumbling under his breath, while Tavlin held the lantern over the bow, just in case of more slugmines or other obstacles. Soon he needn't have bothered, as illumination gradually bathed the walls in brighter and brighter light, slow enough so that it didn't pain his eyes, and at last they came within sight of the mouth of the tunnel. Moss hung down across the aperture like tattered drapes. Beyond stretched the eerie dark waters of the cistern chamber, wreathed in mist, and out of that mist, far away, loomed the eerie facets and towers of the Temple of Magoth, Herald of the Outer Lords. Low, ominous music swelled out from it, and contained within that music was the Song.

Don't think about it don't think about it don't think …

Fingers trembling, Tavlin shoved in his earplugs—which, he had learned, had been dipped in an alchemical resin created by the Ualissi—and Frankie shoved the plugs in his ear-holes. Millicent did not ask for any, nor had they brought any to give her, and in any event she only seemed to swell with light and grow more beautiful as the Song bathed her. They hadn't moved any closer to the mouth of the tunnel for fear her illumination would give them away, and now Tavlin ordered Frankie to move them back just a little more. The frog-man did, grumbling and swearing.

At last he said, "Tav, how can we go in there with her along with us? I mean, really." Tavlin could hear him through the earplugs, though Frankie's voice was somewhat muffled.

Tavlin chewed the inside of his cheek. "Actually …"

"Yeah?"

"She was kind of helpful with that guy back there. He thought it was the real Lady for a moment and bowed to her and everything. Maybe she can help us inside."

"Shit, Tav." Frankie shook his head pityingly. "You think she's on *our* side, don't you? Poor dumb chump. Well, it's easy to get confused by a pretty face, but that's *terminal* stupidity, my friend."

Tavlin examined Millicent, who stared, enraptured and angelic, at the Temple. She certainly didn't seem like someone opposed to whatever was going on there.

"Millicent?" he said, but she paid him no mind. "Millie? Hello?" He snapped his fingers before her eyes.

"Yes?" she said, but her attention was still fixed on the Temple rearing from the foul mist like a lover rising from a consort's bed.

"Do you mean to betray us when we go in?"

Frankie snorted. "As if she'd tell us. Shit, Tav, this is a mess. I thought she'd've pulled a runner by now. Face it, I'm going to have to go in alone. Just tell me what I need to know and I'll do what I can when the shooting starts."

Tavlin didn't answer. He was staring, imploringly, at Millicent. Slowly, very slowly, as if feeling the weight of his gaze, she swung her eyes to him. They were very blue.

"Yes?" she said again, as if she hadn't heard any of this.

Tavlin counseled himself to be patient. "Will you betray us, Millie?"

She blinked, as if confused. "*Betray* you?" Then, impishly, she smiled, and when she did she looked even more beautiful, and very young. Tavlin heard Frankie sigh. "Tavlin Two-Bit Metzler," she said, "if you die, so do I. I am *bound* to you. Don't you remember? Silly." She touched the tip of his nose, and he flinched. It was the first time she'd ever touched him since she'd choked him. Her finger was, strangely, warm, even though she had no real flesh, and it gave off a slight electric tingle.

"You tried to kill me at least once," he pointed out.

"Yes, but that was when I was still … coalescing. Gathering. Now I'm me, and I've come to understand what that means, at least in part. And if you die, so does my link to this world … perhaps any world." She shook her head, blond locks swaying, both serious and mock-serious. Her eyes were very solemn. "No, Tavlin, I will not betray you."

Tavlin turned to find Frankie watching her with wide eyes. When the frog-man realized he'd been caught, he spat again and said, "Why couldn't she have been stuck to me? Honey, if you get tired of Two-Bit here, why don't you relocate to some spicier real estate, maybe to someone a bit more frog-shaped. You wouldn't believe it, but I can hop like a motherfucker. And the things I can do with my tongue ..."

But she had lost all interest in them. Once more she had turned her full attention to the Temple. As one, Frankie and Tavlin did, as well. It *glowed.* And the Song ... Tavlin felt it tugging at him, even through the plugs.

"Easy," Frankie said, laying a hand on his arm. "Keep it together."

Tavlin hadn't realized it, but he'd taken a step forward, as if meaning to walk across the water to the alien-looking structure. He sucked in a breath and slapped his cheek, hard. The pain brought him back to reality.

"How long do you think we'll have to wait?" he said. The plan was for Boss Vassas to launch his assault from the other direction, drawing the cultists' attention toward that side so that Tavlin and Frankie could slip in from the rear and do what needed to be done.

"Fuck knows," said Frankie. "Could be a minute, could be—"

Distantly, half-muted by mist and earplugs, came the pops of guns.

"Could be now," Frankie said, but there was fear in his voice.

* * *

More guns answered the first, a great many of them. In moments it was obvious a full-scale battle was taking place on the far side of the Temple. Tavlin pictured Boss Vassas leading an armada out from the two tunnels on that side, the two fleets joining, then speeding across the cistern lake through the mist. Cultists would be in the doorways, windows and landings of the terrible structure, firing on the mobsters, and their pet monstrosities would be assaulting them, as well, perhaps from below. Tavlin imagined the insectile G'zai rising from the deeps of the lake and dragging the criminals overboard with their whip-like tendrils or simply blasting them apart with their organic weapons. Hopefully, as planned, the Ualissi would have joined the fight and would be countering the G'zai with their own inhuman devices.

"Now!" Tavlin said, shaking himself. "We go now!"

Frankie revved up the engine and the boat shot across the water, foul vapor swirling around it, seeming to hide strange forms. Something with a tentacle breached the surface to port, then sounded. Tavlin screwed the silencer onto his pistol, knowing it was only good for a couple of shots. *This is it. Dear gods, it's come to this.* His heart thundered and he could hear his pulse behind his ears, behind his eyes, feel it dance in the sweat on his forehead. They were going straight into the beehive to kill the queen. Or at least to take away her prize honey.

He glanced back to see Millicent facing forward, eerie serenity on her face as she beheld the Temple and basked in the Song. Tavlin could feel its tremble in his bones along with the chop of the water. He kept expecting gunfire from the windows, but none came, and he knew then that Vassas's raid had been successful in drawing many of the defenders away. But they could not *all* be away.

Frankie halved the distance to the temple, then quartered it, and Tavlin felt it rearing over them, all strange angles and alien architecture. It hurt his mind to look at, brought an itching to his frontal lobe. The Song washed over him, soothing him, telling him it would all be all right, that soon Lord Magoth would arrive and the world as he knew it would be gone, replaced by something superior. A new reality, a new existence.

"Soon," he heard himself say. Startled, he swiveled to see if Frankie had caught the word. Instead he saw Millicent mouthing it, too: *Soon.*

Her eyes found his, and she smiled joyously. He did not smile back.

Soon, she mouthed again.

Frankie drew them up to the rear dock. Tavlin hopped out and tied them off. Frankie and Millicent joined him on the docks, which creaked underfoot, and Tavlin was reminded that even the cultists had access only to cast-off materials.

Finding a door, he shoved it in, then led the way inside. He had stepped into a hall, and footsteps pattered down it. Toward him.

Frankie and Millicent entered behind him.

Two men rounded the corner ahead, evidently a patrol. Both carried shotguns and had a belt of grenades strapped about their chests. *Havictus*, Tavlin thought. *He sent them here.* The Octunggen had realized the weakness in Temple security as soon as the attack was launched and had sent these two, heavily armed, to reinforce the existing pair.

Tavlin didn't think. He raised his silenced pistol and shot one in the chest, just above his belt of grenades. The other leapt to the side, ricocheting off the wall. He brought his shotgun up. Tavlin fired at him, but the man bounded back the other way. His fingered tightened on the trigger.

Frankie barreled into him, knocking him against the wall and sending the gun flying. Tavlin jumped to help Frankie, but the frog-man already had his knife out and was stabbing the cultist in the belly, again and again. The dying man gasped and sank to his knees. Blood poured from the wound. Taking pity on him, Frankie slit his throat, then began rooting through the two bodies. Tavlin watched on in awe and revulsion and guilt, staring from time to time at his smoking gun. *I just killed a man. Again.* Knowing the silencer was done for, he removed it. It would only hinder him.

"If you wanna throw up, do it now," Frankie said, reading his expression.

The worst part was that Tavlin *didn't* want to throw up. He realized he could kill a man and not even feel sick about it anymore. He almost felt sick over the fact that he *didn't* feel sick.

"Lookit this," Frankie said, and held up one of the shotguns. He grinned ear to ear. "I'll have to keep this. Boss said he didn't have one to spare." Next he held up a belt of grenades. "I'll take this, too." He strapped the belt, which contained five grenades, around his torso. "Want the other?" he asked Tavlin.

"No thanks. The fewer explosives I have stuck to my chest the better."

Millicent was staring down the hallway, evidently enraptured by the sound of the music.

"Come on," Tavlin said, not sure whom he was addressing. "Let's hide these bodies." They nudged open a door, found that it was empty, and dragged the bodies inside. The room was normally occupied, it seemed, and the closet was full. There were three robes, and Tavlin and Frankie each donned one.

"Hopefully these are still in style," Frankie said, straightening his new attire.

They emerged back out into the hallway and continued down it. When they hit a stairwell, they went up, meaning to penetrate as deeply into the Temple as they could. Distantly Tavlin could hear shooting, lots of it, but the sound seemed muted somehow. The Song engulfed him, swelled against him, devoured him. It was coming from the center of the Temple, where the great open space was, and laced with it were the chants and singing of the congregation. Surely the

Lady was leading the ceremony. Was Havictus there, as well?

The stairwell ended on the third floor, and they took another hallway, going toward the center of the structure.

"You sure this is the way?" Frankie said.

"This is it," Tavlin said. "I think. My memory's still a bit fuzzy, I'm afraid."

"This is the way," Millicent said, her voice at once distant and confident.

A group of half a dozen priests rounded a bend and filed down the corridor toward them. Tavlin and Frankie slowed, lowering their heads. Tavlin moved a hand toward the gun in his pocket. Hopefully their robes would fool the priests, but he didn't want to bet on it.

Millicent glided forward, not seeming to touch the ground.

The priests gasped and bowed, first the one in the lead, then the rest of them.

"My Lady!" the head priest said. "What are you doing here? And you're … so different …"

"We just saw you in the Great Chamber!" said another.

Millicent smiled dreamily; Tavlin could see the smile through her transparent head. "Now that the Time has come, I am changing. I can be in multiple places at once."

They murmured in awe and bowed lower. Tavlin dropped his hand away from his gun, sharing a look with Frankie, who appeared just as admiring as he felt. Millicent was a fast thinker, it seemed.

"Filip said he saw her in the tunnels a few weeks ago," one of the priests said. "Another Lady, like a ghost. She helped capture a heathen and bring him into the Order."

"Bless you, Lady," said the head priest. "May we be of service to you?"

"No, carry on."

She drifted down the hall, and Tavlin and Frankie scurried after her. After a few moments, the priests rose and shuffled off the other way.

"Nice thinkin'," Frankie said. "But did you have to send them off? Mebbe we coulda used them."

"And maybe they would have seen through the ruse the first chance they had to talk to either of us," Tavlin said. "Just keep going."

Millicent slowed as the corridor spilled out into the Great Chamber, that huge open space in the middle of the Temple that was as tall as the building itself, all three stories. Circular in nature, balconies ringed it, and priests in their finest robes knelt along the railing, bowing to the great space in the center. That space seethed and roiled, the fantastic energies of some other dimension ripping the open air in the heart of the Temple apart. It looked as if the air were at war with itself. Light spilled out from half-glimpsed fissures in the fabric of reality, bathing the faces of the congregation, but it was an otherworldly, unnatural light, Tavlin could see for the first time, and the Song that accompanied it was equally loathsome, like the rustle of a billion insect wings all at once, susurrus and trilling, rising and falling to the ripple of unholy light.

Now Tavlin felt like he was going to throw up. Frankie looked ill, too, and his buggy eyes had gone even huger as they stared at the unwholesome glow emanating from the flexing, twisting space ahead. Millicent, by contrast, looked entirely sated and satisfied, her ghostly cheeks somehow flush with life and vitality.

Her counterpart, the real Lady, led the singing of the priests from a projection that thrust out from the third-floor balcony, spearing into that open space alive with otherdimensional energies. Somehow she seemed taller than Millicent, and she was certainly much more solid. Tavlin could only see her profile, but even so he could tell other differences—a certain coldness, an arrogance about her that marked her apart from the odd, disconnected but somehow humble Millicent. *Careful*, Tavlin cautioned himself. *Frankie's right. She can't be trusted.* He wished there were a way to banish Millicent, if only because she drew so much attention, but alas there did not seem to be a method to do so.

The real Lady, Esril, cool and poised, did not just sing. She was quite occupied. Before her, at the lip of the projection, stood a bank of sinister-looking consoles, some sort of complicated apparatus or series of apparatuses. The air blurred around her, hinting that she was using her otherworldly powers, as she worked on the most vital-looking component while three priests beside her worked on others. Sparks flew, and light pulsed from the machines, which resembled the carapaces of Carathids, the massive insects that used to roam the surface world many millions of years ago. The machines' various stalks stuck out like bugs' antennae. Prominent in the bank of machines before the Lady was a glass bulb dripping some strange mercury-like fluid via a curling tube into one of the consoles, which chugged and shimmered, and as it did reality twisted ever more violently in the center of the Great Chamber. Whatever that console was doing corresponded to the breaking of reality.

"That's it," Tavlin whispered. The three hung back near the mouth of the tunnel, just peering out, not eager to be seen. "That's the machine bringing Magoth over. That fluid …" He swore. "That must be the Formula."

"You mean what was in the canister?"

"That's right. It's some sort of liquid—like quicksilver. Sophia was right." Tavlin shook his head. "I don't understand it, but that's what's going on. They're feeding the Formula into that machine. And look, I see cables running from the machines to the outer walls …"

Frankie nodded, licking his lips with his long tongue. "That's right, this whole place, it's supposed to, what, like reflect some other plane or whatever, right?"

"Right. The Formula is channeling into the walls, aligning them, not just physically, but on some other dimension, making this space correspond to that other sphere. And when it snaps into place …"

"Hello Magoth."

Tavlin swallowed. He scanned the machines, the Lady, then the priests and congregation, When he did, he felt his sweat turn cold. The twisting of reality in the center of the Great Chamber had robbed his attention, diverting it from other interesting details of the gathering; namely, that there weren't just humans here. No, interspersed among the human adherents of Magoth were G'zai—tall, chittering, and insectile—as well as other inhuman creatures: dripping, black Suulm; the lizard-people of the Naderhorn; spiked, shelled beings that Tavlin didn't recognize; the long-necked, graceful Hoosings; and other, less easily understandable entities.

"It's a gathering of demons," Frankie breathed.

"Hard to believe they could all worship this … thing. And all welcome the destruction of this world."

"*Transformation*," Millicent said. Her voice came fast and shallow, as if she were breathing hard in excitement, almost randy, even though, technically speaking, she had no lungs or any reason to breathe. "They're transforming the world."

"Thought you were on our side, honey," Frankie said.

She smacked her lips. "I … am …"

Frankie's jaws tightened. "What next, Two-Bit?"

"I don't …" Tavlin's eyes went to the fluid swirling down into the machine. "If it was just a matter of getting the Formula into that thing, they could've done it hours ago, back when Havictus first delivered it. But apparently it takes time. Millicent, can you explain it?"

She blinked, slowly. "Did you say something?"

"Can you tell us more about the Formula, Millie?"

"Oh. Yes." She smoothed out her phantom dress around her phantom hips, collecting herself. "The Formula is powerful, Tavlin, and can only be released a bit at a time. That's why it was kept in the canister, which was specially wrought just to contain it."

"Yes, I understand that much, and I've felt it, too. That canister, or whatever was inside it, gave me terrible dreams."

"Yes, the Formula is quite potent. They can only feed a bit of the holy fluid into the machines at a time. They will be keeping the rest nearby, in some storeroom, and only bringing out small doses as needed. But obviously it is almost spent; otherwise this gathering would not be here. It must be almost done—"

"Wait, what's this?" Tavlin leaned forward. The Lady, the real Lady, Esril, had summoned a group of priests, who seemed to have been expecting her, and was speaking to them in a voice too low for Tavlin to hear over the sound of the Song and the humming of people and machines. The head priest she was speaking to nodded, bowed, and led a group of five other priests down one of the halls.

Tavlin snapped his fingers. "That's it! She sent them off to get the last drop of the Formula, I'd bet anything on it."

"You might just be," said Frankie. "But then you are a good gambler, or you used to be."

"I still am, Frankie. Trust me. They must keep the canister in some secure location, some place designed to resist its effects." To Millicent, he said, "Do you know where that is?"

"I ..." She bit her lip but didn't answer. Either she knew and wouldn't tell them or else she didn't know and didn't want to admit it. Either way, Tavlin could see Frankie grinding his teeth more forcefully. The frog-man's distrust of her was becoming more apparent. What was worse, Tavlin didn't blame him.

"Let's follow them," Tavlin said, meaning the priests just now leaving the Great Chamber. "They'll take us to the Formula. We grab it and get the hell out of here."

They retreated down the corridor, found a cross-hall and fell in right behind the group of priests as they swept past the intersection. *This is it*, Tavlin thought. *This is our big chance. We can't fuck this up.* The priests hit another intersection, turned right, and marched down the hall to a room at the far end. There they knocked on the door. A panel slid back, a face peeked out at them, and the door opened. The priests filed inside, one by one.

"Hurry," Frankie said. "Before they close that door."

He and Tavlin rushed forward as the last priest entered the chamber. The room had appeared brightly lit, but as soon as they crossed the threshold darkness engulfed them and the door slammed shut behind them. It sounded very heavy. From an intercom, a voice sounded, and Tavlin shuddered at the familiar international inflections of Havictus:

"You didn't really think it would be that easy, did you, Mr. Metzler?"

Somewhere Havictus laughed, and that was when poison gas began pouring into the room.

Chapter 20

“A trap!” Frankie wailed. He pounded at the door, but it didn’t budge, and the echoes sounded metallic. “I should’ve known it was a fucking trap! But how did they know we were here?”

“Maybe Millie’s acting wasn’t as good as we thought,” Tavlin said, to which she made no protest.

"Or maybe that guy you didn't kill woke up and got lose," Frankie said, accusing.

Darkness draped the room, but Millicent was still with them, and her faint glow illumined the walls in pale, flickering blue-white. By her light, Tavlin could see what was surely toxic gas billowing into the room from grates along the wall near floor level. Hate filled him. *Havictus. I’ll kill you yet, you bastard.*

“Where did the priests go?” Millicent said dreamily. Of course, she could afford to be dreamy. The gas likely wouldn’t effect her … unless she’d been telling the truth about dying when Tavlin did. In that case she would have excellent reason to help them escape.

“A secret door!” Tavlin said, realizing what she meant. “They must have gone out through a secret door.”

He and Frankie leapt at the walls, feeling every nook and cranny they could find with groping fingers. The deadly gas swirled around them, growing thicker and higher. Tavlin sucked in a last clean breath and saw Frankie do likewise. Holding it in, Tavlin stepped back from the walls and shook his head at Frankie, and the frog-man returned the gesture. If there were any secret panels, the cultists had hidden them well, or perhaps Havictus had, if indeed this was his trap. Desperate, Tavlin sought some means of escape.

Something caught his eye. He pointed. At the top of the wall to the left was another air duct grate, but this vent had been sealed, presumably when the other one had opened, which meant that there was fresh air in that duct … and possibly a means of escape. But it was several feet beyond Tavlin's reach.

"Can you jump to it?" he wheezed at Frankie.

"Watch this."

Frankie dropped the shotgun to free his hands (though Tavlin could see that pained him), coiled himself … and leapt. Tavlin gasped to see him shoot through the air, propelled by his powerful frog-legs, and grab hold of the vent. He wrenched off the cover—that was one good thing about junkheap construction, anyway—and stuck his head inside. He took a deep breath and turned back.

"Clean air!"

"Can you fit inside?" Tavlin said.

"I … think so …" Frankie spoke even as he wriggled into the duct. It was a tight fit, but he was well-lubricated with slime and somehow made it and was able to turn back around. "Jump, Two-Bit!"

Tavlin jumped, and Frankie's hands fumbled at his—missed. Tavlin jumped again. Frankie's hands found him. Tavlin's fingers slipped off the grease. Tavlin knew he only had enough air for one more jump. He gathered himself, leapt, grabbed … started to slip …

Frankie's tongue darted out, incredibly long, and stuck to his jacket over his breast, and pulled. Tavlin rose a bit off the ground … not enough …

Millicent, floating weightlessly, pushed on him from below. She didn't possess superhuman strength, apparently, only the strength of a normal girl her age and size, but it was enough, combined with Frankie's help, to drag Tavlin up and into the duct. Frankie withdrew, making room, and Tavlin shoved himself inside. Millicent flowed in after them.

Tavlin drew in a great big breath, then swore. "I can still smell the gas."

"Shit," said Frankie. "I shouldn't have tossed that cover away."

Millicent flew down the duct, then returned. "There's another vent in the next room. Come, I'll show you. Oh, and I grabbed this for you." She pressed the shotgun into Frankie's hands.

"Thanks, hon. Maybe you're not so bad."

They followed her to the vent in the next room and peered through the grate slats to find the small chamber vacant. Tavlin kicked in the vent and they dropped down into the room. One of Tavlin's knees protested as he landed and he reminded himself that he wasn't as young as he used to be. The door was unlocked, not that that would have mattered, as it locked from the inside. The three poked their heads out into the hall, a different one than that by which they'd found the trap room, and stepped outside.

"Think these are still good?" Frankie said, fingering his disguise as a priest.

"I don't know. Something alerted them to the fact that we were here." Tavlin picked a direction and started down it. "Either those priests weren't fooled earlier or they found the bodies."

"Or that guy woke up."

"Yeah." Tavlin didn't know why he felt guilty about not killing that sentry. *I spared his life, damn it.*

"Either way, they know we're here," Frankie said.

"Maybe they think you're dead," Millicent said. "Me, too." The thought seemed to make her sad, and her face made a pretty pout.

"Thanks for your help back there," Frankie said. "I complain, but you make a hell of a flashlight." She didn't reply, and Frankie frowned. "Think Havictus knows we got out?"

Tavlin had been wondering the same thing. "I don't know, but if he does he'll send people after us. I guess it's inevitable. I'm sure he'll crack the door of that trap room as soon as he can suck the gas out."

"Or maybe he won't wait. He could send in a team with gas masks." Frankie grumbled under his breath. "Anyway, where's Boss Vassas? He should be inside the Temple by now."

They could hear gunshots coming closer, but they didn't seem to be coming from the first floor interior of the structure, which is where Vassas would be striking from. The corridor turned. They were along the outer wall of the Temple now, and a series of balconies jutted from the hall. People occupied them, firing down on someone below.

"Boss!" Frankie said, bounding forward, but Tavlin dragged him back. "Let me go, they're firing on the Boss!"

He was right, Tavlin realized. This was the front of the Temple, and these were its defenders raining lead down on Vassas and his gang. Edging forward, just slightly, Tavlin took stock of the cultists and was able to peer out of one of the front windows. Sure enough, Vassas and his people were on the water of the cistern lake below, but they were stymied by several broken-apart, overturned boats, as well as inhuman limbs that rose dripping from the water and dragged them under—the G'zai, Tavlin was sure. The

Ualissi might be helping them beneath the surface, but the G'zai were still taking their toll.

Worse, he saw, one of the cult's priests, probably a high one, was wielding a long back iron scepter, like some sort of magic wand, and using it to devastating effect. The man stood at one of the balcony railings. He would wave the scepter, which blurred with extradimensional energies, and each time he gestured one of the mobsters below would begin to vibrate, as if in the grip of some personal earthquake, then erupt in blood and gore, like an egg shaken to the breaking point. Tavlin saw one man shatter apart and spray a fellow gunman—actually, a gun-woman—with blood. The woman wiped away the blood from her eyes, popped up from behind a jut of broken boat and fired at the cultists along the balcony, then ducked back down again as a volley sailed over her head and dimpled the lake behind her. Her round found a cultist at the balcony, and the man pitched backward, blood flying.

Boss Vassas and his people had taken refuge behind the overturned boats as best they could and, like the woman, were returning fire. But none of the mobsters could hit the priest with the scepter. Tavlin saw what must be a bullet streak right toward the man, but the air shimmered around him and the bullet flared into embers, then vanished.

"That scepter's protecting him," Tavlin said. "If we could take him out, I think Vassas could advance. Everyone else is hunkered down, but not that priest."

"I ain't making no rush at that asshole," Frankie said. "Those Octs would mow us down before we got five steps.'"

Indeed, Tavlin saw that several of the people on the balcony did not wear robes but suits. Frankie was right, they had to be Octunggen. Some of Havictus's crew had survived. And they would be more skillful with their weapons than the cultists.

"I can get though," Millicent said. "Their bullets can't hurt me. And I can penetrate whatever is shielding that priest, too."

"How would you kill him?" Tavlin said. "*Can* you kill him? You're not very strong. Do you have any powers, like Esril does?"

"I … don't know. But …" She pointed at the knife stuck through his waistband. "I wouldn't need any powers with that."

He almost laughed. "Take it." He pressed the knife into her hands, or rather she plucked it from his, as he never felt her flesh.

"Look at her go," Frankie said, as she swirled away, making for the scepter-wielding priest. "Our own little murdering angel."

The Octunggen saw her. Spinning and raising their submachine guns, they fired, but their bullets just punched through her, striking the wall on the other side and showering wood fragments but doing no other damage. The other priests and cultists saw her, too, but their pistols and shotguns could do nothing.

The priest wielding the scepter was too preoccupied with his slaughter to notice the cries of his cohorts at first, but he turned as Millicent slid up behind him. He gestured with his scepter. Millicent stiffened. Her arm came up. The knife glimmered in her fist. Started to come down. He gestured again. The knife slowed. His free hand came up, meaning to wrest it from her phantasmal grip. Her brow furrowed with concentration. She renewed the downward plunge, shoving the blade into his chest. He gasped and reeled back, blood pouring around the wound, and tumbled off the balcony to the foul waters below. Something grabbed him and hauled him under with a large pincer.

Frankie and Tavlin cheered quietly. Vassas and the other mobsters cheered more loudly below, and Tavlin heard their motors revving as they renewed their advance toward the Temple. The Octunggen and cultists at the balconies fired at Millicent a few times, but, seeing that the shots weren't effective, rushed to the nearest stairwell to join the fighting downstairs. Soon Millicent occupied the balconies alone.

Tavlin and Frankie crept out from around the corner, the Song crashing and thundering around them, ever more potent now, and Millicent joined them as they pressed down a hallway.

"Where to?" she said.

"I don't know. Back to the main room, I guess," Tavlin said. "No, wait. What we need is to figure out where the real storeroom is—where they're keeping the real Formula. Obviously it's here somewhere. They set up that trap because they thought I might have remembered it was kept somewhere and wanted to lead me to the wrong place. But it *is* here somewhere, and the Lady *will* send for it. The Formula obviously isn't fully administered yet—otherwise Magoth would be here by now."

Frankie fingered his knife. "We need to find a cultist."

They hit a large cross-hall that appeared to go back toward the heart of the Temple and started down it. They hadn't gone twenty feet when a pair of priests bustled toward them, and the clergymen stopped in shock when they saw Millicent.

"My Lady!" said one.

"No," snarled the other. "That's the false one. Didn't you hear the—?"

His words vanished in a scream as Frankie leapt on him and plunged a blade through his eye into his brain. Frankie could leap *fast*. He had dropped his shotgun to the floor.

The other priest stumbled backward, a cry on his lips, but he tripped on his robe and went sprawling to the floor. He started to scramble away, but Tavlin flipped him over with a foot and straddled him about the chest, pinning his arms to the floor with his knees.

"L-let me go!" the priest said, his eyes wide.

He tried to buck free but Tavlin held him down. Frankie was approaching, his knife dripping blood onto the tile. Around them the Temple thrummed, shook, seemed to twist and flex. The Song was growing louder, more violent. Magoth was close. Very close.

"Tell us where the remaining Formula is being kept," Tavlin said. His knife was gone, so he drew out his pistol and placed it to the man's forehead in case the fellow needed motivation. The man, like all the cultists Tavlin had seen, was a mutant, and his right ear had vanished, replaced by an ear hole, and his nose had shrunk to a scale-covered nub. His eyes were all black. Still they managed to look frightened.

"If I t-tell you, you'll let me go?"

"Sure," said Frankie, but he didn't sound convincing. Millicent floated beside Tavlin, but she offered no help, only stood there glowing and basking in the Song.

"We'll let you go when we get to the storeroom," Tavlin assured the terrified priest. "We have to be sure it's the right one."

The priest swallowed. He had stopped trembling and Tavlin was afraid he was rediscovering his spine.

"If you take the Formula, the ceremony can't be completed," the priest said. "The Great One can't open this world to His Delights."

"Fuckin' shame," said Frankie.

"I don't know if I can be the one responsible—"

Frankie crouched low and stabbed the priest in the upper arm. The man howled and thrashed under Tavlin, almost throwing him off. Tears leaked from his eyes.

"Now take us to the room," Frankie said.

The man nodded wretchedly. Mucus flowed from his nostrils, mixing with the tears, as Tavlin released him and helped him up. One of the man's hands flew to his wound and cupped it, applying pressure, but blood still leaked between his fingers.

Frankie snatched up his shotgun.

"This way," the priest sniffled, and lurched down the hall toward an intersection. They took a right, continued down it to another intersection and hooked a left. The Song crashed and thrummed and battered the Temple around them, and something deep inside Tavlin ached to join it, to give in to the beauty and the majesty of the Herald. Looking sideways, he could see those same thoughts reflected on Millicent's face. The difference was that she was giving herself over to it. He could see her start to sway in the direction of the Great Chamber.

"Millie!" he snapped, and she blinked. "Don't listen to it! Fight it! If we surrender to the Song, we're lost."

She blinked again and shook her head. She flashed him a smile, but it was trembly and uncertain. "Thank you, Tavlin. I'm … better now."

He frowned. The Song swelled. Below them, gunfire sounded, as well as the crash of grenades and the wails of injured men and women. Boss Vassas had finally arrived and was giving battle to the cultists on the first floor.

"Good luck, Boss," Frankie whispered, apparently hearing it, too.

At the next intersection they saw a small procession traveling up this hall. At its head was a priestess wearing brilliant vermillion robes and a fancy circlet on her head—some sort of high priestess, Tavlin supposed, but not *the* High Priestess: that was the Lady. Behind her marched several priests, the one in their center holding an iron staff with a translucent, fluid-filled bulb at its top. The fluid looked like quicksilver, but it moved as if it were alive.

Tavlin had no doubt that it was the Formula. The Lady really had needed the last drop of it, he'd been right, and this high-but-not-highest priestess had been sent to retrieve it from the real storeroom, not the decoy.

Tavlin shoved the bloodied priest toward the group and lifted his gun to point at the high priestess while Frankie pointed at the man with the staff.

"Hand it over," Tavlin said, "and no one gets hurt."

The procession stopped.

The priestess stared from Frankie to Tavlin, then to Millicent. "So it's true …" she said. "The Lady *has* been doubled."

"Give us the Formula," Tavlin repeated. "I don't want to have to kill any of you."

"But we will," Frankie added. To illustrate his point, he fired a shotgun blast at the ceiling over the priests' heads, showering pulverized wood down on them. They flinched and coughed. "Now hand the fucking thing over!"

The priestess blinked. Ignoring Frankie and Tavlin, she spoke instead to Millicent: "Lady, if some part of you is still really you, stop this. Listen to the Song. Embrace it. Do away with these fools and escort us to the Great Chamber, where the Glory will begin very soon."

Millicent watched the priestess as if hypnotized.

"Fight it!" Tavlin urged.

"Shit," said Frankie, as he reloaded his weapon. "I *knew* this would happen. I should've come in alone."

"Embrace it!" the priestess told Millicent.

Millicent wavered.

Frankie shot the priestess in the head with the shotgun. Her brain—her entire skull, really—spattered onto the priests behind her, who screamed and reeled back. Several ran. The headless body spouted blood from the neck, wavered and collapsed, one of the legs still twitching. Frankie chambered another round and shot one priest in the back. The man flew forwards. The rest scattered. The one bearing the staff containing what Tavlin assumed were the last drops of the Formula turned to run, too. Frankie shot him in the lower back. The man screamed and fell, the staff thudding to the ground.

Several of the priests had been armed, and these finally summoned their courage and turned to fire at Frankie, but he was already throwing a pair of grenades from his liberated grenade belt. They arced through the air, landed at the priests' feet and exploded, throwing the clergymen, or what was left of them, backward.

All this took place in seconds, before Tavlin could react, but he came to himself when Frankie grabbed the staff and brought it to him.

"Use that shit," Frankie said, and Tavlin knew he meant the nullifying agent the Ualissi had given him, the one that had been concocted using the black jewel, among other ingredients.

Nodding shakily, Tavlin shoved his gun away. His fingers sought out the precious vial in the inner pocket of his jacket. He had peeked inside earlier; the fluid was copper-colored, thick as honey and smelled like rotten meat. Beside him, Millicent stared at the bodies sadly. The surviving priests had fled around the corner and were out of sight, but the man who had been carrying the staff was trying to drag himself after them, leaving a trail of blood behind him. Tavlin was half-tempted to put him out of his misery—no one could survive a shotgun blast like that—but he had a world to save, so he refrained.

There! His fingers closed around the vial . . .

"I don't think so," came a voice to the side.

Havictus stepped out of the shadows of the cross hall, automatic pistol clutched in hand. His ice blue eyes sparkled coldly beneath his thick eyebrows, and his heavily lined face was locked in the grimmest expression Tavlin had ever seen.

Chapter 21

A rush of hate filled Tavlin, like a dry river bed suddenly flooded with rainwater. This was the man who had killed Sophia. It was all Tavlin could do not to rush Havictus right then, never mind that the bastard would kill him instantly.

Frankie pivoted, clearly meaning to shoot the Octunggen spy, but Havictus was faster. His gun roared, and Frankie's shotgun spun from his fingers. Frankie swore and sucked on his digits. Apparently Havictus hadn't wanted to risk killing Frankie and having him drop the Formula, which he still held in his left hand. Its glass container probably couldn't tolerate much more.

"Hand that over," Havictus said, echoing Tavlin's words from moments ago. "Do it and I might just let you all live."

"Bullshit," Tavlin said. "You'll kill us as soon as the Formula's safe."

Havictus pointed the gun at Tavlin's head, but he spoke to Frankie: "Give it to me or I shoot him."

"Don't hurt Tavlin," Millicent said, her voice sounding as if it came from far away. Her expression was all dreamy abstraction again. "I wouldn't like that."

Havictus ignored her. To Frankie: "Hand it over!"

Frankie took a step toward him.

"Don't!" said Tavlin.

Frankie took another step—Tavlin could see his rear leg muscles bunching—and *leapt*. Havictus swung his gun, but too late. Frankie barreled into him. The gun fired wildly, punching a round into the wall. Another bullet hummed through the air by Tavlin's side. The two crashed to the floor, rolling and punching. The staff flew toward the floor …

… but was caught by Millicent. She stared at the bulb containing the quicksilver fluid longingly, and the silver light played strangely on her phantasmal features, actually seeming to touch her, unlike the light of the flash. Frankie and Havictus rolled right through her, biting and kicking. The gun had tumbled to the floor.

Tavlin held out his hand. "Millicent, give that to me."

She stayed where she was, eyes on the bulb containing the fluid that could damn the world.

"Millicent!"

No response.

Frankie and Havictus rolled back the other way, Havictus groping for the fallen pistol. Tavlin yanked out his own gun and tried to get a bead on the Octunggen, but the two were constantly changing positions, one on top, one on bottom, then flipping. Blood spattered the floor.

Tavlin strode across the intersection, wrenched the staff from Millicent's unresisting hands and slammed its metal length over Havictus's skull. The spy groaned and went limp. Tavlin tore the bulb loose and held it aloft.

Frankie extricated himself from Havictus and climbed to his webbed feet, spitting out a tooth on the way. "Took you long enough," he said. Then, to Millicent: "And thanks a lot, sweetheart."

She still gazed at the bulb, her head seeming to bob with each slow, languid slosh of the living quicksilver.

"Let's end this," Tavlin said. He shoved the pistol through his belt and pulled out the vial containing the nullifying agent. All he had to do was unscrew the top of the bulb, uncork the vial, tip it into the bulb's open top, and this would all be over.

"Wait!" said Millicent. Panic had entered her eyes.

Tavlin sighed. "I'm not going to stop, Millie. This is *it*." He started to unscrew the top of the bulb . . .

"That's not what I meant."

"There they are!" cried a voice, and Tavlin pivoted to see the Lady, the real Lady, Esril, marching toward them at the head of a column of priests, G'zai and other inhuman things.

"Do it!" Frankie told Tavlin. "Hur—!"

A gun thundered, and blood burst from his abdomen, some of it striking Tavlin's front. Frankie gasped and sank to his knees, then toppled sideways. Behind him Havictus, holding a smoking pistol, climbed to his feet. Tavlin would have shot him but both his hands were occupied, one with the vial, one with the bulb.

"Stop him!" he said to Millicent.

For a moment she wavered. Then, finally—*finally*—she seemed to reach a decision. She would, at last, fall on one side over the other.

She chose Tavlin.

Even as Havictus mounted to his feet, Octunggen swears coming from his mouth and his blue eyes blazing, she unleashed a banshee howl and flew toward him. Her arms lifted, her hands curling as if to throttle the Octunggen spy. Havictus fired at her, but the bullet passed right through her, coming perilously close to Tavlin.

She halved the distance between them. In moments she would be choking the life from Havictus.

His free hand thrust into his jacket and withdrew something, some sort of metallic sculpture or device; it looked to Tavlin like the seal or emblem of some religion.

Seeing it, Millicent screamed. Her form rippled, like water boiling, and she faded out of existence.

Tavlin stared.

Havictus, snarling, lumbered toward him. He wouldn't risk shooting Tavlin till he had possession of the Formula-containing bulb. Behind him, Tavlin could hear the Lady and her minions coming closer. Below came the rattle of machine guns. Vassas had fought his way to the second floor, by the sounds of it.

Havictus was very close now.

Tavlin shoved away the vial and reached for his gun. Too late. Havictus made a fist and smashed him across the jaw. Even as Tavlin was hurled back against the wall, the Octunggen's hand snaked forward lightning-quick and grabbed the bulb containing the remaining Formula from his hand.

Tavlin hit the wall, hard, and slumped down it. Above him, Havictus grinned. In one hand he held the bulb, in the other a gun. Behind him Frankie twitched on the ground, one hand over the exit wound in his abdomen. Blood pumped from the entry wound in his lower back, and pain etched his face.

Tavlin tried to crawl toward the intersection—it was only a few feet away—but Havictus kicked him in the belly, and Tavlin grunted and slumped.

"You're not going anywhere," Havictus said.

The Lady arrived.

"I believe this is yours," Havictus told her, and with a flourish he presented the Formula to her.

Unsmiling but with obvious satisfaction, she accepted it.

"Do you require any sacrifices for Magoth?" Havictus said. "I wouldn't mind seeing this one get eaten." He indicated Tavlin.

"I require nothing further," the Lady said, and the spy nodded.

She turned about, rejoined her party, and they streamed back toward the Great Chamber. Havictus's large square head swiveled back to Tavlin. His eyes burned with a cold light.

"Farewell, then." He took aim at Tavlin's head.

Millicent flickered back into existence behind Havictus. Like Frankie, she wore an expression of pain. Her form still a bit unsteady, she wrapped her hands around Havictus's bull neck and squeezed.

He bellowed. The gun fired, but wildly, and a cloud of dust billowed from the wall. Tavlin scurried sideways on hands and knees. He reached the corner and hurled himself around it just as Havictus fired again. A bullet whined through the air where Tavlin had just been.

He yanked out his pistol. Sweat drenching his hair, he popped back out and fired off a shot at Havictus. The Octunggen, grappling ineffectually with Millicent, swore, but the round didn't even come close. Tavlin fired again. Dust billowed from the wall near Havictus's head.

"Damn you," the Octunggen said.

He dug out the symbol again and thrust it at Millicent. She was prepared this time, and as soon as he started to flash the thing, whatever it was, at her she separated herself from Havictus and drifted away. This was evidently what he had wanted, however, as he wasted no time in retreating down the hall. He was being fired at by an opponent behind cover; there was clearly no more sensible thing to do. Tavlin loosed two more rounds, hastening him on his way, but again missed. Havictus turned back and returned fire, keeping Tavlin pinned, and when Tavlin chanced to look out again the Octunggen was gone.

Tavlin rushed over to Frankie. Crouching, he gently turned the mob enforcer over and assessed the damage. The frog-man had passed out, but he came to when Tavlin removed his own jacket and Frankie's belts, both his leather one and the one that carried the grenades—three left, Tavlin saw. Tavlin wrapped his jacket around Frankie's waist and tightened the leather belt around it, staunching the flow of blood.

"That should help," he said.

"Thanks," Frankie wheezed. "Fucking Oct … son of a … bitch."

"Yeah."

"Is he going to be all right?" Millicent said, drifting over.

"I don't know." Tavlin looked at the grenade belt, then strapped it across his own chest. "I hope I don't need this."

"Go," Frankie said. "Get 'em for me."

His green skin looked very pale, Tavlin thought. Almost yellow. "I'll try." He stood.

Frankie tried to move toward the wall but collapsed in agony. Tavlin bent again and helped lift him to it, where he could lean his weight. To his surprise, Millicent assisted him; she was finally coming out of her odd paralysis. They left a trail of blood in their wake.

Tavlin shoved the shotgun into Frankie's arms. "Keep your eyes open."

Frankie met his gaze. Soberly, the frog-man said, "I will."

They nodded farewell. Both knew this was probably It. Throat sore, Tavlin turned up the hall in the direction the Lady and Havictus had taken. The fighting sounded very close now, definitely on this floor. Guns cracked and popped from down a hallway. Reluctantly, Tavlin moved away from Frankie toward the Great Chamber. The Song crashed around him and Millicent floated at his side. She seemed even more serene than before, at peace somehow.

"What was that thing Havictus did?" Tavlin asked her. "That symbol?"

"I … don't know. Some sigil from one of the pre-human races, I think. They had strange gods, and some of them are allied with the gods of Octung. And Octung has always befriended the old races. They have strange arts. Strange weapons." She bit her lip, looking unnerved, and he asked no more questions about it.

A group of cultists moved into view ahead, appearing from a side hall. They were firing backward at an unseen enemy and several flattened themselves against the wall of the corridor Tavlin was in. They didn't see him but shrank against the wall anyway. The others continued backing down the main avenue. One ducked behind a pile of bodies and returned fire. The ones along the walls returned fire, too.

Tavlin crouched, back still against the wall, and sidled back toward the nearest intersection in the opposite direction, meaning to take cover around the corner, though having to go in the wrong direction to do it. Millicent followed. Just when he didn't want to be noticed, she flared brighter than ever.

"What's that?" he heard someone shout, and one of the cultists looked in his direction. Tavlin rose and moved faster. Before he could take cover around the intersection, however, the sounds of fighting erupted anew, and he turned to see that Vassas's forces were overrunning the defenders, shoving them back and up the hall. The few in Tavlin's hall fired back. One fell, then another.

"It's all lost," Millicent said, dreamy once more, the change so quick as to be abrupt. "She will be reaching the Great Chamber even now. With this fighting, we'll never get through."

Tavlin gritted his teeth. "See if we don't."

He ripped two grenades loose, bit the pins off them and hurled them forward, first one, then the other. They landed in the intersection and exploded, flinging two of the cultists backward. There were none left down this hall. Smoke billowed in the intersection, and there were shouts and cursing on both sides. Both seemed to withdraw, though there was intermittent popping of guns. A few moments later someone shouted from a distance, "There! They've gone around!" The sounds of the men stalked off through the halls.

"Brilliant!" Millicent said, as Tavlin marched through the smoke and out the other side. "You cleared them all away."

Tavlin didn't believe in false modesty. "I was always quick on my feet."

Ahead the tunnel spilled out into the Great Chamber, and he paused on the edge of it. The fighting had reached this chamber, too, and what had been an orderly ring of priests and adherents, some of them inhuman, was now a writhing mob grappling with Vassas's people. A group of the Boss's fighters was advancing from a hallway, firing all about them, but they were running out of bullets and having to use their guns as clubs. The priests were mostly unarmed, but there were armed guards and Octunggen among them, and these returned fire. Apparently Vassas's troops had split up or become fragmented during the assault, as others that Tavlin recognized as serving the Boss were stumbling into the Great Chamber from other halls, some retreating and under fire by its defenders. These ran straight into the unsuspecting priests and desperate hand-to-hand fighting broke out. More hand-to-hand fighting took place as Vassas's people and their opponents began to run out of ammunition.

Separating Tavlin from the projection the Lady had just reached—the one containing the banks of machines overlooking the empty space—was a writhing orgy of punching, shooting, gouging and biting. There was no more orderly advance or carefully orchestrated fallback. It had become a brawl.

In the center of the Great Chamber the air shook and thrummed, twisted and ripped, and, just vaguely, Tavlin could see an awful form begin to materialize. Then, more clearly, like a mirage on the desert crystallizing …

Tavlin gasped.

Dear all that's good, no, please no …

Magoth rose, fully a hundred feet high, a colossal being that made no sense to Tavlin's eyes. At first he thought it resembled some sort of flower, a tulip perhaps, graceful and fluted, a long tubular construction just blooming at its top so far above, and tapering gradually to an almost pointed bottom, which hovered impossibly off the floor. But then he saw the tendrils sprouting from its sides, coiling and curling gracefully, as if moved by the currents of some unseen body of water, and he became aware of vaguely squid-like properties about Magoth as well, strange limbs and orifices, but all of it symmetrical and breathtaking, heavenly and gorgeous. The whole substance of the being glowed brightly, but softly, throwing its pearl-white light across everything, even the struggling combatants. But, though Tavlin saw it, and felt the shine of its light, he realized that the being wasn't as solid as it at first appeared. It shimmered, just barely, here and there, but mostly he perceived a sort of ghostliness about it, as though it were part phantom, part flesh. Or perhaps a phantom *becoming* flesh.

In the center of the gargantuan mass, Tavlin saw a sort of face between massive, ungainly limbs, and a dripping orifice ringed by terrible eyes. Another eye gaped inside the orifice, huge and black and multi-faceted, like a fly's. *The Eye of Magoth.*

The Song crashed in Tavlin's ears.

Shit, it's almost here.

"Hurry, Tavlin!" Millicent said.

Tavlin sucked in a breath. There was no time to waste. Though dizzy and off-kilter, he waded into the morass of the fight and clubbed one priest over the head with the butt of his pistol. It was amazing to him that anyone here could concentrate with Magoth hovering in the center of it all, bathing them in his/her/its insanity, but somehow they were able to focus, and he made himself close his mind off to the presence of Magoth, too. There was business to be done.

Ahead of him the Lady was throwing switches and preparing to insert the Formula bulb into the pedestal the previous bulb, now empty, had rested in; she had removed it, or one of her priests had. Two still helped her, and one G'zai. More G'zai took part in the fighting.

One of Boss Vassas's men barreled into Tavlin, knocking him aside, and Tavlin started to curse him but then saw the blade buried in his back. He let the body fall. There was no sign of the knife-wielder.

A G'zai reared before him. A segmented limb slashed at his head. He ducked, fired into its abdomen. Ichor spurted out. It stabbed out again, apparently not phased by the blast. Tavlin aimed at its snapping mandibles and pulled the trigger. The insectile horror wilted backward as what passed for brains erupted out of the back of its head carapace.

An acolyte of Magoth leapt at Tavlin, blood-covered knife glimmering in her hand. Tavlin stepped aside. As he moved, he stuck his leg out, tripping her, and she went sprawling. The knife jumped across the floor.

Where was Havictus? Tavlin scanned the mob for him but couldn't see the Octunggen spy. Maybe the bastard was dead. *He better not be. He's mine.*

A cultist, who crouched over the body of one of Vassas's men soaked in blood and holding, of all things, a ceremonial-looking sword, climbed wearily to his feet and stabbed at Tavlin. Appearing from nowhere, Millicent knocked the thrust aside. The man slipped in blood and fell.

Tavlin punched him in the face and stepped out onto the projection that the Lady and the machines occupied. One of the priests tending to the machines turned, a wrench in hand, and swung at Tavlin's head. Tavlin recoiled, sweat flying. He raised his gun. The priest leapt—

Tavlin shot him through the chest. The man fell. Only one bullet left. Tavlin swung the pistol toward the Lady, but the G'zai next to her lifted a tentacle and a squirt of something acidic whizzed past Tavlin's head. He jerked to the side. Fired. The G'zai slumped across one of the machines, fluid leaking and raising sparks.

The final priest on the projection bent to a corpse on the floor and wrestled the rifle out of its hands. Before he could aim it, Tavlin struck the man over the head, then bent down, grabbed him by the legs and hurled him backward, over one of the machines and into the empty space where Magoth was taking form. There were no railings on the projection, only machines. The priest howled and fell three stories, surely to his death.

Tavlin spun to the Lady.

She punched him in the throat.

Gagging, he reeled backward. She kicked him in the knee. He screamed and collapsed to his other knee. Either she had exhausted her otherworldly energies or had no time to bring them to bear on him. She plucked something up from one of the consoles—a screwdriver—and coiled her arm to skewer it though Tavlin's eye and into his brain.

"No!" Millicent said.

Appearing before Tavlin, she caught the descending wrist of the Lady, stopping the deadly screwdriver.

The Lady's eyes blazed; Tavlin could see them through Millicent's ghostly form.

"You dare defy *me*?" the Lady said, spittle spraying from her lips. "You *are* me, you fool!"

"No! I am *me*."

Millicent punched her in the jaw with her free hand. When the Lady tried to throw a punch of her own, she surprised Tavlin by connecting her fist to Millicent's cheekbone. It didn't pass through Millicent like others attacking her had done. The Lady *was* powerful.

"Keep her occupied," Tavlin told Millicent.

He climbed to his feet as the two women wrestled each other, the Lady trying to free her arm from her twin's grip. While they were busy, Tavlin pried the bulb containing the Formula loose of the pedestal.

Before him the image of Magoth, occupying the entire central space of the Great Chamber, rippled and seemed to rage. The orifices squirmed and pulsed. The ungainly limbs thrashed. The Eye blazed darkly.

Stay right where you are, Tavlin thought. He started to dig the vial containing the nullifier out of his jacket pocket. Before he could, someone wrenched him around by the shoulder. A huge fist crashed into his nose. The world dimmed, went dark, and when it snapped into focus again Tavlin was sliding down one of the machines, Havictus bending over him.

"I don't think so," said the Octunggen. He kicked Tavlin in the ribs, then tore the bulb loose from his fingers. Tavlin swiped at him, but the attempt was feeble and Havictus didn't even seem to notice it.

Havictus plunged the bulb back into this pedestal and flipped a switch, then another. The machines hummed louder, the quicksilver fluid in the bulb slowly being channeled down various tubes to the machines, which then passed that energy or information through the many cables and into the walls of the Temple itself. The Song filled Tavlin's ears, his whole being. In the middle of the Great Chamber, the shape of Magoth solidified.

Millicent was struggling with the Lady, but she was winning. One hand still wrapped around the wrist of the hand holding the screwdriver, but the other had wrapped around the Lady's throat. The Lady scratched at Millicent's eyes but this time her fingers only went right through Millicent's ghostly features. She wasn't able to draw breath. Wheezing, eyes bulging, she sank to the floor.

"Millie!" Tavlin choked out. His ribs burned.

Millicent's attention shifted, saw Havictus at the controls. Fear filled her features. She flew at him, hands crooked like talons, ready to throttle him, too.

With one hand, Havictus yanked out the sigil he had used on her earlier, while with the other he flipped another switch. His gaze never left the console.

Millicent screamed. Her form rippled, blurred, and started to vanish. Just in time, she drew back, but it was as if she had lost strength. She was sliding down, *into* the floor, vanishing from sight.

"Millicent!" Tavlin said.

Her torso disappeared, then her upper arms, and finally her head. She was completely gone. Havictus chuckled, but still he did not look up. The Lady clutched at her throat with one hand and tried to pull in breaths, but she made no attempt to rise. Behind her the battle was fading, the cultists unable to cope with Boss Vassas's veteran throat-slitters and brass-knuckle-wielders, but that wouldn't matter. In moments Magoth would arrive, and It would tear reality itself apart.

Tavlin reached out a hand, groping on the consoles. He found a lever and used it to pull himself partway up.

Still not turning to look, Havictus lashed out with a backhand slap, and Tavlin flipped over onto the machine, then slid off and hit the floor again. He groaned. The blow had aggravated the pain in his ribs.

The world blurring around him, he dragged himself toward Havictus, hand over hand. The killer of Sophia would *not* win.

The Lady struck at him with the screwdriver. He kicked the blow away.

Havictus, huge, took up his vision ahead. *Murderer*, thought Tavlin. *Bastard muderering motherfucking son of a whore!*

Havictus, sensing him approach, began to lift a boot to bring it down on Tavlin's skull, likely killing him, when all of a sudden ghostly blue-white hands shot out of the floor and grabbed onto Havictus's ankles. The Octunggen glanced down, startled.

"What the—?"

Millicent, for it could only be she, yanked with all her strength, jerking Havictus's legs out from under him. He fell with a cry, whacking his square head on the machine. Tavlin reached him. Climbing to his knees, Tavlin grabbed the back of his jacket and lifted him, then slammed him forward again, striking his head, then once more. Blood cascaded from Havictus's huge forehead over his shaggy eyebrows and into his piercing blue eyes.

Havictus lurched around, and Tavlin was dismayed at the presence in his gaze. The Octunggen was barely stunned. What could stop him?

Havictus made a fist and swung it. It was a slow swing, but Tavlin proved even slower, and the blow caught him in the temple and sent him sideways, slamming into another machine. Sparks erupted.

Behind him, he could hear the Lady scrabbling on the floor toward him.

Gathering all his strength, Tavlin socked Havictus in the gut. Havictus breathed out sharply. Made another fist. Fired it back toward Tavlin's already-broken nose. One more good blow there would lay Tavlin out, he knew it. He jerked back, just missing the swing, and threw himself forward. He did the only thing he knew to do. He grabbed Havictus by his great craggy face and plunged his thumbs into the Octunggen's eyes. Havictus bellowed and arched his back. Both his fists came crashing down on Tavlin, a rain of hammers, and Tavlin's consciousness dimmed. His thumbs were pulled back before they could blind his enemy.

The Lady stabbed Tavlin in the ankle with the screwdriver. Tavlin yelped and kicked at her, but missed. Millicent floated up through the floor, grabbed the Lady by her foot and hauled her away.

Tavlin punched Havictus in the crotch, slowing the punches for a moment. The two rolled about, punching and kneeing each other, but Tavlin knew there was no question who the winner would be. Havictus was just too strong and too well-trained.

Think, Tavlin told himself.

He had only one advantage, he realized: his hands were fast.

He used them now.

At last Havictus delivered a crushing blow to the side of Tavlin's head, and Tavlin let himself be knocked to the side. He rolled and lay crumpled against a machine while Havictus's bloodied hands found purchase on the central console and the spy hauled himself to his feet, grunting and swearing for every inch. Streamers of blood trickled from his nose and lips, and his eyes seemed exhausted. Still, they gleamed with victory as he flipped the final series of switches and mashed the last series of buttons.

Tavlin crawled away, his heart thumping against his chest. *Any second now.*

In the heart of the Great Chamber, Magoth grew solid, and Tavlin could feel this space, the inside of the building, start to align with that other reality, Magoth's realty. Hair stood up all over Tavlin's body, and he tasted something acrid in the back of his mouth.

"You lose, Tavlin Two-Bit, you worthless card player," Havictus said over his shoulder, flipping a switch. His fat finger hovered over another switch, perhaps the last one.

"There's something you're forgetting," Tavlin said. He had to force the words out. Still, he savored them.

"Oh?"

Tavlin held up the pin of the grenade. "I cheat."

Havictus's eyes widened.

"For Sophia," Tavlin said.

Havictus opened his mouth just as the grenade Tavlin had thrust into the inside pocket of his jacket exploded. Gore rained outward, and Tavlin threw his arms over his face. Chunks of meat and spatters of hot blood struck him, and he felt something warm drip down from his hair and into his ear. When he opened his eyes, there was little left of Havictus, only a pair of legs leaning against the machine with a bit of pelvis jutting up from them, all raw and red where it wasn't blackened.

Havictus, at long last, was dead. Tavlin breathed out a sigh of relief. *Rest in peace, Sophia.*

The blast had caught the machinery, too, and fire leapt upward in a bright sheet. The Lady stared, and all the fight seemed to drain out of her. Millicent stopped wrestling with her. Around them, the fighting slowed. The air changed, the planes passing out of alignment, and the hairs on the back of Tavlin's neck lowered back to their proper position.

In the center of the Great Chamber, Magoth, which had been so nearly solid moments before, now faded, then rippled into nonexistence altogether. The door between the dimensions had closed. Sparks flared from the machines. Plugged into the walls, the walls began to shake, too. The floor trembled under Tavlin.

"We've got to get out of here," he told Millicent, whose eyes were huge. He stood, wiping pieces of Havictus off of his face.

The Lady recovered herself. Shrieking, she flew at Tavlin, the screwdriver aimed to impale him through the temple. Tavlin had no time to react and Millicent, caught off guard, could not help him.

A great boom ripped the chamber, and the Lady was thrown forward onto Tavlin. He fell back under her weight, but it was a dead weight now. Smoke wafted up from the great black-rimmed hole on her back.

At the beginning of the projection stood Frankie, holding the shotgun with both hands.

Tavlin laughed, half hysterical. "I thought you were dead!"

Frankie patted his gut, which was still bound by Tavlin's jacket and his own belt. Blood had seeped through it, but not as much as Tavlin would have thought. "This?" Frankie said. "You forget, I'm a frog. I'm half bile and half gas. That asshole didn't hit anything vital."

Tavlin embraced him, and Millicent smiled. Around them the surviving cultists were fleeing, and the mobsters weren't far behind. The Temple shook and pieces of ceiling material cracked off and plummeted to the floor. Tavlin saw one strike a priest and another crush a G'zai.

"Let's get," Frankie said, and Millicent nodded.

"One thing first," Tavlin said.

He limped back to the central console, hauled what was left of Havictus to the side, and stretched out his hand to the bulb. The blast of the grenade had cracked it, but the quicksilver fluid hadn't flowed out of the fissures. Just as the Ualissi had warned, the Formula was sentient. *Alive.* Even as Tavlin reached for it, the mercury-like substance spun up from the open top of the bulb like a cobra about to strike.

Tavlin poured the contents of the nullifier on it.

The Formula squirmed and thrashed. Smoke rose from it. For a wild moment, Tavlin feared that the Ualissi had been mistaken—worse, that they'd misled him. But then, mercifully, the quicksilver turned gray, then rust-brown, then black. It stilled and cracked apart like charcoal, scattering across the consoles.

The Formula was dead.

"It's over," Tavlin breathed.

Frankie pulled him away—and just in time. The floor split open where he had just been standing and tumbled away, taking two of the machines with it.

"Hurry!" Frankie said.

Half-supporting each other, the two fled through the halls, Millicent at their side the whole way, as the Temple broke apart around them. Some awful energy was building inside it. The dimensions had almost merged, and though they hadn't, they'd touched. There had to be some consequence, and Tavlin didn't want to be around when it happened.

He and the others joined Boss Vassas on the docks out front. The Boss was bleeding from a wound on his arm, and he looked pissed-off and in no mood for reunions.

"Get in," he shouted to Tavlin, gesturing to his boat. One of his men was revving its engine. Tavlin and Frankie didn't argue. They tumbled into the boat as he pulled away from the docks. The others in the Boss's little armada did, too, and Tavlin could see stirring in the water and supposed the Ualissi were leaving, as well, hopefully leaving many G'zai corpses in their wake.

The boats shot away from the Temple just as a pink energy suffused it, encased it. Pink light filled the whole cistern chamber, and an awful howling, as of unimaginable energies grinding away, the machinery of the cosmos itself being bent to its breaking point, and then there came a great roar. Tavlin looked back, once, to see the Temple being pulled into nothingness, and he did not turn back again.

EPILOGUE

Tavlin laid the last flower, a white rose, on the cement spot before the vault containing Sophia's ashes. It was the same vault holding their son Jameson. They would spend eternity together, mother and son, just as she would have wanted. Tavlin had placed the other flowers down earlier, during the service, but he'd kept this one back, wanting to hold onto it for as long as he could. Somehow placing it here felt like a goodbye, his last gift to Sophia. *You deserved so much better.*

"Sure you're okay?" Frankie said. He was the only one who hadn't left with the others—well, all except for Millicent, but she had pulled another of her vanishing acts. It had been a nice service, given by a priest of the Church of the Three Sisters, and many of the women of the Twirling Skirt had attended, and not a few of the gang from the Wide-Mouth. Boss Vassas himself had stood in the front row; there wasn't enough room for a seated gathering.

"I'm okay," Tavlin said.

Frankie eyed him doubtfully. They had faced combat together and emerged from it closer than before, perhaps even friends. Good friends.

"You sure?" the frog-man said.

"I'm sure."

Reluctantly, Frankie nodded and turned to leave the little cemetery. He still moved a bit gingerly, but he was healing well.

"Two-Bit?" he said, turning back.

"Yeah?"

Frankie frowned. He started to say something, then seemed to think better of it. He nodded at Tavlin. Tavlin smiled and nodded back. Frankie ambled away, leaving Tavlin alone in the cemetery. A flail fluttered overhead, spraying mucus, but Tavlin ignored it as he pulled out a pipe and lit it. For a long time, he smoked and stared at the little vault containing all that he'd ever had for a family in this world. He was all alone now. *Well, almost.* When his bowl was empty save for ash, he made his way down the walkways and out of the cemetery. Fog swirled around him, and it seemed as if the sounds of Muscud came from far away. Someone was shouting at someone else; another was singing. Music came from nearby. Just the same, it seemed to filter in from a thousand miles away. Muscud was back to normal, at least, or as close to normal as it had ever been.

He wasn't aware of her beside him until he knocked out the ash from his bowl and started to tuck the pipe away.

"How long have you been back?"

Millicent, floating in the fog next to him, only shrugged. "Not long."

"Did you attend the ceremony?"

"I think so. I'm still trying to get used to this life, if that's what it is."

"Thank you for your help back at the Temple, by the way. You chose me over your own people. You were gone before I could thank you."

"They weren't mine," Millicent said. "My people, I mean. They were *hers*."

He tilted his head. "Are you free now that Esril's gone?"

"'Free?'" Millicent seemed to ponder the question. "I'm still bound to you, if that's what you mean. You're my anchor to this world. If I became untethered … I don't know what would happen. I would die, I guess." She shook her head, her pretty blond locks swishing. "Anyway, I don't want to leave."

"No?"

"No." She looked very serious. "I'm where I want to be."

"That could make my life very complicated, you know."

She only smiled. "What will you do now? Return to the surface?"

"No. I see now that my place is here. Trying to live up there had been running away from something. But I'm back now, and I'm staying."

She twined a finger through her hair. "Will you be working for Boss Vassas again?"

"No. I'm done with that life, too. Time to start something new."

"Like what?"

"Well … being back, seeing the problems the folk down here have to deal with, I can tell that they need help. Someone to face down their troubles when they can't. Also, there might be some money in it, who knows?"

"What do you mean? Like a police officer?"

"Ha! No, I was thinking more like a private detective."

"A *detective*?"

"Why not?"

She looked troubled. "There are things down here, Tavlin. Things tucked away, hidden from the eyes of the surface for countless years. Magoth was just the start of it."

He was wearing a hat, and he tilted it back now. "There's an office available downtown. I was thinking of moving in. Boss Vassas paid me what he owed me, and it's enough to get started. But … I'll need a secretary."

She raised her eyebrows. "You want to *hire* me?"

"Actually, I was hoping you'd work for free, at least for now. I don't actually have any money to pay you with."

"That's okay. I don't need any money, and I'm not sure what I would do with it." She sidled up next to him, and this time, he could swear it, he felt her brushing against him.

He stepped aside, just a bit, and cleared his throat. "No."

"So," she said, sounding chipper and not at all put off. "When do we start?"

"I thought I'd head to the office right now and begin setting up."

"Well, let's go!" She tapped her chin. "I have some ideas about wallpaper …"

Side by side, they walked on through the fog, which brightened around them as they went.

THE END